entropy

For my dear mother, Willie Mae;
and my darling husband, David Hutchins

EN TRO PY

BONNIE GREER

First published in Great Britain in 2009
by Picnic Publishing
PO Box 5222, Hove BN52 9LP

ISBN: 9780956037039

Designed by SoapBox, www.soapboxcommunications.co.uk.

One great part of every human existence is passed in a state which cannot be rendered sensible by the use of wideawake language, cutanddry grammar and goahead plot

JAMES JOYCE

Secrets, passwords, return tickets.
We wander in the labyrinth

ENTROPY: ROBERT REHDER

1

...chaos is come again...

OTHELLO

Lately, it had returned again, what she could only call chaos, that thing which threatened to swallow her alive, and which she had come to know was the true legacy left to her by her ancestors who had tried to bury their legacy in hope, in a surface happiness, in God, in music and in a stance in the world that went by every name except what it was.

What it was, to her, never had a name except that temporary one she had given it, yet the time had come when she must name it, just as she must ask herself who she really was, who really were these women with her now, old friends, each one, like her, for some ancestor, a promise fulfilled.

A promise fulfilled, she thought as she looked at them, these black women, like her each the flower of centuries of suffering and death and struggle; each a little history of hard work, tenacity, and faith; living sites of remembrance marking epochs of pain and struggle, and death; all of that culminating now on a cloudy Sunday afternoon in September in an elegant tea shop on a lovely common in South London; Bach, the backdrop both to their daintily half-eaten cakes resting alongside their exotic teas; and to their conversation, the light, trivial talk of women who had known one another a long time and who understood how to nurture one another's myths, and hasty, spur-of-the-moment lies, the latest of which had just been watered down by yet more pink champagne which helped to bathe their tales and stories, and put a glow on their lives; but now, as she sat with them, she used this latest toast to allow her to go over in her mind the letter that she knew by heart: "There is this thing that has been a part of you and me for centuries, for always, Janet Bookman Baker. Where are you? All the letters you wrote to me, I read them, every one, over and over. Where are you? Who are you? I thought I knew, but not now. You haven't written anymore to me. Is it because I've begged you and begged you to come and see me? Was it too much? Janet, I can't see my face in the mirror anymore. You've made me vulnerable and I'm afraid. I don't know how much time I have left and I still have the other musician to bring to the orchestra. Please forgive me. I'm so frightened of the disorder of the world."

The disorder of the world suddenly rushed back, accompanied by a chorus of sucking teeth, as Janet's next door neighbour, Tomas, entered the café, oblivious to anyone but the blonde hanging onto his arm with whom he was in deep conversation; her face fixed on his, the women's faces fixed on them in anger and disgust and resignation at what one of them muttered 'typical black man'; Janet suddenly shocked to find herself – with a rapid violence – hating these friends from her childhood, hating them for their contempt of this man who had come to dominate her thoughts during the day and her dreams at night; this obsession, too, part of what the letter-writer had let loose in her, and using the excuse of a champagne headache, she said goodbye, kissed them all, promising to meet again next month, and left the café quickly to escape across the Common.

With The Flotsam and the Jetsam

I'm going to lose my job. I know it. But I have to keep going. So, I keep going:

"We're always running through life, and don't tell me it's because you're so busy. Forget that. It's an excuse. I mean, where are we running to? Have you ever stopped and asked yourself: What am I doing? Where am I going? That's Taylor Made's Big Thought for the night. Now here's the big question, the really deep and existential question that philosophers have been dying to ask since the dawn of time: Has anybody actually slipped on a banana skin?"

I know that I only have to wait for a few minutes to get my answer. That's the kind of audience I have.

Five minutes later somebody calls in.

"Well, I have."

"Right. Tell us about it, Sir."

"I wanted it to happen. So at first I tried sliding on banana skins in various states of decomposition. Sadly, over time I had to give up and take the skins to the compost heap."

"And?"

"But as luck would have it, one day I walked into my local supermarket, simply talking on my mobile…and slipped on…A BANANA SKIN! I was thrilled and delighted!"

I played the new "standing ovation" recording that I play now just to keep the audience – and me – interested.

"Thank you so much!"

My caller was in heaven.

He'd reached his goal at last and could die happy.

He could. But I was on a banana skin, too.

And I wasn't happy.

I could smell what was coming.

I was going to be out of a job soon.

I had been sort of warned by Jess.

Jess-Jessica has two names that you don't pronounce the way they're spelled which doesn't matter anyway because all of her friends call themselves "Boo" and "Eezz" and "Icky."

She's the top floor's representative on earth, somebody you never see because she's always having treatments.

But when Jess emerges from her aromatherapy and heads your way, you can smell the toast burning.

An authentic Notting Hill chick, the kind you see at nine in the morning walking up those hills, dressed in a fake leopard skin coat, jeans flapping around her ankles, high heels, and with that hollow-cheeked gym-bulimic look, and bad boob job that makes the implants sit on her rib cage like heads of two bald-headed men stuck on a prison wall. That comes from being deeply into competitive skinniness.

Her idea of fresh air is walking down Ladbroke Grove with her phone plastered to her ear screeching "last year I was rubbish but this year I'll be great".

Here she is standing at my cubicle flicking her hair out of her eyes, about to speak when I cut her off.

"Yeah, I know what's happening. And I also know that I got this job because the boss's ex-wife read my novel on a spa holiday."

"It's shit, Anna…

"You don't have to apologise."

Dead air.

Bad thing in a radio station.

Her eyes kind of well up.

More dead air.

I forgot.

I make the signal that I'm listening.

8

Because no matter what's going down, my real purpose in her life is to listen to: "Anna, (take your pick: Tom, Dick/Harry) dumped me."

"That was two months ago…"

I end up comforting her all the way to her natural habitat, the toilet, a place you don't want to go to with Jess. She constantly veers between constipation and the far shores of diarrhoea and it is truly shocking how somebody who doesn't eat can be so full of faecal matter.

Me? I am the Fat Friend. I am used to this. I was the Fat Friend at my school, Roc. It's always good to have a Fat Friend. Having a Fat Friend makes it unnecessary for a slender but unfit person to have to go to the gym or diet. With a Fat Friend, thinness is instant. If you have a FF, you can look great next to your porky mate. The FF is seen and at the same time unseen by all and sundry. You can shine by comparison while the FF hovers in the shadows.

I used to think that in some past life I was Casanova because I had all these beautiful girls around me all the time. My punishment as Casanova in a past life is that this time I'm not into women.

But being fat has its rewards.

You can eat what you want.

Your invisibility allows you to see…everything.

If you had met me a few months ago, I would have said that

experience had taught me that it was necessary for somebody like me to go through life making an effort to create connections with people who demonstrated an interest in a subject or subjects which interested me. That would make me look connected, like I was plugged into what most people were plugged into.

I had to practise this, otherwise I would have had…nothing. So all of my gab and loud laughter, it's my front, my way of saying: "Don't freeze me out. There's something in me that can't engage with you." There's something in me that's always watching and weighing and standing back. When I was a kid, I discovered that it was best for me to shut down. I have been, since the age of ten, an expert at self-protection.

Throughout my whole life until now, any connection made was for that moment, when the need arrived. Even when I fooled myself into thinking it wasn't.

I became an observer of the human zoo. When I felt like it, I joined the zoo, but only on my terms. Nobody guessed.

Now, there are things I want to tell you, have to tell you – both of you.

A story was given to me.

But you know that.

You know all about it.

There's always a story.

And mine?

I'll tell you what suits me to say now.

When I first came to London, I fell into a radio job. I became a late night personality. My show went out at 4 a.m., the time people die in hospital.

That suited me since as far as I'm concerned, the cultivation of absence is the best solution to all problems. Radio is the best medium for that. You're there and you're not. People can invent you.

I can invent, too.

I can invent that person out there in the ether who connects with the real me, who knows the real me. Better than I do. That person doesn't email or call in with some pithy observation. You could have coffee with the person who really knows you. The person who really knows you is that calm part of you, that understands who you are and what you're here to do,

Ok, that's straight out of Mills and Boon, but that's what I long for. Maybe my voice will be recognisable to someone in that way that when you hear a voice, just the tone, you know that this person is for you.

Is you.

Until that person shows up, I remain very dedicated and conscientious about my show. I took the whole thing seriously.

If I had an author coming on to plug, I'd read the book, not the synopsis like one of my guest "critics" once did.

That was unbelievable.

This 'Presenter's Friend' guest critic picks up an outline at a bookstore the afternoon of the show, skims it over two cappuccinos, and then on air bullshits his way through as if he'd spent seven days in quarantine reading the thing.

I know all of this because he bragged about it before he went on air.

But the guy is famous, and people hang on his every word, and if he likes the book it shifts a warehouse of pulp.

Fate takes care of him though.

He got glassed in a pub in Cornwall because of something he'd said on the show.

All good.

My last show before I got THE NEWS was a big one.

There was Hugo Michael Power.

Well, he called himself Hugo Michael Power.

His pen name is a homage to Ireland about which he writes and sells loads of books. Except that he isn't Irish. He looks Asian, but no one knows. That doesn't matter, but he's never been to Ireland. He saw no need to do anything so mundane as visit the country which has made his name and fortune. After all, he'd read lots of great Irish novelists and had the feel for the whole thing. Irish people tell him he has the feeling and sound and landscape right. Even when he takes other writers' plots to achieve his goals, that's ok.

It's homage.

His book *Dirty Protest*, is set during the hunger strike of the early eighties and is the story of a young man who returns to Ireland to confront the father he had never met, and who had turned IRA informer.

I start gently:

Me: You haven't even been to Ireland. You don't know anybody in the IRA or connected with the IRA. Do you even know any Irish people? This is pastiche, Hugo.

Hugo: The critics loved the plot.

Me: But the plot is *The Charterhouse of Parma!* Of course they like it!

Hugo: What's your point?

11

Me: What about visiting Ireland?

Hugo: Is going there a requirement?

Me: You kind of want to get it right…

Hugo: Stephen Crane never saw the American Civil War, he wasn't even born when it happened. Kafka never went to America. Brecht never saw Chicago.

I could have said that he was talking about three geniuses, but it would have been pointless.

Then next up to the plate was Charlie 'Moondog' Custer, the inventor of Okie-existentialism.

Old Charlie had smuggled over on the plane some homebrew which he called 'two-buck chuck'.

He had beat security at three airports.

The guy is a brilliant writer, too.

Me: Charlie, you're a brilliant writer. Thinking 'Don't get pissed on air, Charlie. Please. My job's hanging by a thread as it is.'

But he's in monologue mode and bits of his voice make me nostalgic for my native Midwest. I want to go to his country, Charlie Custer land that resembles America-but isn't. It's all his.

But I've got a show to do.

The Samaritans depend on me.

"Charlie, you're a brilliant writer".

Truly, I am intoxicated by his over-the-hill outlaw aura, his face like a Crosby, Stills and Nash cover come to life right in front of me. The thanks I get for my tribute to his brilliance is Charlie trying and failing not to vomit on-mike into his paper cup full of cheap studio wine, while telling me that I'd been in Britain too long because I over-pronounce my 'Ts' which would be considered the height of pretension if I had talked like that back home in the Midwest.

I explain that if I didn't articulate the 'Ts' my listeners might think I was saying 'rider' like in 'bike rider'.

I tell him that reading his stuff is like staring into klieg lights, it's so bright. I tell him that I've got burnt irises from being inside his beautiful, prairie prose.

Without skipping a beat, Charlie essays into a discussion on 'slickness', his word for a writerly affliction that in his eyes ranks right up there with 'charm', 'accessibility' and 'trendiness', qualities that could insure a writer a 'whippin'. From him.

We finish that, and next take a trip into his creative mind, what he refers to as 'the torture chamber' filled to overflowing with the flotsam and jetsam of other writers, ("but I'm not so stupid to let the seams show. I didn't take creative writing classes, I didn't go to college, I don't hang out with writers. I like real people; critics are my toilet paper.")

"Tell me about the torture chamber."

The torture chamber consists of half-remembered conversations in bars, on park benches, and in peep shows; screaming ex-wives and girlfriends; the recriminations of children and parents; the sound of the gunshot, the shape of the exit wound – he has an obsession with self-inflicted bullet-induced deaths, courtesy of Ernest Hemingway's "shot-gun sucking denouement that was consistent with the man's prose as was good old Camus' head-on with his publisher sitting at the wheel".

Custer is a guy so wrapped up into Hemingway and the Hemingway mystique that he started urging everybody within the sound of his voice to re-read *The Sun Also Rises/Fiesta*; finally spinning out and stating on my live radio show that what he really wanted was to blow his own brains out and have them scattered from one end of Illinois to the next, fertilizing all the corn and the corn fed; his 'Sermon On The Mount' delivered in an Illinois patois which got my console lit up like Oxford Street at Christmas. But I didn't care because I was sitting in the same space with a god of hard, true, clean writing and truth in packaging.

I had ended the show with just plain people I liked or who I thought were interesting or weird or both: like the guy who brings in listeners' emails but who always says he is actually a poet. He read his work on air. He should keep delivering emails, but he did say something worthwhile: every poem is an answer to another one, even one that hadn't been written. As all real art is.

Do you think that every life is the completion of another, or the extension of another?

My next guest is the woman who owns my favourite Greek restaurant, the one I always stare at when I'm hungry.

She talked about Greek culture.

I said something about the Greek royal family. She stopped me.

"The Greek royal family? Do you mean 'So and so of Greece?' Anna, retsina is 'of Greece.' Ouzo is 'of Greece'."

At one point as guest after guest came on, I could hear my neighbour's words in my head:

"Nothing is made anymore but talk. Hot air. Bullshit. Talk, talk, talk, talk, talk. And don't forget service. We're all in service. There are as many servants – let's call it what it is Anna, – in this country as there were in the 1860s!!!"

At last, the show is finally over.

Exalt, somehow, in the potato's sorry life...

ON THE SUBJECT OF FLOWERS, RIMBAUD

Across the Common, her heart pounding from anger and from seeing him again, Janet found refuge in the bookshop owned by the man who always dressed in blue Shetland sweaters and who never greeted anyone except those who interested him – being much too busy arranging his bric-a brac and his precious, leather-bound volumes; a man who had been a great admirer and intellectual sparring partner of her late father, Milton Bookman, constantly quoting him to his customers, extolling the wonder of his great West Indian bus conductor friend whose devotion to the great works of literature had never failed to astound him; why a man with his knowledge had been wasted collecting fares on a bus rather than lecturing at university was one of the injustices of this world, he would say, no one he knew had more to say about The Holy Koran, The Bible, The Torah, Dante, Milton, Montaigne, Plato, Socrates, Chaucer, St. Augustine and a raft of others in the Western Canon; the man in the blue sweaters always greeting her with this litany like a praise-song, but this time, without his usual digression, he told her that he had something for her, something that she might find interesting, something authentic.

"'Authentic'," she mused, would have been the only description tolerated of the "'Café on the Common'", once simply the local caff, now a place where she and her friends could drink champagne, where they could talk, laugh, be together and be who they really were, be beyond the colour of their skin, which had, for the most part and beyond their will and control, made their fate; now they were simply a part of the new look of the café, a place very different from the days when they were all growing up and it had been run by Luigi, a South Londoner born and bred out of generations of South Londoners, who had taken his name from the stage name of a favourite uncle who had

15

been an acquaintance of Marie Lloyd; the café had been, in those days, a place her mother had forbidden her to enter because she did not consider the English to be exceptionally clean, now it was just another enclave in the nostalgia circus that her community was slowly becoming, the café's 'authenticity' consisting of windows full of cakes covered in white sugar icing topped with red cherries; cakes that reminded her of nothing more than those cupcakes with red cherries baked by her best friend long ago, a friend who had not gone on to the glittering academic career and beyond that Janet and her other friends had, that friend having failed the 11-Plus, an ordeal whose anticipation had made Janet wake up screaming in the night; in passing it she had been freed from the fate of her best friend, but not from her guilt.

Janet had noticed that Bev had been the first to arrive at the café for their monthly reunion, early, always a little ahead of the game, ready with a hug and kiss and fresh news, this coming together her idea, a way to keep them – all of the old girlfriends – connected she had said, now that they were in their mid forties and fading fast, heading for the time when sex would have to be paid for because men no longer saw you; important, therefore to stay in touch, important to keep up with growing children, troublesome siblings, ageing parents, racist employers, and those ever -present treacherous white women who feigned solidarity only to go on to take their promotions and their men; the others arrived, and with the second bottle of champagne came the usual ritual of contempt against the can't- live - with -them -can't- live- without-them black men, the exception always being Janet's own husband, Sam, still gorgeous, they raved, sexy, and much better looking in his glasses than she was in hers, the paean abruptly ending with the entrance of Tomas and the sucking of teeth.

The sucking of teeth, that most dismissive of sounds, pulled Janet back from her reverie as the shop-owner handed her a 19th century daguerreotype of a black woman; a woman with a solemn and rigid bearing in the style of studio portraits of the time; the subject dressed in a high-collared frilly blouse and a long black skirt, her hair pulled back into a bun, her right hand resting primly in her lap, her left pointing to the bottom of the photo and the inscription: 'Les Larmes de la Reine' and beneath that the word "Elmina"; before she could ask, he had his research at the ready: Elmina was the name of the infamous slave fort on Ghana's Atlantic Coast; the word in the photo, was however not referring to the slave fortress but to L' Orchestre d'Elmina, the name of one of the most famous brothels in Paris during the Second Empire which flourished throughout the Franco-Prussian War, the Siege and the Third Republic, finally disappearing altogether before the First World War. He enjoyed, he said, the fact that the prostitutes gave the name 'orchestra' to their brothel. They named themselves after instruments, and had in their number a quite extraordinary creature known as 'The Flute'.

'The Flute', he continued, his voice lowered to a whisper, 'could bring a man to kill himself at her request, after one night of pleasure'; this daguerreotype, he concluded, had been buried beneath piles of detritus; he had made for it just as the local 'roots woman', Mrs. Coleman, had reached it, not at all happy about his taking it; following him out of the shop, telling him that the picture belonged in the possession of a black woman, not the likes of him, a black woman who, through it being in her possession, would discover what she had been searching for; anyone else, she had said ominously, would get nothing but bad luck, particularly, especially, in his case since his shop stood atop an underground river at the very spot where there had been a medieval shrine to a miracle-working Black Virgin, a shrine destroyed by zealots in the time of Henry the Eighth; her knowledge and her rant had made him decide that it was best to give the picture away, better than having a crazy old lady with her wild superstitions haunting his shop.

His shop and what she had been given there, had brought Janet back once again to the matter of time, its obligations, its trajectory, and its meaning; all of this playing on her mind as she walked in the direction of her home in Morant Bay Road, unable to ignore any longer what had been apparent to her for some time: the quiet unravelling of her once orderly and perfect life.

Her once orderly and perfect life had lately taken a battering: a call from her mother, demanding to know when she was coming 'home' for a visit, she having to remind Gloria-Loretta for the umpteenth time that the West Indies was not her home, she had been born and brought up in London, her passport said United Kingdom; and then there had been Ayesha's question – 'Mummy, are people connected?' coming after a day of coincidences that she could not now recall but the feeling still lingered; Ayesha, clearly demanding an answer to her question, although Janet had learned very early on that her daughter did not ask a question because she wanted something as mundane as an answer, since asking questions, for Ayesha Bookman Baker, was simply what human beings were meant to do, after all, how else could they define, order, and live in the world; unsaid but obvious ever since Ayesha had learned to properly form a sentence, ever since then, Janet's day had begun with an onslaught of questions and observations, Ayesha, her only daughter, picking the world apart, examining it, taking no one's word about the scheme of things, relying on her own tools and natural gifts; it seemed to Janet that not having an answer to this question had suddenly crystallized the unravelling inside her, and made her see that she had to find an answer to that question, to her life, she thought to herself as she looked up at the sky.

A malignant life of its own

It's five a.m.

Char Bingham, one of the work experience people walks up to me. She's punch-drunk from having to work on the evening shows and then sticking around for late night.

She's muttering: "1,000 quid to get my teeth whitened and then after a week it's gone. That's mental."

The teeth are an aberration because Char lives in the 50s. She's got a complete collection of *Hancock's Half Hour* and knows nothing about Reality TV, downloads, etc. All this is mixed with a hippie thing. When asked about her choices she says: "any person who doesn't see the interconnectivity of all things, you need to make an ocean between you and that person".

Char's the full ticket of organic, vegan takeaways, like them she can smell bad if left alone after six minutes. She wears prairie dresses; cheesecloth; she re-gifts: repackaging gifts she receives and then giving them to other people when she has to take a gift somewhere. There are her muslin and capes, except for when she goes down Hackney Wick Market to 'be grime' when she's bored, the prerogative of a woman whose brother is a member of the Bullingdon.

What truly perplexes me about her is that even though Char is poor, she's always got stuff. She steps out of the 50s to go online looking for sample CVs so that she can re-configure hers, especially under the section called 'interests'.

She doesn't have a life. Just 'interests'.

Cal, who usually looks like he sleeps in a box, comes in for once all pressed and clean.

An omen of badness to come.

Cal's signs of anxiety are legion: the bitten down nails; changing which side he combs his hair on a daily basis; his need to have nightly reality checks with the life-size models of Charles, Diana and Camilla standing guard in his place. Ever since the day he brought some mail over to the girl across the street who now thinks she's having his baby and keeps ringing his bell to talk names, he's had the cut-outs to help him. But that's nothing compared to the problem he's got with his ex.

They started writing a novel together, 'Urban Exchanges' which is nothing more than their emails. The relationship ended. She found someone else. But they have to keep writing the book because they have a deal that'll pay off their mortgage.

"Anna, this novel has a malignant life of its own. It won't go away. We can't get rid of it."

It's 5. He reads the headlines.

Hasn't anybody ever told him that the only headline most people want to hear at that hour is 'Doctors find cure for death'?

He starts arguing with Frank, the veteran newscaster:

"Look Frank", he's saying, "…see, the difference between your time and mine is we have degrees but we had to pay for ours. We have to figure out how we're going to pay off massive debts. It's no fun having only 50p to live on after working all day. It makes you think maybe what you should have done instead of study is to buy scratch cards or something. At least if you win, then you can move out of the bedroom you've been in since you were a child. And it would be great to stop living the 'not new, but glue, make-do' existence, and buy a pair of trousers once a year instead of going down to Oxfam. The thing is Frank, this is my problem and all of my friends', too: see, ever since I was little, I knew that I was destined to do great, important things. I also knew that it wasn't going to happen through academics or nine to five. I'm 27 now. I know it's over. I'm at the age when an athlete peaks. Kurt Cobain, Jimi Hendrix, Janis Joplin all died at 27. You go to school and strive and then you reach 27 and wonder why the hell you did it. Because somebody made you? Look at me, Frank! I'm fiscally conservative, but I'm socially liberal, so what political party speaks to me? Ok, if I had to, I'd say I'm conservative with a small 'c'. I like saying it because it gives you more of a mental work-out. If you're conservative, you have to be that much more up on your facts. Being liberal at university, everybody's that. Being conservative – you just have to know more and be on it more. It's not like the way it was when you were my age. Back then people came and organized you. Now you organize yourself."

"Somehow", I think.

My boss, Dan The Man himself emerges from his cave and summons me.

His diet, which consists mainly of junk, along with his sedentary lifestyle has given him an unhealthy and life-threatening paunch, the whole mess resting on spindly legs which accent his weak shoulders.

Soap and Dan are not mates, which didn't bother me, being allergic to it myself from time to time.

Dan smiles. In his way.

I feel sorry for him.

His tiny blue eyes reflect the utter boredom and tedium of his life, the horror of his three divorces, and his complete devotion to a life behind glass, watching presenters, producers, and other sentient beings send forth his programmes into dead air.

Generational congestion is his main preoccupation. He finds great comfort in the kind of world where grandparents mow lawns and walk around in aprons, moms cook the food and give the kiddies baths every night while being available for daddy and their candlelit supper, with good, legitimate sex later. The guy wilfully ignores real life staring him in the face: Grandma and Grandpa spend thousands on rock concerts and climbing the Himalayas; middle-aged women hang out on Saturday mornings at Top Shop; there are Internet mogul-kiddies and pre-teen girls with massive couture collections including skimpy bras and t-shirts that say: "Too Many Boys So Little Time"; tons of tweenies who get facials and manicures every week.

For him, none of it made any sense and was looking more and more like the abyss.

I know that feeling.

There are times when I wonder what it must have been like to be young when youth meant something.

In his office, Dan's got these vintage posters: the iconic Farrah Fawcett, but with dart holes on it; groups like T-Rex; one of Roxy Music he put up two thousand years ago when he was trying to look cool to his glam-rock assistant who has since become a High Church Tory in the shires.

He asks me to sit down which is a joke because there is never anywhere to sit in Dan's office. Boxes and bags of tapes from old rockers are all over the place, still coming in tribute to his DJ days, over forty years ago on an off-shore boat. On the top of my boss' 70s metal file cabinet there are half-drunk Coke bottles older than me. Complete crap clutters his shelves while every available inch of space is filled with CDs for review, ancient literary magazines, yellowing newsprint, all artefacts from the youth he never left and that has gone into legend in his mind. He has prog rock vinyl originals, some with the original Roger Dean artwork which he hopes will be his pension.

Dan and I have something in common: disorder follows us.

If people like Dan and me simply stand still, a pile of chaos gathers. My flat looks like a storage space. I share my little bed with my daily shopping. So I feel at home in his office.

We both see the new girl in the office at the same time. We see her because she's unlike us: very neat, systematic, orderly and handles things with meticulousness.

One of those high-end Afro-Brit girls, all extensions and lipstick.

I called her "Miss Africa".

I used to make fun of her.

Didn't think much of her.

I was wrong.

Very wrong.

Dan starts making small talk.

Then, if I was around small talk, I'd make some comment and drift away. If I stayed, I'd just nod and go `yeah, yeah' absently and the person would eventually stop talking and be gone.

My boss is a guy who loves statistics, especially doom-laden ones: like how the over 50s now have £8 out of every £10 in the economy and can look forward to enjoying their wealth for several years due to longer life expectancy.

People in my age group, 25-29, can look forward to eight career changes and work until 75, and as for the NHS…

He is a guy famous for his lack of timing, an unfortunate trait in a radio man. He demonstrates it again now, as I perch on his desk, the only clear space.

"Look, Anna. I'm sorry to tell you this but the programme after your next…"

I panic. "This station will soon be known as", and he elongated this, "'Flooooooow Radio'. Easy listening. Music to commit euthanasia by. End of fucking story."

This was bad.

I had to stay in a job for now.

"Wow, but…"

"The numbers, Anna."

"But you always said this show was never about the ratings."

"I used to work for the Beeb, it's my automatic response. Oh, and one more thing and you won't like this, they're giving your slot…to Jake Simpson."

"The shock jock?"

"Listen to the pilot."

"The WHAT?"

He flipped a switch.

A woman's voice in a mangled imitation of an American accent purred through the room accompanied by what sounded like the soundtrack to a soft porn film from the 70s.

"It's *Emmanuelle*!" I say. Well, I had to say something so that I wouldn't get sick.

After she finished, along came Jake Simpson. He did a one minute reading of *The Canterbury Tales*. Then some reality TV person came on and talked about her first novel. I mean, how she dictated characters to a ghost.

"Ok, Dan. I get it. Stop the torture."

"That's the way it's going."

Yeah, but not yet, I told myself.

The guy I was renting from – I had a tiny place near the British Museum – was a designer from Nottingham who had decided to come back from New York where he had been living very happily for twenty years because his dinner party joke had got unfunny real fast.

His green card said 'Nottingham, Ukraine' because he'd told the clerk who wrote down his information that he was from the UK. Suddenly, the police get really interested in him. Because even the NYPD knows that there's no Nottingham in the Ukraine, so who was this guy and where did he really come from and why was he covering up where he came from. Soon, the FBI would drop by to chat on a regular basis. He was starting to feel like there was a special room for him at all the airports, internal and foreign, that he landed in. His emails were being read. He thought he'd left England permanently. But now he had to come back.

Me, I didn't have anywhere else to go, and that would be doubly true if I had no job. Plus, I didn't want to go back home to Chicago with my folks thinking that I'd been a wash-out in London.

I didn't want to think about them just yet. Or what they were going through as voluntary hostages in their own home, doing time for what my Mom calls 'the failed dream of the flower power generation.'

I didn't know what she meant. Then.

Dan was going on about 'Flow Radio' when I stopped him with an idea right off the top of my head. I talked him into launching a contest on my show called 'Tell Me A Story'. That way he could see how many people were out there in the ether listening. And the contest would give me time to figure out what to do next.

He said ok, and I announced it the following night.

I thought we'd get a trickle from the truck drivers and morticians, but by the first week there were 2,868 entries in and counting. My intention was to stretch it out as long as I could. Dan couldn't fire me until the contest was over.

And then, she came out of the blue.

But you and I both know that she had always been there.

Right from that day when my life stopped, and another began.

The world, according to Mallarme, exists for a book…

The sky was like a Constable, its fat, turbulent clouds suddenly disturbed by fitful shafts of light, creating a landscape which quickly became a Titian red-gold, then changed again and became dark, speckled, low, glowering, full of the promise of an autumnal storm, a sky shot through with a peculiarly London beauty, which for a brief moment, as Janet Bookman Baker stopped and looked at it, erased the fear of the city of her birth.

Fear of the city of her birth, especially of its river, had been with her for most of her life and made her now turn suddenly towards it, determined to try once more to face it; to simply stand overlooking it, a river, she had convinced herself, which had come into being according to one of the numerous superstitions from 'back home"; "Golgotha", they call it, a name born of the ancient fear of deep water, of its expanse and the possibility therein of transcendence; a fear intended to be erased with the coming of the gun and the Bible; but it had not happened, at least not in her case; the river held an attraction-repulsion that she would have to face and soon, if she were ever to regain control of her inner life; a spiritual woman with cowrie shells in her hair had told her once at a fair that she had knowledge bred in the blood and the bone and that this knowledge would soon crash past her education, good taste and natural reticence and become manifest, but first, she would be taken briefly back to when the water ran crimson from the Slave Coast to The New World, where it ran all the way to London her birthplace.

Her birthplace was actually a hospital not far from where she now lived; she taught at the local university, once a polytechnic; everything in her life contained within a few miles, within the known, believing that in taking several degrees, marrying an accomplished man, together buying one of the biggest houses in the area and producing two exceptional children, she had freed herself from the relentless hunger to tear down her own life and rebuild it again.

Again, she thought of her daughter, too fragile and more beautiful inside than her pride would ever reveal; her hair uncombed, growing into a huge, unmanageable forest only available to be washed and oiled, no combs, no chemicals, already like Milton Bookman's people, already a big woman and in time big-hipped, too, heavy-breasted, a body inherited from centuries of women who bore children to be sold, who squatted and bent down to plant and harness what was not theirs; her face and body and hair not considered beautiful by the standards of the country into which she had been born, a reality that would make Janet cry from time to time; frightened that Ayesha would not have the patience to wait for the discovery of her qualities by others when they were so apparent right now to anyone else who cared to look; frightened that this failure to accept her daughter on the part of society would make her youngest child difficult, ugly, rendering her life harder than it ought to be; Ayesha, right from the beginning had refused to be restrained by all the elements set up to restrain her, daring the world to come to terms with her, not her with it; just like the American girl who had boarded Milton Bookman's bus that summer day three decades ago, a mysterious girl, a kind of exterminating angel carrying a suitcase that had been battered and worn.

Battered and worn, not beautiful, her father had told her, welcomed to London by the blunt refusal of a hotel room in Earl's Court on racial grounds, leaving her to walk the streets on a wet August day searching for a friendly face and someone whose voice she could understand, and she, out of fear and desperation, finally taking refuge on the first bus she saw, Milton Bookman's bus, the 903, on the very day that he held his monthly book club; Madame Bovary being the book of the month; the discussion that day centring on an analysis of the romantic, trivial mind and its need for constant gratification; the girl interrupting to say, in her southern-tinged American accent, that Madame Bovary's mind was not trivial and that what she was searching for in the guise of the love affairs and fine things, was the woman she held inside, the woman who lived and breathed away from the definitions of society, her death an act of courage, a way of keeping allegiance with herself, and that to mock her, call her silly, was not to understand the lengths that a woman then and now had to go to live her life all the way to the end, as Hemingway would have said; in saying this, Janet's father had said, this young woman had struck him as being the only person who had ever known him; known him for just one brief afternoon and then vanished, gone forever. A spectre in Janet's childhood home, a place of half-lives and shadows; a place whose atmosphere had created a melancholy in her that certain men had found attractive and which she had been accused, from time to time in her life, of playing upon; a 'Modigliani', one smitten boy at university had said, so taken with her that he had asked her to visit his family in Edgware, but that would have entailed crossing the river and when she had told him her fears, he had told her of how London had always been considered an infernal place, a place of fires, a city where a hopping demon reigned who could leap from house to house with fiery hooves, how he himself had lain awake as a boy waiting for conflagration; but nothing glorious had ever come to Edgware, except her, if she would; she imagining one day that he would arrive at her bedroom window like a fiery angel and carry her over the great watery Golgotha to his magic kingdom of Edge-ware and she would walk through green fields and wait for him, peering behind bevelled glass that cast rainbows whenever she moved, living with him under the high, bright sky of Edgware under an unimpeded sun, happy in the relief and the release.

The relief and the release could have happened if only she had said 'yes' and taken his hand, but she had made her father's choice, and remained in the places she knew, her streets.

Her streets, the ones she had known all of her life, felt alien now as the day began to close in, her tiny world suddenly a cauldron and she a victim of the present, riding with her father on a bus that had never stopped. Contemplating a life she could never name.

Contemplating a life she could never name was one of the reasons she listened to the radio in the early hours of the morning, smoking her clandestine cigarettes, becoming more and more dependent on a voice in the ether, in the void, an American voice, her phantom sister, black like her, a voice that sounded free, untroubled, secure in the world, beautiful, noble and clear about her destiny and purpose; imagining the presenter of the arts show, Janet fashioned in her mind a woman she had never met, forging her into a higher image of herself, the woman she was not: unashamed that she, Janet Bookman Baker, had become that most pathetic of creatures, unashamed that she wanted to know this Anna Taylor, her interest now dangerously close, she knew, to an obsession, this construction of Anna Taylor, her total belief in her undoubted graciousness and peace, seeming to have always been in her life, yet the mystery was that Janet could not remember how she had first come upon the programme, only that she had been mesmerized by a fierce panel discussion on the notion of circularity. Anna without doubt a strong woman of mature years, a woman of wisdom, a woman sure of her place in this world, a woman who could help her answer her daughter's question, help her answer Abena Assantewa's questions; in her mind she could see them together reading Professor Assantewa's letters over coffee, wondering together why she had chosen to write to Janet; their conversation segueing into the issues of the day, and above all they would talk about the art of fiction – "only the great ones are worth the trouble" Milton Bookman would often say – she imagining herself with Anna, interjecting interesting bits of information, such as it being Boccaccio who had attached the word 'Divine' to Dante's canonical work, not the great poet himself; in time revealing everything that she knew.

She knew that Anna Taylor would one day be in her life, wise, a woman who knew herself; it would be Anna Taylor who would free her from peering into the chaos.

That Tragic And Beautiful Mixture

I think that you can come to the conclusion that 'chaos' is my middle name.

Also, I could say that my personal goal is to be forgotten in a memorable way.

A more sensible goal would be to marry a man with a strong future, and pass my genetic material around in the most efficient and effective way possible. But I figure that at this point in the life of the world it is too late for me to care about the environment, war, the plight of child soldiers, AIDS, etc.

I have always known that I have a very brutal nature which keeps me responsible.

Another thing about me is that I prefer older people as friends. Not for their wisdom. But because they're usually full of regrets.

You asked me for the truth.

There are things I want to tell you, have to tell you – both of you.

I have a story here.

I think that after you hear it…I don't know what will happen after you hear it.

My story:

There's always a story.

The time before I came to you, I lived in London because of my first novel, "blk/wimmun/sistuh/ luv". Ok, it was an arrogant joke, not written but typed out on Diet Coke and Doritos in three weeks, just to see if I could. I gave myself a word count, stood in the bookshops, read a lot of pulp, then I finally sat down and did it. Next I sent the manuscript to the first publisher my eye fell on in one of those writers' guides and two days later I got this excited call telling me I was going to be a star.

Then I got scared.

I started seriously thinking about saying it wasn't me who wrote the thing but this guy I knew from college and who I had totally nothing in common with called Brent Caulfield the Third. The guy was desperate to do literary conferences, festivals, readings, book reviews, think pieces and get a chance to go to Yaddo. He would have done anything to have a novel published just to say that he was a writer. To get mentioned in The New York Review of Books was the Holy Grail. It was about the bling, not the work.

But by the time I'd done the rewrites, I had come to the conclusion that Brent and I did have something in common: like him, I've never been inside a ghetto in my life.

Except the one growing in my parents' house.

I could have written about how my mom has decided to take in all of the baby mothers and their children; the molls, and the 'laydeez', too, and give them all shelter in the only house still intact on the street – my childhood home. This is her penance for having 'dropped the ball'.

I could have written about how my dad is fighting Alzheimer's and sleeping with a Glock under his pillow, but they say that the first rule is write about what you know and I don't know anything about that except what mom writes to me, when she does write to me. If I had signed my manuscript Brent Caulfield the Third it would have been politically incorrect for the publishers to have published the thing because of its subject matter and to have not published would have been dumb after three weeks of concentrated rewriting.

I was half-right and half- wrong.

Anyway, the publisher who had accepted the book probably would have had a problem with it if it had been an Ivy League Caucasian male writing about a black girl called Sistuh Luv even if it was good; but it was ok, even cool that a middle class, university-educated, privately-schooled black girl, the daughter of two academics, writes the story. Like black college students who don't have American slave ancestry are now what's hot, I was acceptable. Even desirable. Marketable. A little tightening here, some rewriting there, and it was published.

31

The book got a lot of hype, and tours, and readings, little awards, all for the following immortal prose: "'waz I goin to fine wha I waz serchin fo inna dark reces ugh ma…'"

I couldn't look at it again, let alone stand up and read it. But I had to. I Couldn't say: it was a joke. Honest.

The book got lots and lots and lots of flak from African American women's groups accusing me of creating a damaging and inauthentic character.

Then it got weird.

Out of the blue, a famous female rapper with a three-picture deal called me up to tell me that my inauthentic novel happened to be the story of her life. 'Sistuh Luv'was the name of the inner self she'd channelled.

She was convinced that the only reason she was alive was to do my book, which she referred to as 'The Project'.

Apparently, we'd been sisters in another life or something.

However, sisters or no sisters, she insisted that I get a special ring tone just for her because she didn't like waiting when she called somebody.

I decided to flee to London and work on my second book. Since I'd taken and spent the advance, I had no choice. Writing a novel overseas is better than doing real work.

London was my safe haven. It was the place where I could hide out. I could be a sleeper in my life there. London lets you vanish. What it requires, I could give. I had decided to lose the United States, lose Chicago. Let it be foreign to me. Feel what that was like. Exile.

I was thinking about that again, when at the end of the first week of the contest, right after I went off air at 5 a.m., I was told that I had a call from Paris.

Jess gave me the call. Told me to go to her office.

Never been in here. It smells like lavender and there are flowers all over the place. Like an ashram.

I take the phone. An American woman's voice, Black. I can tell.

"Ms. Taylor, bonjour. It's Dr. Abena Assantewa here. I'm submitting a story for your contest."

I almost stopped breathing.

Abena Assentewa was one of the biggest radical academics in the States in her time, the 60s and 70s.

She'd been a Black Panther, on the run from the FBI when she was my age, had her face on 'Wanted' posters, the whole deal.

I got an early taste of how deep she was when my mother brought one of her books home when I was six and Dad grabbed it and burned it in the backyard. If something like that happens when you're a little kid, it makes an indelible mark. Especially when you come from a highly cultivated, snooty family like mine with relatives on both sides who don't celebrate Martin Luther King Day because they think he was nothing more than a class traitor out to ruin the annual cotillion season and force all the debs into Afros.

After the burning incident, I found almost all of her books and read them in my bedroom at night under the covers, books like 'No Fire Next Time' about the diminution of the reputations of Richard Wright and James Baldwin in America; 'The Lucky Peninsula' about Europe as a peninsula of Asia and how in denial Europe is of that fact.

Every time a new book came out, I rushed and bought it. My favourites were 'Dead White Females' on how being posthumous is a great career move for a woman; 'Improvisation: The Art Of the African In The West, How It Was Lost, And Why It Must Return', 'A Lament For The Loss Of Abstraction, Wit, And Wandering'.

My mother read my copy of 'Lament'. Which surprised me because she usually floats away from stuff and into other stuff.

She's in her own sealed world, even in the one she has to live in.

When I was a child, she was really into the arts, theatre mainly. Then one day she had a seizure and three weeks later she was totally obsessed with numbers. She spent something like six months absorbed in math books. We both thought she was going crazy. I asked her what was up and she looked up from one her books and said something like 'numbers are my friends' and "the butterfly effect' has been vulgarized, Anna…'

Then one day, without me even saying anything, she said: "Abena Assantewa will leave these shores one day, go on her way. She has to. She has to keep moving until she can come to rest. You see, daughter, as young women, she and I fought for the masses. I wasn't in the streets like her, but I did my part, too. But what we didn't do…I don't know how to say it – but what we didn't do was individualize ourselves. WE became individuals, 'me' people. But we didn't evolve. We didn't help anyone else to evolve. That was our job, but we dropped the ball. I know from reading her book that she knows this. She will have to, in her own way, face this and rectify it. So will I. And so, my daughter will you. As my child."

And just as my mother said, she disappeared.

But she didn't disappear from me. Inside.

Or from you.

Abena Assantewa is talking to me. "Ms. Taylor, my mother used to tell me bedtime stories that she'd make up herself. Now most little girls got told stories about princesses and Prince Charmings and Cinderellas and things. But my mother knew who her slave ancestors were, the women and the men, each of them and their stories, and she was part Native American, too, and knew all of that side. She knew that no matter what, that was what she was and we are. That 'tragic and beautiful mixture' she called it. She knew her past, so she set her stories in the future. Always the future. She'd spin her story out night after night as if she was afraid to get to the end. As if something would happen at the end that she could not face. Ms. Taylor, are you still there?"

"Yes, ma'am…"

"Good. Nowadays silence and introspection make me scared of my own shadow. My mamma would say, 'Child, every woman has a duty to write her own ending.'"

I said, "A duty?"

"Yes. Excuse me. I haven't been able to sleep very well. I can't sleep because I'm going over things. Waste. Time lost. In my case, I had to get older to know what I needed to know. If you live long enough, and you want to see, you'll notice a pattern. There's always a pattern, shape being made. Ever since my husband died, I've sat all day trying to find our pattern, our shape. For a while I couldn't do anything. Couldn't read or write. I couldn't see the words. He died close to my sister's death. There

34

is a pattern there. I know it. Or maybe not. Maybe we fool ourselves believing that there is more than ourselves. This is how I think all day. Grief is a strange thing.

I like hearing your voice. You sound like a strong, wise woman, but I know that you're not. I don't mean that the way it sounds. That voice is your mask. We all have one. A mask. In your voice, I can hear my sister's. Little bits of her. My late sister who I had judged so harshly and used that judgement to define my own life. Now that I have discovered that I was wrong, I have to make atonement to her, and also, heal what's left of me. Your voice. I am touched and chastised by the sound of it. Please forgive my opening up to you like this. You don't know me. It's just that when I heard you for the first time, you brought back to me what I haven't done in my own life.

My sister. I came to know her when it was too late. She was in a coma, dying of what our family has inherited from the centuries of…well, centuries of it. You know, lately there has been a melody in my head, Ms. Taylor. I want to set it down. And now I have found the two musicians who can play it. I know this sounds mysterious. Please forgive the mystery. I'm so used to hiding, so used to obfuscation.

If you read the story that I'm making up for you, you'll understand. It'll come every day at this time. Wait for it. Wait for me."

Those were the first and only words that Dr. Assantewa spoke to me. To recall them now is spooky, like a dream.

As soon as she finished, she hung up and the fax machine began, the first instalment of the story started coming through.

I felt like she was watching me.

I put the story in a plastic bag and left the station.

I got home and washed the dishes, the first time in weeks.

I cleared off the sofa bed, put my clothes and old Cheeto bags on the floor and pulled my coat around me. I was suddenly cold.

I hesitated for a minute. Then I began:

"Imagine.

Orwell was right.

There will be a 1984."

1.

Jody Carlyle bent down to see if the child lying on the ground was alive.

Impossible to know whether it was a boy or a girl. It was too dark and the child was too dirty.

"Face it, bitch!"

A cluster of feral children suddenly appeared, surrounding her.

She was in the NPF, the 'No-Parent Family' enclave, where the children belonged to no one. They were united by their poverty, by the risk it took them to stay alive. If they interested investigators and observers of the enclave, like herself, then they would be fed properly and kept alive to live another day.

The faces of the feral children were old and hard, their eyes wary and cold. They looked like old people with the bodies of children.

Jody Carlyle knew that she had once been in a place like this.

She had lain in her own filth. She, too, had searched the faces of the people around her, desperate for a friendly look.

She had also known something else, known it for a long time. Her parents had left her in a NPF.

They had abandoned her.

And she hated them for it.

They had left her in a world of categories based on generations:

There were the Nonas, born in the late nineteen forties – the wave of baby boomers. Nonas were me-orientated pleasure-seekers, people who refused to get old and die. They were the motors behind the gerontology boom that dominated society. Above all, Nonas were dangerous because they had reverted to their childhoods. They loved to play the games of their childhood, especially Hide And Seek in which they could "disappear", morph. You never knew where you stood with a Nona. You could never trust one.

Octas, the former punks of the nineteen seventies were money and status-obsessed.

Septas, born in the mid sixties and nineteen seventies were dry, analytical and driven, dedicated to fighting the hedonistic Nonas.

Those born in the eighties had refused a label. Now in their 60s, they were the ones having babies.

Nonas, Octas, Septas, made so much noise, demanded so much. Millennials and those born after them, like her, were essentially worker bees, supporting their elders who seemed to be going on forever.

Putting grey in their hair no longer worked for her generation. Too many people were doing it. Even grey hair wouldn't help the young ferals surrounding her. They were doomed.

This was life in the year 2044.

Someone was talking to her. He had been talking to her for a few

minutes, but this was the first time that she heard him:"…easy to cultivate groups of people to be antagonistic to each other. Antagonism is in our nature. We'd fight over a feather floating in the air. Look at these kids. Sometimes what they're fighting about is upfront, but most of the time it's very subtle. We'll drop something in to them like: '5,000 years ago, your people fought my people' and they pass that message down.

It's the 'Ancient Outrage' technique. 'AO' is really popular because you can massage the facts a little bit and then watch 'em explode! In the old days people tolerated gang warfare, it went on for a long time. Then the government got smart and thought: 'Hey, don't fight it. Let's use this negativity. Make it tangible, measure the energy that two kids fighting release. What negative space do they leave as the positive space they create is filled with their violence? We can use that negative space which people thought was unusable."

"Entropy."

"A little bit. We're working on using it, seeing if it can be used. If we can harness that, we'll change the world. I've got a feeling some people already have, but they're the so-called 'primitives', so we don't bother. Those 'miracles' that people have talked about? That's the use of entropy."

"I don't understand."

He smiled.

"If a ju-ju man tells you that he can see the future, believe him. He's using entropy."

He was talking in such obscurity that she knew two things right away: a) that he was a systems man, and b) that he was high on 'o'.

Jody Carlyle recognized a fellow junkie.

There was no question that he was addicted to the 'feel-good' pheromone oxcymorcin, just as she was.

He had the tell-tale constant smile and bright, shiny eyes.

Oxcymorcin.

One of the people she would always be grateful to was a Septa, Dr. Melanie Farbesh. Professor Farbesh had wanted to bottle the loving and trusting feelings she felt while nursing her children. She had worked on a formula for decades before finally making her breakthrough a few years ago.

Dr. Farbesh had discovered how to take a big hormone like oxytocin – the source of her loving emotions – across the blood/brain barrier in order to create a drug that could make anyone content and happy at a profound level, at will.

Many people took it instead of taking the trouble to have sex. It cut down the need to encounter other human beings, the risk of contamination, and the need to enter other environments.

For Jody, it kept the questions at bay.

All she had to do was take it and enjoy.

She was addicted to it.

She enjoyed inhaling it rather than injecting it. She did not like piercing her flesh. There was always the risk of infection.

It was only with the help of 'o' that she could witness what she was watching now, a particular form of sport known as 'The Ugly Hours'.

The systems man was still talking: "…they call entropy 'disorder'. But nothing is disorder. Disorder is the order that you can't see yet."

He stopped talking. When he spoke again, his voice was very low.

"You'd think somebody'd want kids who look like that. Blue eyes, blond hair. I haven't seen a blue-eyed blonde little girl for years.

Except for you."

At last, Jody recognized the voice.

He had been one of her trainers.

"Well, looks like the morph rumour is true. I didn't even recognize you,"
Jody said.

*He was so involved that he did not hear her question. He continued above
the enclave's din.*

*"…take our handmade environment: 'Ubiquity.' We need to think that our
24 hour wrap-around surveillance keeps us safe. But the 'Uncertainty Principle'
reminds us – no system can be both consistent and complete. In other words,
the antidote comes into being when the poison is made. Nothing is 100%. But
we don't want to remind people of that. Besides, 'Ubiquity' is, to put it crudely,
playing games with our brains. We don't have a clue as to what's really going
on. We never have. 'Ubiquity' just uses that to make the world it wants.*

Hey, we could be in the middle of World War Three, but who knows?

*You and I know it, that's who. We know about 'Ubiquity'. We know what
HC-5 is for. We know. FSD likes HC-5 because it's not built on a boring
grid, like most American cities. HC-5 is like a head of broccoli, bumpy, each
section growing out of another with no apparent start-up. It just does. Used
to be called London, England. So ok, London is fractal, the city is shapes born
out of shapes, born out of shapes, born out of shapes. Nothing but a series of
feedback loops. Good place to do our experiments, test out our theories, find
guinea pigs. Speaking of guinea pigs…"*

*He produced what looked like a tiny mirror. She looked in it but couldn't
see herself.*

"This is sending a signal to your brain. Look into it again."

Jody did. The face she saw there was his.

*"Now", he continued, "we know that humans can remember up to 10,000
faces. This function happens in the anterior temporal cortex, which I am
manipulating…"*

He touched her ear.

*"There, the right fusiform gyrus just behind the ear reacts to a face that it
recognizes even if that face is changed a little. The inferior occipital gyri at the
back of the brain are the ones sensitive to slight changes in morphed faces, say,
on screens. The brain is hard-wired to pin a single identity to a single face. You
damage any of these parts of the brain I've just referred to, you've got a crisis."*

"What kind of crisis?"

"Dementia patients with damage to the anterior temporal cortex, for instance, have a problem putting a name to a face, while damage to the right fusiform gyrus can cause an epileptic to believe that several faces belong to the same person. Now, and this is the great part: in HC5, we are learning how to adjust and play with those areas of the brain. In our research there, we study patterns like the tendency toward unconscious herd hysteria. Remember those stabbings and shootings among black kids in HC5 at the beginning of the century. We call those kids 'extreme feedback mechanisms due to acute fractionality'.

With this mirror, we can disorient our enemies. Placed in the places where they get together, the distortion will start to build up in their brain and we will have incapacitated them. They won't be causing mayhem to themselves or anybody else because they'll be too busy trying to figure out who they are. We're also working with this on the ferals here. It's looking very promising."

"Is that all we do? Keep people in cages – virtual and real?"

"Whoa, Nelly!" he yelled. "You're our star pupil, Jody, the rising Tool in Elimination Systems. You are absolutely key to what we're doing. You know what really turns me on? In fifty years, we'll know everything about human beings, even before conception. We can eliminate the troublemakers before they hatch. That'll be far out!!!"

"In order to make our lives safer. Cleaner...", Jody said, "we Ultras...What we don't need or want, what might hurt us, we eliminate."

"Yeah. Elimination Systems!"

Jody watched the children tearing each other apart.

She closed her eyes.

The oxymorcin was wearing off.

She had to get to her apartment, her haven.

She hurried home through the Special Network created for Ultras like her.

When she arrived, the man who had saved her life, who was the only real parent – the only father she had ever known – was waiting for her.

Control...

Waiting.

The only person who made her happy.

DANTE, THE DIVINE COMEDY

Something inside had told Janet Bookman Baker to simply be happy, not in the big things that she sought: peace of mind and the all-encompassing passion her father had had briefly that summer years ago, but to be simply happy with the minutiae of the life of a woman with a busy husband and two growing children; content with this plan as late as last summer when she and Sam and the children, along with a young Polish student from down the road, had planted the new garden; Janet radiant and full of life – before the arrival of Tomas Saddler next door and the return of the chaos she had thought she had laid to rest.

To rest, even for just a moment, would have been welcome; but as soon as she unlocked the door and turned the knob, there would be, among other things, the question of Lucas's schooling to consider all over again, along with the undeclared battle between her husband and her son.

Her son, Lucas, eleven months older than his sister, precocious like her but very different, and, unlike her, from a very early age, lost in the world of his beloved equations – he detested computers, great workhorses, but not subtle enough-always with his beloved numbers; a boy especially devoted to the Number Three, the number in which he had spontaneously grouped all of his toys in late infancy, adoring it for its symmetry, its clear quality – to him like sleigh bells ringing in the snow, or sometimes fragile and metallic like the sound of a young tree, yielding, its thin wood bending in the first strong wind of spring, a light rain falling on its leaves; she remembering how he had burst into tears at the age of eight when he had first understood the triangle whose shape he would gaze at for hours if allowed to, along with equations, musical scores for Lucas.

Lucas, always to be found bent over his pen and paper, the lovely curve of his neck so like Milton Bookman's; his sharp, dark eyes, like her father's too: always bright.

Always bright, even that day a week ago, when, after being chased home from the library, he had come through the garden entrance, silent, wiping himself down, refusing to discuss what had happened, demanding that she say nothing, do nothing, not be his mother, not be his defender; she standing aside, letting him do the things he had to do in his own way; those bright eyes shining; making himself a sandwich in silence, then sitting down at the kitchen table to eat it; quiet for too long a time, and then, looking at her, his face radiant, he had told her that being chased by the local "mandem" had been a good thing; the "soljahs" having given him a chance, while sprinting through the streets, to empty his mind, to watch the theory he had been thinking assemble itself without his assistance; ready now, he had said, his mouth full of bread, to work his idea straight through.

Through his own natural curiosity and dogged determination to understand all that he could about everything, he had, while running, with his empty mind, brought together his primary mathematical and scientific interests in a beautiful way to begin to understand his tormentors.

His tormentors, he had said excitedly, were brilliant products of The Second Law Of Thermodynamics – Entropy; this idea coming to him after he had stumbled upon the Law, and shortly afterwards, had had a strange but wonderful feeling that human beings were bundles of information, information being what the Second Law describes, and information in itself is neutral, just as $E=mc^2$ can be used to warm homes or make atom bombs and since we are all bundles of information, we are all connected; something he intended – along with quantum mechanics and the idea of the universe as a membrane –to study at university.

At university too he would develop a non-sociology based science of the enslaved basing it on the way in which his ancestors had used the very sweat from their labour as a feedback system through which they developed a profound art, music, philosophy, including ways and means to stay alive.

To stay alive, he had said to her in his run-on sentences, had been the first goal of the enslaved and in doing so they had created something new, something which had African culture as its root and matrix, but had, in fact, extended that culture.

That culture, Lucas had gone on barely stopping for breath, she terrified that he might choke on his sandwich, but not daring to bring his discourse to a halt and risk one of his tantrums, was a kind of mutation – new; confident in his suspicion that something had changed during the Great Slave Crossing because of the Number Three – as in the number of typical ports of call of the Triangular Trade: the slave station on the Atlantic Coast of Africa; crossing to the New World where the slaves were deposited; and the return trip to the Atlantic coast of Africa with calico, mirrors and guns for the Africans – all of this involved in his interpretation of the 'Three Body Problem'.

The 'Three Body Problem', he would say over and over again to help her understand, concerned the relationship involving the sun, moon and the earth: just as the sun disturbs the attraction between the earth and the moon, the attraction between Europe and Africa had involved a 'third body', the enslaved, the enslaved becoming possibly mutationally different from those back in their homeland as a result, perhaps different from everyone else on the earth since 'The Three Body Problem' caused change; he therefore preferring to be referred to as 'black', a more accurate name for that change than 'African'; black being more indicative of the fractal nature of the slave experience; his own physics theory, his own equation in which he hoped to explain the special nature of the Diaspora; this theory was the closest to his heart.

His heart, Sam had said the last time that Janet had brought up the subject of Lucas' schooling, told him that Lucas must attend school in the community with black boys like himself, not at some public school in deepest Wiltshire; tuck box and trunk, name tapes, and black loafers; and that peculiar 'Imperial Inner Silence' which

Sam detested, that public school sureness, that in Lucas' case would be false, an illusion; more determined than ever that his own son would not sound like one of the ruling class over the telephone, then turn up in the flesh a living contradiction; and the gulf between her and her husband widened each day, until now they had no conversation, and there was nothing between them but the routine of their lives and a loneliness that had a special quality which could only exist between a husband and a wife.

'Between a husband and a wife', her mother would say, lips pursed, while dusting down her beloved glass figurines of 18th century English shepherdesses –Gloria-Loretta continuously attempting to shape life, define it, make it into something manageable; Gloria Loretta, a quiet and resolute atheist, confident that if she were wrong she could, at the Pearly Gates, successfully explain her way out of it; totally appalled and repulsed by an England and a London that had let her down; life in a city with a filthy, turbulent river and people like the Saddler family next door – he a former professor of mathematics who never changed his trousers, a German, a white man with his Negro wife, a woman, like her, from The Island who, dead husband or no, should never have allowed her little son to grow up in a house where she slept with and kissed and washed and cooked for a white man, husband or no; railing against them every time she cleaned the budgie cage – poor little Jaspar, huddling in terror at the assault on his environment, taking the brunt of it all, his treatment instilling in Janet a fear and hatred of zoos, circuses, caged creatures.

Caged creatures, Janet thought as she looked in on the children, surprisingly watching telly together, their heads close in a complicity she had rarely seen; thinking of her mother – it was mid-morning for her back on The Island – Gloria-Loretta up early before the heat and humidity in order to get her kitchen started; running her guest house on her own, a legend on The Island already; once confronting a potential robber with a gun, she almost mannish-looking in her big hat, trousers, loose shirt, not the feminine 'English Lady' in her tiny shoes, gloves and handbag that her father had married, not the woman betrayed who had never directly spoken about the weekend her husband had disappeared, not the woman who had never, except once, openly displayed her inner rage, a rage nevertheless that had consumed the house, making her husband more withdrawn, and Janet aware of the unspoken, aware of the erotic that had turned in on itself.

On itself, and of itself, her father's lost weekend that rainy two days in her early adolescence when he had not come home from his job on the bus, had been the defining moment of her life when her childhood had come to an end and she had faced the onslaught of a wider world, a world beyond her control; a chaos that had been set into motion by Janey Francis, a woman also from the Caribbean like her parents; a whirlwind who owned a shop called 'Taken As Red' in which every item was either red, had the word in its title, or both; Janey Francis with her long red locks, her sparkly, bright carnival dresses worn every day of the year, her dark shining skin, her eyes inquisitive, naughty, in contrast to the carefully guarded eyes of Gloria-Loretta; Janey Francis, a woman who could create legends by the casual sweep of an arm. Janet, over the years and even now, standing outside of her shop from time to time, watching her through the windows; Janey Francis, a woman always laughing, her big Island music creating an atmosphere that kept her shop crowded and welcoming and warm; a beautiful woman with beautiful things; Janet growing up outside her window, watching her, weaving in her own mind stories of lost African queens, black-skinned pirate women on the Caribbean Sea, warriors, devils, the divine.

Divine Janey Francis, no mystery at all as to why Milton Bookman had gone to her, no mystery at all as to why her own childhood had become a battleground of silences; and now, to find herself in a place that she could not name. She could not name the years that had gone by, a decade now, after her father had been found dead on the Common, a book in one hand and a rain-soaked letter in the other, amongst the few words legible had been the word 'child'.

Child and woman her father had called her, she pretending not to understand when he said it, even to be offended; nevertheless it had become increasingly obvious that her life had been a series of actions and reactions that filled in the outline he had created, books being all that mattered, great books, those who could not understand had not taken the time to read, had not taken the time to listen to others; his route from Westminster Bridge to the far fields of Plumstead taking the journey every day in his rolling kingdom, the tiny, tight world of the Routemaster, red-clad and red-bound on the old Pilgrims' Way.

The old Pilgrims' Way suited him when he had been full of the promises of the Mother Country; in the end he had been a man left to create in his own mind what the meaning of his life was while listening to his passengers, absorbing and discarding the short and the long view; not frightened by the real world around him: the cold, the greed and the indifference – indifferent to the air suffused with horrid smells day in and day out; in the beginning squatting down to the floor often, so that he could breathe, the old imperial centre dingy and hopeless when he had first arrived clean and shiny and with hope; a man too full of knowledge for his own good.

His own good – that which would serve Milton John Bookman at the deepest level – would always include a past which would enable him to live in the present; yet to her Milton Bookman was a Lord Byron limping to a Greece which would never understand who he was, which used him for its own purposes; and she, after the weekend of his disappearance and return, watching his life year by year, day by day broken on a lonely shore of his own making.

Making as best he could a world for those who boarded his bus and handed him their grubby coins and notes; who smelled of drink and of poverty; of cramped rooms and bad cooking, whose eyes were flat and faces closed and hard; how could they know that it was Balzac who had made it possible for him to serve them and 'Pip' who had matched his own life.

His own life was for him the only real measure; he had taught her that, but she had lost it, and her father, not being an academic but only a bus conductor, only a man who read when he could, collected what he could, built his own library book by book, often from recommendations from his regulars, who like him, worked with their hands; he, Milton Bookman, son of a man who had worked the sugar cane fields, he who had been taught by his semi-literate father to read for England, knew all too well that there were those who assumed that a man who worked with his hands, who took fares every day in all weathers was invisible; incapable of the trick question he would pose to any passenger who claimed to have read literature at university, any university; what did Cervantes and Shakespeare have in common besides being the greatest writers the world has ever produced; Milton Bookman the tall, thin black man with the El Greco eyes would, in a traffic jam, amuse himself by conducting a discussion on one of his favourite subjects, etymology, or some obscure fact: the name Iago being a corruption of St. James; the French dish 'Coquilles St. Jacques' named after the sea shell which was a symbol of St. James and the Milky Way; pleased at his passengers' astonishment, pleased that they had mistaken his ready smile and his jolly voice for ignorance and buffoonery, not knowing that he was descended from a long line of people who by necessity, could read eyes, facial tics and souls; climbing the winding staircase of the bus with an air of victory, staring out of the front window of the upper deck, like a monarch of the route; Janet unable to forget the day she had ridden with him and had seen him in his glory, supreme and moving down the long road in his bus, which had always been a metaphor for his own life.

47

She Showed Me The Horizon Line

I call myself posthumous.
I found a man dead.
My dear friend.
I saw him. But my parents told me I didn't.
I call myself posthumous.
Because of my nanny.
She's the reason, too.
I'm sorry, but I had one.
Me and her. She and I.

Me sitting at my own little table in the corner of the kitchen, listening to the stories she made up for me.

I was a hyperactive kid who couldn't stop talking and the only thing that shut me up was a story.

Her stories seemed spontaneous to me. But like everything that looks easy, she worked hard at them. I know that now by the quality of them.

She created whole worlds for me. Imaginary animals.

I really liked the animals. My own bestiary. Have you ever had your own bestiary?

Metamorphoses. The scariest thing. But I loved it. They talked, too. I can remember how they talked. But I'm not sharing that with anyone.

The stories. No matter how elaborate or far out, were always stories of caution or warning.

My nanny thought I'd wind up plunging into the world head first.

She wanted everything to be neat and clean and safe. Everything around me was neat and clean and safe. The treachery of that.

I found refuge in the stories. After all, my nanny was trying to save my life. For what that was worth.

The stories had morals like:

Don't cross the street until the light is green; Don't go home with strangers; Don't lie.

Never tell lies.

Never forget that a story can change direction, can change its nature even in the middle of it telling itself to you, just turn like that, and you have to follow it because that turn is the story breathing and living.

You don't have to understand it. But you can feel if it's right.

And always to say my prayers at night because there's a God up there and He's keeping tabs. He's benevolent, she'd tell me, not some old guy ready to squash me like an ant if I don't do what He says. My nanny's God was not a dictator and a somebody with a fiery sword. He was born in a bestiary.

My nanny always said to me that in the beginning, the word was made for the people.

Not the people for the word.

The world hadn't been good to her. She had wanted to see the world. "Like a proper coloured girl", she'd say, "in a big hat and travelling cases, lovely shoes and a handbag made out of gold. I wanted a Prince Charming to erase the bad nights, and I want that for you, too, Anna. I want your future to be full of light and the sweet smell of your own accomplishments. I want you to love God because God holds you in His hand with the greatest poise and He never interferes, not even when you ask. Because He loves you, Anna."

She slept in my room with me whenever my parents were fighting. She'd hold me close and the smell of the kitchen and Ivory soap and the garden and sometimes Chanel Number 5 – her main luxury – bathed me and made me feel like a human being.

I was ten and my nanny was about twenty. That's really young when I look back now. She was younger than I am. How could she carry so much at such a young age? I can see her face. I can see that she was young, too young to have so much sorrow and also so much compassion.

The world hadn't been good to her. But she was good herself.

A big word, good. A big concept, goodness.

When you're a little kid you don't have preconceptions. You're not cynical. Cynical about what? You spill your guts 24/7 because this is childhood. And I'm not saying she was a child. She just listened to me, that's all. She didn't look down or treat me like a second-class citizen because I was three feet tall and needed a nap every day.

Her point of view was my point of view. You don't have any other window to look out of as a kid because adults have the ability to take you to that window, open it and show you what they want to show you unless another adult takes you away and says 'Look this way' and when you look, you know, although you can't prove it, that what you see is what they want you to see.

She showed me the horizon line from my window in the early morning. She told me that the sun was the same sun that had shone on everybody who had ever lived. Jesus walked under the same sun we were looking at, and the same moon.

Stuff like that.

Then there was that she had an older sister she never saw, or more to the point, who never saw her. No contact, even though she would leave notes. I hated that sister for not contacting her.

I hated her sister for that.

There was no way that I could find inside myself to understand her or forgive her.

Now look at me.

I'm here.

Waiting.

Just waiting.

I'm waiting. Me and my story. Waiting.

You know, you don't know what being an only child means. You have a sister. Like I wish I had. So that I could have told her what I had seen, what I knew. That day.

I couldn't tell my parents. They were caught up in their own melodrama. I didn't exist. As their daughter, yes, for sure. But not as me. Whoever that….

I can still see it:

I go out. I need to get out, get some air. I'm a kid who needs fresh air. I climb over the fence that divides our house from Carl's. I go through the basement door that he leaves open for me and the alley cat that he feeds.

I look all over the house. It's dark, but I can see that he's not there. I'm scared but I don't know why.

I walk out the door to his garden. I see his whiskey bottle on the bricks he is using to make a pathway.

I walk further into the garden.

It is summer in Chicago. The air is heavy. I can barely breathe.

I want to take a bath. I can see myself in my bubble bath, my bestiary playing in my head. We are frolicking in the soap and the bubbles, my animals and me. Laughing. They are telling me to come under the bubble bath to their land, to where they are floating in joy. In peace.

I count my steps as I walk further into the garden. One. Two. Three. Numbers are comforting and it is here that for the first time, I discover this.

Two squirrels are in a tree, fighting over a walnut. It is so still. So still.

There he is.

I find him.

He is sitting in his kitchen chair. The one he likes. The one from his dead mother's house with the ornate back. 'The brothel chair', he always called it.

He never told me what a brothel was but I remember now, as I walk toward him, that he said, "Long ago, Annie. In this city called Paris. You'll go there someday. One day there was a house of women. Some folks would say they did bad things, but you know what I say? I say that they were free. They were powerful ladies, could make the sun set, the moon rise. They had been slaves and the daughters of slaves. They had powers that made them vanish in thin air in order to escape the lash. They were great understanders of the cosmos. They could see the holy rhythm beneath the madness and the ebb and the flow, and it kept them whole. My grandmother was the child of one of those women and my mother her child, and I am my mother's child. And you, Annie, that's you, too. You'll find out and when you do, I want to see your face. Our folks, all of our folks – from those winos out there on the corner, to the preachers, the rag lady – we came out of Africa but were not deserted. Remember what I'm sayin', ok?"

And now I do. Word for word for word. Because I can see him clearly now.

It looks like a crown of thorns on his head, or roses. He is smiling. He is still.

I tell my parents. They tell me that I have found a sleeping man.

I want to believe this too.

With that mess at home, Mom and Dad send me away to school. Roc was the place where I felt sheltered and safe.

The full name of the school is 'Our Lady Of Rocamadour'. It is located in the Michigan woods, on a trail that was a part of the old Underground Railroad, the name for the series of safe houses that runaway slaves used.

Roc was and still is a group of buildings made to look like a medieval fortress in the South of France, whitish-brown and pretending to be on mountaintops.

It was created by an order of black French nuns that had been founded right after the abolition of slavery by the Commune of Paris during the French Revolution.

They were Jacobins in their soul and their goal had been to educate the daughters of the free and the enslaved.

After Napoleon re-established slavery, some of them went to Haiti to teach girls there and to fight for L'Ouverture.

Eventually some of them emigrated to America and began to teach freed and enslaved young girls, and to work as part of the Underground Railroad, providing safe houses for those who ran away from enslavement.

They survived the war and set up a school in Michigan dedicated to 'creating the whole woman, with an eye on her ancestors'.

Roc did not allow the fashions in language to penetrate its walls.

Something they called 'English phonics' and Latin and Greek were taught in the morning followed by French in the afternoon with madeleines and tea; American history – especially the history of slavery; the Emancipation Proclamation which freed the slaves in those territories in rebellion against the United States; the Constitution; the Federalist papers; the poetry of Whitman; the works of Melville; Richard Wright; James Baldwin; W.E.B. Dubois; Zora Neale Hurston.; Toni Morrison; and the Women's Brigade in the Paris Commune.

We of course studied Catholicism.

But at Roc, we studied it as a continuation of the religions of Egypt.

The bishop made spot checks on us a lot. But he couldn't touch us because we could recite anything he wanted.

We had heard of another group of black nuns, who had broken off from the Order that had founded Roc, and who had remained in France.

Eventually they left the Order altogether, and ended up setting up a brothel in Paris on the Ile St. Louis.

An act that somebody like Luis Buñuel would understand completely.

It was they who were said to possess a Secret brought over on the slave boats.

Nobody knows what that was.

There some kind of a medal struck in Paris at the end of the 19th century especially for those in possession of the Secret.

There are supposed to be pictures of it around.

But I don't know anything about that.

But Montgomery Tourlaine did.

Before I came here and found you, I lived in the same building as he did.

He lived across the hall from me and we usually met in the corridor.

I mentioned this alleged picture to him one day and he told me that he had met a blues singer in 1970 in Kansas City who wore one.

Her mother had brought it back from Paris after World War Two.

She'd joined to help the black soldiers there, and when she found out that the black service women were put near the white service men and nobody gave a damn, her mother had gone AWOL and met a black woman in Paris who gave the medal to her. But the blues singer wouldn't tell him what it meant.

Montgomery Tourlaine.

Born into gentility in Alabama, he came to London in the mid-sixties to go to university. By the late seventies he had written two novels while doing graduate work at Oxford.

He also took a job reviewing books to help him finance his third novel, the one about his father who escaped Berlin after Kristallnacht and ended up being moved around London during the war because his family were 'enemy aliens'.

He never got around to finishing the third novel because he got a job on a daily, writing about other people's books and their gossip which paid more money than he had ever had in his life.

Soon after getting that job, Montgomery (he hated 'Monty') met his future wife at a drinks party and they married soon after. She began producing babies every eleven months, so Montgomery moved them all into a big house in North London, then the schooling began and he took another job writing a column in which he pedalled recycled arts rumours and the cheap opinions of his drinking buddies.

The column eventually enabled him to buy a place in the country, send the family down there, and take a small flat in central London near to where he drank, in the building I eventually lived in, the building a good place to install a young girl who was studying creative writing at some university and had already been given six figures for thirty pages of her first novel.

Montgomery had decided to move back to America with whatever kids wanted to go with him, and take over his mother's clothes factory up in New Jersey.

He'd been working on his farewell to London, a novel he provisionally called 'The Pundit,' "the adventures of a tall skinny American kid who had high hopes about literature and his place in it but ended up a hack."

"Why did I do it? Money. I wanted the profile, the name. Money begets money, fame begets fame, you get addicted, hooked, and what happens? IT happens, Anna. Obsolescence. Pointlessness. You think: 'Yes, I'm going to provide a service. I'm going to put my two cents into the argument, but do you know what? Nobody wants your two cents. They don't want to know. All they want to do is talk. Talk, talk, talk, write their opinions, be visible, matter. Critics? Real ones, ones who have made it a calling, a vocation?

Do they exist?

Am I one?

Are you kidding?

You know what we have now in place of criticism? Punditry. We have people and I'm one of them, who think their opinion is what the world revolves around. Their opinion! Years of work, of blood, sweat and tears are destroyed every minute of the day by punditry.

Someone is anointed by the powers-that-be and suddenly he's all over the airwaves. What's the problem with that, they can learn as they go, they can bone up on the run and who suffers?

Culture suffers!!!!! Civilization, which is always hanging by a thread at the best of times, suffers!

The world is full of people who walk around with their heads crowded with statistics, little facts, useless rubbish, praying that they can get on some quiz show or into some talent contest.

And have you noticed? Everybody's got an opinion. The Kiwi who cuts my grass spends hours telling me what he thinks of the latest movies. I'm giving him my column. I've had it. I'm heading back to New Jersey to sell shmatte to New Yorican totty. That, Anna, is honourable work. Listen to me. Go back to the States. It's a beautiful place. It's the last place. Get out before you can't look yourself in the mirror any more."

"I never can see my face in the mirror anyway", I wanted to tell him, but Montgomery's conversations are not made for give and take.

We're in the hallway as usual. I pull my coat around me. It's cold. His world is cold. He has no landline, no mobile, no internet. The Luddite's Luddite.

Most times I just can't take Montgomery.

I can't take his despair or rage.

I've never been inside his place.

I don't want to be.

I know that he wants a response from me.

I just can't figure out what it should be.

I wear big coats all the time.

No matter what the weather. Big coats with Don Corleone shoulders. I wash when I can remember to.

And the books of Abena Assantewa, they always kept me sane.

Do you think that I can say that to her at the appropriate time?

I told myself that my nanny had died the night Carl Cookson died.

I told myself that she had walked out into the night. In leaving me, she had condemned herself to a terrible death. Or maybe she had gone to some foreign land where she got amnesia.

For years and years I made up my mind never to say her name. Not even in my head. Never.

I am ten years old when I bring the shutters down.

I let in no light. No fresh air.

And I know what I saw that day.

No matter what my parents said.

To save myself, I wove my own fiction.

I compensated my mind, nourished it, defended it, against the time that I found Carl Cookson.

My defence against the onslaught of my parents was to weave my own story of that moment:

I am walking through a maze.

I know how to go through the maze, how to navigate its turns and its twists.

I am walking.

There is something sweet in my nostrils, something warm and evil.

I arrive at the heart of the maze. Carl is seated on his kitchen chair, a crown of thorns and roses around his head.

I like him. He sings the blues in his backyard all day. He plays jazz at night.

I sing to him: 'My nanny done gone and my friend is dead' to the strains of a crying guitar.

That's how I made it through.

I hold this myth in my heart. My myth.

Nobody asks me why I don't want to go to church anymore.

2.

As she waited for Control to speak, other words came back to her:

"As a new Tool in 'Elimination Systems', I can now inform you that you have come into parts of your inheritance as an Ultra. That inheritance is knowing one of our secrets: we artificially create what people consider reality. We base this reality on our data. We do this in order to make lives safer. Cleaner. There you have it. We know where all the 'lost ones' are. There are a lot more and you'll be let in on them as time goes on…"

Suddenly, she heard Control's voice in her head complete the sentence: "…at 'Elimination Systems' what we don't need or want, what might hurt us, we eliminate. Welcome onboard.".

Control was inside her mind.

Jody closed her eyes. The oxymorcin was wearing off.

She had to get away, get out of the all-powerful 24 hour surveillance system, 'Ubiquity'.

But how?

Control was making himself comfortable. He had an air of quiet power overlaid by a subtle menace. He had allowed his hair to go slightly grey, but his skin was still firm and fresh. His face had all the mischievousness of a child, especially when he smiled. He was the best example of a Nona she had ever seen.

And she loved him. She loved him for what he had done for her. Control had saved her. But they were not close. Control was cold and it always seemed as if he were harbouring a secret. Someone sinister.

Someone who could kill her.

Control began talking to her in his homely way as if he had been with her for hours.

"Jody, you know, I was just sitting here thinking that there are sounds from my childhood that I really miss. We don't HEAR things any more: like coins in a pay phone; cash registers; adding machines; ticking watches. Watches used to have sound. Maybe I'll bring all that old stuff back."

"You can."

"And you know what? One of the problems with the good old US of A is that we don't have any…ruins. We need ruins! They instil pride. I told folks at the time of Ground Zero and New Orleans that they should have been left as they were But who listens to me?"

She laughed.

"Yeah. I guess they don't call me 'Control' for nothing."

He uncoiled his long body.

"I just got back from London. I hate like hell calling that town HubCity5. Means nothing to anybody but those damn digital pen-pushers. Used to be a great place."

"What'd you do there?"

"Well, first off", he smiled, "I had a great meal: The Red Meal Special: 'to give everybody a little boost in these tense times'."

She had never heard of the wine nor the dishes he was talking about as examples of food and drink to 'make you happy' "Guigal's 1978 Côte Rôtie. La Mouline", he said, "Aw, it reminds me of some of the legendary Rhône Valley wines from 1929. Oh, and there was a sublime Pauillac there, too. 1945 Mouton Rothschild".

He was lost in reverie for a moment. Then continued, "In 'Les Misérables', Hugo refers to 'the good wine of Mauves'. You know, I think that this could be Hermitage because a lot of red wine in 19th century France was "hermitagé", or fortified with Hermitage which had had a vineyard in Mauves since 1480. And then there was the stupendous 2025 vintage, the one that came after everyone got back on their feet following the weather catastrophe of 2012, when everything changed forever…

People back then liked to demonstrate their knowledge of food and drink. It was a one-upmanship kind of thing. Like their possessions. During the years following, people accumulated so many things that rented storage areas became second homes, most of the living space then *was given over to possessions. People shopped and shopped. Women especially collected shoes, hundreds of pairs. Possessions, designer labels, money, those things really meant a lot."*

Jody laughed. She could not imagine how a pair of shoes could make a person feel safe and happy. Only 'FSD' could do that and that was available to everyone, rich and poor.

All thanks to the President of the United States, Thelma Louise Hess.

President Hess was one of the famous Hess Triplets: math and musical prodigies, linguists, sportswomen, and Chess Grand Masters. All three had been found in a giant moses basket floating down the Missouri after the great flood that had almost wiped out St. Louis.

They had been three little black girls that no one had come to claim, so they were raised on a farm by the descendants of Norwegian immigrants.

They were so sheltered that they did not see an electric light until they were seven.

Thelma Louise had run her campaign on the platform of 'Full Spectrum Dominance'.

FSD was known by its official name only by those deep inside government circles. The name was finally brought out by President Hess into the light of day with a speech on the site of The First Outrage: Ground Zero, New York City.

"Let the word go forth today: that the only way to protect ourselves is to turn the world into ourselves. We must create a world of our institutions. We must create a world of our language. We must create a world of our laws."

President Hess had completed the task begun in the early years of the century.

Control was quiet for a moment.

Then, "You know", he said, "the food was all red. Red, the colour of energy. There it was: tagine of lamb with couscous; frijoles negro con pescado from Cuba; black eyed peas with fish and tomatoes, red chillies and prawns; smoked red herring; mullet; curried ackees; snapper; and to finish, sorrel drunk straight down. A great meal in a great place. Any place that can monitor its citizens 24 hours a day, awake, asleep, even before birth, has to be a good place to be."

And Control told her his real business in HC5.

They had taken a young hunter there, one of the people who found and captured those considered to be enemies; the Undetectables, the subversives. He had become one himself. In the end, he had confessed everything. He had had an English friend who had decided to return there after England had lost its seat on the UN Security Council following the break-up of the United Kingdom a few years ago.

He had eventually told the hunter that his real reason for going back was to join the movement called '39, 40', the numbers taken from Clauses 39 and 40 of Magna Carta. He had been sent the relevant sections from it: 'no free man shall be taken or imprisoned or deprived…except by the lawful judgment of his peers or by the law of the land', and the other: 'to no one will we sell, to no one will we deny or delay right or justice'.

The Movement had pointed out that the Data Protection Act of 1984 was the source of a grave problem, the Act not having been rigorous enough to prevent the creeping powers of the Information Commissioner set up in the UK at the turn of the century.

And there had been more information sent back to him about how Magna Carta had elevated the rule of law over executive power; how the revolutionary Americans had called on Magna Carta to guarantee their rights, John Adams stating that the brutality shown towards the colonies was against 'the great charter itself'. The ancient Fifth Amendment resembled in large part Clause 39. Magna Carta had underpinned American Habeas Corpus. When it existed.

I don't blame him. Just a kid. A post-Millenial. After everything that was done to him, know what he said? He felt safe in England. That's what he called HC5.

Oh, and the real highlight of the trip: I met some guys working in 248 dimensions, or trying to. Mathematicians. Some of them are tiny, like fairy wisps from a storybook. Do you know that mathematicians say the word 'beautiful' more than artists do? Anyway the word from them is

'Deep Symmetry'. That's what God is."

He was quiet for a moment.

He was reading her.

She thought of wiping her mind, but it was too late.

"Kid", he said, 'You always let things bother you. Too much introspection is bad."

He was lost in thought again.

"Those feral kids. Look, they'd make more money entertaining people than scrounging in the streets. But they're used as…gladiators. And their life expectancy… Those ferals are in the way. The world is full of collateral when you're trying to keep order. We have to be the ones who have a monopoly on violence. Hey, you're 'Elimination Systems' now, young lady."

"I was a feral", she said.

"You? You were special."

He ran his hand over the surface of her table. Words appeared on her bare wall.

"Have you seen this?"

The words read: 'We the privileged, the most beautiful, the most powerful, the most desirable people on earth reject our birthright, reject it all. Those like us seek to solve the world situation in the most non-violent and direct way that we can: we will commit self-genocide. We will not reproduce. We will be the last. We will cease to be.'

Jody thought: everyone, Ultra and non-Ultra, knew that manifesto. It belonged to the Stockholms.

She remembered the information on them: 'Stockholms are well-brought up, moderately wealthy to rich kids who identified so viscerally with what they call the "oppressed" that they are considered to be cultural victims of the 60s "Stockholm Syndrome", a Nona-era sickness. It is the psychological condition which caused victims to identify with those who victimised them. The Stockholms are considered the most dangerous because they cannot be profiled. They are the ultimate victims of ancestral mismanagement. They have declared war without weapons. They refuse to breed. The most extreme of them actively advocate the extinction of those like them. This cannot be allowed to happen. These young people are the best and the brightest. They cannot be allowed to go rogue. Our job is to find them.'

Control watched her.

He had more to say.

"'The Blueberry Farm' Books."

"'Blueberry Farm'? I don't understand. It's just a..."

"Children's book? You want to know the truth about those delightful kiddie books ? They're code. Every word, every sentence, every character."

"Code? Code for what?"

"Before the French Revolution began, the revolutionaries published their tracts on the other side of porn stories: the naughty priest having sex with the poor country girl while Sister Mary Whatch-a-ma-callit peeped through the open door waiting her turn. But the purpose of these 'libelles' was this: you turn the page over and there you find: 'Down With The King.' Jody, the 'Blueberry Farm' books promote VEC-"Voluntary Ethnic Cleansing." A suicide manifesto. We've analyzed them. All of the Stockholms' slogans are anagrams of dialogue from the book. Now if the ferals want to take themselves out, who'd care? But not the ones who read these books, not the Ultras."

Jody thought: "Rosy cheeked Mrs. Haze, her dozy husband, Hal Haze, and their talking tabby, Bonhoeffer? Subversives?"

Control stood up to his full height.

It always surprised her how tall he was.

"You're going to Paris. I wanted to come here and tell you myself."

"Paris? I'll need a swimsuit. Paris is flooded, Control."

"They're really enjoying it. Last time they had anything like it was January 1910. It's a fashion moment, everything is Belle Epoque, Edwardian, Art Nouveau, old boats from back in the day..."

"At least it'll be pretty."

Control laughed.

"Don't worry. You'll be where it's dry. You're going to meet the author of the 'Blueberry Farm Books', Saronia Miller. She wants to come home. You're bringing her back. You'll meet Charles Andromache, your contact. He'll have a little get- together for the expats. Anita Collins, alternative therapist, will be there, also known as: Blanche Rose, her nom de guerre. She's the head of the Stockies in Europe. Their spiritual mother. You know, her dad was a Supreme Court justice. Now she fights what he tried to defend. Kids today!! But I look at it like this: our species likes to tear down what our elders have built. Anyway, we're slowly poisoning her."

Jody did not react. She did not want him to read her mind for the moment.

"I'm going to meet Saronia Miller?"

"A fan I see."

"Every little kid is at some point. Why doesn't she just go on her own?"

"Not that straightforward. She's a big deal over there. The French use her as a poster girl for their asylum system. Their President is descended from African asylum seekers. Their issues are her 'thing'. So, our fellow Americans who don't like what's going on here, go there. They always have. But we don't need the hassle with the French right now. Not while we're wiring Paris up."

"We're there, too?"

"If you can't beat the system, be the system."

"I'll remember that."

"Right. Saronia Miller, who, as you know, writes the books, will be there. You bring her to Lon…HC5. That's it."

"Why me?"

"She asked for you……"

"Why me?"

"Her husband's very sick. It's unhinged her. Go along with it. Truth is, he's dying, but nobody knows it. He's kept it secret. We've made sure that he can't be treated anywhere but HC5."

"Is that it?"

"Oh, and you'll have a new Regular in Paris. The Regular will find you".

"How will I know who it is?"

"You'll know. Anyway, it's gay Paree. Paris. I was there in the 60s. The

64

60s! We had lots of dreams, lots of goals. I didn't wait for my dreams to die. I killed them myself. If you have any, you will too, in time."

Control looked out of the window at the guard box and the darkness beyond the gate of Jody's section.

'When I was a kid I used to be like those ferals out there... I wanted to destroy everything, pull it down. I knew even then that kids, they're the real oppressed people. If I were a kid now, my only aim would be this: Pull it all down."

Control was quiet again. His eyes were closed. "I used to love the theatre when I was a kid. Especially this one play: 'The White Devil.' There was this great character in it. He had a line – I can't remember it. But I loved that line. It was me. What was that line?"

Jody waited.

In the quiet of Control's memory lapse, she saw in her mind's eye, the Image again.

The Image that appeared when she least expected it.

Someone was sending it to her.

But who?

And why?

...his former name
Is heard no more in heaven...

MILTON, PARADISE LOST

Wiping things down, shining up surfaces, she suddenly saw her father again re-reading Paradise Lost, saying some of the words out loud; stopping, Janet fanned herself with her hands, the house much too warm, the way Sam and Ayesha liked it, and she and Lucas did not; thinking of her reflection in the mirror, always vague, not lyrical like the eyes of Dr. Assantewa whose photo she had first seen on the back of one of her books, a big woman, full-lipped and broad-nosed, with the jolly face of a Botticelli angel dipped in chocolate; Janet stopping, suddenly staring at her perfect kitchen, everything in its place, like a photo in a lifestyle magazine, antiseptic, pristine, remote, deciding then and there to bake a pie from scratch; carefully measuring the flour, then rolling the dough made from it, fluting the edges, cutting the fruit into pleasant shapes, sifting and kneading, laughing a little at the thought of escaping inside this pie as the lights next door in Mrs. Saddler's garden came on, the ones Tomas had installed to show his burgeoning handiwork; pleasing, the idea of lights and Tomas, stringing them alongside the border of his mother's hedge, his powerful body like a rippling stream, almost female in its contained power, like Ayesha's, asleep after her bath, her mouth open, a small halo of spittle on her pillow, surrounded by her golden-haired dolls; her little daughter stating that dolls were for dreaming and how could she dream about something that looked like her; perfectly logical if it had not been, when she had first said it, so alarming, that comment combined with the names that she had given to her blond, blue-eyed dolls: Adjua, Abena, Akua, Yaa, Afia, Amma, Akosua; the lone black doll she approved of – a no nonsense, plain-faced antique doll that Janet had found in a second-hand shop and had begged her to take- was given the equally intriguing

66

name of Léopoldine, all of them dressed in Ayesha's latest obsession, red and its various shades and permutations: magenta, rose, maroon, raspberry, vermillion, crimson, cranberry, cardinal, claret, berry; she and her dollies tucked beneath the blanket; Ayesha in her own way, a woman already, already sure of her way; but what of Lucas, what of her son; what was the purpose of her life if she had nothing to give to him, could not help him because she could not help herself; could not see the future, prepare him for it; if only someone could appear to tell her the future that they saw – Lucas had told her that the future was mutable, as was the past, something from physics that she could not understand, once again. Janet recalling how he had, the other day, taken her on a kind of tour of his room; the blackboard covered with equations, clothing littering the floor, books and comics teetering on his chair and his windowsill, everything seemingly haphazard; Lucas explaining that it was the way it was because there were more disorderly states than orderly ones; and that within the chaos of his room there was an order, full of links as it is in all chaos, invisible to those who did not know his system, a pale reflection of that present but hidden order he sought continuously.

Continuously, like some mad magician, he had raced through it, delightedly pointing out the reality of it: what seemed to be a discarded sock whose heel, on closer inspection, pointed in the same direction as the mismatched one lying beside it, both socks pointing to a drawer covered over with science magazines hiding a small pile of clean socks.

Socks and books and clothes, and so the symmetry had unfolded, Lucas' room slowly and beautifully becoming a system composed of hidden signs beneath a surface anarchy whose rhythm and purpose created before her eyes a hidden landscape; that day, it had been her child who had helped her understand that the world, life, had more connections than she could know; and that if she would only strike out, move forward, look for those connections, she would not be cast adrift. Now, looking in on him asleep over his equations, breathing heavily through his mouth, congested again, another little cold coming on again; Janet momentarily bathed in that feeling she always felt for her babies at twilight, a deep, unnameable thing like lust without sex, like hunger with no need for food; always grateful to be a mother, but particularly at this time between the end of day and the beginning of night: 'the hour of the wolf" the French called it; love too shallow a word to describe her need for the smell and feel and heat and sound of her children; Sam, once in a moment of rare candidness, had said that he had never quite felt so alone as the time Lucas was first put into her arms.

Arms entwined and kisses, all of the paraphernalia of bedtime was over, when, suddenly, Janet remembered something from one of Abena Assantewa's early letters; it had been a paean for a time when the world looked containable, when the good seemed to be on the ascendant and youth had had a purpose; a time, she had written, so easy to mock now; so easy, too, to mock the youthful arrogance of her generation, the Baby Boomers, they who had believed that their kind had never existed before: not after 1848; not after 1918; not after 1945; they had been desperately wanted, born with a skull and crossbones above their cribs and a mushroom cloud on the horizon; her own youthful assertions and expectations now turned to dust, buried with her late husband and her dead sister, she now standing on the shore of her life, gazing across the wide, unbearable sea of it, waiting for the ferrywoman and the riverine goddesses from the Mother Country, waiting for them to come to escort her to the other side, but there was one last task unfinished, undone.

Undone, she had written, by her attempt to complete a story; the story a debt she had to pay; then she had ended the letter abruptly, begging Janet's pardon for being so obscure, obscurity being a luxury for her.

A luxury for her – time with Sam in the evening – Janet Bookman Baker worked carefully and meticulously: preparing the fresh pasta from the Italian deli on the Common, putting together the olive oil and tomatoes, the organic mince ground at the butchers, the baguettes and a good, dark bottle of Amarone – 'the bitter one' – from a grower that they had been introduced to on one of their evenings out; fresh roses on the table, candles, their fine china; Sam on the telephone in his office, his voice tense and secretive, she pouring herself a glass of wine, surveying the kitchen's wide and bare expanse of white wall, the glass door leading to the patio and out to their Japanese garden, the blankness and neatness of it a metaphor for their lives; the uncluttered and systematized surroundings light years away from her childhood of flock wallpaper, the mantelpiece crowded with family photos, the crocheted throw on the couch, the electric fire, the big chair Milton Bookman sank into every evening in the 'cosy corner', she and her parents sealing themselves in, warming themselves with their own heat; but Janet was becoming aware that she and Sam had lost along the way something they could not retrieve except in a kind of kitsch, prisoners of their success and their assimilation, 'Role Models' and 'The Perfect Couple', profiled and interviewed in all of the black press, Sam headhunted by all the major parties to stand, the successful, the beautiful, the radiant and glorious Bakers.

'The Glorious Bakers', examples for all, that was the way they had been toasted at the recent party Sam had thrown for their wedding anniversary when they had danced to 'Soul ll Soul', the way they had at their wedding and Lucas had recited a poem and Ayesha had sung a song of her own composition; Janet crying so much that she could not cut the cake, her hand trembling as Sam held it, the knife in her hand, the guests applauding, Lee 'Scratch' Perry, Sam's boyhood favourite, suddenly blasting black anarchy from the sound system, he dragging her to the floor, the knife still in her hand, a man, her man, still sexy, still loving, while in his arms she thought again of the passage in Madame Bovary where the little Norman dances at the great house in the arms of a stranger, and Sam's arms were becoming the arms of Tomas Saddler, rendering the moment cheap and sad and melodramatic and she cried again for the triteness of it all, while everyone laughed and called to her to be happy, to be proud.

To be proud was what she had a duty, an obligation to be, pride being the sole object of the life her father had striven to make for her, but everything in her life had been, even then, becoming smaller and smaller until she could not cross the Thames for fear of being swallowed up by it, but somehow, she had to; Abena Assantewa was scheduled to address a conference in Central London although obvious from that last letter that she was undoubtedly ill or in a deep malaise; if she could travel, despite this, from Paris to London, Janet could try and find a way to cross the Thames, to travel to her, but how, how could she face it? And suddenly, the laughter of the young Muslim family who had moved in across the street into her childhood home rang through the kitchen, followed by, right in the glass door at the entrance of her garden, the bold appearance of a fox

A fox, undoubtedly one of several regulars that would strew rubbish in the street just before dawn; there had been repeated sightings, talk of extermination, while she would quietly leave food out with an anti-mange concoction in it; listening intently for the fox when she couldn't sleep at night, when she would rise and go to her study, smoke her clandestine cigarettes, waiting, anticipating that small explosion of savagery in the night, the rattle of rubbish cans, the wild, uncontrollable force of nature making its way, disrupting the tidy reality of the road, its complacency invaded and disturbed at night by a wild animal; she noticing the occasional tree limb that grew back with an unnatural quickness in spite of recently being cut; the grass that recently had begun to snake between the cracks in the pavement; and she could feel, running beneath the street, the dead river whose name she did not know, a ditch actually, deep down, which her mother, Gloria-Loretta, could feel from time to time and which would frighten her, make her say that London sometime soon would be swallowed up by all the water that it held back; those dead rivers and streams and ditches would someday burst forth like all secrets; Janet Bookman Baker, standing in the twilight in her kitchen, longing to tell her mother – if she could tell her anything now – that she lived for that day, because then she could peer into the abyss.

The abyss – that was Gloria-Loretta's threat to her whenever Janet had made the decision to go her own way, even something as trivial as wanting to turn the opposite corner from the one her mother had chosen was enough to start a rant; her own choices and decisions predictably rendered damnable by a mother who would not let go; now independent of her mother's thoughts and wishes, it seemed to Janet that in her way Gloria-Loretta had been right in her discontent; that all her mother had wanted was to spare herself the grim post-war construction, the greyness of it all, the corridors of gloom that passed for the high street in her day, and above all that methodical, exacting prose of the suburbs; her father, by contrast had discovered a jewel in the local library: *Othello*; consequently remaking his bus depot into a South London Rialto by sheer virtue of his topics of conversation; the depot a marketplace and centre of gossip in which a black man, who had more inside him than anyone could suspect, would set out each day to meet his fate; all because of a gift from his mother, like the gift that Othello's mother had given him: a handkerchief, given to him before he had boarded the old troop ship to his new life in England; a piece of his mother making the journey with him; and the life she had given him, unlike Othello, he had never given away, not even to the woman he had married.

The woman he had married, with her melodramas, constant rebukes and odd self-protection, had propelled them both into a world in which Milton Bookman had turned Old Father Thames into the Adriatic at a Renaissance Venice; drumming into his only daughter and only child that *Othello* was not demeaning and racist, the key being the poetry, Shakespeare having written nothing more sublime, except in his sonnets, and certainly not for any of his other characters; this poetry for a black man, a stranger, a member of a race that Good Queen Bess had described as 'creeping' into her realm when it had been Queen Bess herself, born on the left side according to the Old Church, who had crept in; irrespective of the times, Shakespeare had conjured Othello up and out of himself; himself a stranger in a big city, a city that stripped him down every day, Shakespeare putting that feeling into a black man; defiantly elevating a black man, celebrating a black man; the Bard, a country boy like himself, living in the dank air of his writing place, most likely setting out to mock a black man but because his genius had intervened, had created instead this Othello who was himself; created out of a mutating language – mutation the only way forward, he had said – and Shakespeare, 'the upstart crow', supreme master of the three-way conversation that is theatre – even his monumental ordering of words and sound nothing in comparison to one second in the company of a Jamaican rum seller; yet in putting together, in metre, the consciousness of a man inherently more noble than any in the world in which he moved; the great poet-playwright, through his psychic forge on the Thames, his engine-room of creation, had bestowed more upon this island-nation than it could contain; and that heat which had been thrown out as a result of his sweat and toil – Lucas would have called it the 'information' as pertaining to the Second Law – it was the heat that had sent out the ships and the men with Bibles, since no truly great piece of art ever ends within the boundaries of itself; in the end it was Shakespeare himself who had helped to create the Great Triangle that deposited Othello and his people in a Western place; the immortal poetry's coming into being had brought real Moors to England; and Milton Bookman had come too, on this wave that had not stopped for four hundred years; her child's articulation of these links, his understanding of them both terrifying and confusing, her father had once admitted to Janet that he had set out to find this magic William and his sceptred isle, and like Othello, had vowed to tell his employers on his last day on the buses: 'I have done the state some service and they know it.'

As she sat in the growing darkness, Janet felt a strange connection to that time just before Milton Bookman's death when she, early in her pregnancy with Ayesha, and against the advice of her doctor who had told her to stay in bed, had gone instead to a rare book auction: the selling of an entire library of books from a country house, books she had intended to share with her father, but which, she had known would be for herself alone since he had said once, in complete seriousness, that women collected books and men built libraries; at the auction sitting next to her had been an old lady with an odd body odour, like dried roses that had been pressed for decades between the pages of an ancient

Bible, the smell causing her to have a violent and continuous sneezing fit; conscious that she was the only person like herself in the room, conscious that she had begun to annoy everyone; she had stood up abruptly, pressing against the chair of the old lady, who turning a tombstone gaze in her direction, made a remark on the lines of 'another one of them about to come into the world'; her hard eyes fixed on Janet's swollen belly on its thin frame, a comment so crass, and said in such a polite and low voice, that Janet had not understood what the woman had said until she was out in the street; the comment suddenly coming back to her, unsettling her, making her feel vulnerable, alone, holding momentarily on to a wall to stop the feeling of wanting to storm in and beat the woman, the books she had bought tumbling to the pavement and no one helping her; looking at them on the ground; wanting her father suddenly, wanting him to appear and stop the feeling that was overwhelming her that the old woman's comment had been not just a hostile one but one filled with jealousy at her fertility, at her very person and that of her unborn child; their proximity, their reality had bombarded the old woman's senses causing her to drive Janet out; she somehow, some way, had made it to the front door of her house, all the while with a strange need to, above all, secure the glasses she wore, never taken off except for sleep; she held them to her eyes just to keep seeing, thankful as she unlocked and opened the front door, for their aid in clarifying things, thankful that they had helped her to see; an involuntary laugh had erupted with such force that she had had to sit down, recalling Sam's constant insistence that she buy a new pair of glasses; her reluctance to do so out of vanity and annoyance, now understanding why he had insisted; happy, joyful that she had taken her husband's advice, happy and joyful that she was going to have another baby; listening for Lucas upstairs in the care of the baby minder, safe in the knowledge that she was away from the evil woman at the auction, sitting in her house, in her chair; stronger through what had happened at the auction house; and before she could tell him what had happened, he had died; the remembrance of that lingering through her supper with Sam, hanging in her mind as they made love; keeping her awake that night; part of her washing and preparing breakfast for Sam and the children the next day, and on to the university, to her office, seeing her pregnant self again, hurrying across the courtyard of the university, slowly realizing that it was not her but someone else, she a decade later, a university professor, staring at the young people congregating below, their youth and the advance of science rendering it unnecessary for most of them to wear glasses, she thought; removing hers, wiping them, keeping them off, relying on her kinetic intelligence, touching the edge of the desk, imagining the location of objects, unsure as always, whether her bad eyesight was real, or a wanting to block out the world just as her father had done, wanting to be blind, as he had once said to her had been his dearest wish so that he could know Milton's vision of God, so that he could be the black version of an ancient, Celtic, sleeping king.

An ancient, Celtic, sleeping king had been her father's model, a royal man of adventures and great deeds performed before he had gone to the mountains and vanished; his connection to it he had promised to tell her, and she had waited, but he had died without telling her, on the Common, his eyes open and turned toward the sky, his body gazed upon by strangers, his face frozen like an African statue, the little King Charles bitch that had discovered him dying herself the following day, the result of an enlarged heart, a condition, her owner had said, common to the species, but Janet knew that the animal had been a funerary gift, dead in order to live and accompany a king, and being her father's only child, her duty had been to go to his makeshift library, open the drawer that contained the things Milton Bookman had said he would leave her, and bring them to her office at the University for safe keeping.

Safe keeping, the irony of that, because they may be safe with her but not from her; ten years after his death, Janet still found herself unable to be away from them for long: the sepia-toned photo of him on board the ship that had brought him to England, looking like Humphrey Bogart; her father so young, waving into the distance, smiling at his future; and there was his bus conductor identification; the notes made for the book on Othello he had never written; she now sitting in her office alone, Simon, who shared space with her off to a class; sitting, hearing her father's voice, praying that she could be rid of the sound of his voice, the deep, melodious bass-baritone that could at once both break her heart and make her angry; not understanding, never understanding his sudden death, shocked that the thought of him lying dead in public could still make her cry, still make her rage at God; through her tears reading the sentence in which he had written that he believed that Othello and Iago were welded together by their opposition, a bond which had inevitably led to a violent collision which had its roots in Othello's needing Iago to take him to the final realization of himself; the reason that Shakespeare had never allowed Iago to explain his actions was because Othello was Iago, was Shakespeare talking to himself; finding herself in the still of her office cursing the fate that had rendered his mind silent, that had made the world consider him nothing more than an undereducated black man fit only to take fares on a bus; what was the point of it all? He thought himself nothing, his life bound by the perceptions of others; and she knew something, something that her father had not written, and that Othello could not face: that his true tragic flaw was his exchange of himself for the acceptance of others, for respectability, quiet and order; during the long weekend in which Milton Bookman had not come home, he had faced this fact, a fact that she had never faced until now; and through her tears, she could see once again, spelled out on the yellowing piece of paper that her father had always carried in his pocket and which had been found alongside his body on the wet grass, the light rain reducing it to a word; and suddenly now, the mystery was becoming clear to her, the word slowly emerging in her mind like a developing image, that lone word which had to have been a part of a poem: the word still left on the paper was 'child'.

3.

Whose child was she?

She lived and worked in this world of 2044, but did not belong to it.

She belonged to the people who had made her.

Whoever they were.

Now she wanted a life outside of subterfuge, privilege...

How would this end? Jody asked herself.

Would she be able to do what was expected of her in Paris?

She could always refuse. That was her privilege as an Ultra.

But the penalty for turning down a direct order from Control himself could be the gradual diminution of her very existence.

It could mean expulsion from the special enclave reserved for Ultras with her special 'domus' which contained an 'icebox', a large area which was surveillance-free, the ultimate privilege.

She could be herself there.

Whoever that was.

What she did know for sure, based on medical tests, was that she was between 27 and 29 years old.

But her youth was not an advantage.

Youth now, in this year of 2044 meant poverty, hard work, grind.

To be young was to be like the impoverished countries in which the average age was eighteen and falling. Young meant a low-skilled existence.

Nothing.

Many people her age greyed their hair in order to try and get jobs and respect.

Many young people worked as Hunters.

Jody had once had a lover who was a Hunter.

She would bring him to her domus, to her ice box where they could not

76

be seen or heard. She would give him high grade 'o' and they would tell each other everything.

Gradually, she had come to know his story:

He had been conceived to do his job. Ever since he was a child and had been told his destiny, there had been no real relaxation for him.

After his brief education was over, he was first given jobs to do that the robots, who did all of the drudgery, couldn't do. After that, he had been taught subtle things like how to check the eye movements of suspected people for signs of lying as well as tonal changes in voices. Eventually he had come to learn that he and others like him existed solely to protect society against what was believed to be an infected, dangerous world.

They talked together about life in a world obsessed with tracking enemies, rounding them up, destroying them.

Everything was scrutinized. People were assessed even before birth through biochemical methods. The pre-born who were suspected of possible future criminal or subversive behaviour were destroyed in utero.

If the assessment could not be exact, the newborn was surrounded by gadgets at home; by clothing, even food that constantly sent back a stream of information to FSD until the day the suspect died.

But no matter what was done, there were always those who slipped through the net.

There would always be Undetectables, outlaws.

She told him that she knew this because she had learned that there was a mathematical proof that proves through rigorous logic that nothing is foolproof.

She talked about matter and anti-matter. There was the Earth they lived on, and a mirror Earth, invisible to us, but it had to exist according to the Proof. Matter and anti-matter.

She liked to imagine, she would tell him, that on this other Earth her ancestors thrived, her parents, as well as her other self.

And his other self.

There they were happy.

Over time, as she came to trust him, she would tell him more of what she learned in her training: Elimination Systems was experimenting with hormesis. Hormesis was based on harm and the theory that a little stress on the body was good. She was being taught that harm kept the body young and functioning. Years ago it had been discovered that young rats kept at 23C increased their life span by 5%.

It had also been discovered that exposure to 41C – the temperature reached during a fever – for an hour twice a day could provide anti-ageing benefits.

At that temperature, closely monitored, cells could keep their shape and the number of damaged proteins would go way down.

Hormesis, she told him with disdain, was another part of the 'Fountain Of Youth' project, an obsession with the Nonas.

Now in their nineties, the ancient 'baby boomers' who ran society were determined to find ways to continually reboot the immune system.

They had set the entire society to work in their pursuit of youth and longevity by creating new techniques of exercise, based on semi-starvation on a very low calorie diet; raised body temperatures; electric shock; radiation; hyperthermia; everything to create heat in order to shock proteins, as well as the use of neutraceuticals: food that acts as medicine; small amounts of pesticides; toxic drugs; and the avoidance of prevention and suppression, the approach traditionally used. Now medicine was using small amounts of poisons in stimulating antibodies as a better approach in fighting disease and ageing.

And because they were in an icebox, they could ask questions they could not ask anywhere else: were they alive merely to serve the old and the ageing with their fears, their goals?

Were they doomed, these Pandemic babies, born after the First Pandemic which followed the silent biological attack of 2012? The attack that had changed everything and made everyone afraid of contamination, literal and metaphorical.

Neither of them had had parents. He had never, and hers had mysteriously died.

She had resented their deaths all her life, and their deaths had made her who she was.

There had been another orphan who had lived with her at one time, *a child whom she had treated so badly that the girl had ceased to speak.*

But Jody could see, even in her silence, the great goodness of the child, her love.

Whenever she would share 'o' with the Hunter, she would talk about meeting her one day, and of reconciliation.

He finally said to her: "There is no reconciliation. We're out here alone, Jody, and there is no connection to nothing. We might as well be Stockholms."

Even in the safety of her icebox, Jody had quaked with fear to hear that word.

"Jody?"

She heard a voice. Through the haze of the 'o', the Hunter vanished, and she thought about her 'homey', its warmth and familiarity.

By 2044, Internet Protocol had become obsolete.

All information had created convergence. And convergence had gradually become the ultimate convergence: Ubiquity.

Ubiquity had created mobile surveillance devices whose cuddly, generic name was 'Homeland'. Homies spoke in the warm, sweet voice that people needed. Everyone loved their homey.

Scientists had long ago known that a voice implanted in a device could, in a particular tone, in a particular timbre, change a mood, build up rapport over time.

These soothing voices had been created years before from the recorded voices of people who had randomly joined phone surveys and talk-backs on various anodyne subjects. The happier, more pleasant voices had been harvested, decoded and their elements used to mimic the sounds in Homeland.

Some of the voices had been put inside the robots who had increasingly taken over the drudgery of everyday life. They were beloved, too, because they could mimic the body gestures of their owners at the subtlest level.

Jody knew that the robots' rapport created empathy and empathy created compliance. It was not difficult to understand the principle.

Nor was it difficult to see that every appliance, piece of clothing, toy, everything had been created and was being used for three purposes and three purposes only: surveillance, data collection, and elimination of those believed to be enemies.

"Get people", Jody had been told during her training, "to willingly police themselves. That's the Holy Grail. Sit back and let them do it. Give them friends. Homies take the trouble out of going through the rigour of human relationship with its possibility of defeat and depression. Depression could foment discontent. Discontent could become trouble. We have our hands full fighting enemies within and without. We at Elimination Systems use innate human conservatism. People don't like change. They like their own sound, their own stink. Comfort, familiarity, tribalism, no risk."

"Jody…"

She could not make out the voice.

Maybe it was something else, something planted in her domus to test her, challenge her. Keep her on her toes.

Small was now invisible and invisible was the must-have.

Hidden, unseen, quiet, anonymous were the goals.

Only the poor and the ill-educated wanted the obvious, the visible, the known and the big.

Jody closed her eyes.

She needed to find out who was trying to contact her.

The voice did not belong to her homey.

Or that other one which would come from time to time, and which she knew, somewhere deep inside.

This was something else.

Had the 'o' so blighted her ability to tell the difference?

"Jody!!"

Was it the voice of Audrey Carlyle, her late, adoptive mother?

Could it be her?

"Jody", her adoptive mother, an expert on the brain had told her: "the fact is that no one knows where they really 'are'. Reality is a kind of agreement, to put it simply. Now, Ubiquity, the surveillance system we live in, uses the brain's tendency to project itself into the future. The brain does this on what you might call 'idle'. This trait is an evolved thing. It

helped our species to survive. We learn what we know by projecting the past into a future based on the past! We do this by utilizing various scenarios: if a sabre-toothed tiger had once attacked us, we put that experience into the future and from that develop strategies of survival.

Survival, as for all species, is key.

Jody, the past is constructed. The past and future are not very different as far as the brain is concerned. Those in power are in control of the past. The past is not neutral. Find your own. Own it. Defend it."

"Jody!!!"

She knew the voice now. It was her Regular, Maisie.

"Lay off the 'o'."

"I'm ok, Maisie."

"Then stop."

"When I get back. When I get back."

Becoming A memory, A dream

After my nanny left and Carl Cookson died, my mother upped and fled, taking me with her to Maine in the middle of the Fall.

I loved the trees, the red colour of the big, fat leaves. I used to walk and walk through the woods, pretending to be a guy with patches on his jacket and a pipe in his mouth – a writer!

Walking, walking down a long passageway, full of reds, all sorts of reds.

I even saw the shade of Carl's head wound.

In my mind.

Maybe that's what I was looking for. But instead I got falling leaves all tumbling at my feet.

Me in Maine, revelling in the surprised faces of the people who had never seen a little black girl before. Except on television.

I didn't really understand what had happened to my family and why.

Something like that sets you up for a lifetime of mourning.

A little while in Maine and then we went down south to a beautiful house full of lace and shade and good cooking.

There was a woman there with big, fat, silvery braids that rested on her chest and a big smile who hugged me all the time and smelled like sweet spices. She was my mother's mother, my grandmother.

By then I was building that wall around me. I could feel her love but couldn't do anything about it.

Mom vanished into a bedroom and slept all day and cried when she did not sleep.

But me, I planted flowers in the garden and walked to the sea.

There was a jar of red earth in my grandmother's kitchen.

I asked her what it was.

She said: "Africa".

After her death I learned these facts: she had gone to Ghana in her youth, to the Atlantic Coast. To Elmina, the slave fortress.

I remember the photos of her in the old slave dungeons.

She had scraped out some earth from the walls and brought it back. She left it to me. I left it with my mother before I came to London.

It was not easy to carry.

Mom lost a lot of weight at Grandma's house.

I gained a lot of weight.

Never lost it again but I didn't care.

I loved my grandmother's food: the fried chicken, the biscuits and honey and butter.

My weight, and the fact that I was big for my age and not very graceful repelled my mother. And the coat I started wearing all day, even to bed. That, too.

I wore it even in that heat.

Then, that's when my face began to not exist.

I pretended that I could see it when I looked in the mirror.

But I really couldn't.

I still can't.

This all started so long ago.

I couldn't stop eating so Mom packed and took us to the next stop: New York City.

We lived in a railroad flat: an apartment that went straight back, like a railroad car.

She enrolled me in the local school where I picked up Spanish as fast as I could.

A communal garden was outside of our window down below and every morning the old ladies came out and planted vegetables and flowers.

Once a week Mom and I ate in one of the Ukrainian restaurants off the local park, beautiful rich soups and thick bread.

She liked the docks by the Hudson River because of the way the streets curled around themselves down there in the Village.

She'd take me there early Sunday mornings, to acclimatize me to the Big Apple and its ways.

We'd greet the tourist buses along with the disco-goers stumbling out of the clubs. Our early Sunday mornings.

She became a playwright for a while, not very good, but she was pretty and her stuff got noticed.

By the time we'd been in the Apple for almost two years, she had a kind of success with a play set in Paris during The Commune of 1871.

The play was called 'The Queen's Tears'.

It was about a black woman who had the power to pierce the veil between life and death. She gained this power through the suffering she had endured as a baby at the bottom of a slave ship. The suffering had altered her genetic code. She knew that she should do good with her power.

But she couldn't.

Mom wrote a line where the woman Léopoldine says: 'As long as I live and beyond this life, I can never be reconciled.'

I asked Mom what that meant. She said it meant exactly what it said.

"And you, Anna, never will be, either. Or me."

Mom said that she had dreamed the story one night from beginning to end and wrote it as it came to her.

She didn't change a word.

She told me: "Anna. Never change a word of a story that comes to you. Because, as someone said; 'All that we know is that we face one another…in this place.'"

'The Queen's Tears' attracted a famous Puerto Rican playwright named Manny. He and Mom fell in love. He told me that Anna meant Beloved Of God.

My father was becoming a memory, a dream.

New York City was good, the actors and the storefront theatre, the rehearsals.

I liked rehearsals more than the performances because I liked to observe the accumulation of detail.

Life goes by too fast. You can't see this in the everyday. But it happens. A play slows it all down. Then you can see.

I watched Mom work at night: rewriting, stopping in mid-sentence to listen to a voice in her head. Happy.

Manny was brilliant, a guy who had been friends with Miguel Pinero and together they had both come from that Nuyorican thing long ago. Mom said that they had principles.

We ate at a table every night, a proper meal, with napkins, knives and forks.

Manny sometimes cooked, he and Mom reading each other's plays to one another, arguing, but not in the vicious way she did with Dad.

If I'm honest, Manny spoiled me for a man.

He was very honest and vulnerable, too.

When he laughed, he laughed with his whole face and when he had his asthma attacks, he let us see him struggling for air.

He called me Negrita.

He said I had to learn to let go.

And one day, right out of the blue, Mom said that she was too happy.

So she went to Mass to repent.

Just as the priest was telling the congregation about the sin of Eve and how Mary had come to redeem mankind, I felt something warm running down my legs.

I put my hand under my dress and pulled out a finger full of blood. I showed it to Mom and she took me out right away, making a lot of noise and moving fast while I tried to hold my legs together so that I wouldn't drip.

She wiped me down in the ladies' room, put a wedge of toilet paper between my legs and with me waddling like a duck, took me out and we got a taxi home.

An Asian driver stopped for us. I left blood on his backseat in spite of Mom making me to sit on the Sunday newspapers.

She announced while we were in the taxi that we were never going to church again. She couldn't get over the priest putting Eve down.

Eve, she said, was the inventor of human curiosity, not transgression.

Nothing I could understand at the time.

The whole thing at the church had disturbed her.

A week later we were off again.

We made it to Tucson where Mom discovered that she was pregnant. But she lost the baby.

She didn't – never did – talk about it.

She'd been there before.

Mom had been married to my Dad for twelve years before I was born. She had a daughter before me, perfectly formed, but born with the umbilical cord around her neck.

This last dead Manny-baby had been a girl too, a sign that Mom took to return to Chicago and my father and our comfortable home with our library and my own room.

Little kids are essentially conservative. And since I was growing up with two radicals, two baby boomers who saw the world from the Left and the Right, through their own ancient filter, well, I just froze myself in the middle of them, not sure which one I should imitate.

Before I was born, my father was kicked out of the college at which he had spent half his life, after it had been re-named, becoming Marcus Garvey University. His dashiki-wearing co-educators voted him out because he had come into the place one day wearing a suit and tie.

He opened his own storefront right across from the storefront the Black Panthers used to feed children breakfast. Every morning at the same time, my Dad would open up just as the Panthers would and they'd stand glaring at each other and waiting to see which kids would show up and where they would go.

Dad sat at a podium with his glasses on his nose reading from Cicero while student volunteers from the college who'd stood up for

86

him served breakfast to little ghetto kids. The Panthers would read from Mao's Little Red Book or an Eldridge Cleaver tract on revolutionary rape or something and he would counter with Shakespeare, because he said, if Castro can have Romeo and Juliet read to his cigar rollers, little black kids from the ghetto can hear it too. He also read Peer Gynt to them and I can't even begin to imagine what they thought of that. But he loved the trolls. He called them the heart of darkness of the European imagination and said that every black kid should be acquainted with trolls.

I dreamt about them.

He finally fell out with the Black Students Union at Garvey, calling them "a self-indulgent, incautious, ungrateful, unhistorical rabble, un-teachable, ignorant, ill-mannered and a recruitment poster for the Ku Klux Klan".

He collected newspaper clippings about himself and read them to me before I went to sleep every night. I could recite them by heart.

Mom had been his student in the mid-sixties and had fallen in love with him because he had stormed an anti-war rally where Mom danced topless trying to "bring down the spirit". He ran down a grassy hill, took the microphone and called everybody a bunch of "afro-fascists, homosiduals, femi-nazis".

A real wedding-crasher. Mom's type.

The deal was sealed when they got into an argument in class over the existence and value of what Mom called 'African American Vernacular English' which Dad called slang and therefore useless, and she told him that she knew all that she needed to know about language and that's when he asked her to tell him the term that describes when 'pater' became 'father' and 'piscis' became 'fishes', a linguistic mutation when the 'p' became 'f'.

She couldn't do that and that's when they fell in love.

He tried to turn her into a chocolate Pat Nixon, but the stillborn daughter ended that.

Funny to say this now, sitting here, waiting, but…everything I've ever done, every fucked-up, every ok thing, too, was because of him. To make him look at me, not just his projection or his creation. At me. And Mom wanted that from him too. She dragging me all over the place, trying to get away from him was an attempt to get him out of his own melodrama and look around. There was a wife and daughter there.

I was just an appendage to the drama between them, the whole thing was about them. I was the by-product. I'd ask myself in those days why she had to keep moving. She doesn't want to deal with the past, while my dad's past is being obliterated. He's a creature only of the present.

My dad took it in his stride when we came back.

He had expected us to return home. All that really mattered was his academic standing anyway.

Maybe I'm not being fair here.

Now he's up in his room back home, talking to ghosts.

Ghosts.

Listen: The guy was like a mountain, far away, distant. He'd go away and be gone all day, sometimes just riding the local buses, studying people.

When his dementia began to set in, he would go out and sit on a bench in the park, stating his views on life to the air.

This guy, my dad, once he was the head of everything, the first black this and the first black that in his day.

Now he's dead, but he's still alive and we have a living form of grief.

Mom hides in her good works giving away every inch of our living space to strangers.

She said to me once: "Your father and I, we owe these kids. We didn't make a future for them because we were too busy making a present for ourselves."

Crackheads have taken over the leafy street of my childhood and now my home – my former home, has chaos encroaching closer and closer to the front gate, leaving slums and destruction in its wake as if the whole block has been bombed. While our house – my parents' house – is the only one left standing.

Its white picket fence, its drive for two cars, the lawn and the big front door which honours the seasons: Christmas wreath; gobble-gobble turkey poster; jack o' lantern; all of it standing in the middle of the rubble and the destruction of a neighbourhood that once had elegant Edwardian white stone houses where servants worked and ladies never wore rouge.

Or so my parents were told when they moved in at the end of the sixties, before I was born and knew what loss was.

So she lets in everybody, every kind of kid.

Except me.

In time, I had to go. I used the excuse of going away to write a novel. Writing a novel is always an excuse.

There was no room for me.

There never was.

Carl Cookson.

How could I be so consumed with feelings for him when I was so young?

He was mysterious, hiding away somewhere just below what I could see.

What I could grasp.

See my point here?

Everything that has really touched me has been just out of reach, or in the future.

Like Abena Assantewa's story coming by fax to the station every day at the same time. She was out of reach. Once.

I always liked that distance until…there's a guy who comes and goes.

He lives in my building part time. His real home is across the river in South London. That's what a friend in the building told me. He still lives with his mother there.

I'm so curious about him because he comes and goes.

On his mail his box name is spelled "T-o-m-a-s". He's not German, he's black. I mean he could be black and German, too. But I don't know. He never speaks, but he does smile at me.

That smile.

I've followed him.

He reads the poetry of Wilfred Owen at the local coffee shop.

I want to ask him why.

I've never seen a black guy reading Owen.

For some reason, I want to talk to him about my mother, about how she teaches math to gangs and their molls and how my father cowers upstairs with his arsenal and waits for the darkness to descend.

And when it does, I think about her. Not my mother. My nanny.

Her name was Earlene. I told myself that I'd never say her name again.

Earlene. A common name among the people I come from.

Earlene.

Once she took off the ring her mother had given her and threw it into the lake.

"For the river goddess. Our ancestor. That way you'll cross the great water someday."

Cross the great water, all so that I can sit in Dan's office, reading the rest of the stories with him like he cares about it, about anything but his drugs.

Cross the great water to be with Dan The Man.

God.

But, as the story kept coming in, inch by inch, my face began to return in the mirror. Slowly. Not totally yet.

I didn't know who would be looking out from that mirror at me yet.

Or how the story would end.

2

*One thing can never be undone: having neglected to run away
from one's parents.*

WALTER BENJAMIN, ONE WAY STREET

Walking through the Common, Janet went over the rest of Abena's
last letter in her mind; no mention of the conference there, only of her
late sister, about whom she couldn't stop thinking; a woman for
whom she had never had any respect, a woman she had considered
beneath her who had ended her days as a cook at the school that they
had both attended as girls, and she, too busy on a lecture tour on the
need of feminism in society to be with her sister and only sibling at
the end; and arriving too late, there had been nothing left to do but
to sit beside the body for a few minutes, and submit to the tales that
the nuns and schoolgirls told her about her sainted sister; and, after
evening prayers, returning to her sister's room to study her face in
death, later discovering amongst her things a closely written journal
in which she had recounted her life, the everyday incidents, her work
at the convent, her cooking, and the help given to one elderly nun in
particular; and also, there in her sister's journal, there had been an
entry about a journey she had taken in her youth which Abena
Assantewa had investigated, putting together bits and pieces until the
information had yielded an address and that address had led to
another, she needed to bring her sister's journey to the conclusion
that she herself would have wanted; but above all, the journal had
revealed her sister's deep love for a little girl who had been in her
charge; how every night, she would tell the child a story, a cautionary
tale about the consequences of playing with matches, or getting into
cars with strangers; the stories had been their bond, their lifeblood,
until one night, she had had to leave the little girl abruptly, leave her
without her cautionary bedtime story, and that she had regretted this
above all, above all; she, Dr. Abena Assantewa, feminist, black

93

nationalist, public intellectual, great author and professor, had been humbled by the love and the simple goodness of the woman revealed in the diary; and since that day she had been haunted by two things: the need to deliver one last story to the child, in memory of her sister; and the deep feeling that in her life of sacrifice and love of others, her sister had not found love for herself; so she was busy now, with what strength she had left, writing one last cautionary story for the child that her sister had had to desert, hoping that it would express something of the great love that her sister had possessed, and something of what she herself had learned in the wake of her sister's death.

Janet suddenly saw Mort Finklestein, one of her father's old passengers, scuttling along in his perpetual black suit, a book in his hand, muttering to himself; a man who often ridiculed her and Sam, black people like them, he had said, were a total mystery to him and a disgrace to 'the community'; far too posh. He knew what he was talking about having been an old 'comrade', with the POUM, who had fought in Spain and had known Orwell: 'a smelly man', he had called him; they smiling as the old comrade paused when he said the great writer's name, his face skyward and one-eyed as a result of the war; recounting once again how he had caught some glass during a train bombardment; Mort Finklestein a man who had always, like a lover, been true to Orwell, true to the old ways and the old times when there were such things as principles and truth; a big fan of Anna Taylor's programme, because, to him, she sounded like a wise woman, a blues woman; he had told her this once when they had had him over for Sam's special Sunday roast; always, he had said then, making sure that he stayed awake to catch Anna Taylor, staying awake in the dead of night not difficult when you had seen what he had seen in Spain; his life now consisting of days sitting in his tiny front room with the radio blaring; burning the little lamp with the bullet hole in it brought back from Madrid decades ago; Mort had been the man who had taught her how to read Hemingway, especially the brilliant early work; Hemingway a writer, he had said, you read for what he does not say, the tension and drama is in the restraint, the way he forces words out, spare and deceptively simple, a man in which all of the senses existed except that of smell, because smell, as Proust demonstrated, was the strongest sense of all; Hemingway whom love and the possibility of love eternal and unchanging, had kept alive until the words got lost amidst the medication and the fear until they couldn't find their way out; he had also told her about Joyce, how the Master had said that he would never write a book again like "Dubliners", neat and measured; words were like life itself, Finklestein had told her: tumbling, half-realised, scatological, straining, a failure in the end; most novels 19th century constructs, Victorian and Edwardian machines of consistency; even Dickens had been moving away from that; read he had said, the beginning of Our Mutual Friend; the novel no longer 'novel'; Finklestein, a man who loved Auden but hated him too, for writing that he had hoped he would not run into any surrealists when he went to the war in Spain, what else had Spain been but a battle of the surrealists against the beasts; telling her, from time to time and for no particular reason, that fascism was where the Western world was heading, fascism being the desire for safety and order; fascism was wanting Daddy to take care of everything; pull the covers over your head while Daddy heads out with the shotgun to sort the baddies out; Mort, railing against them for throwing a dinner party once for a group of local black achievers; how he had yelled, could any black people be called 'achievers?'; they were betraying the millions who had died under the whip and the hangman's noose, the gun, the dog and the chains, betraying them all by eating and drinking and not fighting.

She watched him as he disappeared out of sight around the side of 'Mrs. M's Hair and Beauty'.

The last time Janet had been in the salon there had been an African American woman from Detroit who had needed her weave done; and who had made everyone laugh as she described how she had escaped the clutches of her lecherous pastor, fleeing the Midwest while lugging an entire suitcase full of medicines on her first trip to Europe which to her meant Britain, Britain meaning England, England meaning London; before she left she had made a will; not setting out on her transatlantic flight before her family back home had in hand the number of an air ambulance – just in case something had happened, in a country where the surgeons were addressed as 'Mr'; told over and over again by her brother-in-law who had been to London several times on business that she was not landing in the middle of the Sahel, that in fact the services in Britain were more civilized than their own, at least you didn't have to have your medical insurance number tattooed on your wrist in case you fell unconscious and you couldn't tell anyone what it was, plus the care was free; but the African American woman had heard about the killer viruses and the mixed wards and the horror of sleeping next to some old, farting, snoring, male stranger; that reality alone enough to will her to stay healthy, she had laughed; better to have the things you know, she was saying as her own hair was being parted and Korean hair weaved in, better to have the circumstances and the kinds of medication that you were used to; then if you died, you died of known causes; anyway, better to die back home – back home she could have her wake held at her favourite soul-food restaurant; then, suddenly, out of the blue, the woman from Detroit stated that she would like, one day, to experience all of herself, even for just five minutes; experience all that she was without censure or judgement, and then turning to Janet, her eyes full of tears like a sad clown, she asked her if she had understood what she had said; Janet too shocked to reply, had merely nodded and buried her face in a women's magazine but she had not forgotten what that woman had said and now as she went over the question in her mind, she saw Mrs. Monk. One of the long-time residents of Morant Bay Road, Mrs. Monk had lived there long before the local Council had changed the name of Trindle Way to one in honour of a Jamaican rebellion against the Crown; Mrs. Monk had protested, demanding to know what was wrong with the old name of Trindle Way, that name had a long history, Mrs. Monk complaining that events and history had forced her to be the local historian, the living repository of history, the one accumulating memories: memories of weddings and family celebrations, garden fetes and that sense of safety and belonging; she had put herself out and about instead of hiding in her house; and as she spotted Janet and made her way across the road towards her, Janet jumped into a cab just as its former passenger began to close the door and soon found herself once again outside Janey Francis' shop; 'Taken As Red', the storefront radiant as usual and lit by cranberry-coloured fairy lights; the shop a worthy addition to a street called Electric Avenue, the fairy lights emitting a deep red glow as if the shop were on fire; holding her handbag close to her body as a group of young men walked past, she heard Janey Francis' voice and turning, she saw her through the windows of a pub, dressed in her trademark crimson dress, surrounded by a crowd singing 'Redemption Song' at the top of their lungs in the high afternoon, a chilly breeze settling in the passageway Janet was standing in, driving her inside the pub, catching the eye of a man, who, flirting with her, motioned her over to Janey Francis' group; Janet declining, not sure what she was going to do next as she stood in the middle of the pub; suddenly the man, breaking away, a man comically short and powerfully built, asked if he had seen her before, insisting that he buy her a drink, tugging on her sleeve like a little boy, Janet pulling her coat to her body, panicking now, looking around for assistance, the singing from Janey Francis' table growing louder, and she finally pulling away as calmly as she could and out into the street, making her way through the crowds in the direction of the mini-cab office and the bus stop, whichever came first; her mind filled with thoughts of her mother who had been humiliated by Janey Francis; her mother – if she had ever mentioned Janey Francis' name – would have added that London had ruined her, made her cruel and brazen; London, dark and evil with its stygian river, even the reason hundreds of South Londoners survived during the war down to something hidden, underground; in this case a secret tunnel underneath one of the areas worst hit by the Germans; an area running from St George's, under

97

Borough High Street, to London Bridge, then on under the Thames and ending in a ghost Tube station at Pudding Lane, where the Great Fire had started; a section abandoned because it was on the wrong alignment when the network was expanded, a tunnel given a name appropriate for anything to do with London: The Deep.

Her father had told her about The Deep years ago during the one and only time she had ridden on his bus, the 903; she had been ten years old and on that day, she had been able, for the first time in her life, to observe her father objectively: his broad head, broad shoulders, happy in the company of his passenger/friends, conducting his book club in between his duties; the club reading aloud from their chosen novels, defending passages, even whole sections; she had been excited by the passion of it all, everything on the bus that day had been overwhelmingly exciting; the highlight of it being the arrival of a woman dressed in a telephone box-red dress with blood red roses printed all over it; a woman too sturdy, too strong for such a delicate dress, which made her look dangerous, alien; wearing her big, carnelian-coloured picture hat at a jaunty angle, her scarlet heels at a ludicrous height, her laugh so deep and rich that Janet had stared at her in wonder, as did her father who had led The Lady In Red onto his bus like a queen; her presence altering the entire atmosphere, her deep, dark skin full of a light which seemed to illuminate everything; illuminate above all Janet's father, Milton Bookman; that had been her first glimpse of Miss Janey Francis, clearly a woman capable of giving her father much joy; impossible to forget having seen him so happy that day, surrounded by his friends, the miracle of hearing him laugh out loud; on his bus a completely different man from the one at home; a man silent, seated at the dining table, a book in his hand, his glasses balanced at the end of his nose, his lips silently mouthing each sentence, lost in another world, lost to his family; Gloria-Loretta chattering away about the soaps, or the market, or the newest neighbours, black people inevitably, who in her opinion had brought the neighbourhood down, lowering the price of everyone's property, a disgrace to the race; Milton Bookman oblivious both to his wife and to his only child; and Janet, that only child, sitting in the middle, her head down, eating the unappetising food cooked with Gloria-Loretta's usual haste and indifference; her mother ranting on about London, how she could not understand it; husband telling wife to read the beginning of Our Mutual Friend to learn everything that she needed to know, which caused another explosion centred around his failures in general and the lost weekend in particular; he finally retreating to the room beneath the stairs, to Wordworth's translation of the sonnets of Michelangelo; to The Decameron and Chaucer and Skelton; Andrew Marvell; Donne and Campion; Defoe; Diderot; Voltaire; Molière; Rabelais; his thoughts on them in the notebook he had left behind and which she kept in her office at Jennie Lee University; a notebook which revealed another attempt to write a book of his own, this one on the subject of individual genius, genius that could be explained neither by theories of race, nationality or politics, miraculous; Janet, always unable to read what he had written without weeping; grateful to be now in the mini-cab, grateful that it reeked of stale food and cigarettes, grateful for the distraction, pretending to listen to the driver's complaints about the road and his boss, her eyes closed, the thought entering her mind that she might need to return after all these years, to finally talk to Janey Francis; gazing out of the window, Janet saw a child who reminded her of Ayesha; reminded her of Ayesha's question: a question that she could not answer for her daughter when she herself was so unmoored; seeing that day eight months after Ayesha's birth, when she had washed and dressed herself properly for the first time in six months, had left her two babies with Mrs. Saddler and walked to the southern foot of Lambeth Bridge, staring at the river beneath her, telling herself that if the good Archbishop of Canterbury was in residence – even though she was a member of the 'True Faith' and he the head of a rebel communion – nevertheless, he would, in charity, come out and assist her across, complete with mitre and cross; she, that day at the foot of the bridge praying aloud in the dingy sunlight that he would emerge from his palace behind a procession of the Black Madonna, Our Lady

Of Walsingham, walking behind a congregation filled with candles and drums, bells and colour, an Italy on the Thames; but no colourful procession emerged that day, only Janet crying her eyes out; a nice old lady asking if she was alright standing still like that at the foot of the bridge; the blessed onslaught of sudden rain driving Janet back to Morant Bay Road; once there, soaking wet, she had run to Mrs. Saddler, hugging her babies to her, all the while Mrs. Saddler soothing her, telling her that her own son was away in the Army, and that she prayed that no more wars would come, particularly for little Lucas' sake; and Janet, grateful for Mrs. Saddler's words, for her warmth.

Afterwards, she had plunged into re-making the kitchen into something 'French country': the natural wood floor, large wooden table which could double as a working surface and family dining table, cast iron pots and pans suspended over it – some of them found in antique shops on the Common that she had insisted that she and Sam search through together; then all of her cookbooks, row upon row of them stacked in shelves all around the kitchen; her prize was a Victorian cookbook filled with Tudor recipes for peacock and swan; her favourite cookbooks were the ones covered by Sam's greasy fingerprints, he often sipping a fine vintage wine while cooking and playing his favourite Herbie Hancock or Wayne Shorter or anything arranged by Quincy Jones simultaneously watching his tapes of Vivian Richards and other legendary West Indian cricketers; and when he really needed to make an elegant dish, he listened to an interview he had found with Sir Garfield Sobers; Dame Cleo Laine – whose voice sounded to him like the way the finest Châteauneuf-du-Pape would sound if a luscious black wine could sing – playing in the background; cooking being his joy, his escape; the great happiness Sam took in arguing with the cooks on television, challenging them to make rice and peas better than he could, weighing up men versus women – his theory being that women were the cooks and men the chefs because women made food to keep the race alive and men made food as a kind of contemplation and act of war; she saw herself watching him in the kitchen; this perfect, beautiful man to whom she had never revealed herself, never bequeathed herself; but what she hoped was to leave behind two children who could go through life unaided and alone, not formed by any definition except their own; this, what she had wanted for them all of their lives; all of their lives, she had attempted to achieve this with her methodical building up of their destinies; confident, in the days and years before they were born, that she would be a successful mother, mothering being her destiny after all; she had dedicated her life then to nurturing the next generation; but now she knew one truth: now she knew that she saw nothing ahead, nothing at all, only one torturous day after the other; with that revelation to herself she stopped the mini cab, and walked across the Common to the Café; taking her reserved table, suddenly craving a cigarette, instead drinking a glass of water to quench the craving, asking for another; waiting for her son, this being the one afternoon a week they spent together, just the two of them doing nothing, being nothing except mother and son, revelling in the pleasure of one another; but now she had no emotion being too full of emotion, sitting at her and her son's favourite table, the one in the corner facing the door; a chill suddenly coursing through her body at the possibility that she might not be able to accomplish her task of raising him, that she was not up to the task, that she would have to watch life engulf her son, sweep him away, and all that she had planned and dreamt of for him – for both of them – come to nothing; the way she had felt on that bright, sunny day, a year or so after the bridge incident; a day on which she had been scheduled to receive what became her first award for community work; on the way to take the children to their nanny, all of them dressed beautifully, she, happy and proud, catching a glimpse of the three of them in a shop window; she staring at herself, her children, reflected back to her, and at the same time seeing a taxi barrelling down the street, the taxi clearly trying to run the lights, her reflection staring back at her frozen in her mind; and without any feeling or warning, she had taken a step toward the speeding vehicle, longing for the feel of the taxi slamming into her body, the release the impact would give her, for a split second she longed for it, longed for her and her children's destiny to change in a flash; but instead she chose to step back out of harm's way; no one noticing what had almost happened except an old man who stared at her for what seemed an eternity, knowing.

She knew that this memory meant that somehow she had to let her dead father go; she had to escape from him and his influence, live her own life – whatever that might be, perhaps as soon as she and Lucas got back home, she should immediately ring Gloria-Loretta, ask how the new roof was coming on and if the rains had lessened; and her mother, as usual, would barely say hello before launching into the gossip about her community, an oddly endearing bunch of 'Happy Valley' types, who with their savings and British pensions had become the local rich; and like the returnees they were, had developed peculiar habits, feuds and loyalties; her mother chattering away as if Janet knew everyone there, and she finally would have to gently remind her mother that the reason for her call was because her late husband had been dead now for ten years; and she knew that this announcement would cause a slight pause on the other end in which Janet could hear the birds in her mother's garden, and some words that resembled a prayer which would be followed by her mother's quiet goodbye in that voice that could be like a girl's; Janet would feel then a brutally triumphant feeling run through her chest, proud that she would have defeated her mother for once, made her become quiet, pensive, revelling in her moment of power, and then after saying goodbye too, she would go into Sam and undress, put on the pyjamas that Ayesha and Lucas had bought him for his birthday, pull the extra fabric around her, and slide in beside him, kissing his forehead, making herself feel a strong desire for the man whom she knew had endured uncountable snubs and insults day in and day out and who, more than anything, simply wanted to arm their only son against a world that would surely try and break him down; the thought of Sam's care for their children made her love him – the way love is given to a faithful creature; she was not a faithful creature, not in the conventional sense, not in the way Gloria-Loretta had been; her life

102

as a mother was true, but her life as a wife was false, a sham, a kind of product of the lives of her mother and other wives she had observed; dear, gorgeous Sam, a man out of her mother's dreams, her mother's dream of the perfect black man: intelligent, superbly educated and going places; no doubt, she had said to Janet soon after her first date with him, Sam Baker was a man who would take silk; a measured, calm man; a man she knew who had a penchant for taking the cases of people he did not understand; people who teetered on the edge of chaos, as if he had wanted to not save the person, but instead have a part of that chaos, revel in it, bathe in it.

Janet closed her eyes as she drank her tea, waiting for Lucas, seeing his latest obsession: prisms; elliptic planes; modular forms that danced before her eyes; but the words had no meaning whatsoever to her although for Lucas they had become a new reason to live, along with his sudden ability to imagine how the Fourth Dimension worked; ecstatic at this burgeoning understanding which had come – he had told her in his usual over-excited fashion – at the same time that a star had gone supernova, allowing science and him to better understand gravitational waves, a Fourth Dimension reality; his Midlands granny had rung Janet just the other day, overwhelmed by him, by his sayings and comings and goings, she had already made him into a legend, the star of her bingo nights, it was she who constantly suggested that he have an IQ test; when he had first heard about this, Lucas had rung her up, pointing out to his darling granny that it was indeed possible to get a perfect IQ on what would inevitably be an imperfect IQ test, perfection not being possible in an imperfect world, a beautiful realization, he had said to her, almost too beautiful for him to say, a realization that had the ability to make him cry with the beauty of it; and as he told her, the Midlands granny too, had burst into tears, but not because of the exquisiteness of the theorem he had just told her, but because she couldn't now boast about his official IQ because he wouldn't take a test; Sam had overheard the call to his mother, and had become angry, insisting once again that Lucas needed to be grounded, emphatic that he did not want Lucas to end up like his nephew in the City whose only experience of black people outside his own family was with the waiters at cocktail parties, the security guards at posh private nightclubs, the cleaners in his office and, when he could wake up in time, church; the lack of black people in his life other than his family hardly, the nephew had protested, his fault; there simply had been no black people on his postgraduate course or at the parties or resorts that he had developed a taste for; at the age of twenty-seven even he could see that things had changed a great deal since his Uncle Sam's time.

Sam had warned her over and over, that time was not on their side; she and he had to move quickly and decisively because, although it was true that the community surrounding them was full of children who lived a Lord Of The Flies existence – there were even children living rough—nevertheless Lucas had come into the world a black male; he had obligations to a past and to a destiny, to a continuum; it was ridiculous and absurd that his son could end up one day having no idea who he was or what he was as the result of some ridiculous and inappropriately posh education deep in the English countryside whose chief result, for Lucas, would be a fundamental estrangement from the community in which he had been born and raised, causing him to end up a confused stranger, part of some mythical multicultural Britain which – Sam had said without a hint of irony– he was not totally convinced that Lucas, and Ayesha, too, for that matter, should have anything to do with because it implied mediocrity; all this, in his view, making school in Wiltshire unthinkable; generations would come and go, he believed, before black people could truly become accepted and seen as individuals in the UK; after all, Sam had concluded, attending a local school had not prevented him from going on to university, taking his law exams, enduring the endless round of dinners he never ate, in order to become a barrister and finally a QC; getting himself before that into the right chambers – and not a leftie-radical one either – going on to take silk, proving himself in a case in which he did what one associate had called the 'counter-intuitive thing' by defending a Portsmouth widow against an attempted murder charge, a woman who had gone to Africa and returned with a gloriously beautiful young man, a former child soldier, who had turned out to be addicted to designer clothes and called his wife 'mère-femme' right up until the moment he had tried to strangle her in her sleep; she claiming tearfully on the stand that the reason she had stabbed him as he exercised in their front garden was because he had done so in full view of the hungry, young divorcee across the way, another potential victim; her story and her performance propelling Sam into the limelight, the publicity eventually the source of his becoming a kind of spokesman and commentator for 'the community'; the community, he had often said over and over, kept him steady, kept him real; the community held him to account; but she wanted –and this she could not make him understand – Lucas' community to be the entire nation into which he had been born and was being raised; Sam's desire seemed to her to be Lucas' surrender to what he saw as the destiny of his skin colour, and the fact that Lucas was a black man in a white man's world and had to come to terms, as fast as possible now, with that dynamic.

And she could see now, slowly sipping her tea, the day that Lucas had asked why Sam should worry about him thinking that he was something he was not, because we all are something we are not: creatures of the present: our bodies are in the present, but our minds are in the past, we cannot help but live in the past, hold on to the past, the past being our very nature and he understood his father's fear for him completely because all Sam knew was the past; Lucas's statement had been followed by a row between him and Ayesha; Ayesha, as usual, funny with it, her bright wise face sombre, her voice droll, as she commented that she understood Lucas's banging on about there being nothing but- the- past-how-can-we-know-the-present and there-are- more- disorderly-states-than-orderly, because his room was an example of this, always so messy; her daughter, funny and wise at the same time and all said with such alacrity, that she and Sam had laughed simultaneously.

Janet was suddenly aware that Lucas was now seriously late; she hated texting him because it embarrassed him; but what if he had been met again at the library by the local mandem?

The Café had a queue outside and a small scrum of youngsters hanging around the window looking at the pies and cakes on display, blocking her vision, so she did not see Tomas Saddler enter and walk up to her until she heard his voice above the din and his request to join her.

Her hand trembled as she nodded, pulling a chair out for him, watching him sit down and take off his jacket, rubbing his hands together to warm them in one graceful and lithe motion; his eyes shiny and moist from the cold wind, he had a hint of blush just underneath his dark skin, his lips slightly chapped, and a tiny mole at the top of his right cheek, one she had never seen before.

Before he had come here, he began, after ordering an espresso for her and a hot chocolate with lashings of whipped cream for himself, he had been to the British Museum to see the Benin bronzes, noticing for the first time, he said, the violence with which they had been wrenched away from their original setting and that somehow, he had thought looking at them, the jagged edges of the sculptures made them part of where they, as a people, had been and where they were now; they seemed to him to represent the Diaspora, wrenched and torn away from its natural home; mesmerized by this insight he had found himself spending the entire morning just looking at them, almost going into a trance and believing that he himself had made them, a kind of madness that overtook him from time to time, just as his desire to escape to a desert, to vanish, was just as compulsive; New Mexico or the Sahara, in the Sahara perhaps he would follow the old Salt Trail, taking along a copy of the holy Koran which must be beautiful to read in the desert; or take a copy of the holy Bible to the Southwest of the United States; the Torah he would reserve for Sinai someday; holy books are for the desert, the silence; lost in thought, wiping the cream from his mouth after a hearty drink of hot chocolate, Tomas Saddler moved back again to his first thought about imagining himself to be the creator of certain things and at times, the author of certain things; the way he had felt when he had first read Robert Louis Stevenson; and when he said that, suddenly his eyes

106

became as big and innocent as Lucas', and he laughed, begging her not to read anything into the revelation that the Stevenson book that affected him the most had been Dr. Jekyll and Mr. Hyde, a work, through the beauty and precision of Stevenson's words, that had pulled him inside it, had made him one with the writer with such force that he had not been sure that he himself was not writing it even as he read it; Janet, watching him talk, the way his mouth moved and his eyes, wondering if what she felt for him had to do with the feeling that they, in her mind, looked alike, exactly alike; that he was, in fact her twin, her lost other half, the male version of her; Sam had always been and still was a separate person from her, but Tomas was her; how had she not seen this before; Tomas still talking about his affinity with Stevenson, she seeing herself nodding in acknowledgement, saying that she, too, had felt this kind of deep affinity, not with a book but with a woman who had written to her, a woman she admired and had never met, whose letters had arrived out of the blue like a miracle, finding herself wishing that the woman had been her big sister, someone so close to her that she would not be able to tell where one of them began, and the other ended, the only sort of relationship that mattered, and now she was coming to London and she did not know what to do; Tomas looking straight into her eyes, she told him that she was afraid to leave the community, afraid to cross the Thames, afraid of everything; a revelation so intimate that she felt herself blush.

Yet she knew that Tomas had sensed that she had exposed a deeply hidden part of herself, he telling her – his voice so low, so quiet that she could barely hear it – that he understood and in, she felt, an acknowledgement of the opening up she had just done, he told her that the woman who had been with him in the Café when she had last seen him – when they had last seen one another – was nothing more than a friend, a former colleague from a primary school he had briefly worked at, and unlike him, a teacher in her blood; she was on her way to Australia with her husband – to the desert – and they had met up for a farewell lunch; Janet listening intently to Tomas's account of their time at the school; how she had supported and defended him when he had fought to allow some older boys in the school – black boys – to stay in his class of five year olds after the boys had been temporarily thrown out of their own class; he and his friend had gone together to tell the Head that if all the boys who disrupted other classes could come to his, they could quietly read in the corner, and if they did, this would be a triumph; that no matter what, he would stay with them, never let them out of his sight; too many of them did not have full-time fathers, or any father-figure at all, having them with him for the day – a small gesture – had made sense to him and his friend, and would make a big difference in the lives of the boys; but unknown to them both, himself and his friend, this gesture had been another nail in his coffin at a school drowning in regulations and initiatives and charts and schedules.

Ironic, because schedules were what his stepfather, Tomas Saddler Sr. hated, he continued, the reason he had left Germany, a too precise and orderly land for him at the time, much different now; he himself had gone to Germany after the man he called his father had died, he had especially liked Berlin, the people were real – did she know Berlin? The story was this: Tomas Saddler Sr. had come to London where he had met his mother, and him too, when he was a baby and called Nelson; promptly adopting him – his own father having died shortly after his conception – changing his name to Tomas, he delighting in his name because it was so Germanic, loving the shock that always occurred whenever he showed up; seeing his name and his presence as a way for anyone encountering him to push the boat out further – his motto – that motto also served by the war memorabilia left behind in the apartment that his late stepfather had left him in Bloomsbury; he had been shocked at first by the proliferation of things concerning the First World War, but in the end, those things had taught him so much; and – Tomas, leaned closer to her, the smell of the chocolate on his breath mixed with tobacco enveloping her, lulling her into his rhythm – she listening closely as he went on to tell her that it was through his step-father's collection that he had learned many things, his step-father, through his artefacts, had explained to him the way it had been; objects were important as a means of thinking and reconfiguring the world; his stepfather's things, in miniature could be considered twee and a bit embarrassing, but miniatures had given him, like his stepfather, comfort, being containable replicas of reality, bits of life that could be held in the hand, important to him, this containment of reality; after the Army and his tour of duty during the first Iraq War, he had fallen in love with the desert there, even after coming upon a jeep full of incinerated bodies; he had, like many former soldiers, decided to travel and had gone to America, which he had liked very much because everything – door handles, for example – was so sturdy, so solid, particularly in Chicago which looked as if it sat on the shore of an inland sea which was in fact a lake; Michigan no comparison to any lake he had seen in Europe although some day he would like to see the Great Lakes region of Central Africa as soon as war stopped there; then Tomas shifted back to the subject of the desert, his face growing softer, his eye never leaving her; the desert, he was saying, inhabited his dreams; from time to time, he was invaded by images of white space, a blazing sun, desert blooms; in his dreams the desert encroached on his mother's garden, up to the front steps; the desert blew into his hair, into his eyes, and he, in his mind, turned his face towards its distant boundaries every morning, walking out into it, walking, walking, walking without end, into the void that had no memories and no future, then – was she imagining it? – a shaft of light rested on his face as he told her once again about the apartment his step-father had left him in Bloomsbury and where he went for refuge; inviting her to visit him there, as soon as she crossed the river, because he knew she would and soon; and without hesitation, he wrote down the address and telephone number on a tiny slip of paper, a slip of paper so small that his writing was almost imperceptible, his hand light and swift.

Swift was the only adjective Janet could apply to Lucas' sudden appearance at their table, his eyes bright and shining, his hair damp from running, kissing her quickly then turning to Tomas, identifying him quickly as Mrs. Saddler's son who he had seen working in the garden, quickly moving on to ask him if he liked bees and before he could reply – typically Lucas – explaining to him that the genealogy of bees followed the Fibonacci Sequence, 'the queen bee mates only once – producing unfertilized or fertilized eggs – then through parthenogenesis – the unfertilized eggs become drones – and the fertilized eggs become queens – causing a female bee to have two parents – and a drone only one – the queen – she has two grandparents – three great grandparents and on and on…the bee pattern', he gasped, 'follows the beautiful Fibonacci Sequence of one, one, two, three, five, eight, thirteen, twenty-one, continuing on until it bears a closer relationship to pi and these numbers', he said as he finally sank into a chair, 'are so beautiful' that he can barely speak of them, the Fibonacci Sequence itself, in his mind being a bright gold with a throbbing rose base, the Golden Ratio having a beautiful tone, but if he had been a Muslim, he continued, it would have been easier, since their religion does not allow them to depict God, they had to turn to mathematics, further developing the pentagon and hexagon by manipulating numbers and becoming friends with the Golden Ratio; Lucas talking as he usually did without waiting to see what effect he was having on the person he was talking to, pouring out everything, emptying himself to a new audience; and Tomas sitting there patiently and listening in a way that Sam had never done; warmly responsive without talking, a true teacher and lover of children, and it was clear to her, clearer than anything she had ever known up to now, that the three of them were the same, united, connected, whole together, and it would be for them, and this connection that she would cross the river, that she would go to the other side.

Hen Night.

Other people started arriving, most of them suburban types because this is a suburb.

Over the next five hours I am deep in suburbia, hard by Heathrow Airport, under the flight path, watching.

I pop outside before the festivities start so that I can get some fresh air.

I stare at the bright lights and the rainy streets.

I wonder what I look like on the inevitable CCTV cameras that are overtly and covertly watching me.

I wonder if whoever is watching me is wide awake.

If whoever is watching me cares.

I wonder how many times I have been photographed that day, and since I live in a country that has more CCTV cameras per head of population than any other, I decide to wear red one day, something consistent and special, to give the people who watch me something to talk about later in the pub as they swap my many images like baseball cards.

I am only doing this hen night thing because of Joanne, the one person at the station that I have any real connection with.

This is because Jo is monosyllabic, a hindrance, you would think, to her job which is booking the 'talent' for my show, but she's got a connection with the new owners, so…

She always has a smile and a laugh even while talking to the most pompous person which helps me a lot at 4:30 in the morning when I begin to fade and need a boost to make it to that last half hour.

Joanne is just twenty, and like you, has a big future ahead of her.

Which is what older people always say to kids as a way of distancing themselves from having to engage with them and tell them the truth.

I am assuming that you are Jo's age – early twenties and since I am twenty-seven and have entered officially what make-up people call 'the ageing skin category', I can say what I just said with a small bit of credibility.

Jo says that she likes me, but what I believe is that I am just material for her American Studies course.

At 3:30 in the morning, when I don't have much strength and I'm staring at the studio clock and the big television screens on the back wall, and the sports guy comes in to talk about sports for fifteen minutes, Jo tells me about her course and her life.

What I like about this is that her conversation is pretty much the same: 101% self-involved, which I find soothing and which, I guess if I think longer about it, is the reason I like her.

Sample:

"…American Studies is what I'm interested in. I want to live there. It's really hard doing my subject because I have to defend it a lot. People think it's a hopeless subject, pointless, stupid, but I tell them it also contains English and history and film and politics, I always have to apologize for what I'm studying."

And no matter what we're talking about, the conversation always gets around to her overdraft:

"…I have to deal with the negativity around my American Studies course, plus I'm always worrying about having to start digging into my overdraft, something I really don't want to have to do. The loans are bad enough. I know they say you'll only be paying off a little bit to start off with – but then how long is it going to take me to pay it off? And if I'm earning a lot, they'll take loads. I'm going to be poor forever."

So what's her solution?

She gets married to a guy whose dad owns a string of Balti houses.

This leads me to Patti Smith.

You probably haven't heard of her, but she first started making music in a far away time, my parents' time.

At least this is what I surmise from all the evidence: the films, clothing, books, music etc.

Everyone has a magic past, a place where life was better, more fun, and mine is the late sixties to mid seventies when Patti was Queen and everyone understood what she was about.

In those days, a student went to university and was given money to go.

There was no such thing as poverty except the poverty that came out of being young and a student and living for your books and your fun.

When it's really bad, I go to the V&A and look at the sixties clothes and in my mind, put myself inside them.

There was meaning then.

People had collectives and made things work, challenging The System etc.

Not that I would want to do that, but it's wonderful to contemplate.

Then you didn't have to take on burdens that stretched into your old age, you weren't expected to be striving and acquisitive and focused and driven. You just learned things.

After the V&A I go back to my place and play Patti.

I pretend that I'm pulling up the pavement stones on a street in Paris.

I am not doing that with irony, but with feeling and hope and intent.

Feeling, hope and intent.

I like to think that I could recognize these sensations if they came into my life today, welcome them too.

Back to Hen Night.

Inside I order a double vodka.

It is actually a brilliant evening here at Legs 17.

I admire the 70s wallpaper, and the upholstery which is pretty worn out and the seats which sink down when you sit in them. You don't have to crave smoke because you can smell it in the walls.

There is a naked woman writhing in front of the hens to badly amplified music with one of her high-heeled feet on our table.

One of the hens is shouting at the woman, telling her how her husband is addicted to places like Legs 17, that he spends £100 a night in places like Legs 17, and she wants the dancer to know that.

The hen turns to us, wiping the drink from her mouth and announces that she is going to find a twelve-step programme for men addicted to these places, she will do it, wait and see.

Human feedback is getting to be too much so I try to wipe out everything by pretending that I can see their auras, something easier to do than trying to imagine their molecular composition in colours.

The woman complaining about her husband's addiction has a red aura, deep crimson red with yellow flames shooting from close to her skin.

As the red light moves out it becomes orange, which tells me that she is somebody who loses her temper due to some malfunction in her ovarian area – she probably does not get enough smears out of embarrassment, etc.

This leads me to think about Montgomery Tourlaine and the book that no one will publish called *Britain In Excelsis*.

His main thesis is that GB is basically a suburban, middle class society and that you have to calibrate everything from that.

Not to know that means that you essentially don't get it.

The visual art – including clothing, design and some music – is a kind of aberration and can trace its descent in terms of attitude, defiance, point of view, etc. to William Blake and is at natural odds with the way things really are.

Montgomery Tourlaine figures that if you home in to about 1889-1914 then spiral out from there, attaching bits and pieces as various waves come and go, then you've pretty much got GB down.

The hen's anger and even the club's existence owes itself to what Montgomery Tourlaine's book is about, but I can't point that out to the pissed women in Legs 17 because I would have to shout, which I don't like doing.

I leave and look for a Tube station.

There is none since Legs 17 is in a place with no Tube so I wait for the bus. A woman sits down with me on the bench and it is soon apparent to me that she is a homeless person.

I read somewhere that you can divide homeless people into two categories: those who want to go inside and those who do not.

I try to look for signs as to which category the woman sitting next to me is in.

She is reasonably clean and bundled up. I am actually grateful that she does not smell because this would have been too much sensory overload for me at the moment and I am not sure how I would handle it.

She carries shopping bags from big Sloane Street designer stores barely crinkled which fascinates me and she also carries a big striped suitcase which is stained and tells me that she needs to get herself indoors and is right now heading for shelter.

Out of the blue she turns to me and tells me to follow her to the Tube station.

She can't be bothered with waiting for the bus.

I walk next to her.

I offer to carry her bags because she looks pretty old to me, somewhere in her fifties, but she refuses which embarrasses me, because I know enough to know, having slept on many couches, that your possessions, the ones you wind up still having, are important marks of your existence and continuity.

I wish that I had more of a lack of reciprocity and could turn off at the next corner, but I continue trudging along in the dark and pretty soon in the rain, too, and when I look back on it, it had to be the conjunction of the walking, the rain, the way she just said nothing but she was there, deeply there, that made me think of the kitchen back home and blueberry pie.

Blueberry pie again, like something out of an ironic horror movie, cooking away in our battle front of a home, a staple in our home, blueberry pie the way the peace was made, and order restored.

Mom would be out protesting this or that and Dad would be out trying to rope people into the Establishment, so naturally home life and dinner time especially were not joyful occasions.

That was when she – Earlene – would bake homemade blueberry pie. She hummed in the kitchen, making the pastry, getting the blueberries organized, the sugar, the butter.

I sat next to her and soon, I can make pies, too.

And since my father lived in a world devoid of laughter and joy and trailed this back home with him, the making of the conciliatory blueberry pie, waiting for it to cook, the aroma slowly arising, then the consumption of it, restored some sort of equilibrium, even joy to our house.

When I get back to my apartment, Montgomery Tourlaine is standing outside of the door of his apartment sniffing the air.

He does not like the smell of the wax that the cleaning woman for the flat next door to him uses.

It frightens him, he has said to me more than once, that a curmudgeonly side has lately come to the fore in him and even though he is over eighty, he feels that he is way too young to allow this to happen.

He often tells me about the travails the human mind can suffer at his age, and I straightforwardly tell him more than once, that ever since my father began slipping into Alzheimer's, younger than Montgomery is, I have become acquainted with a living bereavement and the destruction of the human mind.

Oh, and I was joking with you about him having kids. It's just me wishing he had. And wanting that factory in New Jersey to be true too, instead of him being the heir to a great Southern fortune, and that his family is looking for him so that they can put him away in an old folks' home so they can get his money.

Full on Southern Gothic stuff.

This is not true either.

Ok, there's a slight Southern twinge in his voice which, instead of repulsing me, draws me closer to him.

116

And this bit is true, him saying to me:

"I want to go back to the US. But I'm an alien there. I don't know the ground any more. Everything's changed Anna, and I have stood still. It's hard to reconcile myself to this constant coming together, the sharing of thoughts and pictures, the lack of privacy, the lack of desire for it. By privacy I don't mean living behind a wall. Which is where the rich are heading. No, I mean…the fear of being unknown. That drive doesn't sit well here. The English used to be modest and reticent and that was sexy. Now…Anyway, how can I go back to the States? It scares me to see people at shopping centres."

Impossible to see him at my age. He looks like one of those people born old, but I get what he says about the masses and yes, I can feel the same dread from time to time.

They say that nostalgia was first noted in sailors and has something to do with the sea.

I want to tell Montgomery Tourlaine my constant dreams about Earlene; how we are confined in a close space, in a boat I think, at the bottom of it, on the sea, trapped together, but that wouldn't be appropriate.

He couldn't have handled it. So I will tell you.

I am crossing an ocean, more than likely the Atlantic because I have never seen the Pacific. The Atlantic, and my parents are onboard too, throwing dictionaries at one another.

I wander off, being the child that I am, to a cabin below deck and moving past my window is the Statue Of Liberty. I reach out to it, but it vanishes. Alarming enough to dream in clichés, but when I woke up, I tried to elicit sympathy from myself.

But the point that I want to make here is that the Statue Of Liberty has never entered into my dreams, waking or asleep, until recently; the Statue of Liberty, a very funny, even impressive thing, making you want to cut straight to what is underlining the dream which, as you can see, I am trying to do with you. Hoping that in talking to you in my own way without fear, you can help me, since you've been a big part of my life without me knowing it.

And Earlene, too, who has come back to me.

No, no, I do not want to return to those questions about her and that night.

No.

I saw what I saw.

I thought no one else knew, except her, the condition I was in.

But Mom knew.

She has always known, but she has never confronted the damage she inflicted upon me.

Once she came close.

It was after one of our blueberry pie desserts and Dad had retreated to the phone to rally the troops against the latest left-wing outrage.

When he was gone, Mom told me about herself.

See, she knew all that time that I had been sneaking Abena Assantewa's books.

And she wanted me to know that she and Abena Assantewa had gone to the same school, that they were Roc Girls, in the mid 1960s.

When I was there for a little while, Roc Girls were concerned with their diets and fashion.

But in Mom and Professor Assantewa's day Rocs were hellraisers with big brains and big mouths.

Mom and Professor Assantewa were the ringleaders of a group they called The Elminas.

They named themselves after a medal that was kept in a safe at school and whose origins were mysterious.

Until Mom checked it out.

That's when she learned about The Orchestra.

The Orchestra could play the universe. What I mean is that they could reorder what was around them. They could be invisible. And they passed their powers down to their sons and their daughters. This power was something that they had developed, like a hide, after they had survived the slave ships. It was secret. But it was real. And it bound all of the women. And some of their descendants were students at Roc.

Mom was one of their descendants

And Dr. Assantewa.

And me.

Me.

Mom inherited a picture of a woman called Léopoldine.

Léopoldine was a conductor on the Underground Railroad during the Civil War and it was said by some that she could appear and disappear at will.

And Mom had a small statue from Roc.

It was a Black Virgin. Mom said that she could work miracles.

She could connect people who had lost one another.

That's what Mom said.

And when I was a little girl, I believed it.

I believed it all the way up to the day Earlene disappeared.

Weird, what people tell their kids, just to keep them quiet.

Me.

What did Earlene used to call me? 'The Little Girl Lost in The Woods.'

Everyone, I bet even you, knows that tale so l won't spell it out.

But the meat of the thing is that there are crumbs that the little girl lost in the woods finds, and they lead her on.

I was the only one on the block, in the whole neighbourhood, with a nanny, because Mom was too busy saving the world to take care of me, and Dad was too busy undoing what she was doing, all of which left the possibility and the probability of my becoming totally engulfed in my nanny's universe, which is what happened. And being a little kid, well, that was fine and so sometimes on successive nights, because we were alone in the house and with each other, Earlene would tell me other tales about lost females; orphans, lost in a world of closed doors, darkness, afraid of the sea and lakes and rivers.

The point being that hearing all this stuff, taking it in, and not understanding what I was supposed to do with it made me insecure.

There was no one to compare notes with.

I couldn't walk up to somebody and say "My nanny just told me this story about an orphan lost in a strange country looking for her parents, except that she doesn't know that her parents are with her because, I mean, she never met them, plus she doesn't know who she is, and by the way, can you tell me how you would interpret this or why a grown-up should be telling a kid stories like this?"

Of course Earlene told me stories like this because she knew that I didn't understand what she was saying because I was too young, even though in later years, in order to reinforce my disdain for her – fuel it – I liked to tell myself that I did.

I'm told that I have a reasonably high IQ, so I let her stories become part of my DNA.

You have to face a thing like this in the cold light of day. Like accepting that you listen to early Stones and Led Zep because you don't really – not really – have any music of your own.

I don't want to hide anything from you.

Not now while we're waiting for the sun to come up and the aroma of baking is floating around and we are both looking out of the window, and yes I am telling you the story Abena Assantewa sent me, telling you from my total recall, and also from the vacant place in my heart that it filled.

I am here with you.

Waiting for the woman in the next room.

I've always been waiting.

Because you can have nostalgia for a person you've never known.

Or a place.

Or a time you never lived. Except in your imagination.

Like, there was this waiter at Comfort, my favourite restaurant.

A Scot.

He told me once that he found himself after a hard night's drinking, walking around right where we are, here on the Ile St. Louis, and then, bam! There he was, floating down the Seine, flowing right down there beneath our window.

Only he thought…he was at home on his sofa!

He thought he was watching people from the safety of his sofa waving frantically at him as he floated past. I don't know how he put all that together in his brain, but when he saw the bridges coming

120

towards him and then passing over his head, that was when he thought: 'Hey, I'm not at home.'

I could see that, feel it. I missed it and I wasn't even…

There.

Right after that, great big hands pulled him out of the river, not a pretty body of water when you're beneath it, not benign, he told me, but a grasping, living thing.

He told me he saw that, after he got sober and replayed the whole thing in his head. He spent ten minutes telling me how, from that, the revelation came to him about how recent and insignificant our species is in the scheme of things.

So I bring this story up at a dinner I go to, held every third Thursday in the month in what I can only figure is an unconscious homage to Thanksgiving.

To be honest, I'm there because this is the one place where I can get a halfway decent meal.

The Septic dinner.

Septic is cockney rhyming slang, 'septic tank – Yank', for Americans.

The Septics are neither corporates, nor retired captains of industry, nor military, nor are they heiresses or showbiz folk.

They are ex-hippies; ancient youth-quakers, doddering old refugees from McCarthyism, strawberry-fields, summer-of-love-obladee-obladah-types.

You can come face-to-face there with still bra-less Gloria Steinem feminists, warriors against war, against the status quo, and let's all go back to Woodstock.

I enjoy these people.

They like me too.

Unlike most people my age, I do not remind them of their youth.

Unlike many my age I do not see myself as having an extraordinary destiny.

I am not in need of electronic social networking or any of the things of my era, so the lack of feedback, give and take, position, or my 15 minutes, doesn't bother me.

I do not seek nor do I have anything to prove.

In short, I cannot break the old dears' hearts.

At every dinner, after the usual grumblings about the state of their native land, a place they don't have the balls to live in any more, I am introduced to new members like the company mascot I am. I am supposed to say what I do.

We're all still Americans, after all.

I always like to start off with the story of my former partner on radio, a guy called Gordon and how he's an example of Shaw's statement that Britain and America are two nations divided by a common language.

My show had been Gordon's before I came along. It was pretty highbrow, low audience share.

Gordon understood right away why I had been hired: to replace him.

So when I started trying to shake things up a little by bringing on people other than the Great and the Good, he knew that the writing was on the wall.

He finally threw in the towel when I brought on a pompous, adjective – laden, ageing roué who wrote romance novels, and was so bitter and resentful of his lack of literary prizes and dinners and suppers with 'real' writers because he made lots and lots of money writing novels that only women read and was therefore not taken seriously by the literary press etc., even though – as I tried to say to him – women keep the whole publishing thing going and the snobbish thing was a little like women being cooks and men being chefs sorta, totally forgetting that this guy is famous for his lack of a sense of humour and his recreation is putting other people down in handwritten broadsides from his massive offshore estate which I figure can only be somewhere super-accessible like the Pitcairn Islands.

I let him unleash his spleen on my show.

The Septics always like this:

"I was sitting in the park reading over my work, minding my own business, when one of the Breastapo plopped down beside me without the tiniest bit of an 'excuse me' or 'is this taken?' and as the dear yummy mummy whipped out a bulging breast with which to suckle her whelping sprog, I leaned forward and asked: 'Madam, do you mind if I have a little? One gets awfully parched at my age.'"

Me: "So it was good?"

"How would I know? Before I rediscovered the pleasures of the maternal breast, I had driven the shy thing and her descendant away."

So level-headed Gordon lost it after I had the guy on, telling me later that nobody had him on a serious lit show, it was like…he couldn't think of an equivalent.

I was tired and couldn't deal with what he was saying so I went out on to the fire escape and lit up, with him hot on my heels about all the negative mail we'd get, me saying wasn't that good that the slot would be finally getting some mail, period; the most important thing at that moment was that I was blowing smoke rings for the first time since I was eleven, and when I finally got tired of his paranoia I told him he was right and so what?

He left the show shortly after that.

His excuse: he suffered from electro-magnetic hyperactivity, which is an allergy to modern technology.

I hear that he's on disability, stays indoors a lot and wears a tent on his head.

That's my standard story at the Septic dinner because it's too much work to do anything else.

There is always a new guest of honour.

How can I forget Thomas Tramwell, another Englishman in New York come home to London 'to die'?

Actually, he feels that he was driven out of New York after he gave a lecture at the 92nd street 'Y' in which he analysed the name 'Danvers' from Mrs. Danvers in Rebecca. His contention was that Danvers is clearly a play on 'd'enfer'- 'from hell', and that the book is a chronicle of the struggle between the White Virgin and the Black Virgin in which the Black Virgin consumes the world by fire.

Like Hedda Gabler, Mrs. Danvers stayed true to her inner narrative, the myth that played in her head, that drove her. A woman is a hero when she stays true to this, no matter what the outcome is in the outer world. The outer world is not set up to enable a woman to fulfil her heroic mythos except within circumstances that would be seen as negative, evil. The audience hates Hedda and the audience hates Mrs. Danvers, but should they?

So he asked at the "Y".

Another guest of honour was Edward Sexton-Featheringbridge who had published twenty-five novels to deafening silence and then published a thriller based on the mystery of the death of Christopher Marlowe which he wrote mostly as a palimpsest of a couple of Jeffrey Archer novels cobbled together. It became a bestseller with a movie deal, a stage adaptation and various awards, all of which he considered to be twenty-five novels too late. Then there's Calvin Beatty, 'Bitter Black Male Author, American Division', who considers himself 'In Exile'.

Calvin.

I don't know what will un-exile Calvin, maybe the death of all female authors, African American division.

I think: he hates me too, but tries to demonstrate his solidarity by giving me the privilege of showing solidarity with him while he rails : 'They don't let brothers publish. Period. A sistuh can write any kind of mess, but a brother…'

His adversary at the dinner was Joy Denice Fairburn, a fifty something African American hedge fund manager who goes to every party going; divorced by two Englishmen in rapid succession, I had been told, and who tried to take me under her wing when I first arrived with 'useful advice' on how to survive:

"The deal with the Brits is: you always have to make a joke. They love that shit. The joke can tank, but that's better than no joke. If you don't get that you can forget it here. The joke starts with you. Self-deprecation, but don't go too far because then you're pathetic and they despise your ass. Self-deprecation. Say it over and over before you go to sleep at night so it sinks in."

What I did was stand in the mirror every morning and just make jokes to myself about myself: my appearance, my hair, whatever. It worked…for a minute. Oh yeah, most important: 'you've really got to do envy, girl. Big envy.'

Sitting next to her is JD who everybody figures runs drugs and has a theory every week:

"Listen up, people. (Listen up people?)We're back in the Twenties again. Look at everything: these crazy cults, the boom-boom billionaires, totalitarianism, it's all there. And you know what happened after the Roaring Twenties!"

Edgar Van Gelt usually cringes when JD talks. He considers himself a custodian of the English language and is more English than the English:

He cleared his throat after JD let loose.

"Plain speaking. That's what we've lost. It started with the Vietnam War when we cast our lot with another clueless Texan. And then came the women novelists with their mangling of plain speaking. The English language does not sit well with Latinate phrases! Ezra Pound said 'midnight is midnight, not the midnight hour'!"

I turn and look at good old Carl Mikva, who loves to say that he was privileged to have known Brecht in Hollywood:

"That sonafbitch had his plane ticket in his pocket when he turned up to testify at HUAC. Those stupid hicks didn't realize who they were talking to. Next to Freud, the greatest student of humanity in the 20th century. Somebody said him being there testifying to that group was like the zoo keeper being interviewed by the monkeys!"

"Reminds me," said Elsa Wincher, an old lady with a soft Southern drawl and the most beautiful clothes, all handmade in the 50s:

"I was just thinking the other day while I was stuck in a tunnel on the Tube: you know, Hitler was rejected by the art school of Vienna; Castro didn't make the Pittsburgh Pirates; they didn't like Napoleon's accent at military school in Paris; the guy who taught Kaiser Wilhelm to ride a horse when he was a kid just kept kicking him until he found his seat, and I'm thinking…'Yes, it all makes sense.'"

Carl Mikva spits his food out:

"So, what if those sonovabitches'd been allowed in –what? they woulda wound up Mother Teresa? Ok Elsa, so what explains you ? Can you be reduced like that? What about me? I wanted to marry Shirley Temple. She had this kids' show in the Fifties where she used to sing: 'Dreams Are Made For Children' in a fairy costume. I used to write her letters. Does that explain me?"

I excused myself to go to the bathroom and look in the mirror and see if I could see my face, but it wasn't there.

I buttoned my coat. Again and again and again and again.

A few days later, Montgomery Tourlaine and I are walking through Bloomsbury in streets that are more Hogarthian than Victorian.

There are small pools of vomit in the corners of buildings. Girls coatless in tiny, tight dresses, walking in packs, drunk to their eyeballs; packs and packs of people looking for Saturday night to come, roaming, and roaring, London rushing at you headlong and what was once for me love has been for a minute reduced to fear. I am no longer excited by it. I want the grid system and the cars going the right way and this frightens and surprises me.

I think as I'm walking that once I liked the sense of London spinning out of control, London about to slip through your fingers, London on the verge of eating you alive and kicking your bones to the kerb. And that antsy feeling you get when you're away that you're too far away, you're missing something back in London, something is happening and you're not there; those endless conversations over drink that I observe in my usual zoological way, fascinated continually by the intricacies of this island, how dense it is with such a small amount of land mass, a place where everyone is essentially deeply romantic, where their wet dreams are about rough sex with the Queen or a romantic night with their partner; me, usually watching it all, talking about it in my head, talking to you here; thinking while I'm walking with Montgomery Tourlaine that suddenly, out of the blue, I am becoming nostalgic for the land of my birth.

Montgomery Tourlaine understands.

So we're walking and I bring this up to Montgomery Tourlaine who changes the subject by telling me about the London bus system, especially the old red buses open in the back to the elements.

It's like this:

In Victorian days the horse buses did not have route numbers. The way to recognize them was by colour or the destination painted on the side. Then about a hundred years ago, someone came up with the idea of displaying prominent numbers on the early motor buses. After World War Two the numbers 1 to 199 were red central area; the 200s were red suburban single deckers; the 300s were green country buses operating north of the Thames; 400s were green country buses south of the Thames; 500s and 600s were electric trolleys; 700s were Green Line.

The man who told Montgomery Tourlaine all this was this West Indian bus conductor by the name of Milton Bookman, who, in addition to knowing everything about the buses also had a book club on…his bus!

They got to be friends, and one day the bus conductor told him about his great lost love, an American girl, black, who had spent a weekend with him, and after that, had vanished.

He told Montgomery that she was the woman he would have left his family for. He had said that he thought she might have known this. That was why she had left him. Because he belonged with his wife and daughter. He both hated her and loved her for her decision. But she had left him with nothing. Each day was like a chasm that grew bigger and bigger and bigger.

I don't know why his story of the black bus driver and his lost black American love clarifies me.

But it does. Suddenly.

I don't say anything.

As Montgomery Tourlaine and I walk up the stairs to the place where we live, I know that to tell him my true story would be to cross a line, to violate an unspoken pact between us. He talks to me, after all, as a way of disengaging, of keeping his distance.

I've got to keep respecting that.
He had given me useless information.
Just like Montgomery Tourlaine.
Anything to keep me from getting close to him.
I don't know why I remember that story now.
Sometimes I think about that guy.
How he might have ended up.
I don't know why.
But when I think about him, I think about going back.
Going home.
It's like he's telling me to.
A guy I didn't even know.

That's why I'm here. I want someone to explain to me this sudden craving for a place that I can no longer avoid calling 'home'.

4.

The Seine had risen, flooding the entire city.

There was the constant drone of the old-fashioned pumps, draining the river.

There were rumours about the origin of the flood. The large American ex-pat community was said to have proof that FSD had created it in retaliation for France taking in American dissidents.

Others said that this was the 'big one' waiting to happen.

Jody quickly banished the thought from her head.

She counted on her back-up in 'Clean Up And Maintenance', the agency that read thoughts. They could, for a price, erase anything that might get her into trouble.

She depended on the greed and addiction of others to keep her safe.

On the way over, she had read how Paris had been warned about the possibility of floods. But the city, despite repeated warnings, had only taken a minimum of precautions.

Paris had forgotten that it owed its existence to the Seine and that at any time she could claim the city back.

In spite of the weather, Paris managed to look like a film set, just as Control implied it would.

Except that this was not the early part of the 20th century, but the middle of the 21st…

"Mademoiselle Carlyle, bienvenue à Paris! I am Jean-Luc Manet."

A water taxi had pulled up.

A voice came from below deck.

"Drout!"

Another voice from below replied.

"Madame! Excuse…"

The same female voice came again, this time with a tone of exasperation in it:

"I blame all this madness on l'inondation!"

A woman emerged from the cabin of the boat.

"We can do nothing here in Paris! It's absurd! It is as if we are living…what?…forty years ago, at the beginning of the century, in the dark ages when people played games on computers with each other. Were they that lonely then? Or terribly bored? Did they not think that they were leaving their footprints all over the web?! Look what we've done with all of that information!"

"Yes, it does sound strange that people were so eager to expose themselves like that", Jody said.

The woman calmed down and smiled.

"I am so rude! I am Sylvie Verteuil-Désanges. I am here at your service."

She extended her elegant hand.

Jody wasn't sure whether she was meant to shake it or kiss it.

"Manet and I will serve you now. Dr. Andromache will take over in due course. And I must tell you: keep your eye on that man. He is quite naughty, even for a Frenchman.

Ah, you must meet Saronia Miller!! Do you know, you remind me of her? Of course, you are not a black woman, but there is something in your eyes, I cannot deny this. I love the way she looks, masses of dreadlocks, flowing African robes, exquise. It is a pity that her husband is not well. His illness is affecting her. They are devoted to one another, as people who marry late in life usually are. But you'll be happy to know that her area of Paris, where you are going, is nicely drained. And another thing. I know that there were heavy rains, but why is the river continuing to rise?"

Sylvie Verteuil-Désanges turned her head back toward the cabin.

A small black girl emerged.

"May I present Tirian?"

Jody looked at her. She knew in her bones that Tirian had been a feral child.

Like she had been.

"Tirian? That's a pretty name", Jody said. "What's your last name"?

"Tirian has no last name. Just Tirian. She is the one who will be with you twenty four hours a day. And she will protect you."

Jody said, "How old are you, Tirian?"

"Tirian is 10 years old." Sylvie broke in, "She just had her birthday. She is muette. She cannot speak."

"Tirian, you know that I can hear you speaking," Jody thought.

Tirian replied through her thought. It was clear that she did this only when she wanted to and that Jody would have to wait for those times.

"Jody,", she began, "I am ten years old. I've seen such terrible things, war, famine. I've eaten out of garbage dumps, I've learned to use weapons, I've taken drugs to dim the pain of it all. And I've made myself dumb so that they can't touch me. So that I can stay inside myself. And then one day they took me away to a beautiful home with beautiful parents. Who loved me. But they weren't mine. I knew that."

Jody was distracted by Sylvie's voice.

"I feel so sorry for the poor people, they are living like rats. No, not as good as rats. The rats are content. They will die when humankind dies. They are linked to us. Genetically. But we call them vermin. Which, I understand, you eliminate."

"You know about Elimination Systems?" Jody asked.

"I'm not meant to say anything, of course. We are all Ultras here, except for the petite."

"My job is to…I take care of vermin and viruses. Trained from an early age," Jody said.

"Well, I am no fan of Hitler, he was disgusting. But to think of what he tried to do – the horrible gas chambers we do not speak of – but the idea."

"What idea, Sylvie?"

"That society must be pure. Of itself. By itself. This is why the Stockholms, they are so dangerous. People of that genetic excellence cannot simply stop breeding as an act of protest."

"They should be able to do what they want."

"No, what WE want! Now, Jody, I will bring you a pastis, an excellent remedy for boat-sickness."

She disappeared below.

Jody reached out to touch Tirian.

Tirian recoiled.

"I won't hurt you."

Tirian turned and went below.

The sun was starting to set.

And the Seine turned the colour of blood.

The prow of the boat bumped against the quay.

The smart residences facing the river had installed Amsterdam-style hooks with which furniture and goods could be hauled up.

Old-fashioned sandbags surrounded Notre-Dame, keeping the water at bay.

The boatman jumped out first and escorted Sylvie Verteuil-Désanges, Jody and Tirian off the boat and onto the landing. The landing led inside to an hôtel particulier in a street called rue Le Regrattier.

Manet remained on the boat as it moved on.

The courtyard had been drained of water.

Children were playing in it.

Jody remembered the feral children she had been with the other day.

Too many of them had been subjected to the testosterone experiments created to make them better gladiators. They did not know how to play. The constant pictures of angry people shown to them in order to keep them on edge would not allow them to enjoy the tranquillity of playing with a ball.

But the English soldiers who patrolled the feral enclaves back in the States as part of a reciprocal agreement, and whose grandfathers had had urban warfare experience in Northern Ireland, would have shot any child with a toy, something that could be used a weapon.

Porters carried the luggage up the wide winding staircase to the cage elevator.

Sylvie Verteuil-Désanges touched the 'hot spot' near the entrance which read their IDs, fingerprints, irises and photographed them, all within seconds. Another door which at first looked like a wall, opened and they entered another stairway, smaller and darker which led to the apartment.

Jody thought: 'One door opening onto another door behind it and another and another and another. Where does it end?'

The next narrow passageway opened into a wide living space with views of the swollen river.

The apartment was stuffed with fresh flowers, plump cushions, deep couches, paintings, photos, and tall windows that opened onto a balcony overlooking the river.

In spite of its calm, tranquil appearance, Jody knew instantly that every inch of the place was alive. It was ready to tell her all about herself; anticipate her needs; even kill her if it deemed her an enemy of the common good.

The bumblebees that swarmed around the flower pots on the balcony were tiny security aircraft armed with cameras constantly taking photos. The bumblebees had also checked out all the plants and flowers in the apartment for any hint of the work of the 'black biologists' who had taken bio-technology and turned it against authority and nations. People who had the power to wipe out 30,000 people in 10 minutes.

Jody noticed the two tiny boxes, disguised like candy boxes, which were actually powerful computers that ran all the systems in the apartment and could rid it of viruses.

She knew then that she was in more than just an expensive apartment in the middle of Paris.

This was a nerve centre, as 'hot' as any ordinary place could be.

Jody stopped and looked over at Tirian who sat stiffly on the chair, her hands folded in her lap.

"Let's look around." Jody suggested to her.

As Jody's eyes scanned the room looking for the security devices, a woman with long dreadlocks suddenly appeared and began unpacking Jody's things.

Jody recognized her as an Adjuster.

Adjusters were like personal greeters, always present to ensure an Ultra was comfortable, informed and armed if necessary.

Once upon a time, they had been feral children saved from oblivion. Jody studied her.

The woman was well-preserved. She could be anywhere from 70-75.

Sylvie returned.

"Adele, chérie. How's the new baby? You look fantastic!" she yelled.

"This is the last one", Adele laughed. "No more after this! I'm not sure retirement and then starting a family was in the right order!"

"Saronia's at home asleep.", she continued. "Between you and me, she's really a little tired from taking care of her husband. He's very sick. That woman is really, really devoted to him.

Everybody should have the kind of love that Saronia Miller has for that man. It's a shame he's so sick. Somebody said it's because he has a rogue gene."

Jody was shocked.

No one admitted to this. Anybody with a rogue gene could be eliminated under national security laws.

Jody remembered a time from her childhood. She had broken a favourite glass and her adoptive mother, Audrey had yelled: "What am I doing with a kid with a rogue gene in my house!"

"Are you ok?" Adele asked, staring at her. "You look faraway."

"I'm hungry." Jody said. "Tirian, what about…?"

She remembered that the little girl could not speak, so instead she made eating motions with her hand as she tried to discover whether Tirian was hungry.

"Please feed me, Jody. I'm very hungry."

Jody heard her thoughts and smiled.

"Tirian is not deaf. In fact, her hearing is quite good. Extremely good." *Sylvie suddenly said.*

Jody looked at the little girl again. Her face was expressionless.

"Jody Carlyle ?"

Another voice.

Jody turned around.

A small, round woman stood in the doorway, hugging a shawl around her shoulders, dreadlocks tumbled down her back. Her skin was the colour of sable.

134

Jody did not scan her.

She knew who she was.

"Saronia, what in the world are you doing here?" Adele yelled.

Saronia ignored her and sat at the table.

Jody thought: "There she is, the woman who has written the books that every child who can read loves and cherishes – she writes the books that I loved and cherished. When I was alone and scared and wondering who my real folks were, there were her books to keep me warm and safe. Standing in front of me is Saronia Miller herself, author of the Blueberry Farm books. She was like a mother to me.

And I have to turn her in."

Blueberry Farm. That place, those characters had been her true family.

But above all, she had loved the big tabby cat called Bonhoeffer. She would say his name over and over to herself. She had wanted her parents to buy her a tabby so that she could have her own Bonhoeffer, but they had gently told her that it was impossible.

"Jody, the word 'Bonhoeffer' isn't a good thing to sing."

Why, Mommy?

"These books are our little secret. In our family, we're allowed to keep secrets. No one else around here can. But if you sing that name, our secret will be given away. Can you keep quiet for Mommy's sake"?

And she had said: "Yes, Mommy. Anything for you."

She remembered her adoptive mother Audrey sitting at the head of her bed, reading another Blueberry Farm story: She could hear her voice once more:

"'Hal Haze was afraid. There was something important he had to do. The Big Farmer had given him an order. Hal knew that the order was wrong. He knew that he must disobey the order. If he disobeyed the order, he would be thrown into the Creepy World where the monsters lived. But Hal knew what he had to do. He had to disobey The Big Farmer. Bonhoeffer curled up next to him. Whenever Bonhoeffer did that, Hal Haze knew that everything was going to be alright.'"

Jody cleared her mind and turned her attention to the business at hand.

Jody allowed the nostalgia to lull her, comfort her without the "O".

She liked the old-fashioned state of the apartment. And sitting right in front of her, was the woman who had nourished her with her tales of a perfect world where everything had a lovely order.

She found a cold bottle of Sancerre in the refrigerator. She had seen kitchens like this in old movies. She had felt a certain nostalgia for them.

Tirian sat with them, and Adele beside her. Sylvie sat at a small distance apart from the group. Jody poured the wine.

"This is a treat", Sylvie said. "Even my nervous assistant, Caroline might have a glass of this. The woman can't eat or drink anything. Everything to her is contaminated. She goes all the time to this woman, an American, Anita Collins who has a healing business. I say to her : how can you live in the world if you think it is trying to kill you?"

Jody thought: 'Anita Collins. That's Blanche Rose'.

Adele swept her arm toward the direction of the window.

"That river out there. Let me tell you all something: Mamma Seine is trying to wipe us out, before we wipe her out..."

Saronia took a big drink of the wine.

She seemed to be in her own world.

"I swear to all of you," she suddenly said, "My books are for children. They're just kids' books. Why would anybody think they were anything else? Why have they arrested librarians, closed the libraries that stock my books?"

"Libraries, books, librarians, all that is long gone, Saronia. They needed the land for more enclaves." Adele said.

"I just don't understand. My books are for little ones!"

Adele said, "The old days. When you could read what you wanted. You could just buy a book and open it up. Nobody bothered you. Nobody checked what you were reading. Nobody remembers those days. Those that do don't talk about it."

Jody saw her opening. She could make her opening play for Saronia now. She said:

"That's what my parents used to say, I'm told. That's why they left the States and became exiles. I wish that I'd known them. They had a tragic accident. They're dead..."

Saronia leaned forward. Her eyes were watery. Her voice slurred.

"Jody, I'm so sorry to hear that. Your parents were exiles. Like me and…I knew we had a connection. I could feel it when I first met you. I know that you are connected to me. I know it! Your people were activists in the 60s, weren't they?"

"Yes. They were."

"Oh. The 60s! Jody, we had such plans. Our dreams were so big. We had the world right here in our hands. You couldn't tell us that the world would be like this. Not our world. Is it because the good ones died? Or got locked up too many times? Was it our chase for immortality? Our greed for life? We wound up making the same thing that we hated our parents for. Worse. We made a world of control. Us? The 'Free Love Generation'? Us? Us?"

She leaned even closer. Her eyes were big and desperate.

"Jody, I want to say something to you: Bogle, my husband. He can't get the care he needs here. I know that he can get it in London. But we're scared to leave. Someone could kill us. I feel that. I've received assurance that if I go London…"

Saronia stopped herself.

"I can't say anything else. I just want Bogle and me to go back now."

"But you can't go back! They hate you back there! Your books are banned!" Adele shouted.

Her shout was so loud that it woke her baby, asleep in the back of the apartment.

She ran to the baby.

"Look at her. Always running. I had the opportunity to become a mother last year", Sylvie said, "but I had the good sense to realize that Nature gives children to the young because the young have energy, patience, tolerance…and stupidity. Saronia, chérie, you are right. Home is home. There's no place like it."

Saronia stood up abruptly.

"I have to go lie down. I'm not used to drinking wine in the day time and I've drunk too much. Jody, I'm so glad that you're here."

She leaned over and kissed her and left the room.

Jody noticed that she limped.

Sylvie said: "A failed assassination attempt. A bunch of stupid women Hunters posing as fans! Pétasses. We almost got her to HC5 but it was this Anita Collins who warned her. Saronia leapt out of a window! Now you are here, and you have got her to express out loud what we thought was impossible. Also, she never talks about her husband in public! All the years that we've been monitoring them, she's never mentioned him in public. You have made her say his name! This means she is ready now to acknowledge that he exists."

"But if we know about him, what difference does it make whether she acknowledges him or not?"

"Aw. Well, you see, her admitting his existence indicates a change in her emotional state which tells us that she is open. Accessible. To us. The emotions of trust and love are easier to work with. The emotions allow us in, Jody. It is marvellous that she feels so close to you, you are like a daughter to her. This is clear. She will continue to open up to you and when she does, she'll follow you to HC5. And we will take things from there."

"What will happen ?"

Sylvie glanced over at Tirian who was sitting impassively.

"We should have been born like that little one. She is just a witness to the proceedings. Just a witness. What better job could anyone have these days than merely to observe?"

She stood up and walked over to the window.

Jody looked over at Tirian. Observing was all that she seemed to do.

But why would they send her someone who just watched things?

Jody had a sudden urge to clap her hands in front of the child's face to see if this would elicit some response, some sound.

"I wanted to work with kids like you." Jody directed her thoughts to Tirian, "But my dad – my adoptive father – told me that I had inherited rogue genes from my birth parents. Mom changed the subject when I asked about it. I had to go somewhere in my mind to deal with it. That's why Bonhoeffer was so important to me. He saved me."

Tirian looked at her.

Her face was softer.

She had decided to direct her thoughts:

"Jody, sometimes we have to betray people. Sometimes we have to be who we are not. There was someone who loved me very much – my own sister – but I couldn't see that. I hurt her. And then she died. And I never told her what she meant to me. She had a child, a little girl. Not her own, in her care. And I want to reach this child, and through her, say how sorry I am to my sister. And to her."

"Tirian", Jody said out loud. "You have a sister?"

Tirian smiled.

She directed her thoughts:

"That was a test, Jody. We are always testing you. Too much empathy is not good. It might bring people too close together."

Later, Jody unpacked the room spray she had been given as a gift the last time she had been invited to The White House.

The President had been concerned about the amount of oxymorcin being consumed by Ultras like Jody. Now that its consumption was becoming commonplace in the general population, something more subtle and less addictive had to be created for people like her. She had been given a higher, 'super' dose. It had been a gift for her services to Elimination Systems. She had tried to thank the President herself in person, but the Commander-in-Chief had become more and more inaccessible.

Jody looked around the room she had been given.

All that mattered was that she stayed in control of her environment, of her reality.

Jody inhaled the hormone, the super oxymorcin, taking in the warm, loving feelings that it caused to be released within her.

The spray had a jasmine aroma. It was lovely. She sank onto the luxurious bed that had been laid out for her.

She let herself go for a moment.

She thought about how she had been taught that there was no evil, no goodness, only a point of view.

But she had experienced goodness. With her adoptive mother.

Once, they had gone to an ice cream parlour. As they ate a sundae together, she had asked:

"Mom, did you ever meet my real Mommy?"

She could still see the warmth in Audrey Carlyle's eyes.

"Yes Jody, I met her once. And your father, too. They died and you were given to me. Holding you for the first time was the most wonderful moment of mine and your dad's life."

"That day at the ice cream parlour", Jody said aloud, watching the past unravel in her head, "was the day my recurring Image began. And the melody. Something told me to never tell my mom about it. Never. And I didn't. I didn't."

She started to drift, to dream, her brain in reverie mode:

She thought: "Keep vigilant. You can't be sure where you are. You could be being read as a virus. Right now. You could be about to be destroyed."

She sprang up.

Tirian was standing at the edge of the bed.

Watching her.

Jody composed herself.

"Have you eaten?" Jody asked Tirian.

Tirian did not respond for a moment. Then she slowly nodded her head.

Jody took this as a response, a gesture of acknowledgment. She did not stop there.

"So they trained you too", she said to Tirian. "They started on me at your age. You must have a lot of talent, too. For what exactly ? Assassination? At least they let me play when I was your age. Do they let you play? I liked playing. What games do you like?"

She was high and Tirian's emotionless face looked monstrous, enveloped in the growing shadows.

"I liked ball games.", Jody continued, searching the child's face. "But above all, I really loved my dollies. I had black dollies, too. They kind of looked like you. They were beautiful. I loved them. I used to pretend that I could talk to them. I'd sit around and wait to hear what they had to say. I said to them: 'Give me some words of wisdom.' But you know, toys can't do that."

The autumnal evening had begun closing in.

Jody reached out her hand.

Tirian pulled back and moved deeper into the gloom.

"Tirian, when my mother told me that I was adopted and that my real parents were dead, I was mad at them. I thought: 'Why did you leave me? Why didn't you take me with you?'"

Tirian turned and ran out of the room.

The Image returned. She could see two people, from the viewpoint of a child in a crib. There were two huge faces, shrouded in darkness, but there was something else, too.

Their skin seemed dark. That skin slowly became clear while the features were hidden. But it was the skin that struck her.

Jody could feel that this skin was her skin. That she belonged to those two people in The Image. Those two people had always been with her and had now chosen to reveal themselves in a way they never had before.

This Image was her birth parents, and she was them, but what she saw and what she felt didn't make sense.

She felt something else too, something that settled in the pit of her stomach and that was as certain as anything could be in her world.

Jody said to the empty space: "My birth parents were killed."

Jody went to Tirian's room.

She was sitting with her eyes closed.

She opened her eyes and looked directly into her face.

As she looked into the child's eyes, Jody let everything that was running through her mind come out in a rush of words.

Tirian shifted but her face had no expression.

Jody went in search of a mirror.

She studied her face.

The world seemed to be swirling around.

Even with the 'O' surging through her body, it was all beginning to make sense.

Control had clearly wanted her to lure Saronia to HC5 in order to eliminate her.

And she had been the bait.

This could work for only one reason.

She could barely think it.

Her connection to the Blueberry Farm books, the reason they had meant, and still meant so much to her.

Jody had always felt that there was something hidden about her, something secret. In spite of her blonde hair, her blue eyes, she had always felt that there was more, another story, just out of her reach.

The world that always had seemed to her to be comprehensible and stable, had suddenly imploded.

Jody closed her eyes. The Melody had begun again in her head, that Melody was associated with The Image.

She could hear Saronia's words as she had left earlier.

She was tired and sounded old. She murmured:

"Tell me how we keep our connection? What do we do to stay human in this crazy world?"

That Calm is but a Wall
Of unattempted Gauze
An instant's Push demolishes
A Questioning – dissolves.

THE HEART HAS NARROW BANKS, EMILY DICKINSON

Her life had been symbolized by her glasses, shields against seeing, a psychotherapist she consulted once had told her; she, too afraid to return to the woman, had made attempts on her own to venture out from time to time and inch by inch without her glasses, armed with her mother's words that all it took to see properly was an act of will, and a simple marshalling of her forces, and besides, without her glasses, what she would see was what her eyes would want her to see; typical, Janet had thought at the time, so typical of Gloria-Loretta to perceive the world as a complete and total act of will; her mother had said life itself came into being because of human need and not the love and mercy of God; ridiculous that human beings would construct the Divine in their own image, so clear to her that if God existed at all, the Divine would be abstract, ultimately unknowable; her point of view driving Janet even closer to the church in self-defence; living in terror throughout her childhood that her mother would die and go to hell, that she would not have the time to repent; Janet would see herself praying over the coffin of her mother, making endless novenas for the repose of her soul, all the while resentful, angry, guilty.

Death and transformation had been the chief themes in Latoya Richardson's writing; her work was typically undergraduate – derivative; yet her slight collection of short stories had been hungrily lapped up by two Soho-based literary agents thrilled by her multiculturalism and her youth; Latoya smart enough to put them off for a while, aware that her work was juvenilia; not wanting it to

143

come back and haunt her later, label her the rest of her days; so she had gone back to work, Janet putting her through her paces, envying her too, for her fearlessness and her youth; taking her right back to basics, placing her in a pedantic writing class in which the other students did not have a tenth of her talent, refining her; the grounding was necessary, after all, she was black and had to know the way it was and would be: in England, no matter how talented she was, she had not been born of the right family, gone to the right schools, and was therefore out of the loop, off the grid, a transgressor, not free – exactly Sam's point about Lucas – and so, she had told Latoya, that it was best to take the long way, the hard slog; read 'The Greats', only the best, Latoya particularly coming to like Zola's Rougon-Macquart series; Janet admiring of her work ethic, at times enquiring how the writing was going, beginning with that officious clearing of her throat which she affected whenever she was about to say something other than what she wanted to say, had to say, Latoya, looking at her in the hard, clear way she had which hid other feelings too complex to reveal, already a Puritan, a Stylite, up on a pillar in her own desert, alone, a young woman against all the odds dedicated to her art with its own timing and pace; completely wedded to the craft; going along with Janet for the sake of it and taking the English way: the avoidance of anything personal; deflecting anything that Janet might say that could build a bridge between them, chewing on her already gnawed thumbnail as she launched into the story of the incident that had inspired her latest short story:

A white woman – the colour of her skin a necessary component of the tale, Latoya had said – had been sitting next to her on the Tube, a poor, deluded woman who must have thought that she was about to pick her handbag; a bolshie City type who had seemed to be prepared for an altercation, which had surprised Latoya and made her momentarily reticent; but the daemon within that made her write pushed her on; pushed her past her own common sense and respectability into an unknown, reckless frame of mind which could have landed her in jail or worse; it was the daemon who had plunged her into a cold raucousness that had made the men in the carriage look at her and pay attention, knowing in themselves that she, Latoya Richardson, was a young woman capable of extreme mayhem, ready to wreak havoc, to risk all in order to destroy the common weal, to risk all for disorder, evident by how brightly her face lit up when re-telling the incident; a small frisson making its way through Janet too, as Latoya had described the stand-off and its aftermath: how the white woman, born to confidence, had given as good as she got, but not as good as Latoya had; each word shouted to the woman Latoya had repeated again for Janet in the quiet of her office; Janet had known that both of them had revelled in the transgressive nature of the incident, its delicious power; through it, for a moment, to her astonishment, she and Latoya had become kin; talking faster and faster as she retold the tale, practically manic as she told how the other black women in the carriage had secretly smiled, some openly giving her the thumbs up as she insulted the white woman and all who were part of her – the living and the dead; the total pleasure of it all – Janet could not forget it – of Latoya, practically delirious as she spoke of the City woman's backing down, her body quivering from unused adrenaline, the sweat glistening on her forehead; the triumph of Latoya bringing a hush to the carriage; no sound for a moment except the train on the rails, then filtering back was the automated announcement at the station; and some kid's iPod blasting Kurt Cobain; the feeling of exhilaration at the shrill, fingernail-dragged-across-a-blackboardness of it; the air stinking with fear; at the next stop it had emptied as if attacked by the plague, except for that handful of black women who had caught her eye and smiled; she, alone except for the kid with Nirvana; and it was nirvana; happy for the vengeance she had taken, understanding at that moment what a soldier in the heat of battle must feel, the smell and taste and sound of violence with its need to rape and pillage in order to keep the feeling going; she had begun, right there in her seat on the Tube, to write it down in her mind in order to make it true; her only frustration being that she had failed to find her usual pen and scrap of paper; now staring out of the window and abruptly announcing to Janet that she was stuck, she could go no further on her story – already about 6,000 words, more than enough for Anna Taylor's contest which Latoya had decided to enter, confident that she would win, rocking back and forth, rubbing the eczema patch in the crook of her elbow, popping the gum in her mouth; that annoying sound and the aggression of it had spurred Janet on to ask whether Latoya even bothered to listen to 'Taylor Made'; if not she had a few tapes of the programme which she could lend since quite a few of them were interviews with writers about their process including several black women writers who had been on the show lately; Latoya ignoring her, and Janet, in order to get her attention, asked what happened next to her fictional black student Felicia and her love affair with Jack Duncan, her white university professor.

Latoya had laughed, calling her character an 'Englishman without a war'; her body loose, her legs slightly open, slowly rocking back and forth in Milton Bookman's old chair, which Janet had brought in to her office; Latoya challenging her, demanding to know why Felicia should not allow the affair to go any further – was it because of their racial differences, the differences in their ages, that she was unmarried and he had a wife in the suburbs; what about a married woman and an unmarried man; one night, one second together; did everything have to be a question of love? couldn't their coming together be a passage for the other to something else? to hatred, for example; why was everything so tight, so small, so much more insular? here was no real adventure left other than love; hadn't that been what Proust had been about, why had Janet insisted she read all of the volumes if she could not apply, even live, what the novels had taught her? that she and her Felicia had wanted to experience waiting at some eternal Balbec for the love that could only occur in its entirety once; this being the point of her story about the black female student and her white professor – why couldn't she understand this?

Janet re-entered the office she shared with her colleague Simon Eckert. Simon's 'day self', she called it, was a miniaturist, obsessed

146

with order and tidiness, seldom speaking, concerned with his tiny cartons of lethal espresso, his thin paperbacks of intricate fiction, his mention from time to time – when he felt insecure and ignored – of the minor poetry prize he had won twenty years ago which allowed the designation 'prize-winning' after every description of himself; his amazement at the world around him, the encroaching world of things that he could not fathom and which was beginning to engulf him; strange incidents and odd occurrences the norm in an England, that for him, had fallen in love with its own dystopia; convinced that all of modern life existed to keep him confused and bewildered, a topsy-turvy looking-glass world where the Malian cleaning woman could be seen standing in a corner with her mop against the wall, reading 'Illuminations', reciting under her breath the beautiful language; her cadence and pronunciation all the more beautiful because he felt – he knew – that Rimbaud had searched for Africa through his poetry all of his life, hearing it in the voice of the cleaning woman, a qualified teacher back home; he wanting to rescue her from her pail of soapy water; the 'day' Simon bewildered by his need to help this woman, but the 'night' Simon, the one who embodied Rimbaud's words "I am the other", would meet Janet beneath the courtyard arch, often in the rain, to share a smoke, his cigarette poised between his fingers like a Home Counties Sartre, and there he talked of love, not 'happy, clappy love', he had called it, but of obsession, Verlaine-style; once saying to her, in an absent way as if he had been talking to himself, that he liked the French, because they used love to create oblivion.

Oblivion and all the quiet of a morgue, Janet whispered later to Simon, as they were shown into an apartment whose unique selling point was 'quiet enough for a baby to sleep in', much too eerily quiet, she thought, except for the river just outside the window, the whole point of this complex which had formerly housed grain; the river was the main reason the apartments both rented and sold well; the river, a dirty, sludgy green, almost static, so close to the windows that it seemed about to burst through; the river luring her out onto the balcony where she looked at the barges, at watermen plying their ancient trade, with its knowledge of the tides and when to go under a bridge; the Thames, at this point in the river, a body of water that was strictly for business; its lanes another world, its treacherous undertow; what it did season in and season out was known to only a few who dared to enter its masculine domain, dared to embrace its brutal insistence upon commerce and trade and the here and the now.

She thought that she could plunge into it now, lose herself forever, embrace it finally, see for herself if it was possible to walk on water like she thought she could as a child, when she saw the river not as a barrier and a hindrance, but as a passageway to the other side not only of the river itself, but of her life; too cold now to try to do it, to leap, the breeze turning into a wind and whipping her coat around her knees, the sky dark already as the nights began to draw in as the days moved toward the Equinox.

She was grateful later to have supper with Simon in a restaurant whose background music was the blues, deep blues, the keening, transcendental kind that told of long roads leading into the woods where the Devil waited; Simon nodding his head, their trivial conversation about the rise of house prices in the area of his potential new home; then turning to the blues itself and how blues musicians were ripped off, how the doomy blues that had been so celebrated were not exactly loved by ordinary black Americans who preferred the more upbeat variety; funny how a Blues Queen with a big, rolling train and mink and jewels could be shunted aside by the powers-that-be in favour of a lone wolf whose sparseness opened up just enough space in the sound for other people to put themselves in – how people – Simon was in his element now – extended themselves into other people's lives, re-animating themselves with lives not their own, as good a definition of power and oppression as he could think of; his life, he was saying was so tiny, so tiny, just a few hours ago, standing in a flat that for one moment he thought he might rent; leave his wife Glyn, and move into the City and try to make whatever existed between him and Latoya work, knowing full well that that was

148

doomed and he was doomed; right now – a student for God's sake – she could be sitting with her friends in some pub laughing their heads off about him; or he could be an object of ridicule on some website; if it were at all possible, just for one day, to know something about her, to be in Latoya's presence with everything around them unmediated; if that were possible, then he could close his eyes in death with the consolation that for once in his life he had known something, had truly known, releasing him from his provincialism, and into a kind of transcendence.

Simon crying now – it was all hopeless, pointless, too late; then abruptly stopping, shaken; Janet helping him by changing the subject and telling him about the daguerreotype and the curious medal around the neck of the woman in the picture; he blinking as if emerging from some dream and leaning in, in his best pedagogical manner, he began to interrogate her about the picture's provenance; trying to tease out details that in the beginning she believed she could not recall, but under Simon's diligent probing, she began to see in her mind's eye more elements of the picture: the tiny, dangly earrings, and the background: artificial, rigid, conifer trees and mountains rising in the distance; Simon continuing in his distant, professorial manner; placing the photo, in his opinion, sometime in the 1880s and how interesting, he said, to have found a photo of a black woman from those times with a tattoo; who could have possibly been in possession of it; why had they given it away, who had given it away; warming to the subject, he talked about Faluda and the Scramble for Africa; the Congo's use as the personal preserve of the King Of Belgium; that strange, and violent late 19th century as far as people of African descent were concerned; and now, he said in an astounded voice, she had discovered a woman in Victorian dress wearing a medal with Queen Victoria's name on it; intrigued, he asked to see the photo and she, overwhelmed with a sudden and deep desire to protect it, even from him, quickly changed the subject in order to bring back the other Simon, the one she could talk to, the one she wanted to ask how he was going to survive now that he was standing on the threshold of his marriage; and before he could answer a church bell rang in the distance, indicating Vespers; it was time to go, the estate agent having left them long ago; Simon, hurrying to thank her for going with him to the apartment and listening to his drunken, melancholy ramblings, and taking her arm he hurried her out into the brightly lit street, just in time to hail a taxi to take the two of them back to JLU.

JLU had another life after regular hours, a life busy with night classes, another, looser world; Simon's hand was still on her elbow, both of them walking in step across the courtyard to the other side where they would go their separate ways, he almost maniacally re-telling old faculty stories; she laughing and nodding out of friendship with him; complicit in his attempts to bury the last hour and a half, wipe away what he had almost done; Simon, out of the blue and in an oddly conspiratorial tone, asked her if she was going to the Othello Conference – lots of Americans were coming – amongst the more interesting was the hotshot African American professor Bradley Preston who was busy dropping little nuclear bombs in academe with his radical look at everything that had to do with Black History, he had heard that Professor Assantewa, the advertised keynote speaker, would not be there, having been taken ill in Paris; Janet shocked, almost reeling from the news, trying to hide her feelings as Simon babbled on that she must go, she must cross the river and go; he had an intuition that it would be important for her; she must go, he insisted and meet this Bradley Preston; all of this said in a quiet voice that she had never heard before; go, he continued, cross the river, go hear Preston, a man, Simon said with a hint of awe in his voice, who disappeared for months at a time in search of the old quilombos of Brazil, the African mini-states deep in the jungle; and before that, he had explored the mountains of the Caribbean; before that the sea coasts of Latin and South America; next would be the banlieues of Paris – the ghettos; a scholar who looked for maroons in all stations and places of life; living with them, then emerging refreshed with enough material for a new book or lecture or article, a man who dressed in the neat, short-haired style of some jazzman from the late fifties, glasses and all, which made Bradley Preston, in his opinion, much more subversive than some dreadheaded radical you could see coming a mile off; rumour has it, Simon added before they parted, that Dr. Abena Assantewa had personally asked him to the conference; all of this on some grapevine whose source he could not pin down but what matter did that make, she had to go, something was waiting for her; the look on his face made Janet listen without showing emotion; frightened to explore the tone in his voice, moved by something neither of them could name. Smiling and patting Simon's shoulder, without saying a word in reference to his situation or about Abena, Janet turned and walked in the direction of home.

As she walked Janet glimpsed a woman her age and a younger man kissing in a car; the woman catching her eye; Janet quickly moving on; running; finding herself wishing that Latoya was there to talk to – woman-to-woman – about Tomas; Latoya would understand the torment she felt, the anger with herself for her inability to prevent him from disrupting her life in every waking moment, even in her dreams; her inner life so involved with him that she was now afraid that she would say his name accidentally in place of Sam's; this man, who had been the cause of the first orgasm that she had had in her sleep since adolescence; she could tell Latoya, woman-to-woman-about Tomas, she and Latoya were equals, kin; but to cross the student-teacher boundary between the two of them would be worse than what Simon was doing; she knew that.

Standing at the end of the street, the street she had lived in all of her life; the world she had never escaped; Janet saw the daguerreotype again, saw the face of the woman, frozen and still like an African mask; an aura of pain around her; yet her eyes were deep and alive and defiant; they were eyes that Janet Bookman Baker recognized from a long lost memory, one that she could not name, but she knew; and that memory had kept her alive and her parents alive, and the girl who had come that summer decades ago and who had led her to this moment in the rain when she knew that she would have to cross the river, not for anyone else or anything else, but for her own transcendence.

151

Sounds Like Hi-Fi

Funny how much you know when you're a kid.

Then, when you get older, you don't know.

I'm a little kid and I know this:

My dad is in love with Earlene.

Every time he comes near her there is a charge in the air, you can feel it on your skin, sniff it in the air.

I don't know what it is.

But I know it.

I remember even now, even talking to you now, I remember hearing them in his study because at night I lie awake listening to the gang initiations in the backyard on the other side of our house – girls having sex with loads of boys – and I listen.

This is all mixed up with the feeling in the house and I lie there weaving it into a story for myself, to explain it all to myself as best I can.

Carl Cookson has a library, rows and rows of old books left behind by their previous owners.

I read them sometimes and I get ideas. I can create other worlds, leap through time.

Fiction.

My dad says: "Why does a guy like that have Plato ? He can't read."

My dad is wrong.

I know Carl Cookson.

I know what he is and what he can do.

Carl Cookson has been in Korea. Once he told me about how the 7th Calvary had killed a bunch of civilians near a railroad arch and he knew all about this.

The Koreans had worn white to bury their dead, it had all been a part of the fog of war.

His reaction to the whole thing is to bury himself into bee-bop, being a 'cat', and 'staying outside'.

Staying way outside, just working at his job assembling cars, coming home with some rib-tips, fries, and a six pack of 'Hamm's' followed by the Skid Row drink of choice – Thunderbird – as chaser, and spending the evening in his holy of holies with his books and his music: 'Bird', Coltrane, Don Cherry, Ornette Coleman, Wayne Shorter, Betty Carter, Abby Lincoln, Richard 'Muhal' Abrams, Henry Threadgill – the pantheon of 'outside' and reading up on Plato's caves so that he can continue to make sense of the car plant.

Question: Is he an outlaw, somebody I am expected to avoid?

Yes.

So I am with him.

And the woman he loves: my nanny.

I help them be together so that she doesn't have to go in to my father. And hurt my mother.

I love all four of them, it's just that the order of things isn't right.

I-me-I facilitate Carl and Earlene's love.

I am the go-between.

One day, I catch my father trying to kiss Earlene in the pantry and she's had enough and that's why she runs away and her running away is why Carl Cookson shoots himself and I think now, as I'm telling you, I think now that this is why my father's mind is no good anymore.

I tell this story to you, a stranger.

Except you aren't, are you?

You know, I didn't realize how shaky I was until I went for my weekly thing with Blasters.

Blasters. That's what he calls himself.

I think he's in the House of Lords or something like that.

He's old and rich and lives in the country. But once a week I meet him at his apartment in Chelsea and that's how I make my real money.

He's not a trick exactly.

What he wants from me is my critique. He listens to my shows and likes recreating it – in his own way. Kinda.

All week he'll work with a bunch of actors he pays to meet him and they work on a play he'd like to play the lead in.

This week it's *The Man In The Glass Booth* and my job is to watch the performance, then be the critic because the critical response is the point, is what gets him off.

My thing started with him when he rang the station out of the blue one day, saying what a big fan he was and asking if he could take me to an expensive West End restaurant. We had some bad salmon fish cakes which I told him that I thought were bad and he said that was a matter of opinion and he pointed out some celeb sitting close to us who I didn't recognize, and still didn't, even after he pointed him out. After supper and a few drinks, he told me what he really wanted and what he was willing to pay for it. I was just on the point of getting a job pole-dancing when I said: "Hey, do my show with you? Why not?"

We meet at his place in Chelsea, where he ushers me in and takes me right away to the 'Serena Slam'.

Blasters is obsessed with Serena Williams or more specifically, the butt of Serena Williams. He's had a sculpture made of her in action on court. I don't want to go into it, but it's pretty authentic. Actually, the whole room is a shrine to her ass, and what do you say ? You just have to go "wow!" which I do, and which he likes.

He's also got a Serena look-alike who takes care of the business end of things, and we've become very good friends.

I critique the opening performance of his latest play. We argue, then afterwards 'Serena' takes him off-stage – upstairs – where she gives him more of an in-depth critique. I read whatever he's got lying around to read, usually stuff about cars and racing; then he comes down and does what I call his soapbox thing: his take on black culture and events.

We listen, 'Serena' and me, while drinking his Krug and eating his Beluga and don't give a shit because in the middle of it he goes into a trance like that guy in the film Network, falls down out cold and leaves the two of us alone so that we can sit and talk.

'Serena' is very smart and very funny. She's got two kids in public school, all with the help of the few Blasters types on her books, so like they say in London, she's laughing.

She tells me over and over again what a very nice, very sweet man, and a real pussycat he is, a simple kind of guy who likes his activity varied: a little rough stuff at decent intervals – urination, defecation, enemas (his and hers), slapping, talking, listening, crying, but the Beluga is making her gain weight and she's trying to figure out how to get him on something more low-fat.

I don't know – I think it was during Blasters doing his Enoch Powell Rivers Of Blood speech – that I whispered to 'Serena' that I was thinking of going back to the States. She said that she'd never been, but intended to go there soon with her kids, then pop over to the Caribbean to see relatives.

"Is it true about Chicago and the wind?", she asked me in her very affected accent that she thinks is posh. "That they have these ropes on the side of the buildings that you have to hold onto when you're walking? I'd like to see that. And what about the sea? I love the sea. My cousin was there for business, and the first time he saw it he said: 'I didn't know Chicago was on the sea!'"

I try my best to paint a picture of my hometown because my hometown is beautiful to me. America is beautiful to me which strikes me as fact as I talk about the restaurant in Chicago where they insult you a lot, and the blues and the jazz, and the big summer festival on the lakefront with the sun glimmering on top of the water.

"Sounds like you miss it."

"I didn't know I did until I started talking about it."

Later on, we're in the kitchen, taking a break, having tea.

So 'Serena' says:

"Ok, think of this: They say that a cup of tea can only go from hot to cold. Have you ever asked yourself why it can't go the other way?"

"No."

155

"Yes, you did once. You asked when you were a little child. A little child asks questions like that. They ask: : 'Why is the sky blue?' We tell them to be quiet. Well, people like Blasters, they say that there's a law that says that hot becomes cold is the way it is, and that the hot disappears and is unused. You can't do anything with it. You can't make the hot come back to the tea again. Well, what if I say that he's wrong?"

"Ok."

"What if I say that our ancestors could do that? The slaves, we used that hot like we used the food they threw out in the garbage and we turned into our food, like we used the silly dances that they brought over from their country and made us do. We turned them into something else, like we did with their religion. We used what they thought was 'waste'. At every level, even that which makes 'hot' hot."

"Recycling, you mean?" I was lost.

"A little. I'm talking about living in the reality of the discarded. We lived in that state and we survived, because we used it. We used that state to create another thing altogether: like making cricket faster; Toni Morrison's writing."

I say that I don't understand because I don't understand and I don't want to be a hypocrite and act like I do just because she's a prostitute with limited education.

"Are you talking about physics ? Something in theoretical physics"?

"I don't know anything about that. All I know is that I had this dream and that's what I'm telling you. About the dream. I saw people, like, picking sugar cane, right, and it was like they had these phantom people on another, like plane, picking sugar cane, too. It's like if you see a leopard leap, another leaping in another world that we cannot see. So the real people – I mean in our world – our ancestors – exchanged the energy with those other people, who were them, but in another world."

"I don't get it."

"So, like there were people on another plane picking sugar cane at the same time."

"Right and the –I guess slaves, right, slaves – they take the energy generated and use it to make them stronger. Sounds like sci-fi."

"I can't explain it any better than that. There's this little split second where the exchange takes place and if they make it through the exchange, then the slaves…"

"Where are we going with this?"

"That's the secret."

"What secret?"

"The Secret. Some people knew. Common sense isn't all the sense there is, it isn't even holy."

I don't understand what she's talking about. I can't visualize it either. I wish I could.

But I can't forget it. I file it away in the place that I file everything whenever I am here with her.

I leave and walk from Blasters in the rain, me, Anna Taylor, just a bit actor in a grand tragedy directed by Jacques Tourneur or some other great Noir director

I walk in the rain, all the while thinking: what do I do now? How do I proceed, now that I am old before my time, but without wisdom.

I go to the pub.

I'm having a drink with some people from the station.

These are my contemporaries.

£30,000 in debt and blowing cigarette smoke out of their old childhood bedroom windows because their parents don't want to smell it when they come back from pensioners' handball at the gym.

Me and my generation. We are 'Generation Mommy'.

We live on daytime TV.

Job-hunting for jobs we don't want and we didn't get our degrees for.

Life on pocket money.

Our malaise is palpable, and it doesn't help that there are people our age in the City pulling down mega amounts and djing on the weekends for the hell of it.

157

It doesn't help when you're told all the time that you're supposed to be 'out there'.

Out there…where?

Bleak isn't the word.

Bleak's too glib. Too energetic, for what's going on with us.

"I wish some dictator would appear and just like take over…I need a rest."

My neighbour Montgomery Tourlaine said to me once that human beings look for utopias. We want a perfectly ordered future where everything works.

"But, Anna, utopias are for children. Look at a little child. Everything must work, everything must be in order, be consistent for a child. Fascism is the ultimate infantile expression with its corporate state and its assurances that it can keep us safe, make us money, give us sex and food and families and God. They throw the word fascism at the Middle East, but if they look at Mussolini, who was its chief purveyor, fascism is about the corporate state. The corporate state keeps us little kids with our toys. Utopia: back to the womb."

Infantilism. That must be the reason I just turned down Martin Ogboyo from the station, when he'd asked me out, again.

I turned him down – because I chase utopias.

Anna Taylor, just a bit actor…

My favourite group, Random Atomic Acts could sum up my situation perfectly. They've even read "blk/wimmin" and sent me a note indicating that they got what I was trying to do.

They release their music only on vinyl. It's like they live inside my life. Anybody who likes them likes me, knows me. Just say 'I like RAA' and I'm there.

Some guy comes over to our table.

I sip my drink, staring into the glass, trying to see my face in the murky foamy red-green, playing tag with my essence.

And I know this: that I can't run away from what Earlene meant to me, no matter how hard I try. The more I try, the more she is building up on the dark side of myself, hidden away, ready to burst forth

And she has.

I don't know what to do with what I know and with what I feel.

Freeze frame.

In strolls Mr. Perfection ordering a cocktail.

As usual, everybody notices him, everybody discusses him. His clothing, what he eats, what he reads, his obsessions. The weird thing is that he might be hot for me. I think it's because I'm his opposite.

I know all this because we have an unspoken connection.

I understand a guy who knows things like exactly 500 people died of autoerotic asphyxiation in 2005. And that life expectancy varies eight years across the country and is at its longest in Bath.

We will be together, Mr. Perfection and I.

I know this.

I am his funhouse mirror.

I overhear two people talking about buying a flat.

But they're in their early thirties, so not yet.

They want to party before the career kicks off and the family thing and mortgage kicks in.

Most of the cash they make goes on socializing and foreign hols, buying luxury goods, and paying the minimum on the credit card.

In front of me, these people get into an argument because the girl is still at home which allows her to buy a car, take holidays, have money in her pocket, and what's wrong with liking your mum?

Then she directs a low blow toward the guy about his dad who is a metric martyr over some fruit or something and flies the flag of St. George on his roof in retaliation.

The girl is sneering and it gets ugly:

"Sorry, but metric is not new!"

She is telling him that metric units were used to design Trafalgar Square because when the Houses of Parliament burnt down in 1834, the physical standards for the imperial yard, pound and gallon were destroyed. The metric system was considered by a lot of people then to be superior and had had many British supporters, including the architect Sir Charles Barry who had been impressed by the beauty and simplicity of the Italian Renaissance buildings which used metric units, and turned on by that fact he went on to design the Travelers Club; The Reform; House of Commons; House Of Lords with Pugin; the Cabinet Office; the Parliamentary Tower that holds Big Ben; and Nelson's Column.

Overhearing this I'm thinking: Nelson's Column is metric? That's why I remember what was said.

Mr. Perfection walks up to me.

I pull my coat tighter.

I look behind me.

Is he talking to me?

Yes. It is me.

He wants me to come to his place for dinner.

I say yes.

Disgusted with myself.

I go home.

I try to read a book by the next guest on my show. I'm having a hard time because I can smell my neighbour's cooking through the floorboards.

I had never noticed this before. That I could smell my neighbour's food, I mean.

Next I can hear her having sex. I change out of my summer coat and into my winter coat. (I wore a coat all the time then) thinking that would get me back on track.

It's another 9/11 novel and who wants to read about that? Or see it on TV or the movies? It's like playing a rape over and over. Will you understand it better if you make into 'Art'? How about keeping it unexplainable?

The phone rings. I answer. It's Jess from the station. She's in a pub. She's pissed.

"Look Anna. I don't like America or Americans, I'll be honest with you, I think they're all shite."

Brits are weird about America. Love-hate hardly describes it. It's sort of like a bunny-boiler thing crossed with Yellow Brick Road syndrome. I truly don't get it.

Brits never understand that at the end of the day nobody can beat another American at anti-Americanism. Ours is bigger, badder and harder. There are guys holed up in mountaintops in Montana and Dakota at perpetual war with Washington. One of my profs at college had a sticker on his refrigerator that said 'USA Out Of North America.' On second thought, he was from Toronto.

But Carl died in America, my nanny vanished in America. I still love the place, though. It gave me back my life in a way.

The first time a dream about my nanny came, I woke up shocked. I had cast the woman in outer darkness by the time I was eleven. It took one fucking year to exorcise her, but I did it. I made her non-existent.

Why not?

One day she was with me and the next she was gone. She left me.

The way I dealt with that was to erase her from my mind, obliterate her as a human being from my consciousness, like her sister had done to her.

Now, lately she's back. In my dreams. Why?

I'm trying to figure this out while Jess from the station is on the phone going:

"A, I heard the news."

"Yeah, well, that's the way it is."

"I'm really sorry."

Jess's slurring. A nasty sound, but at least she's drowning out the sound of the girl downstairs now on her fifth screeching orgasm.

"All he wants to do is save his own skin."

"Who, Dan? What's wrong with that?"

"Not fucking worth it."

"Point."

"So, listen. We figured out – me and Lucy and Sarah…Television. You'd be great on television."

How do I say to her, without causing offence, that the first time I saw British TV I was stunned at the proliferation of so many ugly people on it. I don't mean ugly like in awful, but ugly like in human beings, the way people actually look in the supermarket, in the street, not extraterrestrial, not shiny, aspirational and unreal, like on American TV

I was so fascinated at first by this parade of real humanity as opposed to plastic that I just watched it for days on end. Real live human beings with flaws.

But TV? I was ugly enough by normal standards – too tall and shambolic; tons of junk food fat and miserable with it, plus lots of hair in the wrong place. Ok, with me, there's the freak factor, but you have to want the box bad to be on it.

"Jess, not me."

"You can't get anywhere without a media presence."

"What's wrong with being invisible?"

"Ring my cousin. He's got a production company. Plus he likes Taylor Made.

As she's talking it occurs to me that I know what the aroma is coming through my neighbour's floorboards.

Blueberry pie.

My nanny made blueberry pie.

That's why I was thinking about her.

My nanny made blueberry pie for me. My favourite thing to eat in the whole world.

I could smell her cooking it as I wrote in my room. I had written a little poem for my nanny.

It was about being a child. Full of rhymes, no meter, no rhythm.

She told me: "Anna, I'll always carry this poem with me."

You know, I had forgotten about the whole thing until now.

Later, I wrote stories. Fiction. A cheap thing to do. Lies.

But my nanny told me that stories are truth. Facts and truth are not the same thing. The truth can contain facts. But facts always contain truth. Always and Can.

I like Can.

I preferred, even at that age, the possibility of improvisation. And wit.

They brought me here.

To you.

There is a knife nearby.

Bits of peanut butter on it do not deter me.

I run the knife over the back of my hand, very slowly, watching the white flesh like the colour of pork beneath and the blood come up and I feel really clean and light. This is a cleansing thing to do. I understand why people were bled centuries ago and how good that must have felt, to get the bad blood out, to start all over again, to make it fresh and ok.

I watch the blood run for a few minutes, then carefully wash the cut and put one of my multitude of band-aids on it.

See, sometimes there is beauty and order in what I choose to do.

Don't judge me. Just listen.

If your friend is delirious and scared, has double-vision and then later is drained and has flashbacks, that's acid; cannabis: stupid, pointless laughs and giggles, steals your food, wants to eat weird stuff suddenly, then the paranoia kicks in; speed is verbal diarrhoea for hours about anything, everything, the teeth grinding constantly and no need for food, definitely no food and after it wears off depression, bad, nasty moods; E – up energy, carefree, sweaty, the pupils dilated, after it wears off-panic attacks, energy gone; coke: total confidence-for about twenty minutes, then – hello – where's the next line, thinking you've convinced everybody you have the flu – except those who know better; meth, total intensity, lots of sex, loads of fearlessness: you could tell a guy off built like the Terminator and standing over you with a Glock down your throat and his finger on the button just like you're talking to your kid brother about not knocking on your bedroom door because you're just too fucked up to gauge the situation accurately and when it wears off you're left with violence, ugliness, weirdness and it's all your own.

Which gets me around to the meth which one of the guests on my show left behind.

Which I do and yes, everything said about it is true.

The libido increases, making me call Martin Ogboyo and tell him that yes, I will go out with him if he doesn't mind me wearing my coat the entire time and when I hang up the phone I don't feel scared of what I have just done.

Blasters goes through my mind next and the real possibility that he had propositioned me once and I had simply blocked it out.

'Serena' told me that sex with him wasn't so bad, that he had tons of energy and the Viagra he used was the best.

Tried it herself.

Sitting in my studio alone I let the meth high bring back images of all those hot Polish boys with the acne and light hair who, with friends from my old school, Roc, I used to drive to Detroit from Chicago to see, big, hunky Polacks with big hands and biceps, guys worlds apart from us little middle class black girls; factory boys from a generation of factory boys waiting for us juicy little black girls from the school with the black nuns hidden in the Michigan woods. All of us on a collision course toward the forbidden.

I had one guy. Chris.

He had a girlfriend who used to stand outside his window listening to us.

She would say the Rosary.

I knew, because he told me, that his dad and brother were secretly in the Klan

He probably was, too.

Which made the sex with him better

I put Chris out of my mind.

I make my finger bleed writing over and over: "Ephemeral ecstasies take their toll while looking for what is important in the realm of"…"Ephemeral ecstasies take their toll while looking for what is important in the realm of"…"Ephemeral ecstasies take their toll while looking for what is important in the realm of"…"Ephemeral ecstasies take their toll while looking for what is important in the realm of"…"Ephemeral ecstasies take their toll while looking for what is important in the realm of"…"Ephemeral ecstasies take their toll while looking for what is important in the realm of"…"Ephemeral ecstasies take their toll while looking for what is important in the realm of"…"Ephemeral ecstasies take their toll while looking for what is important in the realm of"…

You ask, what was going through my mind?

Hmmm. What's going through my mind? The title of that novel by the French author who came on my show – what the fuck is it?

You know.

Him.

The guy who gave me the meth.

Anyway, fuck the title.

He's written a novel with missing pages. Written. With. Missing pages. He wrote the missing pages in. The book skips pages. So you have to go to the back to read a synopsis of what he thinks the missing pages are about. It is about a saltimbanque, an acrobat, who is in the employ of a brothel, a brothel full of black women, free women in 19th century Paris. One of them racks up a lot of homicides that people think are suicides, chick called The Flute.

The novel's narrator is convinced that the pages have been lost in a London hotel room, stolen by the Malian maid he saw lurking around his door – or had he been hallucinating?

His book had to be the result of the ice, what else ? Cause when I do the meth, I still don't understand it, but I get it.

The meth makes the morning come too quickly and my head is hurting like crazy.

Sunlight is coming through the window pretty hard and sharp. The sunlight hurts my eyes, but I have to look out of the window to see the day.

Some little girls are playing in the Square like little girls used to do, no mini-skirts and sparkly anklets, just little girls playing what looked to me like hopscotch.

I knock on the windowpane.

I want them to see me.

I want them to wave at me and to smile.

But there is too much noise in the street and anyway, if you're a little kid, you're told not to relate to strangers.

They will have been trained to ignore me.

At their age, I was convinced that I could disappear.

When I couldn't take the duplicity of all the adults around me anymore, I just willed myself to disappear.

When you disappeared, you would look the same to everyone around you, it would be like you were still there, except that what they saw would not really be you and what you saw of them would be more than you ever could say, ever admit.

Whenever I disappeared, I went to look for Abena Assantewa.

I didn't know where she was, I had no contact with her. But we could occupy the same space when I vanished.

I wouldn't take one of her books with me. No, nothing. Just sit and wait, sit and wait. Sit and wait until she spoke to me.

Will she speak to me now?

I am still looking out at the little girls.

Oh, I remember the title now of that book: 'Jusqu'au bout'.
'Right to the end'.

I think of The Girl With The Kaleidoscope Eyes.

She was said to have been the most beautiful girl to have ever come out of Ohio and find herself in England in the middle of the Sixties, a girl who could have given Bardot and Christie and Marianne Faithfull a run for their money, because, unlike them, she embodied a true, American innocence, a belief and a need to believe in the self's ability to change the world simply by force of will and good intentions.

Everyone had her then and she had everybody and still, they say, she emerged as clean as the driven snow, each time more and more

166

angelic, nothing hard or jaded about her because she never let go of that myth she had burning bright and shiny inside, her own true path,

TGWTKE had self-belief, that complete confidence, that if she stepped into any situation, she and she alone could sort it out.

Even when her ex, Jim Morrison, made a whole load of racist comments, got fat and died in his bathtub in Paris, there she was – I've heard – explaining that he had come from a naval family, very distinguished and the water had got him in the end.

She has no kids because a woman like that cannot be a mother. She cannot procreate. She must be sui generis and leave the earth quietly.

With no trace.

Which is as close to sanctity as I can imagine.

Some rich baronet found dead on the Hippie Trail had left her a house in Chelsea painted pink, which she changed to white in honour of his demise, and she has lived there ever since dressed in kaftans and cheesecloth and long, stringy hair and flowers trailing in her wake. And this is how I have come to know her.

TGWTKE is always topping up. Chablis mostly. Cigarettes. Lots of cigarettes. A joint here and there. All of the time. Her big, baby blue eyes are full of dreams and memories that no one else can enter.

Easy to see how she could have been considered beautiful.

Easy to see.

TGWTKE's had no surgery, done nothing to herself, which is authentic and kind of noble and tough. She's wrinkled and saggy but everything that matters is still there.

They pawed her and clawed her, assuming that beauty has a charmed existence.

They didn't know

She tells us all of the time that we don't know.

She sits at the Septic dinners and tells us that we just don't know.

She used to hide her meals in her hair when she had problems with food.

She couldn't see her body in the mirror because it changed shapes to her and none of them were any good, none of them were to her liking. This started happening in her fifties. A good time she said to me once, for something like this to happen. When you get fucked up like that at her age, that's edge.

Get closer and her breath stinks of smoke and her thumb-tips are yellow.

With her, when it comes, it will be deterioration on a grand scale. The only way.

She can never go back to America.

America isn't there any more for her. It has moved. I didn't say "moved on". Moved. Shifted itself to another spot that she can't get to.

Yes. I know this.

But...

I go to see Montgomery Tourlaine.

I knock on his door, and he comes out. I am pissed.

I talk.

I tell him about how I bought what my parents told me about Carl Cookson, that he was asleep instead of dead.

I had to stay in good with them, I had to have their approval and love, so I sold myself out.

I have crossed a line.

I have violated an unspoken pact between us.

Montgomery Tourlaine is listening but also disengaging, keeping his distance.

He is waiting for me to stop, waiting for me to go back to the way I always am with him.

This man has spent his entire life avoiding what I am giving to him at this moment. Everything about me then and now is on a new planet, in a new world and I am frightened.

Why am I talking to him?

Montgomery Tourlaine has never been a father to me.

My father is rapidly losing any knowledge of me.

Anyway, I take a chance and keep going.

I am standing in the hallway outside our apartments and grinning, trying to break the ice, knowing that what I want from this old man he cannot give.

I tell him that I've been given a job on the critics' programme, Showboat, which I'm going to take because I need the money.

It's live on a boat moored on the Thames, but if I get sick, it'll be ok because they like that on TV now.

He hates TV actually.

His face is totally without expression.

He does not know what to make of me. I have become vulnerable and he looks at me with that look that tells you that you are already part of his past.

"Have you confronted your parents?", he says, with his hand on his doorknob. Anything to end whatever else I might want to say.

I prattle on about my mother's letters on brown linen paper with a photo of Sojourner Truth at the head.

Once she was a revolutionary but now her 'mission', the Langdale X-People, have become involved in a turf war with their bitter rivals, 'The Insane Clowns'. The Langdales are using the house as a refuge for their women and children while the men shoot it out on the streets. Mom is having a hard time getting them to settle down so that they can learn the Fibonacci Sequence, and get some beauty in their lives.

And my poor dad sits upstairs with a gun on his lap, watching everything around him deteriorate. Their house is the only one left standing on the block now.

It will be eaten up by what is creeping toward them.

In the hallway outside our front doors, keeping his distance, Montgomery Tourlaine is telling me something off the subject about, scientifically speaking, there are no other beings out there because if there were, they are either too primitive to know anything or too advanced to be bothered with us, which, to me, makes the story of God coming to earth to redeem us suddenly very reasonable.

Somebody to pray to.

I had stopped praying when Earlene disappeared.

I had stopped believing in the possibility of goodness.

I sit in the dark. The meth is over and I'm angry and scared.

Montgomery Tourlaine slips a note underneath my door.

He asks me to dinner at his place.

I slip a note under his door. I say yes.

I stand naked in the mirror looking at myself.

I could cancel that dinner.

Why not?

I would knock on Montgomery Tourlaine's door and explain that my entire upbringing was concerned with expressing all of my emotions in the most adult manner as soon as possible.

Having been the hoped-for-child, I was accorded a hallowed place and my parents, being totally involved with my development, saw as natural in me what would have been considered in most to be totally selfish, even narcissistic behaviour.

Being the hoped-for-child, the world was given to me. I came to see it as my right, a logical assumption because I was 'the future', for what that was worth.

But Earlene made me see that there was much more than me.

Much more.

What I want to ask Montgomery Tourlaine, if I have the nerve to knock on his door is: does goodness really exist?

What are the possibilities of finding it now?

Had he ever known a good person, or been good himself?

Performed or witnessed an act of goodness?

If so, had it pleased him, angered him, embarrassed him or did he look down on the doer of the good deed?

But I don't go.

I crawl into bed and curl up into a foetal position.

I fall asleep.

I dream.

In my dream, Montgomery Tourlaine's door opens. A swollen river pours out of his door, rushing and gushing and washing me and everything that has to do with me away. I am swimming under water in the dream, swimming near subterranean cities full of gold and silver, diamonds and pearls, silks soaked through and weighed down, and there are human limbs there, too, part of the river bed and also, hidden in the mud and crusted-over jewels: a human face. This face still has features and they are negroid like mine and have what I would call a serene grimace. My recollection now of that image is that the grimace is created by the fear of death and the serenity comes from meeting it and discovering that a friend has been found, not a foe, one so beautiful that life cannot contain it.

And I tell myself in my dream that it might be necessary to stay in one place, just one place, doing what I can. With no cameras. No lights. Quietly. Small.

I am thinking of something Earlene had said to me.

She said: "There is a flame, Anna, that we all have. It is what connects us, and keeps us human. It never goes out."

That was the way it was with Earlene and me.

Shall I tell this to Professor Assantewa when she wakes up?

5.

Jody felt strangely relieved after opening up to Tirian. A burden had been lifted off her. A bridge had been crossed.

But she had to figure out how to save Saronia. How could she prevent her fate?

The journey on the swollen Seine was pleasant and exciting. Jody loved rivers. They were her favourite form of waterway.

She took her mind off herself by observing Tirian reacting to the various floating cafés, and amusements that dotted the river. Even though the child was an agent, like she herself was, it was clear that she had not been exposed to life. She had probably been kept in a hothouse atmosphere, raised to be just short of a robot.

Jody could not imagine what she must have seen in her short life. Feral children were exposed to things that most adults would never see.

Somehow the Sixties generation idea of freedom had become warped, leaving children like Tirian to not have a childhood at all. This made her dangerous, unreliable, and a pawn to powers that even Jody did not know.

She had to stop being unnerved by Tirian's lack of response. She had to stop being concerned about Tirian. Tirian was a tool, a part of the machinery of state. Just like she was.

Tirian smiled at an eccentric small circus on the riverbank. The clown saw them both and waved. Clowns frightened Jody. They seemed to change before your eyes.

But Tirian smiled. She waved back.

Jody stopped herself, what she thought were Tirian's reactions had to be an illusion, must have been an illusion. Tirian was not programmed to have emotions. She must never forget that.

To take her mind off what could get her in trouble if she continued to dwell on it, Jody got to work on her latest health profile.

She wanted to make sure that no new genetic 'problems' had been discovered since she last checked before she left the States.

If she had something potentially infectious that she did not know about she could ultimately be cast out of Ubiquity.

She did not want that to happen until she was ready to go.

Her read-out came in numbers running across the top of a small notebook-shaped digital receiver that she always carried and gave her a constant reading of details such as the security state of her domus and who might be trying to reach her.

The numbers told her that she was fine.

But they, too, could be manipulated if someone higher up had decided that she had to go. If that decision were made, she would never know.

And if that decision were made, she would have nowhere to go.

There would be no one waiting for her, no one to help her.

Except…

She closed her mind down quickly. As an Ultra, she had a two-minute window before her thoughts were routinely read by Ubiquity. She took advantage of that, and switched her mind to the person she was on her way to see.

She went over in her head what she had learned about the contact that Control wanted her to see: Charles Andromache.

Andromache was half American and half French. He lived in splendour on both sides of the Atlantic. The son of an oil magnate, his hobby was trading in Old Masters.

There was a rumour that he owned the famous and missing Portrait of Dr. Gauchet by Van Gogh.

Jody had read somewhere that it had been sold for $90million over fifty years ago and had disappeared shortly after its sale. Portrait of Dr. Gauchet was considered by many art experts to be, rather than a painting of his doctor, a self-portrait of the great artist himself at the end of his life. Jody learned that it was said that Gauchet had suffered from the same depression as Van Gogh.

Therefore the portrait was a mirror.

It was an iconic painting. If the rumour was true and Andromache owned it, it would be a great pleasure to come face to face with the Gauchet.

It was considered now to be priceless.

Jody thought how great it would be see the soul of another person through art, rather than the methods Elimination Systems used: the cold mechanics of the 21st century.

Her thoughts were coming a bit too fast. She couldn't control them.

But it didn't matter.

The "O" was giving her a sweet indifference.

But what difference did it make, she asked herself.

The way she saw it, the whole world was on drugs one way or the other.

Everything was a drug. Even what she was feeling for Saronia. And drugs were merciful.

You were alone in the end, but the drugs helped. Too much oxymorcin was dangerous but at least she had not taken the low road and gotten involved with PEA: phenylethylamine. Phenylethylamine created feelings of attraction, romance and wellbeing slightly different from the 'O'. PEA was one of the ingredients in chocolate, cheaper than 'O', and being developed for nonUltras. Just as crack-cocaine had been developed sixty years earlier for the poor, and methedrine, known as 'Arkansas cocaine'.

Jody looked once again at Tirian.

There was one thought that she could not erase from her mind.

"I know that there's something else going on here. I just want to know what powers she has." she thought. Even more crucially, Jody wanted to know if Tirian knew anything about the new morphing techniques which could change one person into another.

If she did, then she could use them to change herself and Saronia and Saronia's husband. They could escape to where the 'Undetectables' were. They were always within reach, always in the vicinity if you knew how to find them.

She would find them. She would find those who had managed to take themselves off the Grid, out of the System, vanish from the constant surveillance, the only real atmosphere she had ever known.

Jody gazed up to the sky. There was a full moon. As she did so, The Image returned.

But this time, she could see more. She could see the faces leaning over what looked like a baby crib. Her baby crib? She tried to make out what she was seeing in the face of the moon.

How could someone send this to her? Did they have some way of manipulating her brain, some way of influencing it? How was it possible to break into her brain, an Ultra's brain?

Someone or something was trying to contact her.

The 'O' clouded her timing. She didn't know how long she had been thinking what she was thinking.

She could feel Tirian staring at her.

Jody pulled herself together. It was time to get down to business.

There was work to do.

She returned to what she knew about Andromache.

Charles Andromache, one of Elimination Systems' highest operatives, had positioned himself among the dissident exiles, many of them known to be supporters of the Stockholms and even Stockholms themselves.

His reports were always precise and as cold as ice.

Under his real name, Jody had read them as examples of how to do undercover work. He made it his business to know every detail of a suspect's life. He was an expert in the labyrinth and how it worked in the lives of human beings, particularly those who had managed to become Undetectables.

In time, Andromache had become one of them.

A few of the dissidents and Stockholms were always at his sumptuous residence, enjoying his social evenings which featured his sumptuous food, expensive wines, top-of-the line drugs, and what he called 'apocalyptic sex, sex for the last days, sex before the Final Battle'.

Jody knew, without a doubt, that Saronia Miller would often be there. Not for the entertainment, but for the emotional connection. Andromache was such a success in his pose as a dissident writer, a 'refusenik' of the

American way of life, that she knew that she would meet so many people that she would, in the old days, have had to spend a week in de-contamination.

His exuberance became a refuge, an escape hatch for those who had run away from the oppression of their native land.

They did not know that in spending time with him, they had, in fact, gone back to have even deeper surveillance, a greater prison. Andromache's only reason to live was to discover and trap the enemies of FSD.

He was a man without mercy.

The gondola finally arrived at Charles Andromache's address. He was privileged. Much of the water had been pumped away so that some of the ancient narrow streets could be used.

His apartment was located in a courtyard, part of an old sixteenth century royal stable. The place had an air of tranquillity. The security devices were expertly hidden. Classical music issued from hidden speakers in the walls.

Jody and Tirian took the quaint iron open lift to the top floor. It opened to an antechamber decorated in fine paintings. It was clear to Jody that the paintings were wired to provide a security assessment of anyone and anything that entered the room. It was also set up to destroy as quickly as possible any threats to the environment. The entire floor belonged to Andromache.

He took no chances.

Andromache opened the door before they could knock, hugging and kissing them effusively while ushering them into his gracious Parisian world. Jody could feel the room's atmosphere change as she moved through it. It was 'intelligent', picking out her tastes, her wishes, adjusting the light, even the colours of the wall as Andromache excitedly asked her about the States. For Jody it was like being in an environment designed just for her. It was relaxing her so much that she felt herself slowly falling into a dream state. She knew that, in that state, she could be a victim of anything.

Instinctively, she dug her thumbnail into her forefinger with such force that she drew a small amount of blood. The pain kept her focussed.

A beautiful aroma emanated from his kitchen.

A small group of very happy people greeted her as Andromache took her around, introducing her. The drinking was well under way.

The largely Nona gathering ignored the small boy who scurried about pouring drinks.

Jody could see that he was a feral. She recognized him by the fear in his eyes. He had been brought over from New York City by Andromache to work as a houseboy and a guinea pig for his experiments on thought control, one of Andromache's specialities.

"I've been having a bit of a problem with my tendon", Andromache said, segueing into a false British intonation. "Unfortunately, I'm too old to harvest stem cells from my umbilical cord the way lucky babies can do now. And that young man there." he said, indicating the child serving drinks.

One of the Nonas, high on alcohol and whatever else was there shouted: " Oh Charles, darling, your tendon!!!! You can't stop it, no matter what lie they tell us! We're all going to die in the end, darling!!!!"

"Hear, hear!" Charles Andromache yelled in agreement, "But surely the point of life is to always try, my love!"

"Oh do shut-up, Charles."

A man stepped out of the tiny throng, walked past Andromache and over to Jody. He kissed her hand old-school style.

"Michael Feulnière here, Mademoiselle Carlyle. `Michael', not Michel. I think you're wonderful. Look at you. I love it! All that comfort and solace and certainty wrapped up in one young person! Only in America, I say! Charlie, dear boy, does nothing but complain about the place. And he gets wonderful benefits from the United States: they give him a pension; they protect him if he's in trouble; and he does nothing but protest. Me? I love France. I love England. I love the US. They are beautiful countries, strong and good countries."

He turned to look at Tirian standing in the corner.

"Hello, little girl. What's your name?"

Tirian did not react.

"She can't speak. Her name is Tirian." Jody said

"*Tirian. Beautiful and unusual name. Jody, Tirian, when you tire of that old bore over there, come to see me. Some people consider my place a refuge.*" *Michael Feulnière smiled.*

Charles Andromache broke in. "*Nevertheless, dear Michael, I must continue my point. Again, take us Americans.*

In our lust for protection, for safety and surety – and lust is what it is – we are even programming the womb. We are making our own made-to-order human beings. Because we can – while suppressing those we don't like and creating those we do!"

Jody knew that, in the womb, the developing foetus is female by default and becomes male when the gene SRY is present.

"*A large number of brain-related genes are on the X chromosome, and maybe, because the male has only one X chromosome, the odds of mutation for higher intelligence in the male is better*".

"*Is that why so many more males are being born?*" *One of the women yelled from across the room.*

"*Really? Are more males are being born?*" *Jody asked, a little shocked.*

"*Jody, darling*", *Andromache replied,* "*Of course it's all being manipulated! I have my sources on this, so don't ask! We're all sworn to secrecy here!*

And don't look so shocked! You look like one of those hairy old feminists from my day! Populations have always been selecting for males by killing females either in the womb or shortly after birth. But it's been discovered that this crude approach didn't ensure that there were more males. So, SRY is being injected into females along with…"

"*Oh in the old days, too many women were using guys as sperm donors. I did…*", *one of the guests said, drunk on the expensive wine and who knew what else.*

"*Aw yes, no men. The ball-buster's dream*", *Charles laughed.* "*The male's fatal flaw is that we're hard-wired to be attracted to you females. All of the intelligence we may have goes right out of the window in the presence of a desirable female. Or any desirable flesh, male or female. On the other hand, technically speaking that is, women have no sexual preference in the sense that you talk about it in men.*"

Jody averted her attention to the room. Her training had prepared her automatically to scan for viruses. But most importantly, if a virus was in the room, then that meant that the environment was flawed, and if it was flawed, an Undetectable could be in the room. If so, she could bring Saronia here as a safe place while she figured out how to get them both out of Ubiquity.

Andromache was still talking:

"…we want women and women want children. Ah, this male/female preference. Jody, I'd say that you were probably programmed to be female. But you were not cast on a river. It was the vogue after the first Pandemic."

"Babies cast on rivers?" Jody asked.

"Special ones. Just to see how long they'd survive. In the times that slavery existed in the West, babies were thrown overboard to see if they floated. A sailors' game. And, scientists have discovered that for some, a kind of trauma got encoded inside the DNA and made them powerful…"

Jody suddenly said: "I know about this, Charles. I know." It was as if another voice was speaking through her, a voice she recognized without knowing who it was or where it came from: "A mutation occurred. Those suspected of having this mutation were studied, placed in situations to see what they could do, what they couldn't. Some killed themselves, some killed other people, some had great mathematical powers, some could pierce the dimensions, some could take the waste product of heat and energy and make it into something that could change the world. And did."

Jody knew that she had revealed one of Elimination Systems' secrets: that they were experimenting with The Second Law Of Thermodynamics using those descendants of slaves who appeared to contradict it, therefore necessitating a new physics. But not yet. More experimentation needed to be done. Meanwhile, certain descendants of slaves with their special ability were being used to pierce Dark Matter."

"We're not alone, Jody." Charles said.

"I…I don't know why I said that."

By exposing ES's work, Jody knew that she and Andromache had condemned all of his guests who were not Ultras to certain death.

She knew that he had lured her to do it. So that the voice that spoke through her could be released. It was as if she had been a medium for it,

179

and that to lure it out, to have it speak through her was to weaken its power, expose it.

Whether there were other people around was irrelevant to him. Irrelevant, too, was the fact that he had just killed his small gathering of unsuspecting guests. Within the next few days, because of what was exposed in their presence, they would find themselves outside of Ubiquity. Undetectables.

Dead people walking.

All except those he could, because of his position in FSD, request a pardon for.

That happened at certain times of the year and that time was coming up. He could show this group that he was more than the hail-fellow-well-met.

He could pardon Saronia Miller and her ill husband, too.

Did he know that there were other plans in store for her?

Charles Andromache had not stopped talking.

"…therefore it is not we hapless males who pick you ladies, it is you who pick us poor chaps. You select us and we mutate so that we can have you. And all you want from us is…offspring. So we mutate or select, to put it politely for height, bigger penises, wealth, all are mutated in us in order to attract you because these factors make us look healthier and stronger. We want you, and you want children. Therefore, it is indeed you, ladies, who are the more powerful."

"Just remember the motto of our dear woman President, Charles", one of the now condemned women added, her eyes sparkling: `If you got `em by the balls, their hearts and minds will follow. Or words to that effect."

Everyone laughed.

Charles joined the group.

A woman approached her.

"Here she is at last," Jody said to herself. "This is the woman Control told me about. The head of the Stockholms – Blanche Rose."

Jody shook her hand. "I really envy you taking care of Saronia."

"I love her, too. I love her books," Anita said. "It's easy."

Jody liked her warmth and her quick smile. Her hand was soft, but strong. It was easy to see how she could lead anybody.

"I'm a big fan of her books, too. Bonhoeffer's my favourite character."

"Mine, too, Jody. Do you know who he's named after?"

'She can't help it,' Jody thinks, 'She's always got to proselytize, recruit.'

"No", she said to Anita.

Anita's voice grew almost reverential.

"He was named after Dietrich Bonhoeffer, executed by Hitler in 1945. He was part of the anti-Hitler resistance that had begun in the German Army as early as 1937 and gained momentum after the failure of 'Barbarossa', the invasion of the Soviet Union. He was a pastor, a Lutheran. Not perfect, but very influential. He worked in Harlem during the Depression and wanted to stay there, but felt that his work was back home. I like him because Bonhoeffer's Christ was the Christ of the Sermon On The Mount, the Christ of the poor. He said that the best way to know what Christ wants of you is simple – you don't need a preacher or the Pope. Go next door and ask your neighbour."

Before Jody could react, Saronia appeared. Jody did not know that she was there. Her scan hadn't told her. That meant that Charles Andromache, or someone higher, had blocked it.

But why?

Saronia was agitated, shaking.

"I didn't name him after a dead German pastor!" she yelled "I found that name in Scrabble! And now my books are banned!"

"It's not your fault that the Homeland Analysis and Technological Institute runs the White House, darling." Feulnière said from the corner of the room nearest to them.

"And the next thing that dear Michael will say is that the forces of light and the forces of darkness that lurk at the base of the Republic are finally at war. The Puritan longing for the purge, for purification through fire, for Armageddon has triumphed!" Andromache said.

"Yes, that's right," Feulnière said softly. "That's exactly right."

Jody ran a quick check on the name. Nothing called The Homeland Analysis and Technological Institute existed.

Her mind was racing: 'What's going on? Who's lying here, who's telling the truth?'

She suddenly had lost the will to check everyone out in the gathering to see if they had any sort of criminal record or disease profile.

Jody Carlyle no longer wanted to enter that place where records were kept on everyone, where all was surveillance and perfection.

"Jody", Feulnière said, "I know that you have heard of the Flute and I won't bore you with any more information, but…"

"I noticed it, too." Charles Andromache interrupted him, "You resemble her. I have seen images of her. You have legs just like her, long and skinny. What they call flûtes in French. They say that she drank champagne from a flûte. She was also said to be the best at fellatio in all of Paris. That act is called in French the flûte, too."

Andromache laughed and returned to his little group.

But she knew that he was listening.

Watching.

"Charles never misses an opportunity to be vulgar. I apologize on his behalf. You see, it's just that something in your eyes reminds me of the photos I have seen of her. She was fascinating. Chilling, you might say. She used her power for what most people would call 'ill'. Men never returned from being with her – bankers, industrialists, generals, high officials in government, the bishops, nobility. These were her clients. They were all she wanted. No others. After they'd spent a night with her, they took their lives. It was as if they had experienced all of life, being with her. And there was nothing left after that."

For a moment, Feulnière stared at her. Then he quickly broke the stare and raised his glass to the room in salute.

Jody had not felt this confused since her training in which different, conflicting scenarios were put to her as a matter of course.

It seemed that there was another reality at work, parallel to the one that she knew, that she had been trained to understand, manipulate, control.

The descendants of the babies who had been thrown overboard off slave ships held the key to connecting the visible and the invisible.

Could this help her?

There was clearly a battle going on between Michael Feulnière and Charles Andromache. As a part of FSD, Charles Andromache was her associate, her ally.

182

Michael Feulnière was the one to be wary of.

But he awakened in her a curiosity she had never known – and an affinity with the babies thrown into the river; and the black girl with the long, skinny legs who had lived long ago.

Or was she being subjected to one of the random tests that Elimination Systems inflicted on all of their agents?

Had Michael Feulnière been sent to assess her loyalty?

Suddenly Saronia returned. Her eyes were soft and watery.

The room was noisy.

Saronia whispered to her.

"You know", she said, "Jody, you look so much like my people. So much. You remind me of a lost child I knew once…"

She touched Jody's face. Jody could tell that she was drunk.

"I think about my generation marching, fighting, believing that we could change the world. But the world changed us. My husband and I…we're so sorry."

"Apologize for being a Nona, for being born?" Jody laughed. She thought: 'But I do hate you. You made it the way it is. You.'

Saronia stood up. "We made this world, Jody. And I'm not tired of saying so. Anita, we'd better go."

"You're not going to eat?" Jody asked.

Michael Feulnière joined them.

"I must leave, too. It was wonderful to meet you Jody, and your young friend, too. Anita, Saronia, we are all going in the same direction. We can face the enraged Seine together."

"I love the river", Anita said, "even when it's threatening to kill us."

Anita turned to Jody.

"Great to meet a fan of the Blueberry Farm books. Maybe we'll talk again sometime."

Anita took Jody's hand and shook it. Jody could hear the sound of the lift door opening, closing.

Listening to it, she knew that her world would never be the same again.

Saronia's eyes watered. She seemed to be in another world.

"Life, life. I lost my dear sister because I was too busy to be there for her,

183

too busy 'fighting the good fight'. Too busy being a big woman in the world.

I know that she had once, for a time, a child in her care that she loved more than anything. I call her the lost child. Jody, I must find that child. I have to take her in my... Jody, how can I apologize to her, reach her child?

Too busy being a big shot, too busy travelling and... she died before I could tell her... that I wish that I'd been there. For her. I wish...

I have to get back to my husband, Jody. I hope that you meet him someday."

"Saronia, you slow down. I'll take you", Anita said.

Michael Feulnière said: "I have my own private barge. I'll take you home. You'll go home in style. My bargeman even knows the way past the sections of the river where the sewers have made a mess."

Saronia kissed Jody for a long time and held her.

Jody felt a surge of affection that took her by surprise.

She wanted to go with her.

Anywhere.

But instead she watched her until the door closed behind her.

Jody ate and drank with the remaining group.

Later they left, unknowingly walking into the Outer Darkness into which Charles Andromache had cast them.

Charles turned to her.

His face was harder, colder.

"Let's get down to business. The Blueberry Farm Books are Order One, high priority. And you and I are working to suppress them as is – what's her name there? Tirian? Yes, Tirian. The `Laughing Little Kid' over there.

Now, as you know, the entire centre of this for Stockholms is Bonhoeffer The Cat. You heard that right from the mouth of their leader, the so-called Anita whatever-she-calls-herself. I'm sure you know that she is Blanche Rose, their leader. She just can't stop trying to recruit people no matter where she goes. And forget what I said about entropy. Diversionary. An amusing theory, though, don't you think? Forget it. Forget it all.

Now `Blanche Rose'. Why do you think she chose that nom de guerre?"

"I don't know."

184

"It literally means 'white rose', after the White Rose anti-Nazi Resistance inside Germany. The Stockies compare America to Nazi Germany. Can you believe that?

If they weren't so dangerous, we'd send them to get their heads screwed on straight. People like them never figure out that because they're American, they're allowed to be anti-American.

Hitler had the answer. He just chopped the heads off the White Rose Society."

Charles Andromache poured himself another glass of wine.

"It's always the ones born with silver spoons in their mouths. I wouldn't give a damn if they all became extinct, but FSD says some of them have great genes so we need them. I thought science was advanced enough so that we could create the kind of people we wanted.

Oh well, it's not for us to reason why etc. Now, as you can see, Saronia is full of bad memories of her sister and some lost child. I can also tell you that her main concern is to get the proper care for her husband.

Well done, you're almost in her family now. Good work.

I really must hand it to Bonhoeffer, though. The minister, not the cat.

When the Protestant pastors were complaining about what Hitler wanted to do with church music he said: 'Worry about the Jews first. Then deal with your music.' Or something like that. I looked him up. Hell of a guy.

Now remember: our mission is children's literature. That's our main priority, especially now when children's literature is all that people read these days.

It's clear that purging librarians was not enough to keep things under control.

Tra-la, there's always more work to do.

They tell me that you're the best."

"Hi, I'm on escort duty here. That's what I was told."

"Aw, David Frederick." Charles Andromache said.

The most beautiful man Jody had ever seen had entered the room. He was about her age. He was young.

185

"I took that one in as an exile. And so, at last, after a great deal of work, he now knows a little about wine." Andromache laughed.

David Frederick extended his hand to her.

"David Frederick Adams. Illinois. Hi."

"Jody Carlyle. New York City. Hi."

David smiled. *"Charlie here's trying to give me a little knowledge before I go back home."*

"So you are going back!" Andromache said in surprise.

"Jody, can you believe it? He says that he can't take France any more. The women frighten him."

"I love France, Charlie, and especially the women. It's you who can't stand the competition." David replied, without taking his eyes off Jody.

"You?" Andromache laughed, *"Competition? You have yet to understand that for all of their machinations and posturing, women are a Frenchman's means to oblivion. The void. I'd say that all women are a passageway into the void which we poor men cannot access ourselves. And men always yearn for oblivion."*

He laughed and left the room.

David turned to her.

His face had changed.

"Yes, I'm going home. I don't know how, but I'm going to warn young people, all people about what's going on.

I don't give a damn if I'm being listened to. I'm going back to the States to tell people what their parents and grandparents built. The good things. Before everybody forgets and thinks that all there ever was is where we are now. I'm going to be a living memory. I'm going to help those trapped in avarice, in greed, in wanting more.

The more they give us, the more they're gathering information about us."

Before she could stop herself, Jody asked:

"How? How're you going to do this?"

"You build a vaccine. The virus gets smarter. Nothing is 100% foolproof, 100% certain. There's a flaw somewhere, a fault, and I'm going to find it in FSD. I get closer everyday. I know it. I'm going to find the people who know it, too.

186

Jody, I'm an orphan, too. Like you.

Yeah, I know your story. I got the information, don't ask me how.

And Jody, I found out my history. The whole story. I know everything. You can know everything, too. I want to be a part of your discovery. That's why I've go to go back."

"Why do you…"

"I'll tell you why I want to. When it's time."

"How did you find out…"

"It's complicated. But look, I can find out the truth for you. You'll have it, I promise."

"But I need to know why. Why are you doing this? This is risking your life."

"Maybe it's because I see through you. You and me, we've got a connection. I know it. But we'll talk about that later.

Jody, trust me. I'll bring your story to you. One more thing: Only trust what I give you face-to-face. Remember that."

They both looked at Tirian at the same time.

"You know what she is, don't you?" David asked.

"Yes. A feral."

"That and more. They hollowed that little kid out. There's nothing there. That's all I can tell you now."

Later, Jody was surprised to find that she remembered what David had said about Tirian above all. She missed her.

But where she was going was no place for a child.

Ultras like her had their own private clubs. Each one went under the generic name of ` clavis` – 'the key' and there was one in every major city. The clavis provided anonymity. It allowed Ultras to mix with non-Ultras, and the riskiest people of all. Undetectables.

Hunters were also there on a strict 'no-arrest, no-elimination policy', along with those even higher than the Ultras.

Who no one knew.

In a clavis, an Ultra could do what she wanted with whom she wanted in the way she wanted to.

It was possible to risk everything in a clavis.

187

For the thrill of it.

The clavis dispensed drugs which were not available outside.

Jody could get higher value oxymorcin in a clavis.

As soon as she entered, she made sure she inhaled it.

A Nona greeted her. He was dressed in sixties clothing. He had a girl on each arm.

"This place 'll blow your mind! Enjoy, man!" he screamed exuberantly to Jody.

Jody smiled. She needed to relax, have space to figure out her next move, space to see if she could discover who was telling her the truth.

She looked around.

The typical clavis had several layers which could be entered depending on the Ultra's status.

As the high intensity 'O' surged through her, Jody searched for the level on which the Undetectables offered their sexual services. She had never been with an Undetectable before.

At each level of the clavis, the colour was drained away from the surroundings. At the very top level there was nothing left but a smudgy greyish black and dingy white, like being inside a black and white movie.

This was the area of the Avatars and their Begetters.

This place was the ultimate playground for the ego.

Because the Avatars were not 'real'.

They were clone-like entities created in the gloried image of their 'Begetter'-people who had given themselves over completely to extreme narcissism.

Where these Avatars had existed in cyberspace decades before, now in 2044, they were multi-dimensional. They could walk, talk, feel.

It was possible to have the ultimate sexual experience: sex with your glorified, exalted, perfected self. There was no need to interact with another.

Further down on another level in another part of the clavis, she could smell the unmistakable scent of men who had participated in what was a new 'Ugly Hours'. Popular in New York City, it had clearly spread to France.

This UH involved men and sometimes women hunting down, rounding up and bringing to the authorities various people accused of minor misdemeanours, by any means necessary, as long as it was bare-handed, that is, with no weapons or those no more sophisticated than the archaic ones used in the early part of the 21st century.

This new UH was purported to be a cross between an out of control police auxiliary from the old days, and an old-fashioned blood sport like fox hunting.

Plebs, the second lowest class, participated in it for the money.

Ferals did it because that was the way they had been brought up.

The activity involved made whoever joined in beast-like, the entire circus guaranteed to raise the sexual hormonal count of anyone watching as well as participating.

Right now, Jody was glad that all of the silly drugs and self-help books that had proliferated in the years before she had been born and that were meant to boost sexual activity had been cast aside in favour of the one tried and true method: combat.

A few years earlier a basic fact had been faced: human sexual activity thrived in warfare, in violence.

As Jody watched the Plebs and Ferals in the arena, she thought of what one of her instructors had said:

"The human gene pool has largely been spread through violence, not love and peace and understanding. We fight. We love it.

Whoever got anywhere through compassion? It is alien to us.

We are upstanding apes, more violent than our simian cousins. Don't forget this."

Jody knew this to be true.

The most daring of those who came to participate came barely dressed, armed with primitive weapons or no weapons at all in order to ramp up the risk factor. At the height of activity, this game generated an odour in the men which had become fashionable and was believed to aid fertility.

Jody could smell it as she entered the area.

The smell made her heart beat faster.

But she decided to move on.

Jody inhaled more high level 'O'.

It came with an endorphin boost which made her feel good.

189

Through it, everyone looked beautiful and happy.

She moved on to another circle.

Only celebrities – the type who had stalkers and for whom people camped out overnight in an effort to see them – mingled there.

Jody recognized the most famous couple in the world sitting in a corner. Even she stared at them.

Suddenly she heard a voice in her ear. She did not know where it was coming from.

Maybe she was talking to herself.

She was too stoned to know.

That couple? Forget them. They don't even see their kids. Can you imagine what it's like not being able to see your kids grow up? Oh yes, they worked for this fame. They worked hard to get our attention, to get us to know them, want them, envy them, hate them. Their work ethic at this was admirable indeed. But the most famous man in the world couldn't even go to his father's funeral last year. Couldn't have an autopsy, either, the image would be all over the place. And who knows where the father's buried? The most famous guy in the world can't even go to his father's grave because somebody would follow him. They'd steal his father's body parts, you see. Anything to get close to the most famous guy in the world.

The circle below the celebrity area was decorated like an Italian circus from the 19th century. Everyone was dressed like a clown. A small, balding man with a bright blue fright wig held centre-stage.

Jody scanned him:

The scan read : 'This circle belongs to him. He has patterned it on his idea of the Emperor Constantine's palace at Constantinople. To replicate it, the man has employed eunuchs, men from the pleb class who have willingly allowed their manhood to be destroyed for the opportunity of steady employment.'

The man in the blue fright wig said to no one in particular:

"…because look everybody, this is what I figure: ok, it's scary, but you gotta have a little bit of free speech. You can't keep people in a pressure cooker, they explode."

190

His circle was crawling with people. So many crowded the space that Jody did not have time to check their disease profile, or their security clearances.

Some recognized her and began touching her, kissing her.

She recoiled from their touch.

A clown whispered: "The Seine right outside the clavis is rising for an inexplicable reason. There are rumours that a curse has been put on it, that something old and ancient is being reactivated. All of you big time Ultras witnessing the rise of this river, have dismissed the idea of a curse on it -on Paris – as superstition."

Jody had been told about this curse on the way over from New York.

The person who had told her had indeed dismissed it, saying that the river was rising solely as a consequence of the 'grand warming' of the earth in general and that all in the City Of Light was calm.

But the City Of Light was not calm. Nowhere was. Jody knew this.

There was something that she could feel, something that was building up and about to explode, something that neither the 'O' nor anything else she sought to use as an escape could stop.

The feeling was there again.

She fled down to a lower circle.

It was dark.

There was nothing there.

Except voices.

Suddenly she could hear running through her head the voice of her Regular, Maisie Blue.

"Listen, Jody. I'm breaking the rules about intervening in your life with my own observations without a request, but don't…"

"No, Maisie. Not this time. I'm not going to listen to you. I'm going inside!

"But Jody, your mission's…"

Jody blocked Maisie Blue out.

She stood in the darkness, listening to the myriad of voices of people she could not see:

They rang all around her:

191

"Our needs, our drives, our excesses, that's what have imprisoned us here. Look at a baby. Look at a child. A mass of all of the history of our species. We've evolved the baby-shape: that big head, that helpless body. So that we don't kill this history of our species."

Another voice: "The various advancements we've made, both internally and externally, have come largely through war. We are in love with conflict, with aggression. Every advance in our homes, the workplace, began in war. Rape in war has made us stronger, bigger, more violent as we have inherited the brutality of our rapist forefathers. And even God makes war. The Christians believe that Jesus will return as a warrior. The Prophet was a warrior. The Israelites had great armies. Lord Krishna is a warrior. Look at it all very closely."

Another: "We're not living in 2044, the Golden Age. This is 444, the Dark Ages. Rome is gone and we are the barbarians. No one listened when they warned about the sun's temper tantrum in 2014. We were too busy consuming, consuming, consuming. Then the sun storm came, and knocked out our satellites, our computers, the entire structure of our so-called civilization collapsed until…until this. We became ill, our bodies turned on us, nature had its revenge and then we came back…ugly…"

Another: "In our minds, the world is a binary world. This is understandable. We have two hands, two feet, two sides of the body. But scientists, mathematicians know that there are more than two dimensions, many more. But our masters and we ourselves keep us in a binary paradigm: 'yes', 'no'; 'either', 'or'. That is not the truth. Just a construct. I find the binary world and its with-me-or-against-me mentality and its all powerful Big Daddy deity versus fount-of-all-evil Devil deeply boring."

Another: "In 'Many World Theory', there can be several gods or goddesses. Who's to say that the Divine does not exist in different ways in different dimensions? I prefer the fifth dimension myself. The music there is beautiful."

Another: "Look at Africa. Many of the states that existed at liberation were essentially run by war lords on one hand, and aid agencies on the other. The others that were not…they had to struggle to be seen as other than very sad places. The search for ideas rather than the giving of constant *aid never happened, so 'liberal interventionism' hitched a ride on the back of military intervention. And Africa now? It's a paradise after FSD took over. We run the continent and 'wham-bam, thank you ma'am,' the people are productive and healthy. You can even take decent vacations anywhere there now. Couldn't do that in 2009!"*

Another: "At the beginning of the century, we were living the way they did in the 1920s: the same economic bubble, the same mumbo-jumbo mysticism passing as economic advice; the same nasty rationalists; the phoney glamour; the madness of celebrity. But the big crash, The Big One, in 2010 stopped it in time. Pulled it all back."

Another: "Common sense doesn't make sense anymore. We must become counter-intuitive. For example, take the idea that emptiness is empty. Common sense says that this is true and it is true — 'on average' as theoretical physicists would say. But 'emptiness' is not a place where nothing happens. Pure emptiness creates a mechanical force. That force is being harnessed now. It is creating speed; agility; improvisation; wit; endurance; music. The Void seethes with creation and annihilation. When we slow down time we can see 'The Dance'."

Another: "We will solve the Measurement Problem by the very act of studying the Problem."

Another: "We don't need interpretation. Be against interpretation. Interpretation is a fixed point. Humankind's greatest desire is to head for The One. Go past that point. When you do, you will discover that the only language that can be used is that of poetry."

Another: "I was reading F. Scott Fitzgerald on the first day of the Big Correction of 2010. The book was 'Babylon Revisited.'"

Another: "There are people who are not governed by the Pleasure Principle or the God Principle, but by a branch of Thanatos — The Negation. Creating ruin is their greatest achievement."

Another: "We wanted bigger presences in the world, bigger toys, bigger sex, bigger money, bigger friends. Bigness. We weren't vigilant. We gave ourselves over to Bigness."

Another: "As we know so far, the building blocks of life are much, much smaller than the atom, they're called the 'quark'. I love the word 'quark'.

It rhymes with `pork' and the word can be found in Finnegan's Wake, where seabirds give 'three quarks' or quacks."

Another : "Yes, I love Finnegan's Wake. 'fin, again'. The end-again. How does it go?"

Suddenly all the voices opened in a chorus:

"Three quarks for Muster Mark / Sure he has not got much of a bark / And sure any he has it's all beside the mark."

Another voice: "There are up-type quarks; down-type quarks. There are three generations, and six flavours of quarks: Up-type: 'up', 'charm' and 'top'; down-type: 'down', 'strange' and 'bottom'. Well, the types have to be called something, don't they? I like 'strange' and 'charm' myself. And they have colours, too, but not colour as we know it, that is, formed by light. You can say that a quark's colour can take one of three values: 'red', 'green', or 'blue'; and that an anti-quark can take one of three 'anti-colours', sometimes called 'anti-red', 'anti-green' and 'anti-blue'. These are occasionally represented as cyan, magenta and yellow."

Another: "The act of observation creates the universe. Take `Yard Bird.' Take Ornette Coleman. Ok, `Bird' played the changes, but Ornette plays the anti-music that exists alongside the conventional stuff. He destroys narrative and instead, asks you to go on the adventure of your mind."

Another: "Take fiction. Most people are reading in the mid-19th century. They haven't even got to Proust, Woolf, The Modern Age of almost a hundred and fifty years ago! Driving a Model T in the age of the car that can power itself on air."

Another: "But Ornette can play his music straight, too."

Another: "Remember: Above all: 'empty' is not empty. While your ancestors, Jody, picked cotton, the sweat of their brow was not wasted…"

"My ancestors?" Jody said. "Mine? Mine?"

Suddenly a huge image of Hal Haze and Bonhoeffer The Cat swamped the space.

The Voices did not stop:

"Hal Haze is the illegitimate son of Dolores Haze. Speak memory!"

There was a pause. The silence filled the space.

A voice that Jody recognized as Anita Collins, or rather Blanche Rose,

194

leader of the Stockholms spoke: "'We call ourselves 'Cell 92' after the cell that the Lutheran and anti-Nazi resister Dietrich Bonhoeffer was held in at Flossenburg Prison. Before he was executed on the personal orders of Hitler. We read the works of Bonhoeffer. He believed in the Bekennende Kirche – the Confessing Church. He believed that we have a relationship with God, not with religion. He didn't believe that the Resurrection was necessary in order to believe. He called the Bible merely the witness of God, not the word of God. He preached in Harlem. He had a church in Sydenham in London, in the days it was London. We believe that Bonhoeffer says to us: My Jesus is not the Lord of Hosts. He eats and sleeps with the least amongst us. He always goes back looking for the lost sheep. He gets himself crucified over and over again. For us. He's always in the Garden of Gethsemane, not sure that he can go out and do that one last big thing. Bonhoeffer's inspiration was Beethoven's last piano sonata. Do you know it? From our study of Bonhoeffer, we Stockholms believe that we are obliged, that we are duty-bound to resist like the White Rose Society did in Nazi Germany. This resistance takes several forms. Some of our brothers and sisters simply walk, like they did in the American Civil Rights Movement. They walk peacefully, no weapons, no harsh words. Just walking to freedom, into freedom, for freedom. Through love and justice. Above all, we do not kill others. Just ourselves. We resist with our bodies. Your ancestors did, too. Be with us."

For Jody, there was no doubt now.

Everything FSD, Elimination Systems, President Hess, everyone – except her adoptive mother Audrey Carlyle – had told her had been a lie.

And she had participated in the lie simply by wanting to be left alone, to be comfortable, and by her need for order.

But.

By walking into this clavis, this Dante's Inferno, she had risen above all that she had been before. Now what lay ahead of her?

What would come next?

It was then that that strange music played in her head again and the final part of the Image returned – The Number. And then the Number appeared. Again.

195

It was the number that she had always recited to herself as a child, a number that had suddenly appeared. Out of the blue one day and came back to her from time to time:

5387.

She said it again over and over, the way she did it as a child.

Suddenly a rush of flamingo pink and spring green light washed over her.

Tiny golden bees appeared.

They were benign.

It felt to Jody like she was being held in the arms of her lost parents.

She could feel her mother's warm breath on her cheek.

She could feel her father stroking her forehead.

She knew that somehow they had always been with her.

And would always be with her.

A voice came.

"Jody, my Jody. The number I have given you is very beautiful. 5387. I gave it to you when you were a baby. It's a Fibonacci Prime. Prime being a number that can only be divided by itself and the number One.

They see our people but they do not see our people. We are invisible as human beings. They think that we have no inner life, no real feelings, no power other than that which is crude and brutal. And we women – we are the deeply feared because it is assumed that we are filled with rage, poison. But I have embraced the beauty of Nature. I have given you, child, Fibonacci."

Jody could not take everything in. She quickly clung on to what she could: she knew something about Fibonacci.

She had always had a fascination with the number sequence.

She had become obsessed with it in her teens and had spent her spare time trying to understand it.

What she knew at least is that a Fibonacci number is a recurrence relation in which each term of the sequence is defined as a function of the preceding terms. 0, 1, 1, 2, 3, 5, 8, 13, 21, 34, 55 etc.

FSD used Prime Numbers as part of what they called Deep Surveillance: their system of spying on a human being at every point in life.

The Prime Numbers comprised the complex codes which created Deep Surveillance."

For those scientists who liked their mathematical equations in forms other than numbers, 'bees' were created and used not only as surveillance mechanisms but because they were, in a sense, the Fibonacci sequence itself. Graceful and beautiful, they made the bitter pill of being watched twenty-four hours a day more bearable.

But they were also a show of muscle, a reminder that there was no hiding place from the all seeing, all-knowing Ubiquity.

For a brief moment, she had been out of Ubiquity. It had lost her, and realizing this, had come to claim her back.

The bees suddenly vanished.

She knew now that she was the prize in a battle between an Undetectable – Blanche Rose – and FSD.

Blanche Rose was winning.

Jody listened.

The voice of her mother continued:

"Jody, I give you, my daughter, a Fibonacci Prime. It is Impenetrability coupled with Beauty. Remember, Jody, if beauty is missing, then it's all pointless, useless. Remember that.

Now, The Prime I have given you is not a wall like all the Primes that have built our society. This Prime, darling, is a key.

You know from your studies that the Prime's fortress nature is what the world of commerce and the military and everything else is built on.

You know, as an Ultra, what those who are not Ultras – the majority of people – do not know: that FSD can predict the sequence of these numbers. That discovery is believed, by you Ultras, to be humankind's greatest mental achievement.

But those above Ultra – above you – know something else.

Something I discovered, gave to FSD and then was trained to use for FSD's benefit: mathematical harmonic frequency. Jody, I could literally hear 5387's frequency!

So I made a little music out of it. For you.

That's the tune that always creeps into your head from nowhere.

It's me. Your mother.

I'm talking to you.

I'm with you.

I have mastered 'All World'.

And I am here with you now. As I always have been. Daughter, I want you to choose 23 or 47."

Jody did not hesitate.

"23", she said, trembling.

"Good, Jody", the Voice said. I like that. 23 is known as a 'Sophie Germain Prime.' She was the great mathematician who was deprived of her glory. Because she was a woman.

Hold onto that 23.

Keep it in your heart.

Jody, we live in wartime. Some say that war is all our species truly knows. But we know love, too. And love can transcend time. It's the little flame. Remember, my daughter: Maintain a scepticism concerning the Official Wisdom. Be impatient with mediocrity. Have faith, Jody, in nature's simple truth.

In the words of the late, great mathematician Richard Feynman: 'You can't fool nature'."

And as those words faded, Jody found herself in another circle.

It was dark, lit by candlelight.

A beautiful boy stood there. Naked.

The boy spoke to her: "My grandfather was born in 1984. He was a boy when the Long War started. His father was a boy during Vietnam. And his father was a boy in World War Two. His father was a boy in World War One. And his father was a boy during the Boer War. And I am a boy during this war. Here, briefly, you were out of Ubiquity. Your mother has brought you here so that you can have a taste of it.

Sometimes being out of Ubiquity looks like the aftermath of the worst war you could think of.

Like a city in the future. It is dead. There are no more rats. Rats depend on humans for survival. They flow with us, mirror us. They are our brothers and sisters. They are gone. Then, sometimes being out of Ubiquity looks like being in what scientists years ago called a particle box. That name is still retained. Look around. That's what I call what we're in now: this stuff –

straight, really thin black lines, like black beams of light just coming at you from all over. It's like where they torture me when they feel like it. See it. There's another me in there. My doppelganger. He's just like me."

Jody saw between the lines an identical naked boy, being tortured by light and grimacing in pain.

"I could save him.", the boy said. "But I know that if we touch – my doppelganger and me – boom! Gone! Matter, anti-matter annihilation.

I don't care any more. There are those who keep me disconnected from it, know that I want to touch this doppelganger because…"

"You're a Stockholm?" Jody asked.

"You see…" He stopped as his voice began to tremble. "That's a simplistic question for us.

Jody, in this state that we are in, there is a corridor, a zone right between these two worlds of matter/anti-matter, a zone where they do not touch and the annihilation does not happen. If I could enter this corridor, then I could re-arrange what we call 'reality'. I could hold that corridor open, stop it from coming together. Jody, I've found out that it is possible to use what is being released in the particle box. You can use it.

That's how you think about things when you're out of Ubiquity. You think about how you can use things. And you realize that this thing called common sense is of no use now. It's used against us. To keep the people down. Out of Ubiquity, you have to be counterintuitive. You can only survive if you're not afraid of that. You can't be afraid of asking 'the wrong questions' and looking at things in the 'wrong way'. You learn that."

"I don't really understand", Jody said.

The boy moved closer to her. His face was urgent. Desperate.

"How do you know what I have been telling you is true?" he asked.

"I don't know."

"Jody, you'll hear this more than once now: There are things that are true, that will always be true. But you can never prove this. Ever. There is nothing more beautiful than this statement. It shows our bravery, our nobility as a species, our courage in the face of annihilation, of never knowing."

The boy was suddenly gone, back into his endless journey outside of Ubiquity.

And with his disappearance, just as suddenly, Jody was back where she had started.

The long-haired, hippy Nona she had met at the entrance of the clavis was standing at the bar, drinking hard. She could see now that his surroundings were made up of the things of his youth, made up of the 60s.

There were go-go girls in cages, long-haired musicians smashing guitars and drum kits on a massive stage. Even a glitter ball.

"Like that?" he yelled at her. "Didn't I tell you that this clavis would blow your mind? The most important thing is: don't believe a fucking thing that happened to you in there, baby. Not even me. You can't take a breath in there without inhaling a high. That's the blast of this whole thing!"

"I have to go," Jody said.

"'Hey, like, pay no attention to the man behind the curtain. What movie's that from?"

"I don't know. I have to…"

"You're a drag. Hey, almost forgot. There's somebody here to talk to you."

Jody turned around

It was David Frederick

He took her to one side, yelling above the blasting music.

"Jody, I told you that I'd get your story. I have. I've found out who your mother is. It's Saronia Miller. Are you listening?"

Jody was speechless.

"Jody, you've got to get to her! Forget this place, it's a druggie haven. Where is she now?"

Her head was spinning.

There was no way that she could tell that what had happened to her had really happened.

She had gone to the clavis to escape. Perhaps she had met the escape that she needed. And that was all it was.

She looked at David Frederick.

"Jody, wake up! Let's get out of this place! You've got to save your mother!"

"Yes. My mother. Saronia. Yes. Yes!"

Across the meridian, I try seeing the other side,
Past rusty containers, waves like welts from the lash
In a light as clear as oil from the olive seed.

DEREK WALCOTT, OMEROS

The bridge at Waterloo, straight, unshowy, concrete, grey; straddling the path between Peter and Paul; the vista cut in two by the bridge itself, that structure of hardness and grit, utilitarian, not made of battle cannon as Janet thought it might be, as it should have been; not peppered with rotting skulls as it would have been if it had existed centuries ago, as a public trophy case for the mighty; Janet Bookman Baker, at last, walking towards the bridge, the air spinning around her, she waiting for it momentarily to settle down; waiting for her heart and her breathing to calm itself; waiting for the sweat that was forming beneath her breasts and under her arms to cease; using the sweat as a momentary excuse to feel uncomfortable; using it to make her want to run back to Morant Bay Road to shower, to scrub and scrub until she had taken off her skin, until she had stripped away the medium through which she had been judged by others whose judgement she had taken on and had used to form herself; Janet, gazing into what she had been brought up to see as a liquid Golgotha, gradually, over time, holding it responsible for her malaise; the Thames, ugly, menacing, threatening, just as her mother said it would be, without question a place where the dead lived; Janet, now petrified, unable to move, looked at the bridge stretched before her covered in people going about their business, people who were swarming around her, some of them looking at her, through her, past her; possible – just possible – she said to herself to be swallowed up in them.

In them, with them, she could match her steps, her breathing; move along with them as if she were one with them; amongst them she could identify a hand to hold, an arm to grab, a back to climb upon if need be; flow with the people; move along; so many people in the world; and on that particular bridge, too, it was possible – if she could just find the courage – to be carried along with them.

With them. Janet said the words aloud as she walked; every step painful but strangely light; as she came closer to the bridge her breathing racing again, causing her to lean against a building like a woman twice her size; for a while she waited there, praying that someone would come along and rescue her; someone would take her hand, cover her eyes, tell her funny stories, lead her across; all the time wiping her forehead, and she, counting to herself: one, two, three.

One, two, three: Janet, walking towards the water; conjuring up images of her son sitting beside the window, just as she had done decades ago, waiting for her to return home; Lucas sitting and watching the long, endless street, wondering, just as she had wondered at almost the same age, when her father would return; Lucas' face, silent and tortured when she had said that she would be away for a while, not a long time, but longer than he had ever experienced before; she would be gone for at least three days; three days, he had repeated, barely able to speak; the first time the number three had been ugly to him; his face slowly crumpling like a baby's, his lip trembling, and it was then that she knew that she would die for him, knew then that she understood what dying for your child meant; thinking now as she pauses at the foot of the bridge, that perhaps Sam was right to want to keep him in the community, how could it be possible that Lucas could live and survive in a world that would have to devour him, as alien life; what would he be, hidden away in the woods, a place that would break him down and re-shape him, make him a stranger to her, all so that he would be able to continue going forward.

Forward, no choice, she thought to herself, she must go forward, she must cross the bridge and not turn back, particularly after the big theatrical parting complete with tears and hugs she had had an hour ago; she could not turn around, return, go back with nothing; by doing that, she could make it difficult for her own children to leave when the time was right, when the time came; but she could not move, she could not go forward; standing as if rooted to the spot, she was suddenly startled by a cyclist, his long, skinny, Lycra-clad leg brushing against her; as she steadied herself, a man shouted, his face red and sweating – not an old man, possibly as much as twenty years younger than her, she thought – his face contorted into a shape that made her recoil, remembering what her mother had said about London, how it could drive you mad, how cruel it was, always rushing forward; moving with the tumult; she heard a dog bark in the darkness of the underpass.

Her heart began to beat faster and her mind began to feel as if it did not belong to her, was not under her control; that she had become part of a collective mind, ancient, somewhere bred in the bone; and now that mind was showing her things: dogs crashing through an ancient bush, dogs too skinny to be healthy, their teeth bared, the sound of them, she knew in the deepest part of herself, was the sound of suffering and death; she, running, out of breath, the hounds after her, all of them crashing through the bush; and she running, running until her heart felt as if it would explode, crash through her chest; this person she sees, who is her in some other reality, one just as real as the one she was in; this other Janet is physically stronger than the self she knows; looking closely, Janet can see that The Other is not female but male; head down, he is praying aloud as he runs to the shrine of a river goddess: Yemanja – she whispers the forgotten name; breathless, yet he finds the breath to sing songs and chants that buoy him, using remnants of the Old Religion, the Old Religion causing his footsteps to become lighter: the power of the old ways raising him up into the air; raising him above the bush, up into the sky, up and into flight over the blood-blackened Atlantic, his very flight reversing the flow of the great ocean itself until instead it flowed up over the Arctic and the Pole; down through Scandinavia; becoming once again

Mare Germanicum – another body of water – and that body of water becoming the Rhine; and the flight of the boy takes her back to thousands of years gone; back to Doggerland – the land connection between Europe and Britain where the mighty Rhine and the Thames were one; and with the force of the boy who she is, with the force of his winged flight out of slavery, the Rhine begins to gather itself and then at London becomes the Thames – "Tamesa" – the Dark One.

The Dark One, the name given by the captives who had not been able to fly, to escape, to the ship that had taken them away from the African coast; and Janet with them now; now a woman once again, a woman lying beside a latrine whose foul contents sway with the movement of the death ship; the slavers housed one floor above the women, the women easy prey, she is easy prey; the travail of those still alive ringing in her ears as she lies there; her eyes unable to penetrate the darkness, the sound of creaking wood and the sound of the ocean like mourning; a woman dead beside her; two other women, noble, and beautiful, and strong who do not speak her language, but nevertheless are her kin in suffering; she, lying between them, instantly naming them Anna and Abena, two names that come to her out of the cries and the mourning in the dark; she desperate for water, and light, and air; but together, she and the two women on either side of her, will stay alive and go across; together; they will make their way up the narrow steps to the deck; together they will see, once again, the wild woman poised on the prow, her black skin radiant in the moonlight, her arms outstretched, calling out to the river goddess, to the queen of the oceans, together they will see her throw her head back, arch her back, plunge into the sea; and Janet, in this vision on the bridge, in this strange reality on the bridge, can see another vision: she is now a baby, floating atop the sea, thrown overboard by her mother in order to save her from her fate; she is a baby penetrating the veil of the ocean, tumbling into the arms of the mother goddesses, and they catch her, and they bless her with a gift; and, because she is a baby and cannot question, she receives this gift, this power and knows that she will survive and have children and her children will have children and through her they will have the Gift that was born out of misery and pain; and receiving it, the baby smiles, closing her eyes.

Closing her eyes again, not sure that she could take any more of what the river was giving her, nevertheless she held her breath and allowed the grey water to talk to her again. Seeing that all of the certainties she had come to know were nothing but the shadows of a parallel world, that itself was a shadow of another: a world where a broken glass could right itself, according to her son, a world where her son and daughter, her husband and she herself could be happy; where she could move into another kind of narrative, live there and return again from where she had come; this possible, she knew, by simply crossing this Calvary called the Thames and giving herself nothing to hold onto; and with the images and worlds inside her, Janet Bookman Baker, longing for another narrative, another way to think her story, moves forward.

Forward, suddenly Janet turns.

A girl is jogging, her hair is pulled back. She has an open, clean face.

The girl is out of breath

She slows down.

She leans over to check something on her heel.

She does this cleanly like a dancer or an athlete.

Janet decides to follow her the rest of the remaining distance and to walk off the bridge.

But she cannot see.

She inspects her glasses.

"Take the glasses away. She doesn't need them."

"But she can't see", the doctor said.

"If she wants to, she will", Gloria-Loretta had said. "She will see when she wants to."

Janet adjusts her glasses.

The jogger is gone.

She thinks: if she turns around now, she can return home with the excuse that she must read the last of her father's papers.

She has avoided doing this for a decade.

She turns and standing there is her father: Milton John Bookman.

He looks the way he did the summer he had discovered *Paradise Lost*.

And it occurs to Janet suddenly that his copy of the book has mysteriously disappeared.

But now she can only hold in her mind his face young again, slender again, his eyes bright.

She can see that time again:

This summer is the summer of his dictatorship, the summer he has demanded that Gloria-Loretta read The Poem.

And Gloria-Loretta does read The Poem. All summer. Every day. Every spare moment.

After supper one evening near the Equinox, Milton Bookman asks his wife to recite something from the poem.

Gloria-Loretta looks at him for a long time. Then she speaks:

'When this creation was? Remembers't thou
Thy making, while the maker gave thee being?
We know no time when we were not as now;
Know none before us, self-begot, self-rais'd
By our own quickening power, when fatal course
Had circled his full orb, the birth mature
Of this our native heaven, ethereal sons,
Our puissance is our own"

Janet stops:

"Our puissance is our own"

Power.

Our power is our own.

She remembers the first lines she saw when she opened her father's copy of the poem:

"…which way I fly is hell; myself am hell;
And in the lowest deep a lower deep…"

She closes her eyes.

More words come:

"Full fathom five thy father lies;

206

Of his bones are coral made;
Those are pearls that were his eyes;
Nothing of him that doth fade;
But doth suffer a sea-change;
Into something rich and strange"…

And she thinks again of *Heart Of Darkness*, the book her father had told her was so misunderstood by their people and which he had wanted to write one of his papers on, but time had taken him away and had plunged him into the heart of darkness.

"When you think of me, Janet" he had said once, "take that line from the Conrad, please":

"He who is living is now dead…"

And she sees the words from the book, written on the surface of the Thames, like writing etched on a frosted window, ephemeral, disappearing even as she recalls them:

"The sea-reach of the Thames stretched before us like the beginning of an interminable waterway. In the offing the sea and the sky were welded together without a joint, and in the luminous space the tanned sails of the barges drifting up with the tide seemed to stand still in red clusters of canvas sharply peaked, with gleams of varnished sprits. A haze rested on the low shores that ran out to sea in vanishing flatness. The air was dark above Gravesend, and farther back still seemed condensed into a mournful gloom, brooding motionless over the biggest, and the greatest town on earth…"

Janet says aloud to her father: "He who is living is now dead"
"In these times of ours, though concerning the exact year there is no need to be precise, a boat of dirty and disreputable appearance, with two figures in it, floated on the Thames, between Southwark Bridge which is of iron, and London Bridge which is of stone, as an autumn evening was closing in."

Again: "He who is living is now dead"

And she turns away from Milton Bookman and faces a little girl, so much like Ayesha, but not her.

The girl is in her school uniform and backpack.

She looks up.

She hesitates.

Janet moves toward her.

The child makes a wide berth around her as she carries on across the bridge.

In moving towards the child, Janet has crossed the bridge.

She is on the other side.

"Janet Bookman Baker", said the woman at the hotel as she looked up her name.

The hotel lobby was full of people. Janet held her handbag tight to her body. She looked around to see if she recognized anyone.

The woman smiled and welcomed her. She gave her the key and asked if she would need help with her bags. Janet smiled, too, but did not answer the question. She was holding on to everything.

The lift was tiny.

A gilded cage.

The signs advertising the hotel's amenities were plastered on one wall of the lift.

There was a kind of reflector on the other. She looked at her face

It looked too young and frightened to be her.

A maid came down the hall, carrying a bucket and mop.

To Janet, she resembled people who came from the same place as her parents had. Janet smiled. The woman smiled back, her eyes full of astonishment.

Janet stood at her door for ten minutes trying to make the swipe key work. She had always been terrible about opening doors.

The room was small with a tiny bathroom and tub. The bed was single, covered over with what looked like a tartan. She sat on the bed and pulled out her mobile.

She tried to block out of her head the sound of the hotel generator right outside her window.

It would be hard to sleep here.

She called home.

Lucas answered first. She could hear Ayesha clamouring on the other side of him, insisting that she talk first, she had news.

Lucas sounded like a baby. She had never spent a night away from him before.

Ayesha grabbed the phone from him and talked about how her black doll, Léopoldine, had taken over the dolly kingdom and there was absolutely nothing she could do about it.

Janet wanted to ask her how exactly this coup d'état happened, but Sam was in the background and he had to tell her something, too.

His voice was low and conspiratorial. His case – the woman who had gone on a rampage in the office and wounded several people with a knife – there was some mitigation, he said, as if he had been talking to her five minutes ago.

It seemed that the woman had been racially bullied.

There had been problems with the case, but racial bullying he could understand. He could see the way through now. He could get a good result. His instructing solicitor was over the moon.

Janet took off her shoes and lay on the bed as she listened to him outline the case and its new developments.

She blew him a kiss, asked if he knew about the dishes she had prepared for the children's supper.

He said yes.

She blew him another kiss and rang off.

She noticed that the room had the smell of old cigarette smoke and cleaning things.

The cigarette smoke made her crave one, but instead she took a shower.

She dressed in a black skirt and light jacket instead of the black one that matched it and went down to the lobby.

She fumbled in her handbag, praying that she had brought along her cigarettes. She had. They were tucked behind the pictures of Sam and the kids.

She stared at them for a while, then put them away and went outside to join the other smokers on the pavement.

They were younger, stronger, standing in the slight breeze, puffing away and laughing.

She wondered if Sam and the children could smell it and knew.

Of course they could.

She smiled to herself.

Of course they knew.

They had merely kept quiet about it, that's all.

They loved her.

How extraordinary, she thought, that the three of them could make that kind of pact, hold to it, keep it.

She finished her cigarette, stubbed it out on the pavement and went back inside the lobby.

A man, with teeth much too white, turned and looked at her as she came in. She instantly knew that he was American. There was something about his air and bearing.

She walked past him and overheard him say that he was Bradley Preston and here for the Othello conference.

She turned away so that they would not make eye contact.

Not yet.

The hotel backed onto the river.

Janet Bookman Baker watched the barges on it and the small commuter boats. She wanted to call her mother to tell her that she had made it, she had crossed the river. But that would make her bill too high.

Or maybe she could write to Professor Assantewa to tell her what she had done. Or leave a message for Anna Taylor to tell her, too.

But she did none of those things.

She turned her head instead in the direction of a woman who, in a dress far too small for her, was having high tea by the window and talking to a man who sat across from her.

She was talking about the rats that came up from the river at night to eat what had been left behind in the kitchen.

Heaven for a rat was the river and a hotel full of food alongside it.

Janet turned away.

She could see Bradley Preston talking to two of the conference delegates. He was strong, tall and full of confidence.

He saw her and waved. She looked behind her to see if he was indicating someone else.

He looked straight at her and motioned her over.

She joined the group and he continued his conversation as if she had been there all the time.

A few minutes later she excused herself and returned to her room. She did not turn on the lights.

Janet Bookman Baker lay on the bed and stared at the ceiling.

She thought of those words that had accompanied her across the bridge, and of *The Waste Land*:

"He who was living is now dead…"

Janet took a few seconds to play with the on-off switch on her lights in the hotel room.

When she did that, the light appeared in different places.

There was no rhythm to the flow of light.

She liked that.

There was a box of chocolates on the pillow in a white box accompanied by a note of welcome from the management.

She ate a chocolate slowly as she read the note attached to it. It was bland and written in a childish scrawl. It was written much too fast to be sincere.

She returned the note to the pillow. She returned it correctly to its previous position.

She could smell the scent of a man's unwashed hair on the pillow case Gloria-Loretta had told her how it was with hotel beds.

There was a large envelope on the desk.

For a moment she thought that she should ring the concierge to have someone come to pick it up.

But instead she sat down to open it:

'Some places only exist in the morning: Greenwich Village, almost rustic in the dawn, the cow-path streets meandering toward the river;

Washington D.C., just as you enter it from Virginia, the sun on the Monument and the shockingly small White House; the Jardin du Luxembourg, the part near the Senate, the gravel path dappled with light, the red-dust road out of Accra down to the coast where the slave forts are; a medieval village carved from a rock, perched at the top of a mountain in northern Italy, its square silent except for the church bell.

Other places were best in the afternoon: Soho at teatime, when the air hangs heavy with the stink of petrol and jazz sticks to the bricks and mortar; Marseilles, overlooking the sea from atop the rock where the church with the golden dome sits; Dam Square, Amsterdam swirling around it, and a man dancing with a black marionette.

And some places exist at night: Piccadilly Circus, haphazard, polyglot, neon-obsessed; Edinburgh, the wynds, down into the gloom of the gardens and the shadow of Arthur's seat.

A woman is ending her life far away from home, and now, in its days, she can see the places that she has known, and they have arranged themselves according to the time of day.

There had been other places, too, many others, and in each one she had left a part of herself. Back home, people had been born, and people had died, but she kept moving, looking.

Long ago someone had told her that her destiny was mapped out for her, there were constraints that she must not breach. To breach them would disturb the ancestors, and the elders and those not yet born.

But who had they been, the ones who had told her this, and where were they now that she was making her final journey…alone.'

Janet returned the pages to the envelope. She rang the concierge to tell him that she had found an envelope in her room that someone had left behind.

But no one had been in her room for a few days and besides, each day the rooms were thoroughly cleaned.

Janet read the pages again.

He was obviously not lying to her.

Why would he lie?

212

But how had they got there?

They frightened her. They made her think of Professor Assantewa.

She rested on the bed.

The children were asleep by now if Sam had kept them to schedule.

Ayesha was always the first to nod off. She would be surrounded by her dolls. Nothing would disturb her except her own snoring. That will have to be corrected when she gets older. But who will do that?

She closed her eyes and listened for a few minutes to the TV.

A girl had been shot dead not far from Morant Bay Road. She had been the sister of a gang leader and had been executed, gun to head, at a fast food restaurant. The young reporter in the poison green suit was shouting the news over the siren wail.

The young girl's name sounded familiar. But whether it was did not matter.

The girl was gone now.

She watched herself weigh her emotions.

Her mother had told her once that she should have become an actress. Gloria-Loretta had said that she was a great actress and that she really should consider the profession. At the time she had taken this as another one of her mother's insults disguised as helpful hints.

She was not so sure now.

She looked at the bathtub. Maybe she should have a bath.

The bathtub was spotless except for a ring around it that was barely visible. That ring would have driven her mother mad.

Whenever Gloria-Loretta had the opportunity she would point out how clean the people from The Island were. They were always very clean, dressed in whites like the Arabs in the desert. If cleanliness was a religion, then she would join up. The Island people were clean people who washed their hands before each meal like the Jews and the Arabs.

Did she know that Jews were persecuted during plague times because it was thought that they were the ones who started it ?

They survived, therefore the conclusion was obvious.

Janet laughed out loud as she remembered Gloria-Loretta, a woman who never subtly sent a message. There were no hidden codes with her. If she had died when Janet was small, she would have died, never to be remembered, never to be conjured up because that would have been her wish. She laughed at the people who would claim, after the death of a parent, that they could see them somehow, hear them. That, to her, was African, primitive, impossible. The world was what was seen and nothing more. First you died and after that was dirt. Better to live with what you could see, what you could taste, touch and feel.

Janet knew that she was the daughter of a woman who was, if anything, an evangelist for cleanliness.

She had taken three baths a day and after her husband's betrayal, had taken to washing everything constantly, even her raincoat.

She would run a mental white glove across the surfaces of every new environment she entered. She was a woman in love with the smells of cleaning.

But there had been times, small moments, when she could feel something between them.

She would be at school, frightened about speaking out in class for instance, or worried that someone she liked did not like her, and she thought that she felt Gloria-Loretta beside her, standing there silently, and beside her, her mother's mother and a line of women related to her by blood, strong and silent and proud.

They were there, always there. They had kept her alive and kept her mother alive, too. And perhaps they had brought her here, too. To this hotel room.

The telephone rang.

It was Sam again, asking if she had brought the charger for her mobile.

She could tell that he had been drinking.

But he was elegant with it. Sam was always elegant. A beautiful man.

He was talking to her.

He was saying that all he wanted was to be a good dad to Lucas and Ayesha, just as his father had been to him and his grandfather before him.

He wanted to be a good husband to her.

That most of all.

In the end, the children would be gone and all that would be left would be the two of them. He wanted to make his final journey with her.

He sometimes prayed that he could die before her because he could not bear the sight of her dead, lying in some coffin in the cold ground or a pile of ashes in an urn.

The odds were on his side, women outlived men.

He asked her if she was going to have an early night.

Stunned by what he had said, she could barely answer.

Then she said yes, and blew him a kiss down the phone.

She could see herself, for a moment, lying next to him in bed.

Why did that feel like solitude?

She dressed slowly and left the room.

The Dark Is Good

I want to talk to the producer of Showboat.

Because I don't know anything about the show.

Plus I've never done TV before let alone live TV.

I don't know what to wear, other than no stripes or patterns, which somebody told me you don't do on television.

But he's very busy and as soon as I identify myself, he puts somebody else on the phone, a girl with one of those girlie voices, Eastern European – and sorry for sounding a bit racist here – but I'd guess that she's one of those Russian girls who'd be about six feet tall that you find hanging out in some bar in Mayfair waiting for some of that good old City money to walk in.

But that can't be true about this girl, I think, because what the hell is she doing in TV if that were true?

She chats about the format, about there being a long table, how we perch on stools to talk, the show goes really fast, the robot cameras are on tracks so don't look at them going around and – oh, right – there's no swearing, plus we don't pay much.

And I'm meant to be grateful because it's air time.

My face in the homes of thousands.

Somebody-picked-out-of-anonymity.

And now I count.

I am visible.

I am going to be on TV.

I ask what happens if I get seasick and she giggles nervously and says that she's sure that this won't happen even though the Thames now has waves – what? – and anyway if it happened, it would be good TV and her high-pitched sing-song voice is lulling and I say "ok".

I bring up that I wear a coat 24/7 and never, under any circumstances, take it off except during those rare occasions when I take a bath, which is a very traumatic time for me.

And don't suggest that I take showers because I can't stand water dripping on my head, and to my surprise, Nataliya ("call me Nat, please") says that the host is American like me and is into English eccentricity and even though I'm not English the point is taken.

I say thanks.

I hang up.

And sit in the dark.

Because I know that It is coming on and the only thing that I can do is sit and wait for It.

I call It "Malvolio" because I want to laugh at its yellow-stockinged pomposity.

Its funny clothing.

Its airs and graces.

'Mal' and I have a relationship.

The only real one that I have.

Since I was a kid, It shows up fairly regularly.

Me?

I sit and pay attention.

It stalks the room, lecturing me, watching me carefully, daring me to venture out of the shell that It has constructed for me, and that no matter what I do, how far I go, It will always be there to bring me down to earth and right through the bottom of the Seventh Circle, in the process making me understand the way it really is, and that one day, if I'm really lucky, and keep my mouth shut, I'll come to see the truth and wisdom of what It reveals to me.

I want Its revelation because it has been promised to me for years and years and years and this is the moment that I need to see that revelation; but as usual, there's a lot of finger-pointing, stalking, blah-blah-blah, and it's better to keep my head down no matter what happens.

The dark is good.

Sitting in a corner in the dark is good.

Good to observe something that you have no responsibility for talking to.

Something comforting in that.

Warm and comforting.

Has a zing to it.

I can name it.

I can tame it.

I have the balls.

Will have.

But not right now.

Much too interested in watching the performance that It does and knowing that my coat protects me.

Will always protect me.

Is there any circumstance in which I would remove it?

Yeah, to slip on my shroud.

With the shroud I'll have no choice; a comforting, wonderful thought, a comforting part of the life that I have created and which has created me.

I don't have any fears, not really, just a series of unfortunate circumstances that seem not to want to go away no matter how hard I bury them, make fun of them, disguise them, push them away like little lap dogs barking and biting at the hem of my trousers.

I've been living a story and the story has changed.

That's why I'm here with you.

That's all.

It's like reading a book about someone and suddenly, the style of the book changes, the words that you've got used to change, and you know that the narrative itself is thinking, breathing and you go through it, like moving through Dante's circles, and there are these voices all around you becoming more and more obscure until the clarity comes.

And it will come.

They say that mathematicians are obsessed with two things: pattern and beauty.

I've run away from beauty, and pattern has always been running toward me.

Earlene used to promise me, in her way, that beauty and pattern would come together for me.

She always said: "Just keep going, Anna. Don't give up. Just keep going."

Do you understand?

Now, a moment of silence, please.

It is time to say goodbye to Blasters and I have this sentimental/terrified feeling that overwhelms briefly me.

I have to catch my breath before I ring his bell, not in order to deal with the odours of the twenty-four white Persians that live in the apartment below his, but because I am leaving this sentimental, mental old man, and, while I'm not flattering myself here just trying to be clinical, my leaving will be the end of him.

He'll try and play it cool like anybody would who spent time in an English public school and a German POW camp I guess. But I know him and he knows me.

I walk up the creaky stairs, aware more than I have ever been aware of just how creaky the building is, how in need of repair it is.

There are tales about it once having been a trysting place for Oscar Wilde and his boys, that it had his ghost here in the walls, and I half hope that old Oscar will bust out somewhere in these musty halls – bad thought because I read somewhere that Oscar's body actually did explode with putrefaction after he died – bad thought, bad place I'm in right now, full of the same feelings I had on 9/11 when I had to go to the station to do my show.

This feeling of abandonment and total lack of sympathy.

9/11. It's an ugly day. No contest.

You would have thought that someone from the station would have rung up and said "Anna, look, stay home tonight. Don't come in."

But no, fuck no, nobody.

I come in, and let me say this : NOBODY said anything.

I was numb and it was quiet in there.

Not respectful quiet.

Just, 'let's don't deal with it' quiet.

Just say nothing, just don't articulate, no looking in the eyes, keep it inside, avoid having to deal with shock and grief. Cross the bloody road.

A digression here:

I know this girl who hadn't heard from her aunt in two years.

She calls the police.

They go over to the aunt's house.

No answer.

They break the door down and find her, not her ,they find the fucking skeleton of her aunt sitting in front of the TV.

And there's mail piled up outside the door and it smells bad in there and NOBODY WENT IN TO CHECK IT OUT. Not even my friend's mother, who was her sister not even her, didn't take one second from her busy life watching reality TV and stuffing her face to think: 'Hey, I haven't heard from my sister. I'd better check her out.'

That's the country I have exiled myself to.

Not the whole picture, but, it's an island at the end of the day.

The night/early morning after 9/11.

I have these two authors on my show, very high literary types, very fêted, and we talk about their books as per the subject of the show, and all I can see is the last time I was in Manhattan seven years ago at the top of the World Trade Center – in one of the buildings, I don't know which. It had been my only time there because I couldn't afford Windows On The World. When the elevator door opens, I walk onto the Observation Deck and this is when I really get that Manhattan is an island and Manhattanites have an island mentality which they bury in hardness and sophistication but it's really Bora-Bora with a Barney's on it.

I'm in the World Trade Centre and it's around the time when they had found that mass grave where all those black people – slaves-were buried hundreds of years ago and I'm standing on top of their bones, not thinking that seven years from that moment I'd be living in London having a quarter-life crisis; no, I'm thinking 'hey, I'm just free, I'm young, I'm marvelling at everything and all of life's possibilities standing at the top of this tiny strip of land.'

Ok, back to the studio.

I've got my earphones on so that I can hear these two authors and the way we sound going out over the airwaves, invading people's space.

I'm hearing but I'm not listening because I'm thinking about NYC, about those buildings, all those people minding their own business on a sunny September morning, the graves of my ancestors GONE beneath the rubble; the cops, the firemen, the people washing dishes and taking cars, the moms and the dads, New York City, it was all gone, blown away by some guys who thought that they had the right to impose their point of view on everybody else, on me; led by some dead-eyed guy who thought he'd just end it all and take everybody else out with him, based on a fucked-up reading of a great holy book, desecration, taking innocent lives and messing with God. All I can think is:

'Some asshole has just plunged us into the Dark Ages and I'm sitting here watching these two literary festival wankers discussing horseshit – literally – as the basis of some mighty work about Devon that will be read, in the end, by two and a half people, and they're talking about that ON THIS DAY, and I ask myself: am I over-reacting here, am I being an emotive self-indulgent Yank, is this the Special Relationship? – they're special and we get the relationship? However it goes it's fucked up.

I'm thinking all this dark, dark stuff about a country that's opened its arms to me, taken me in, indulged me, fed me, I love this place, I really, REALLY, REALLY do, I will fight for this place, go to the wall for the UK, I swear, God Save the Queen and I mean that shit BUT-do these guys really hate me and my country so much and you know what? I DON'T KNOW IT!!!!!!! Obviously. I don't get it.

Here I am smiling and nodding and listening to them read from their deathless prose and I'm doing my crappy show while my head is shouting: 'NOBODY IS TALKING ABOUT WHAT HAPPENED TODAY. THE WORLD IS DIFFERENT TODAY!'

I'm sitting behind my mike in this studio that smells of all the bad egg and cheese sandwiches and cheap wine from days and days ago and these two – people my age, already eminent – hot, doing hipsters talk about all the prizes they have won and have been nominated for like I'm not really here, like they're in some bar in Hoxton or Devon and I'm invisible.

Then wow! They start passing gossip between them about some literary festival and how the director was caught getting rimmed by this graduate from UEA AND THEY HAVE BOTH DISAPPEARED UP EACH OTHER'S BUTT WHERE THE REST OF THEIR WRITING MATES HANG OUT, so finally I say -because my head is about to blow off – I say, believe me: very quietly, very meekly, very excuse-me-for living, that actually this is a momentous day, and you know what? These authors just kind of look at me and I think – because it all went fuzzy in my head then, I must have blanked it out, had to blank it out – I think one of them said:

"It's America's turn."

Wow.

So there's my producer – the one who picks his nose, studies it, salt and peppers it, then eats it, the one who can't understand why he went home two weeks ago and his wife was gone – this idiot, is behind the glass nodding his head in agreement with the literary giants on my show.

There are regulations about language on the air in every country in the world and even by the standards of those particular authors' ironic/nihilistic whatever, what they had said was quite a thing to say, so I followed, again as quietly as I could, with a bleat on the lines of: 'what about the people who died, what about the people who just thought they were going to the office, what about the Muslims who died, can't Americans be innocent like everybody else, where is your compassion, your mercy, what the fuck would have happened to you pale, stale, ale-drinking ironics if we'd said in 1940 : Fuck you. We aren't lending you our shit, we aren't giving you jack."

We're here, you and me in this place and it's appropriate to say this, what I want to say 'to mah fella Amureecans is : 'Listen to me very carefully, you dazzled by 'Merrie-Old England we'll fight 'em on the beaches' hicks': No. Wrong. It's not the French who hate us, that's just an unrequited lovers' spat with them. No, it's our perfidious, tea-drinking, genuflecting to the Queen fucking COUSINS. THEY hate us!'

I take a deep breath, because we're on air, but I start thinking like some old vet from Nebraska : 'Good, cool. America is outta here, lock, stock. But not until we dig up our dead.' I can't stop, my mind is racing, I'm shaking.

I'm a presenter.

I have air-time.

I sit and I banter.

Very important.

Banter.

After the show, I go home to listen to RAA.

They release only on 7 inch because their fans can't be bothered with high-speed download shite. They're guitar-based, and one is a Brit who does not sing in an American accent which is a relief and a change. They've done a side dedicated to Serge Gainsbourg's song Bonnie And Clyde mixed with a take of Zazie's version of something I can only understand as 'Death of a Con'-a con is a jerk or maybe a cunt, all depends. They do this without irony and as much feeling as the rendition requires, no more.

Things arrived this morning to review for Showboat.

There will be a mystery tape shown to us for the first time, live on the show, of a new internet phenomenon called Faustina TV about the 'everyday life of an American girl', but that's all I know about it. We're supposed to have some kind of instant reaction.

223

Then there's a bestselling 600 page novel that's a world-wide phenomenon.

It's about the relationship of Dante to his muse Beatrice with loads of detail about medieval Florence so that you come away from it a scholar of Florentine history which is one of the side benefits of these kinds of books.

You can do pub quizzes on the Guelphs and the Ghibellines and which one was called White and which was called Black because you've read Burning Heart.

I decide to speed read it.

Next, there's a blog written by an MP.

Why, why do these people think that we want to know their thoughts?

Isn't it enough that they've wormed their way into our consciousness, coerced us to vote for them? Now they want us to see them on television, watch them eat their cornflakes in the morning on webcams and you just think: 'Why don't you guys serve the people instead of yourselves? Why don't you spend time feeding the hungry, taking care of the environment? What happened to humility?' Why do they think we've all lost faith in democracy? Forget Bin Laden, it's because of THEM! THEY are the ones who have caused us all to think that the whole thing is corrupt, useless, pointless. All they want to do is punch a personal hole through history and the thing is, they don't think we notice this. They think that we have bought the whole thing, the entire sell and that we actually BELIEVE in them. Well, we don't.

This blog, I assume, is an attempt by this one MP to connect with his constituents, to have them believe that he cares, he's like them.

How about a webcam at the cabinet meetings he sits on?

What about posting his bank statements?

How can anybody seriously actually grow up thinking that they want to be in politics? It's like wanting to be a critic, nobody wants to do that.

What these people want is fame.

And I'm going to contribute to this by talking about him on the show?

And I feel disgusted about this but that's the media game.

I read the blog.

And while I'm doing so I think: what if I have a brain haemorrhage in the middle of this? You now what the Hindus say: you're reincarnated complete with the last thought you had. What If I come back with this guy's musings on the London Eye burned into my brain: 'My wife and I rode the London Eye like two peas in a pod…'…With a last thought like that burned into my brain at the moment of my death, exactly what would I come back as? Would I lose the possibility of being reincarnated as a human being? Or would I move lower down the food chain to pond life or politician?

Last but not least, we are to see a play in the West End, an update of The White Devil starring a pop star who's decided that she wants to be an actress.

I dread this.

I don't mind the reverse, which is more interesting.

I try not to judge her before I see her.

This novel opens with fifty pages on the creation of the city-state of Florence, the genealogy of the citizens and I go straight through that part. Since we only have a few minutes with it, I won't talk much and let everyone else get in.

I hate this woman, the author. She makes appearances dressed in 13th century Florentine garb. I think her dog is named Beatrice.

On my last show there's going to be a guy from a men's magazine, a psychologist who works for reality TV shows; a girl born in 1984 who is totally into the 80s as a lifestyle, plus an American professor by the name of Bradley Preston.

An American.

I read his briefing note on the way here:

'Born in November, 1948 on the same day that James Baldwin left the United States for the first time. The highlight of his life after that was standing in the queue and getting a chance to see Sam Cooke in his coffin; followed by enduring a hundred hostile lawn sprinklers on an open housing march with Martin Luther King in his native Chicago. Later he had the 'honour' (his words) of being tear-gassed by the Chicago Police Department in August, 1968 during the Democratic Convention; then, he started a black student union at college; joined the Black Panthers for a minute; tried Islam; left that, and got a few degrees so that he could teach at college level.

Quote: "Recently having to watch black kids other than the ones with an inheritance of US slavery get all the scholarships; observe our soul food cooking become Southern cooking with smiley, nice white ladies selling more books than we do about our food; I just thought I'd plough my own eccentric furrow, look at stuff from left field, and get the hell out of the academy for starters.

I teach here, I teach there. The work I do is like jazz – you can't lock jazz down, you can't retrospect it, keep people out of it because they're the 'wrong' colour or background or whatever, you can't archive it, all that's anti-jazz. Same with me. Make all the dictionaries and encyclopaedias you want, but there's always just that little bit that you can't catch – can't see, and that little bit is the real essence of us, African people in the West. What's kept us alive? Wit, innovation, speed, mobility, the Spirit. We're in this strange land in our Trickster guise. For now. I'm like The Flying Dutchman. Except that I dance."

I think of Montgomery Tourlaine's black bus conductor, of his wanderings across London, of his search for the woman who was in his life for an instant.

Where is he now?

Where is his lost love?

Does Montgomery Tourlaine envy them?

Do I?

What I mean by this is: do I envy the completely all-consuming nature of what happened to him? Do I actually wish that I could have that kind of desire or am I too young to long for transcendence?

Is that type of thing, at this point in my life, best kept within the confines of pop songs and fiction – the beach read division?

I mean, if you think like that now, when there is so much on offer, so many ways to make and re-make yourself, to disappear, to die and rise again, then what does transcendence actually matter?

If I were to remake myself into, say Anna Karenina, just for the sake of argument and see that train heading for me, and I have a few choices in a split second because predictability is what could be coming down that track and is what the whole book was about – moving away from it, I mean: do I keep going so that I ride off into the sunset, the H'wood ending, or take lots of cash like somebody stupid enough to do that before they're thirty thinking: 'Well, fuck it. What I do is good for business', and what the hell would I be thinking something like that for, I ask myself, surveying the work I have to do at every level? And my life. My life.

I earnestly ask myself what it must have been like to have lived in the time that Montgomery Tourlaine and Bradley Preston did when they were my age.

What was it like to live in a generation when being young really meant something, when young was to be envied and not in that desperate, acquisitive, sad way it is today, but when youth meant a certain optimism, a certain belief in the future, in the possibility – by virtue of being young – that the world could be righted, re-shaped?

No one laughed at this last idea then, no one back then was cynical before their time.

Of course they probably did laugh and were cynical, but let me entertain myself.

You and me.

We will be toiling in the vineyard for a long, long time.

We will know war as a way of life and it will be normal for us.

Our parents will be our best friends, not our necessary enemies, people we will turn to again and again and again for refuge and succour.

We know. The world's already gone.

They have lied to us.

Again.

We sit closeted within the only dream that is the intelligent response to the times: Fame. Never-ending. Fame without boundaries.

In our time, fame will have no reason to be, it just will be, and we will push the ante every chance we can, ratchet it up the scale, until…? What?

No one will ask what the world will be like when everyone is famous, when everyone is known, when everyone is jostling for attention.

No one will ask what kind of suicide pacts we will make.

Because we can't ask those questions.

To ask them is to presuppose that we have paid attention to previous generations and we have, only to see that they have failed us.

They have their own childhood issues to address and there is neither room nor time for us.

These people: our parents and aunts and uncles, our big brothers and sisters, are planning to be immortals and we have to sit back, take a back seat, and watch it start.

We-us-sit back quietly eating our beans on toast.

This will be our contribution: to toil; to keep our heads down.

We watch the world unravel around us at the hands of our elders.

We will watch the environment turn against us.

We look up to the sky and either God is up there as Big Daddy or he isn't up there because what's the point if that option is not on the table.

And if I am not ashamed to dream of Big Daddy up there, if I am not ashamed of sitting with you now, watching the dawn start to come up, listening to the church bells and being glad to hear them, then you can listen to this:

I don't want to be fooled when I die because I actually believe that

I will die and this acceptance gives me a certain calm that I enjoy. And if I accept that, then I have to turn my back on what was given to me by my parents and embrace this –well, this Deity who will be waiting for me at the end.

Do you understand what I'm saying to you?

I wish Earlene was here now.

I wish that she was holding me, telling me one of her stories.

Could she have made up a story about us – now?

If I close my eyes I can hear her voice.

I can feel my head against her chest.

I can smell her.

She smells like Ivory Soap.

She loved that soap.

I couldn't smell it for years without bursting into…

Maybe that's why soap and I are not great friends.

I mean, I can't cry every time I take a bath.

Oh God.

God.

Am I invoking God?

I am seeing Him looking down on me.

You know what?

I don't care that He's a white man with a beard.

I don't care.

I am at Blasters'.

He pours two fingers of gin, drinks quickly and faster than I can see him. He has a gun in his hand.

Yes.

It's a silver pistol that belonged to his father, he tells me.

They say there is a way that you can tell if a gun is real but I don't know what that way is.

I freeze.

He puts it to his temple.

I flash forward to this image of his brains all over the place, and me trying to explain the whole thing to the police.

Wait.

Remix.

Maybe I'm not here to tell the police anything.

This could be a murder/suicide.

But he puts the gun down, bursts into tears and that's worse, his face crumples up into that of a particularly vexed baby who happens to look 78 years old.

I prefer the brains all over the place to this.

I turn.

I leave.

Down the creaky stairs.

Past the lady with all the cats.

Out into the air and back to the radio station.

Can't stay away.

The corridor is full of an ugly white light, the night light, the kind that offices have had from time immemorial.

Like Kafka.

Like Winston Smith.

I figure I have a comedy by-pass because this office, no office, makes me laugh.

How could anybody actually study one long enough to make a joke out of it.

Here it is.

I knew it would be.

Professor Assantewa's next instalment, coming through the fax:

6.

Jody studied her face in the mirror.

She wanted to see who she was, who was there in that mirror…

A warm feeling came over her.

David Frederick had kept his word.

He had come back.

He had told her face to face, as he said he would.

He had discovered and brought back to her the most precious information that anyone could ever give her.

It was clear.

She had to make a choice.

Fast.

Jody Carlyle knew what she really wanted, what she had to face: she wanted liberation from FSD.

She knew now, without a doubt, that she had to take her chances outside Ubiquity.

She wanted to be with those who were like her.

She could do this with the help of David Frederick.

David Frederick.

For the first time in her life, Jody allowed herself to have romantic feelings for someone, to dream him.

He would be with her. Help her.

They were both clever. They could find a way of staying on the run.

She knew that there were people out there who were beating Ubiquity all the time.

'No system can be both consistent and complete'. She was lucky to be living in a time when, at last, the Riemann Hypothesis had been proved to be true. Proving this hypothesis had broken open the Einsteinium universe.

231

She knew that no matter how hard FSD tried, Ubiquity would, could never be foolproof.

There was always someone out there breaking the codes, living free.

She and David would find these people, live with them, fight with them.

They would have children, raise them to value their humanity, and all of humanity. Their children would be proper stewards of the earth. They would not be afraid. Together they would read the forbidden works of the martyred Lutheran pastor, Dietrich Bonhoeffer.

His execution was the result of one of Hitler's very last orders. Their children would learn about him and through him they would come to understand, together, something about religion in a world of hatred and greed and war.

It had all come together at once: her real mother; the man she would marry; and in a way, reconciliation with her past in Tirian.

For the first time in her life, she was connected to something other than a system, some large, anonymous machine.

She would talk to David about all of this. He would understand.

And they would have to keep moving. Stay smart.

But together she and David could beat FSD.

Beat Control.

Control had been like a father to her since she had lost her adoptive parents.

He had been an orphan, too, and had some insight into her situation as a double orphan.

His empathy and nurturing of her had given her the confidence to join Elimination Systems. Control had given her a family, a place in the world.

But now…

He must have known who Saronia was.

Why hadn't he told her?

She tried to rationalize it…

Maybe he was afraid that the truth would destabilize her. After all, she was considered one of the most promising agents in Elimination Systems. She had even been told that she was ES' future.

Maybe he had not said anything because she was being groomed to attain the status he had. Maybe she was being prepared to enter that world beyond the Ultras, where everything was known.

Where everything was even more certain than it was now.

All her life, Jody Carlyle had wanted to have that affirmation, to enter the Valhalla of society.

But it meant nothing if her existence consisted of loneliness and alienation.

All that she ever saw was the degradation of human beings. She was witness to things deteriorating.

Now she had the chance to be a part of life.

She laughed to herself.

She was like a child who had opened a treasure chest.

She didn't know anything about the man she was planning to spend her life with.

She would spend the rest of her life getting to know him.

Jody waited, remained quiet, shut her thoughts down.

Tirian was asleep.

Jody bent down and kissed the child on the cheek.

"Tirian," Jody said, "I know why my adoptive mom gave me all that black history to read. I know now. I know who she is."

Jody watched her sleeping.

She thought of the feral children, her people, who lurked outside her enclave.

Some tried, from time to time, to storm the enclave itself. Once she had waited behind her door in fear while the security guards had a running battle with a gang of youths intent on destroying the enclave.

They had been found, after their executions, to have had high levels of testosterone. It had been administered to them so that they would develop into gladiators. It may have led to their deaths.

She would listen to their cries.

She would think: 'What am I doing here when I belong with you? To you? You're where I come from. I belong out there with you.'

And now. To be part of the same people that Control himself had come from, the man who had saved her, a man who had come from a people who had been stolen, tied down in ships, enslaved,

Jody closed her eyes.

There was only one thing to do.

It was then that Michael Feulnière's words came back to her.

'Some people consider my place a refuge.'

Jody contacted Feulnière. She asked him to invite Saronia to his place.

She didn't know what her next steps would be after doing that, but she needed to see Saronia again.

'Mother', she must have said the word a hundred times.

The journey across Paris was more difficult than usual.

The Seine, rather than rising onto its banks, had come up beneath the pavement. There had been a strange surge which had flooded the city even more.

Jody had had to take several boats. Tirian had become listless. She thought that she might have to carry her part of the way.

Saronia had arrived a few minutes earlier with Adele.

Jody tried not to stare at her across the room because she could see similarities.

At any rate, she had made up her mind.

She was going to save Saronia.

At dinner, they discussed the latest news from America: The Blueberry Farm books were now being banned under Patriot Act Three. The few librarians who dared to come out of hiding were allowed to demonstrate in the streets, but only during the Ugly Hours when they were fair game.

The news made Saronia tremble with fear. "These books of mine, they're just books for kids. What the hell is going on over there?" she yelled.

Adele spoke. "It's bad. Saronia, you don't know how bad." She lowered her voice. "The President has enemies. They're manipulating her policies…"

"They? Who?" Jody asked herself.

Adele was drinking the Sancerre at a steady pace. "There's something else you don't know. None of you know."

Michael Feulnière poured another round.

"We're among like minds here", he said, looking directly at Jody.

"He has to be right", she thought. "That's why I came. To be with like-

minds. That's why his place is a refuge. He said it was. He's right. I know these people. They're my people."

"The river", Adele said, "it's continuing to rise. The rain comes and goes, but the river continues to come up through the streets. Someone or something is causing it. That's from the horse's mouth at Météo, the weather service."

Feulnière continued, "Yes. This is known. As you know, we are always told that we cannot accurately predict the weather. This is because it is an example of Chaos. We don't know what the 'strange attractors' are, that is, what are the factors, the hidden factors that cause the weather. Climate change is a factor, of course, but we don't know what else is."

He was quiet for a moment.

Then he said, almost in a whisper, "I believe that those 'strange attractors' concerning weather have been located."

"What do you mean?" Jody asked.

"Those who have taken over the US Presidency have some control of those attractors, and with that knowledge, they can further manipulate reality."

"Manipulate reality!" Saronia said.

Jody realised that she had better close her thoughts down.

But doing it this time was a strange sensation. As if she was fighting something to do it.

Adele poured herself another glass of wine. "You know you've really got power if you can control the weather."

Jody said: "But who?"

Feulnière spoke slowly. "Do you recall, Jody, how you learned at school that the summer floods in Britain at the beginning of the century had brought in North Sea weather in mid-July? You were taught that the jet stream was lower than usual then. Because that was all they knew. At the time. But…could other things – sophisticated weapons being tested secretly, for example – be part of those 'strange attractors' which had caused the floods? There were no gauges, no measures of other alternative answers. At least not for the general population."

Feulnière's momentary silence filled the room.

"We had to accept what our 'wise people' said."

"But?"…Jody stopped and waited.

Feulnière continued. "No one was looking then at other factors which could have caused those floods, factors much more sinister. For now I will accept the possibility of a Fredo involved with secret weapons testing who made an error."

"A Fredo?" Jody asked.

He laughed.

"A generic term for a screw-up. One you have to eventually bump-off. From The Godfather movies. Michael Corleone's stupid older brother. We figure that that was what happened then."

"And later?" Adele said.

"Aw, yes. Later. There is always a later. They learned from the Fredo, didn't they? He had taught them to manipulate the weather. Now they are experimenting with the way sharks use their brains, how cats use their sense of smell."

"I've had that training." Jody said.

This was Top Secret information but she did not care any more.

She wanted to be with these people, with her mother and if she had to trade secret information to do that, so be it.

Jody studied Saronia's face.

They looked more and more alike.

"Another thing. There was a moment, briefly, when France became quite close to America again," Feulnière continued. "But this is not France's natural position in relation to America. France is the critical friend, the country which is the thorn in the side. That is France's special relationship. This President is moving us back to that."

Jody was listening, but she could not take her eyes off Saronia.

She did not try.

"The new President is in danger, too, from those in control of your President in the US", Feulnière continued, "Our President here in France is strengthening the National Assembly and taking powers away from the Executive. Jody, in other words, there are elements in FSD that have taken the knowledge of 'strange attractors', and other things too, to cause the floods in an attempt to topple our President. This is what we are fighting."

Jody was hearing things that she should report.

But she did not.

She looked over at Tirian. She was, as usual, impassive.

Suddenly, Jody could hear Tirian's voice in her head.

"Don't worry, Jody. It's all under control. Don't worry."

Jody stared at the little girl. She thought she saw something in her eyes. Something close to warmth.

Tirian continued to talk inside her head.

"You are the best assassin of your generation, Jody. That's what Elimination Systems does. That's what you do. You won't lose that."

Feulnière said, "Those who are controlling us are Nonas, like me. Some of us take our ludic heritage seriously. We take our 'play' seriously. We humans play you know. We even think that God plays. We Nonas are still the pampered babies with the atomic cloud over our baby beds. We love Hide And Seek. To vanish and appear again in a different guise. This was a big game when we were kids in the 50s, almost a hundred years ago. So long ago our childhood, our babyhood..."

Jody looked at Tirian.

If only she could read her, see through that inscrutable expression etched in pain.

Suddenly Tirian collapsed. Everyone rushed over.

Saronia took her in her arms. Tirian opened her eyes and smiled at her.

Saronia said, "I used to be a nurse. This child is exhausted. Both of you come back to my place. Jody, you need rest, too. Come home with me. Both of you."

Jody held back tears.

They surprised her.

She had not cried for years.

On the barge to Saronia's house, while Adele was sleeping off the wine, Saronia cradled Tirian. The moon was high.

Saronia said softly, "This is a feral child. I can tell. And you, that look you have."

"What look is that?" Jody asked.

Saronia smiled a weary smile. "Oh, you remind me of a somebody I knew once."

237

"Who?"

"A woman. Very young. She was a theoretical mathematician. Whatever that is. I knew her briefly. She was in a group of women who worked in a building I lived in. A punishment building. We were considered to be 'a bunch of loud-mouthed women'. Unacceptable. She was scrubbing floors. With a mind like she had. She told me that she had been part of a group who called themselves The Germains, after Sophie Germain."

"Who was she?"

"A mathematical genius, pushed aside in her time because she was a woman. At the time that she lived, a woman could only be a genius at inheriting a fortune and passing it on to the children of her husband. Germain did none of that. So she never got her due. The Eiffel Tower over there owes its existence to that lady. But you won't find her name inscribed with those who made it happen. The woman I knew and her group tried to rectify that by making some kind of breakthrough discovery in her name.

It had something to do with that scientific thing – entropy. She was always talking about it. I can't understand it, but the group who called themselves The Germains could prove that African slaves had harnessed it. They used it to stay in contact with one another. The Germains were going to go public with this. They wanted to use what they knew to enable people to heal themselves and to stay free."

Jody swallowed hard.

It was time to confront Saronia.

It was time to say it:

'I don't want to know about anyone else. I want you to talk about what happened to me. To us.'

But she did not.

Something else was troubling her.

Her FSD training was starting to kick back in.

"What kind of breakthrough?" she asked robotically.

"I don't know."

Saronia stroked Tirian's forehead as the child drifted in and out of sleep.

"My husband sleeps like this child. When he can sleep."

Saronia went below.

Just then, Tirian woke up from a deep sleep.

She seemed to be another person now, someone strange, someone dark.

The boat was coming up to one of the checkpoints still dotted around the city.

Jody gave Tirian her oxcymorcin for safe keeping.

Tirian took the drug and put it inside a small pouch that she always carried.

Like all feral children who had been taken out of their environment, Tirian carried the pouch like a security blanket.

Tirian rubbed her eyes, stretched, hid the 'O' and went below deck.

The security guards scanned the boatman. They did not touch anyone else on the boat.

The word had come through that everyone on board was a VIP.

When Tirian returned, Jody took the 'O' back.

She allowed herself to relax, happy that they were heading for Saronia's apartment on the Ile St. Louis.

She would figure out things once they got there.

Jody liked the island that Saronia lived on near Notre-Dame.

The river seemed to be more forgiving here. It had not quite overwhelmed the island. There were still tourists. Like everyone else they were enjoying the quaint old-fashioned planks that served as streets alongside the blackish, muddy water.

As she drifted into reverie, Jody recalled all the rumours about the river.

The latest concerned the river washing away a part of the embankment and uncovering a sacred spring blessed by St. Geneviève, one of the patron saints of Paris.

This 'miracle' of the rising of the water had brought not only more Parisians, but believers from Rouen, Nantes, Lille.

People were taking the water up in cups, pans, pails.

Believers had made up their minds that it was St. Geneviève who was causing the river to rise as punishment for their sins.

The appearance of the spring was evidence that the saint was intervening with God.

Crowds of people jostled one another at the river, on it, and in the tiny, narrow streets of the island itself.

There were prayer revivals at the waterside with flagellants beating themselves senseless near the great statue of St. Geneviève on a bridge over the river.

Others said that not a white saint, but the black Mother Of God was responsible not only for the sacred spring, but for the flooding, too. Only She was close enough to God to cause the Seine to do this. Citizens were being urged to make their way to the southwest, to the old Cathar stronghold of Rocamadour, to pay their respects to the Black Virgin there.

The other island was the Ile de la Cité on which Notre-Dame de Paris stood protected by sandbags and the prayers of the people.

As they stepped ashore, Jody saw, as if in a vision, a black woman dressed in a long dark dress, popular at the end of the 19th century. She walked past the boat, her eyes straight ahead.

The woman wore a medallion around her neck.

Jody could see the word "larmes" – tears – inscribed on it. She looked back. At the same time the woman looked at her. Then disappeared in the throng.

As they entered Saronia's apartment, it seemed to Jody that the world of the 1870 Siege of Paris had collided with her own mid-21st century world. A veil had been ripped asunder, letting in a new kind of daylight. She did not question her surroundings.

"This saint thing,", Saronia said, "these madonnas, black and white. And people are out there drinking that nasty water. They're losing their minds. Jody, I'm glad you came."

"I am too."

Jody could sense that Tirian was reporting on Saronia's apartment, doing a risk assessment for her superiors.

Jody knew the child well enough now to know that she had taken in the whole place in a glance.

Saronia stood by the long, wide windows. She held her hands out in the universal gesture of helplessness.

"Jody, I want you to know that my books just come to me, not from anybody

else, nothing. I see things, a name somewhere, and when I'm writing it pops into my head. I swear that's all".

'Is that all you can talk about?' Jody screamed at Saronia in her head, 'Your work! Is that why you left me…Mom!!!!! I hate all of you Nonas! You marched and you sang and what did you make? Nothing but more time so that you can stay alive!'

Jody felt the 'O' really start to kick in.

She felt herself sinking down into that comfort zone where nothing mattered.

Saronia was talking.

"I didn't intend my books to be anything but children's stories. You've got to believe me."

Jody could hear two lovers arguing in the street below. Their voices rose above the prayers of the pilgrims drifting out over the river.

Jody thought, 'I can't move.'

Saronia opened her handbag.

Out tumbled a small white card with a white rose engraved on it.

That was the calling card of The Stockholms.

The Stockholms were never afraid to exploit their reputation as clever, elusive and complex.

FSD had analyzed that Stockies were high risk-takers who clearly felt that the way to hide was to be out in the open.

Including handing out old-fashioned calling cards.

Jody thought, 'She's lying to me. She is writing those books for the Stockholms. That's why she's carrying that emblem.'

"Jody," Saronia said quickly, noticing the change in Jody's expression as she placed the card on the table.

"This card came from Anita. She gave it to me the other day. She said that she wanted me to have it. You met her at Charles Andromache's. She's my alternative therapist. She just came up to me out of the blue one day. An expat like me. A girl from Texas. She said she was a fan of my books. She had coffee with me. All she talked about were my books, how much they had inspired her. The last time I saw her, she gave me the card with the rose on it. It smells like roses. I took it because I…I love roses!"

"Anita's real name is Blanche Rose." Jody said coldly, feeling her body distancing itself from her mind.

The strong dose of 'O' had long ago lowered Jody's inhibitions. She could not control the information that was coming through her from Elimination Systems:

'Of course Control knows that Saronia is your mother. Control knows all. He also knows that your mother is a Stockholm.'

Jody stopped.

Then she said quietly, "And Tirian is assigned to keep an eye on me."

"Yes," Tirian suddenly said in a flat, childish voice, "You want to eliminate me. But you have to disconnect first. Become an animal. A very bad animal."

Saronia laughed. "I knew that child could talk. She just wasn't ready."

Tirian was by now on her feet.

She paced the floor on her stubby, little-girl legs.

Jody turned her attention to the shot of 'O' she had taken from Tirian on the boat. Had it been switched when Tirian had gone below?

Could she be sure that all of this was happening?

Where was her Regular, Maisie Blue? Maisie could tell her.

There was one thing that she was certain of: giving that 'O' to Tirian in the river taxi had been a mistake. In those minutes out of her sight, Tirian had done something to it. It was definitely stronger than her usual dose.

"You're right", Tirian said in answer to her thoughts.

Now the metamorphosis was beginning…

Tirian was beginning to look less like a child and more like some evil troll masquerading as a child.

"How long was Blanche Rose – alias Anita – with you when you last saw her?" Tirian asked, her voice tight like an inquisitor.

The question had been directed at Saronia, and, trained like everyone to answer questions to their obvious superior, she replied : "A few hours, I don't know."

"Three hours to be exact." Tirian's voice as cold as ice.

She was reading something on her inside wrist, turning her hand slightly left and right.

"She's a cyborborg, too.", Jody thought, not caring whether Tirian could read her or not. "She's got other powers that I don't know about."

"Yes" Tirian said, "I do."

Saronia was in her own world of fear.

"Anita – she told me her name was Anita – was with me…maybe…yes, three hours.", Saronia replied to Tirian.

Tirian held the White Rose card.

There was a cry now in Saronia's voice. Her big lion head looked as if it was sinking down into her shoulders.

Jody held on to herself.

She started reciting the lovely Fibonacci Prime that she now knew Saronia had been sending to her ever since she was a child, the beautiful number that made a melody. Maybe the mathematician had given it to her all those years ago.

Somehow she knew that the number and the melody had been fire-walled so that no one could intercept it.

Enveloped in her world of the Prime, she began to call David Frederick.

He could help her.

He could find a way.

But she had no way of reaching him.

And so she had no choice but to surrender.

She allowed the Fibonacci Prime to wash over her with its haunting melody.

She allowed herself to live within the safety of its environment.

Tirian walked over to an 18th century chest at the end of the room.

She yanked open the bottom drawer.

She rummaged around in it, throwing out the linen and silverware carefully packed inside.

She pulled out a medal.

She held it up to the light.

"Is this yours?"

Jody tried to grab the medal. But her arm felt too heavy to move properly. The 'O' was paralyzing, maybe even killing her.

"What does the inscription mean: 'We Made Queen Victoria Cry?'" Tirian asked.

"I don't know!" Saronia yelled. "I write books for little kids! That's all."

Jody could not move. She thought: 'That medal's the same one worn by the woman I saw on the shore. Or I think I did. But I don't even know where I am now. Or my mission.'

Tirian looked at her. "Jody, don't worry. You can go back to your life and your drugs. Your work is done. Let me play here."

"Play?" Jody recalled Feulnière's comment about the ludic nature of humans, particularly Nonas. She couldn't make the bits and pieces that were playing in her mind make sense. But she still had the presence of mind to try and scramble her thoughts.

In her state, this would only last a few minutes. It was an Ultra emergency privilege.

In scrambling she could protect her mind behind a wall of data, confusing it with other input, hiding it from Tirian.

She could tell by Tirian's expression that it was working.

For the moment.

And in that moment, she saw the Image once again, grateful that even now Saronia was managing to send it to her.

In that moment Jody saw once again the comforting image of herself as a baby and her parents leaning over her crib gazing lovingly at her.

She still willed the face of the woman to belong to Saronia.

In the seconds she was sure she had left, Jody thought: 'Maybe this whole thing with Tirian is a test. FSD always tests its people, always wants to know just how far you'll go. FSD has given me back my mother and in exchange for that, I get a loyalty test. Tirian's all part of it. That's got to be true.'

Tirian smiled at her.

She could be reading her mind.

Or not.

Jody had gone through this before.

Her loyalty, her calm and poise had been tested when a person she had taken for a friend turned out to be an enemy. She had had to plan his assassination, as FSD had wanted, but at the last minute she had been told that the whole thing had been a ruse.

It had taken her a week to get her adrenaline back to normal.

Tirian was a child groomed to do the will of FSD.

In that sense she was nothing but a robot, a computer that FSD had trained from infancy

'That's it. You feed her data', Jody said to herself, 'And she spits out what's required. She can be as subtle as you want. But she's got no values, no morality, no aesthetics. She can't see how a situation can change dramatically if you look at it laterally.'

Jody was thinking laterally now.

"Tirian, I know, I KNOW that Saronia is my mother."

Saronia, her nerves shot, burst into tears.

"I knew", Saronia wept, "it would come out some day. I had to give my child away. I had to live my life, Jody. I couldn't have a baby. Please listen to me, honey. I knew who you were when I first saw you. We have this gene in my family that shows up from time to time…Some of us look…well – you are lighter. But you and I are one. I can see in your eyes who you are. I can see it. I can see it."

Jody held herself back. She did not know, at that moment, whether she hated or loved the woman who had birthed her, then given her away for the sake of her ambition.

Her scramble time was running out.

'I have to get her out of here', Jody thought. 'FSD is probably going to snatch her before we leave Paris. But what do they want from me?'

Jody looked at Tirian.

She recalled the words a high-ranking Ultra had said to her once about the thrill of the feral enclave:

'You don't know who or what anybody is in there. They look like kids, but you don't know. One of the deals for all of us who want to go feral is to let Ubiquity play poker with our brain. So they can study the effects. You go feral. Who knows what's going on in your head.'

Jody felt the scramble begin to wear off.

Before it did, she thought: 'Tirian. Tirian. I can't let you go. No matter what.'

...she turns the bow of her head
for a last look at her own familiar shore.

JUST MARRIED, GRACE NICHOLS

The hotel was filled with delegates for the Othello conference, and as a result it had become a kind of Shakespeare fantasia. The boat tour advertised on the lift wall was called Full Fathom Five.

Bradley Preston was seated holding court in the lobby, Rabelaisian, with an expansive manner and a hearty laugh, he was surrounded by women.

Janet assessed the situation.

The women with him were her age and older, academics, some decidedly blue-stocking.

She walked over to the circle and found herself a seat on the periphery.

The man was like Santa Claus and the experience was like being in Santa's grotto where Santa would never let you go and you knew that the presents at the end would be outstanding.

"There was the issue", he roared, noting her presence, "of the playing of 'Othello.'"

"Orson Welles," he began, turning his full attention to her, then looking away at a rapt woman with the face of a Pekinese, "had played Othello as a hot-house Arab trapped in a sauna. His make-up had been better as Rochester in Jane Eyre. But Welles understood something about the Bad Ending, about the man who had it all and had blown it. That knowledge made his Othello very good. It came from somewhere.

Olivier's performance, on the other hand, could be best summed up as a little bit of Paul Robeson as seen through the eyes of a BNP member: deep 'Ol' Man River voice', lips, eyes, nappy hair.

Yet Kenneth Tynan had described Welles – the better performance – as 'Citizen Coon'. Really shocking that he had got away with it in

246

the sixties. No wonder Enoch Powell had made his 'Rivers Of Blood' speech. That and Old Larry, old 'Fire Over England' Olivier – 'Once more unto the breach, dear friends, once more...' strutting and fretting his hour and more on the stage done up like the brother of Mammy, in Gone with The Wind.

To him, Olivier had played a better Othello in *The Entertainer* when he sang the gospel song on that bare stage. That moment was worth every single line in the film.

Then he laughed so loud that everyone in the lobby looked his way. That was what he wanted. She liked that.

"Now", he said in his big voice slightly slurred by drink, "it is politically incorrect for anyone other than a black man to play the part, and since the brothers don't have enough chances to play leading roles as it is, far be it from me to take work away, but let's get past the employment issues and today's tastes for discussion's sake and look at the real deal: Othello isn't real, it's a role, a part, a construct, a cathedral of words, a treasure chest of cadences, abstract, cold, on the page. Now a white man in black face, not playing black just being himself, would demonstrate the beauty of the words, the whole edifice and you'd be more engaged. Desdemona played by a man – because that's who would have played it in the first place – or a sister in a blonde wig – an obvious wig. Like Brecht says. Wake up to what's being done to you and see how awesome the real play is. Forget making it 'real', 'authentic'. It's a trip inside Shakespeare's mind. Though I'd get shot down by the brothers and sisters for saying this."

"One other result of political correctness," he said, slurping his drink down, "is that Iago has become the star part. What if Othello is white and Iago black?" He laughed again. "Everybody in Shakespeare is Shakespeare anyway. Or nobody. The English" he said, waving his arm across the lobby, "think that Shakespeare sprang from them." That was when he laughed the loudest.

Janet leaned forward, looking him in the eye in a way that she had not looked at anyone for years. She asked him who Shakespeare belonged to if not we English?

247

"'We English?'" He smiled and she smiled back.

He asked her what she wanted to drink and without thinking she told him a tequila sunrise. He smiled again and asked the waiter for two to be placed in front of her.

She drank the first one quickly, cringing at the bitter aftertaste.

The drink made her head spin instantly.

She heard Bradley Preston say Anna Taylor's name.

He said that he was going on her show and he needed fortification.

Janet sipped the second drink, watching it disappear over the rim of the glass as she held it to her lips.

As soon as she put it down she told the gathering that she was a friend of Anna Taylor's.

She told them how they would meet for tea at the weekends, and, taking one of Lucas's new enthusiasms, she said that they discussed 'branes', the membranes that hold universes.

Janet finished her drink in silence. There was jealousy in the air. She liked that.

It was just her and Bradley now.

The two drinks coursed through her head. They felt good.

She asked Bradley Preston if it were possible for her, in this day and age, to give her son – her black son – what he needed to keep him free, without the full stops.

Bradley Preston smiled.

He told her that he did not know what 'full stop' meant.

Unable to sleep, Janet rose and made herself a cup of tea with the electric teapot on the desk. She watched the daylight spill over the windowsill as she drank the tea.

The sound of a trolley in the hallway loosened her from her grip on the tea cup, and without thinking, she dressed and took the lift down to the lobby.

Bradley Preston was sitting alone drinking and reading the papers.

He had the look of a man who had not had much sleep.

He waved to her to join him, then motioned to a waiter to come over.

Bradley Preston described the eggs he wanted and the cold, fresh mineral water and the bacon, almost burnt – American style.

The waiter returned too quickly with the eggs.

Bradley Preston sent them back without inspecting them.

His big, gregarious face had grown hard. The lack of sleep and the small stubble on his face cast a pall over his features. She could see vestiges of sadness she had not seen before. It had to be partly down to the early morning light.

The eggs returned, and not looking at them, this time, he declared them perfect.

As he noisily ate, he told her about his grandmother who had raised him. Her eggs were the best in town, he said. She went on to open a restaurant just to sell her egg dishes. He served there. It was more of a diner than a respectable place to eat.

It was the mid-sixties then and white people drove past at night with shotguns and attack dogs. He had learned at an early age to load a gun, a good American thing to do.

His grandmother had kept a gun in her cash drawer, no larger than the palm of her hand and fully loaded. He had seen her shoot a man once, the impact of the bullet had spun him around like a top.

He had known her by one name all his life, but at her funeral he had discovered that she was called something else. It was explained to him that people of her generation never told anyone their real name. This kept down the possibility of maledictions and the wrong deity knowing who they were.

He had grown up in a house full of women.

Because of that, he knew who women were, what they liked, what they needed to do.

Once his grandmother had cooked a chicken, put it in a bag and led him to the nearest street. She meticulously found the cross point of the street and instructed him to place the bag of chicken there. When he asked why she told him it was to help him with his music.

Janet watched him lean forward. He whispered the word 'devil' and said that the Trickster with the crooked leg and the top hat came to the crossroads – the devil is what the white man had turned him into – the Trickster took the offering and in return, gave the gift of music.

She laughed out of shock and embarrassment at what he said. She changed the subject to her children. She said without thinking that her husband expected their daughter to be the first black woman Prime Minister. Ayesha, her daughter, she said, was neat and a perfectionist. Three schools wanted her. She had insisted on having white baby dolls and giving them Ghanaian names.

Bradley Preston slowly ate his eggs and said that he thought that made sense. He liked her daughter. He liked her incongruity. Did Janet have a husband who thought precision was the most important thing?

He ordered more coffee and complained about the eggs. He told her that he had spent the night talking about Dante and then challenged her to give him the English for the following from Dante: Lasciate ogne speranza, voi ch'intrate.

Janet smiled. This was one of her father's favourites. They were both quiet for a moment. The voices of their fellow Americans filled the air.

"My father told me that no one knows the exact translation of that line", she said.

"But you do", he laughed. "You do."

She blushed.

He changed the subject.

He was due to give his lecture the day after tomorrow and did not know what to say.

His desk was decorated in index cards, but the words had no meaning.

His niece, he was saying, was a doctoral student at a university in California, a big woman who studied tiny worlds. Her latest project was to learn more about the Big Rip in which the universe's expansion is infinite and ultimately fatal.

Her idea is concerned with something she called a black sea in which the universe humans belong to emerged.

Her idea is that there is a God, but a God who is only a part of our universe, who belongs only to us.

It is possible, she had told him, that this God pulled us out of the black sea.

And there are strings which, according to her, give us more than three dimensions to contemplate, add to this, she had told him once over Thanksgiving dinner, that there is membrane or brane floating in four-dimensional space that we belong to. Weird girl. But he liked her.

His niece, he said, had been a girl who had lost her father and her brother to gang violence and according to the ways of his family, he had taken on the obligation of bringing her up.

There had always been the possibility that she would walk away from her studies. She suffered from depression and from time to time felt it necessary to leave human beings to find solace in her quantum world or in her four dimensions.

He had taken what he had understood from her and applied it to his theories about the Diaspora. "What if" he had said "they – our ancestors – had been able, through the sheer force of the brutality meted out to them, to enter other dimensions either through trance or music, the spiritual, or sex?"

Janet thought: 'Has Lucas been saying the same thing? Is that what he's been trying to tell me? Is that the reason he wants to study this, why he has to go away? Is my allowing him to go away the way in which he can break through? To answer this question?'

Bradley Preston suggested that they go sit in the garden to catch the last of the summer and the rising sun.

On the way there Janet told him about Lucas.

Janet told Bradley Preston that her son was like his niece, they were so full of internal conversation and both believed that mathematics

251

was ultimately about connections, symmetries. Bradley told her that his niece thought the job of mathematics was to find love, to find beauty.

One of the hotel guests, an elderly man impeccably dressed in a suit with a cravat, sat feeding the pigeons. The garden was a tiny oasis that she did not want to leave. She said to him that on the other side of the wall was London, as devouring as her mother had said, as Earlene had said, in so many words, in her letter to Milton Bookman.

Janet could say the name now. She could remember the name of the American girl who had changed her life. It had come out as she sat with Bradley Preston.

Sitting with him, she could see herself on the day after her father had died. She had found another letter amongst his things. It was in a childish scrawl on lined paper and signed 'Earlene'.

In the letter, Earlene had written that she could not take Milton Bookman away from his family. She had come a long way to find the man she had wanted and needed. She knew now that he existed and that was enough for her. She had written that she was leaving behind the thing that had meant the most to her: a small statue of a Black Virgin. She had taken it without permission, but she had felt that she needed the statue to accompany her on her journey. Now her journey was over. Everything she had brought with her from the States she was either leaving with him or leaving behind, on a park bench, anywhere where her things could be found, could be used.

And then, on that other scrap, there had been the poem, a little poem she had said, about being a child, written by a little girl she used to take care of and who she loved more than anything in the world.

She was working now for people who needed her.

Happy that she had found him. Happy that she had left him to live the life he had been destined to live.

But there would not be one day, one moment of her life when she would not think of their brief two days together. And they would be the last things that she would remember before she died.

For years Janet had blocked out those letters, that name. She had hidden them in a place she could not reach.

She had allowed her mother, and eventually herself, to carry on believing that her father had been in love with another woman. It was a good story and made things easier because it was explainable. Adultery, whether of the body, mind or both would give her mother a focus, a mission. Her mother could aim her hatred at a woman who it was possible to run into everyday. That way there would be an order, a straight line leading away from the chaos her father had inflicted on his wife and daughter, turning an unmanageable, impossible situation into something manageable, with a plot that could be understood.

But nothing in life was in a straight line.

Was it all that banal, that true?

'…but this is wondrous strange.', Milton Bookman would have said in response to what she was now admitting to herself. He would have quoted Hamlet, anything classical as a means to distance himself from her emotion.

"Do you know Caravaggio's portrait called Medusa with the shocked screaming face, and the blood dripping from the base of the head?" she asked Bradley Preston.

He laughed and asked her if she knew any calmer paintings. There was one at Tate Britain called The Schutz Family and their Friends on a Terrace, a picture of an 18th century family, serene and confident. But there was something in the eyes of the young woman on the terrace. He also felt the same way about the Rossetti painting, The Beloved. He liked the black child in the centre of it. Rossetti had painted the image several times, completely fascinated by it.

He came to London every other year, he said, rented a flat and made sure that he saw paintings. He was going to see the painting. She should join him.

Janet turned to him. He had heard everything that she had not said.

"Just remembering something. Last time I taught here – ten years ago, but that's not that long ago in the scheme of things – I made the almost fatal mistake of calling a room full of black kids English. I thought that being born in England made them English, but oh no. 'I'm not English, sir'. So I asked, 'Well, what are you? Are you British?' A reluctant yes. I said: 'Caribbean?' And that got the biggest negative response. Then one of the gangbangers did a mime of a Caribbean man walkin' slow, talk'n like this and I said: 'Yo, little brother, you talkin' about your father and your grandfather.' And he looked at me and said 'Yeah, that's right.'"

When Janet finally got to sleep that night, she had a dream.

In it, she made a list of the books that her father had left behind.

She wrote the list over and over in order to make sure that she had got it right.

She re-stacked the storage area where his things were kept, dusted it down, placed boxes in new, more accessible places.

She unpacked his clothing and re-packed it, carefully putting things away according to colour and pattern.

She patiently ironed his Sunday shirts, folding them carefully.

She searched every crevice of the storage space, looking for everything that belonged to Milton Bookman.

But it was futile.

The boxes and crates, the bags and baskets did not stay where she wanted them to.

They moved, and when they stopped their minuscule movements, the room had been re-configured and in a prominent place, resting on the large box that held his key books, was the rain-soaked letter found in her father's hand.

The letter with one word visible: child.

But the morning came too soon, and she had to shower, dress, eat quickly and race to the river again, to meet Bradley.

Why had she accepted Bradley Preston's invitation to meet at the Tate?

Still trying to answer the question for herself, Janet stood on the steps waiting for Bradley to finish his conversation with two Americans he had bumped into near Rossetti's The Beloved.

Bradley and his fellow Americans had spotted one another immediately, first of all by the amount of space they had taken up both literally and figuratively as well as in their practically identical array of sweeping hand gestures, clearly a national trait, as were their big voices, loud even in whisper. Janet was fascinated by the way their American eyes had of devouring the painting, not half-looking at it the way some middle-class regular from the Home Counties might, not too directly, terrified at the possibility of making eye contact with a stranger and the danger that it might involve – conversing with an unknown.

This was the complete opposite of the American trio with their American gaze – expansive, proprietary, challenging, greedy and in a curious way, innocent, as were they, the three of them.

They were new friends, the entire encounter beginning when one of the women had asked directions and instantly a connection had been made, easy, natural, familiar, all three of them bonding in the twinkling of an eye. The silver haired, pink-cheeked ladies in their sturdy walking shoes, jeans and pressed blouses, big-hipped and solid-footed were enchanted by the tall, erudite black man. They were easy with him in a foreign place, instant friends.

Bradley's height balanced out the width of the two women, all three now forged into a national unit, she unsettled by their instant solidarity. Janet watched them, talking together like old friends, laughing, exchanging points of view, the women having obsessively researched everything about Rossetti, including his opening of his wife's coffin to retrieve old love letters. But above all, the three of them loved the poet's inner turmoil, so un-American the women chirped.

Amazing, Janet thought, that the painting had brought them together, now swapping anecdotes like old gossip about some mutual acquaintance.

One of them, the one who kept clutching at Bradley's sleeve to get his attention, pointed out that she found it interesting that Rossetti had been a kind of piggy -in-the-middle between the painter Whistler who had supported the Southern States during the American Civil War and Rossetti's own brother, an abolitionist who had deplored Whistler's stance. Without skipping a beat, Bradley added to the conversation a little anecdote about John Ruskin's remark that the only reason a black boy should exist was to be background in a Renaissance painting. This bit of information one of the women quickly took down in a small notebook.

The way Milton Bookman had always noted anything new that he had learned.

While she was doing this, her friend pointed out that Bradley's information vindicated their refusal to read Ruskin, now on their list along with Thomas Carlyle after they had discovered that he had written something entitled *The Nigger Question*. Their refusal to have anything to do with the work of Carlyle and Ruskin, the note-book wielding one said, yet another bond, she trilled, that forged the three of them together along with their obvious love of London and all things English.

If he had been with them and had observed what she had observed, Lucas would have stated that his Chaos Questions – 'strange attractors', 'initial conditions' – were the real state of being that had made it possible for the three strangers to meet in front of a painting at the Tate in London, thousands of miles from home, all three with the same point of view about the era in which the painting had been done.

Lucas would have set up a model of the three Americans, revealing their closeness in age, education, their common language and nationality, their shared view of England and London as places of culture. On the surface, Lucas would have said, the black man and two elderly white ladies would have been thought to be miles apart. But they had had a bond, an invisible one, which had brought them together at a particular moment in time and it was those 'strange attractors', those 'initial conditions' that were his obsessions.

Nothing was really an accident.

Watching the three Americans together added to her growing understanding of what had happened to her since yesterday and what was still happening. Janet was slowly beginning to understand.

As Lucas' world view assembled itself in her mind in a moment that had flashed like lightening, the new friends were busy with one another, their jumble of words spilling out with the excitement of three five year-olds sharing their day out at the zoo, breathless, excited, laughing together as they exchanged email addresses with the speed of lovers who had only had an hour together. The louder of the two women insisted that they all meet in Taos, New Mexico in the near future, then head out for the desert together and get lost in the blinding white of it, perhaps go to see Georgia O'Keefe's work since they never tired of the big, white vaginal lilies. O'Keefe was bigger in spirit, the meeker of the two said, than the entire British Isles. American art was bigger, better anyway.

Bradley laughed loudly and Janet laughed too at the thought of a vagina bigger than John O'Groats. They all laughed so loudly, so wickedly, yet for such different reasons that they took themselves out to breathe in the afternoon air with its definite chill, a hint of October in the air, and further decay.

Janet, standing at the top of the museum steps, surveyed the three Americans until the stairs of the museum became covered in students. She distracted herself by counting them, her head spinning with the growing awareness of just how her life had unfolded: how her father's death had set her off on her journey across the water by setting up in her an unquenchable restlessness; how Tomas had lured her across, spurred her on; her mother's journey across the river and back home had at once freed her and set her an obligation: to go forward in her life with the same resolve Gloria-Loretta had shown; and that Bradley Preston had come to take her to another place within herself and without. Even that all of this had come to her on the steps of an institution built on the blood, sweat and tears of her people.

Later on, after they had returned indoors, Janet Bookman Baker studied Bradley Preston. She studied the length and breadth of him.

She imagined how he would look in bed. Beneath her. She imagined his skin against white sheets, her legs astride him, his face changed, filled with the same vulnerability she had seen in that fleeting moment while he examined the Rossetti, The Beloved. It was as if he lived there, too.

That look was there again as he listened to his new friends discussing how the painter had lost himself in the face of the black child at the centre of the Pre-Raphaelite masterpiece, how Rossetti had re-painted the portrait years later, striving to get right the black child who looked out of its frame with a wisdom beyond his years.

Along with her growing desire for Bradley, Janet had another thought: she wanted Lucas to be like this American, a man whose parents – or loved ones, whoever had been responsible for raising him – had so clearly given him the run of his life, who had shielded him and not betrayed him the way she was betraying her own son by giving him over to his father, sacrificing his humanity to her husband's masculinity.

Back standing on the steps of the museum, coatless, oblivious to the autumnal breeze of Pimlico, Janet told herself another truth that she had been unable to face.

Her concern for Lucas had less to do with him and more to do with her own need to make atonement to black men through her only son. She had sacrificed herself and Lucas to make up for what her own mother had done: the gradual whittling away of Milton Bookman in her quest for perfection.

But Gloria-Loretta's drive for order was an attempt to mask and ultimately stifle what had been wild and visceral in her.

Gloria-Loretta had grown up rough, a throw-away child who had not, in spite of her airs and graces, known her parents. She was not 'hand-raised', as the old people from the Island referred to their properly brought up children.

The woman she had called her mother and Janet had called grandmother was not related by blood to either of them. No one would tell Gloria-Loretta who her parents were, and once, when an itinerant preacher from Jamaica had walked down Morant Bay Road one Sunday preaching that all black people were maroons, escapees to a place of safety, if not in fact, certainly inside and that this constant flight had created a malaise that manifested itself in many ways, Gloria-Loretta had run out of the house and chased the man of God off the road.

"Who are we?" was his constant refrain.

He had said that black comes in every hue under the sun and as truly black skin moved towards extinction – just as white skin was moving that way – it was time to reflect on the consequences and the way forward that the reality of that dying skin colour presented in a white world.

He had returned one Sunday, right to their door, to tell Gloria-Loretta, in a gentle voice, that she was too conventional a mother and had found herself trapped inside a tale not of her own making while at the same time resenting but nevertheless bound up in what white people thought, what white people did, how white people saw the world. She had been a woman obsessed with proving to them that she was better than their estimation. This dilemma had imprisoned Gloria –Loretta and since she was the woman of the house and therefore its light, her husband and her daughter were imprisoned too.

The proof of this had been the bitter argument on an evening soon after Janet's tenth birthday, when Gloria-Loretta had threatened to return to The Island: and Milton Bookman had replied casually, as if talking to someone in the middle distance, that The Island had been built upon genocide, that sixty percent of all those enslaved out of Africa had been taken there to ensure King Sugar's reign, to ensure Great Britain's supremacy. Didn't she know, he demanded, that the Royal Navy had been deployed not to free the enslaved, but to keep the French away from their lucrative areas, the whole Abolition thing in 1807 had been about the supremacy of the Royal Navy on the high seas, not the enslaved, their ancestors who spent their lives being lorded over – and much worse – by the convicts and debtors from the Old Country who had been placed above them?

Her mother had been shocked by her husband's small outburst, but Milton Bookman had carried on, telling them both that The Island, its imported slaves and its domestic ones, were routinely exploited by tinpot seigneurs in white hats while their ladies were protected from the blistering sun by the bodies of black children. He had asked her how she could dream of a land whose people had been forced to suffer the dregs of the earth, English and Scots and Welsh and Irish people who had come to The Island with nothing, were nothing. They had been people with common vowels, used to trading in dank rooms filled with chimney smoke back in the Old Country. They were a people who had exchanged all that for the fresh air of a stolen land. They had come for the warm breezes of an alien sea, come to uplift their own circumstances through the suffering of others, feeding off acre upon acre of human beings.

And now this – Janet laughed to herself on the stairs of the Tate. The irony of them all meeting there, all of them the descendants of chattels to King Sugar – Bradley Preston, the American tourists, Lucas back home in Morant Bay Road, and herself. They were linked because of the drug that had created fortresses and fortunes, that had put the white in the Union Jack, in the Tricolour, the Stars and Stripes. That had whited the sepulchres of those who had told themselves, Bible in hand, that they had gone to The Island where Gloria-Loretta now lived for noble purposes.

These citizens of the British Islands had left behind a people struggling to find a human space in the legacy left them by their Old Country ancestor-rapists.

It suddenly all came rushing in to Janet: the woman in the daguerreotype; and those nineteenth century plantation photos she had seen once of old black men with the bodies of young men or had it been young men with the faces of old men, men distorted in their natural processes, all of them treated like little boys whose only purpose in life had been to keep the master's fire alight.

They had come from a people partially in the New World, partially in the Old, for them, time stopping, then starting again anew in a strange land.

The fact was that The Island was always in her mind, like it had been in her father's mind.

There had been a photo he had never talked about but that he had kept and referred to as one of his artefacts.

It had been part of a group of photos taken in the Thirties of people he never spoke about, but who resembled him. They were posing in tropical whites beside a gleaming Bugatti, sunlight projecting violently off its chromium. A black woman in a white headscarf and white dress stood near it squinting in the sun, a small and shrivelled woman standing beside someone who could only be the man of the family, his arm draped around her, the woman's face similar to the face of the child in the Rossetti; to Bradley's; to Lucas', and Tomas. To her own.

Her father on the day of the big argument had pointed to the series of photos and had said to Gloria-Loretta that it was better to be in London where the bitter truth was evident than back on The Island. Then he had ended his discourse with the dreaded word 'Africa', shouted at her horrified mother. He shouted that their true home was in Africa, but that Africa was gone and they were left to hold on to what had been and through that become new.

What, Janet asked herself, lost again in her own thoughts, lost again in the past, had Bradley been saying about Africa?

He had been saying that the lecture he intended to give at the Conference would not be romantic, not be about kings and queens, but the Africa alive in the favelas, alive in the townships, in the banlieues and the ghettos – kings and queens being the opposite of what he would talk about. There had been no romantic land of bliss and peace, no Africa in excelsis, that place, Janet thought as she listened to him, that Sam wanted Lucas to know.

Standing there, Janet Bookman Baker knew that Bradley Preston would be an aid in her liberation and through her, the liberation of her son.

That new-found liberation led her to the address she had carried with her day and night.

She looked, for a long time, at the building across the street.

The two windows of the flat were narrow and small.

Janet Bookman Baker decided that the building had been a brothel in its heyday, a place where women, ladies of pleasure, were listed in several dedicated ledgers as if they were bloodstock or African slaves, and where they awaited the sons of the nobility.

She stood outside, imagining what it must have been like in that building 200 years ago.

Men, white-breeched and top-hatted, would rush up the steps with all the headlong alacrity of the blood-thirsty hunters they had been brought up to be. They would be still high from killing, the smell of animal blood on their breeches, bathed in the scent of their dogs.

They would impatiently allow themselves to be led through small rooms shimmering in candlelight.

Tallow and other substances would be sticking to the creaking wood floors, floors giving way under the footsteps of gentlemen, laughing gentlemen, breathless with laughter and privilege, ruddy-faced from beef, politics and port.

The themes of the evening would be known in every room, but a purposeful hunter would have had no time to stop. His destination would have been his special room, rumoured to have served as a hiding place for Jesuits during Elizabeth's time.

The hunter would pause briefly to contemplate some man of the cloth who would once have been shunted away in the hunter's very room, muttering his breviary in terror in the same place where the hunter would be paying soon for his 'special assistance'.

His special assistance consisted of taking instruction in the proper use of his chamber pot.

A girl – his girl, the one branded like a sheep by her angry father, the mark on her upper arm considered by the hunter not to be a disfigurement but wildly exciting, so very different from his milk and honey wife back in the country – awaited him.

His station in life had condemned him to a well-bred girl, a weaver and fine embroiderer, a breeder of children, breast milk her only fragrance. But breast milk did not describe the smell of the girl waiting for him whose careless washing and liberal sprinkling of eau de cologne could not disguise the odours of the other men who visited her.

She was his girl, no doubt an escapee from the country, her childhood left on a dusty road hard for London, her country bonnet and her country sash altered and re-arranged in the metropolitan fashion the closer she came to The Smoke.

Janet could see this girl waiting for a man whose very estate her family could have resided upon, an estate they would have worked on all their lives, her inheritance would have been nothing more than callused hands, a mind numbed by work, limited horizons.

She would have told them she was going away to service in London.

The family of this girl from the 18th century, Janet knew, would have been struck dumb by the reality of their daughter's life in the city; but they would have been resigned to her decision to go to leave them to enter that repository of disease and poverty, despair, and godlessness, armed only with her fresh country face, her lack of airs and graces, and her smell of earth and fresh air.

All this would have been inhaled by the nobleman with all the delicacy of a stud facing a squatting mare, his teeth bare, his head thrown back, mounting the rural lass without a word, his breath full of wine and meat, his neck and hands sweaty from his race to the house.

Everything taking place in a house like that – Janet had read Richardson and Fielding as part of her English degree – would have been based on a wager set by the man's friends, usually at their club. They would have arrived at the house drunk, and laughing and free by virtue of their birth. Their birth the opposite of the country lass supine beneath the gentleman, no one thinking it odd that he preferred sex with a girl barely out of childhood, after all, he had paid for it.

He would have taught the girl the words he liked to hear during sex and she would have repeated them parrot-like ,words his milk and honey wife back home in the country would never have whispered in his ear. These words would have been coupled with the vocabulary the girl would have picked up from the other gentlemen

But, Janet thought, even in the throes of passion the man would have been as cold as ice. He would have played a double game with her which would have included correction from a whip kept conveniently in the corner of her room, a white-handled instrument and well-used and wiped clean after each use by a black man. The black man would have wiped clean the specks of blood from the last time the hunter had visited.

Janet can see the whip, the instrument of ritual, cleaned by the man from Guinea. He would have been a source of ridicule for the country whore who had no one else to ridicule. The whites of the black man's eyes would have been hooded like the fires that had to be covered before night fell.

He would have been a man of beautiful teeth. They would have been his pride and joy. A front one would have been missing, the result of the capricious sadism of one of the punters, after he had discovered this evidence of the black man's personal vanity. Perhaps he would have caught the black man unawares, leaving his mouth awash with blood.

But Janet knew that no matter what, his eyes would have remained hooded, hidden from his masters.

In time, the country girl, used up, would have found her way back to her village. Her voice would have been corrupted by inauthentic London tones.

In her village, she would have spoken of the black man's hair. She would have made them laugh, made them gasp in wonder, just as she had done, when she had first seen him.

To her, the black man's hair was like the wool of sheep, a sentiment she would have found so profound that she would have paused portentously after saying it, to allow her brilliant insight to hang in the air.

Yet, Janet thinks, the country girl would have thought of the black man's hair often, particularly at the times when she lay beneath the rough man of good family, 'un-virgined' once again, enduring their charade, watching the black man's head as he bent down to take the chamber pot, watching him raise his head, turn his eyes away from the scene, his head so exquisitely shaped, delicate and small and that hair of his, so thick and strange. The country girl in Janet's mind, thinking of the black man while beneath her master, wondering, as she pretends to be pleasured, whether it would hurt to run her hands through the black man's hair, to press her face against it, to inhale the scent of his hair, so full of the smell of spices and of the sea, the wide ocean, his Via Dolorosa.

No mystery, she would have told the villagers, that the song Baa-Baa Black Sheep had been created.

Yet the country lass would have known nothing of the wide ocean that had brought him in chains to end his days alone, silent, emptying chamber pots, sweeping floors, bringing water and fresh linen, watching what he could not participate in as if he had no eyes, no feelings, no humanity.

She would have known nothing of his working with the gentlemen who came to the house to pull heavy ropes, like church bell ringers, for exercise in the room below and who asked especially for him. He would be there, the bell-ringer without bells, assisting them until his own muscles bulged beneath the tight waist coat he was obliged to wear in the style of a Turk in a seraglio. That would have been his part in the play that unfolded each night in the house.

Janet gave a name to the lone black man that she imagined living in what was now Tomas Saddler's apartment building. She called him Solomon.

Solomon was the name of the picture that Milton Bookman had kept on his desk, a postcard of an 18th century sketch of an enslaved man dressed like a eunuch, his arms crossed, his eyes dead.

Solomon could have lived and died where Tomas Saddler would be sitting now, on the edge of his bed, his hands folded on his lap.

Waiting for her.

Tomas, upstairs behind the window, hidden away with his souvenirs of war, another black man who had refused to continue his ride as one of the Four Horsemen of the Apocalypse.

Tomas had left the Apocalypse altogether as his stepfather had done. To cross the threshold of her life.

Standing there, looking up into his window, she had cast aside the vow that her life was also Sam's life.

Standing there, Janet Bookman Baker knew that she had left that vow on the other side of the river, hidden in the mute corridors of her marriage, buried in the stubborn silence of their communication, the children their only link, the only thing that she and Sam still had in common.

It had been she who had wanted a family. She had been the one who had been determined to make a family life, and fashion it into something completely different from her own childhood. She would use the family life she had created to foster the life of the mind that her father had craved and which could have erased the burden of life in a world that could not, would not, see him.

This life of the mind, this freedom could have been encoded in his grandchildren's genes, allowing them to discover themselves in that space between action and reaction, the space where they could create themselves, the space she had been determined to enlarge for them by her own hard work, her own stability, her Role-Modelness. Her children would have the space that Solomon did not have, nor Sam, nor Tomas. Nor her.

Looking at Tomas' window, Janet knew that all of her life had been a charade, an act, a piece of theatre in which she could foster an illusion behind which the real Janet Bookman Baker lived.

But that was over now.

With one act, the simple climbing of a set of steps, her old life would disappear, destroyed by her like some lust-enveloped adolescent, unaware of what she was undertaking.

She was walking into chaos.

Embracing it.

As Janet walked up to the front steps, a little woman, her dark hair piled atop her head, had come out of the building carrying a mop and pail. She kneeled wearily on the bottom stair, scrubbing the pavement leading up to the steps.

She was oblivious to the people walking over what she was trying to clean, muttering to herself as she scrubbed, occasionally glancing up at the sky as if in search of rain to assist her. She was square-shaped and sturdy, her haunches strangely youthful. The fat on the upper part of her arms moved in rhythm.

Janet would have stayed and watched her.

But suddenly, Tomas opened his window.

Janet saw him.

He did not see her. A beam of sunlight blotted out his face.

Just as quickly he was gone, leaving behind the gentle stirring of a curtain in the breeze, a curtain whose lacy femininity was worthy of Gloria-Loretta herself.

Undoubtedly the work of Tomas' mother, the fruit of one of her visits. Janet laughed to herself. His mother was the sort of woman who would have carefully sifted through the things her late husband had left behind. Janet could recall Tomas Saddler senior. She had seen him when she was a child. He was a man with a melancholy face and grey hair. He had been in the garden, his big belly spilling over the belt that held up his baggy trousers, a check shirt buttoned up to the neck, his small hands tending to the plants and flowers.

He had seemed lost in himself, alone.

He had a sudden spasm in his left hand from time to time, and when that happened, he would wipe his thick brows, still golden with the blond colouring of his youth, with his right hand.

She would study his face in secret from time to time. His was a face full of deep silences. Janet had been confident at her young age that she knew this old man, knew a very deep truth about him. She knew that if they could have spoken, he would have met her at her own level without condescension.

By watching him, Janet had created an act of silent defiance of her mother's disapproval of a family she considered to be in bad taste and out of place. Gloria-Loretta could not allow that much dissonance so close to her.

With every word of condemnation toward the Saddler family that her mother hurled, Janet had secretly come to love them all the more.

Standing beneath the window of one of the dreaded Saddlers like a Juliet in reverse about to call up to the balcony, she smiled to herself to think of how her mother would have reacted if she had known what was destined one day to happen and was happening now:

Janet climbing the stairs, violating with her own body that boundary Gloria-Loretta had so assiduously striven to set up, to cultivate, and to maintain.

And she thought again of what Baudelaire had written, shown to her by her father and which was her first excursion into French:... *Tout enfant, j'ai senti dans mon coeur deux sentiments contradictoires: l'horreur de la vie et l'exstase de la vie.*

She was about to enter that realm of her father who had found there, too, a meaning with no name.

❧

No name, she thought, as she opened her eyes in the morning.

And it made Janet Bookman Baker laugh to think that including everything else she had discovered about him, Tomas Saddler might also be a thief.

With her hair unkempt, her eyes closed, she basked in him.

She watched him as she sat wrapped in his freshly laundered dressing gown, the name of the hotel that had once owned it was emblazoned across its left pocket.

The dressing gown, with its sterile neatness, looked out of place in these surroundings.

It was an item too institutional for his simple room, monkish in its atmosphere in spite of being full of things that had been clearly scavenged from rubbish tips or had previously been the cast-offs from some posh neighbourhood.

Each item's individuality, its quirkiness, threw the white robe, terry-cloth with a belt of the same fabric, into pedestrian relief. The robe could be an indication of Tomas' tendency towards the mass-produced, the anodyne, the anonymous, in contrast to the desk which stood in the far corner of the room.

The desk was heavy, in dark wood and of Victorian design, with a scratched ship's anchor carved on the right side of it. A mermaid with what looked to her like negroid features comprised the straight part of the anchor.

She thought of Tomas – the black man in a white bathrobe.

There he was in a white hotel room, smothered in white sheets turned down at night by a girl from Africa moonlighting from her day job in the basement of a restaurant.

The girl from Africa would be alarmed to find a black man curled up in the midst of the pillows, her pillows, violating her fantasies of toiling in a wicked world with her righteous heart. And then coming to her hotel to find Tomas Saddler in bed trying not to meet the black maid's eyes as she fluffed the pillows, puffing her cheeks in disapproval of him in her domain.

And Tomas would be much too embarrassed to appease her by calling her 'sister'.

He would try to cover up this deficiency by leaving her a tip on a small china saucer. This is what would have been expected of him.

This was his and the maid's relationship in the white room.

And in his rage for the two of them, before he had left the hotel, Janet decided, there had been nothing left to do but steal the bathrobe.

It was easy to imagine it.

It was easy to put herself in his place.

Janet could see herself escaping to some posh West End hotel, a temporary refuge from her children, her husband, her students, her absent mother and her dead father.

She would have chosen an establishment with carved pillars inside and out-a good place to steal a souvenir from – a place full of that air of confident quiet the old rich have.

She would be comfortable in such an environment.

Her hotel would be like a dowager greatly beloved over the ages.

Before and after her time with him, Janet had dreamt so much. She had gone somewhere in her head. Abena Assantewa had called – in one of her books – what had happened to Janet, what was happening to her 'trance, abstraction, that state of being through which the transported African had 'ripped the veil' and entered into a dialogue with the great African continuum. This dialogue had guaranteed their survival. It was always present, just below the surface, ready to be used.'

'It existed', she had written, 'in the long, keening arc of gospel; in the be-bop moment of jazz; the flow of rap; in movement, in speech, in posture, clothing, the eyes. It was there, ever-present, waiting to be tapped.'

And, Janet thought, the crossing of the river had released this birthright within her. She had joined those who had taken the old things to the New World and had forged another thing, too.

The 'old folks', Abena Assantewa had written in her book, 'used to say at wakes and funerals that so and so 'passed on.' Because that is what we did. We passed on, passed over. We crossed the river. And we never died.'

But what could Janet do with this new-found gift? What would it do with her?

For over an hour now she had been watching the light grow stronger, creeping across the uneven floorboards of Tomas' apartment, floorboards painted as white as a New England house by the ocean. Her father had said once that he wanted to build a house that faced the Atlantic where the white-caps were the strongest.

Janet watched the light in Tomas' room, strong but tentative, spill onto the floor, gradually encircling his bed, making shadows on the ceiling with which she weaved patterns above him.

The patterns captured the shape of her father's long back.

Her father.

She sat contemplating Tomas Saddler, how the sweat on his upper arm glistened, the way a scar just below his left breast would soon turn into a keloid, raised and black. The unexpected femininity of his legs surprised her. But his hands at rest were menacing. They were much gentler in motion. She had seen his hands transformed in his mother's garden. And when they had touched her.

She wondered what she would say to Sam if he had rung the hotel and couldn't find her. She had not checked her phone or her text messages.

It was too late now.

Turning, she noticed a piece of paper on the desk, crumpled, then straightened out again, covered in Tomas's handwriting.

Dulce et decorum est pro patria mori:
Mors et fugacem persequitur virum,
Nec parcit inbellis iuventae
Poplitibus timidove tergo.

The paper lay beside a copy of Wilfred Owen's poem, *Dulce et Decorum Est*. She knew the poem. It had been one of Milton Bookman's favourites.

Its last line began with the words, "The old Lie"…then went on to quote just the beginning of Horace's ode. These were the lines that Tomas had copied and which he had placed beside Owen's mockery of those who only extolled that first line, and not the rest of the old lie that Owen's poem was exposing. 'Horace's 'dulce', if read in its entirety,' Tomas had written, 'was not about the sweetness of dying for one's country, but the reality of death no matter what the cause. Death comes, the poet is saying, with a mundane inevitability, sometimes

271

nobly, beautifully, or, as the rest of the poem states, even when a man is on his knees or his backside.'

Tomas loved both poems for exposing the lie of death in war as having a special glory.

Milton Bookman had often pointed out to her that what people needed was the whole poem, not part of it.

The whole poem.

Only a few hours before, they had come together in his scruffy bed. He had been full of what she would name it when she recalled it in later years: a jazz musician's tenderness. He had carved that tenderness through the years, rough-hewn and sublime, rendering it, for their night together, as smooth as silk.

She would never, for the rest of her life, fail to be moved by the thought of him and their night together.

She could clearly see the days ahead, days in which she would be unable to face the reality of the night just passed, days in which she would regret that she had not stayed the morning, the afternoon, the next night with him.

Janet Bookman Baker, the hotel dressing gown falling away, walked over and sat at Tomas's desk. Something had to be said with pen and paper.

Running her hand across the desk's surface, she noticed that it was placed beneath a part of the room where the ceiling gave way to a small alcove. The vantage point enabled her to see, like Lucas' room, the particular accumulation of detail that all added up to the system of Tomas' world.

In the corner was boxing equipment – gloves, a jumping rope, the gear for his head and teeth, some trunks crumpled and flung to the side, a sweatshirt. On his desk a lined writing pad was at the ready. Sharpened pencils rested in an alabaster – coloured can.

She noticed a newspaper cutting of a young soldier, white. His face was like the face of a statue on the tomb of some ancient family, a tomb open only on special days or by chance on twilight walks in the summer in the countryside, its entrance lit by fireflies.

Janet Bookman Baker silently dressed, careful not to wake him. She looked at Tomas Saddler again, the full light of day on his face. He suddenly laughed, the way a baby laughs in his sleep.

'Bradley Preston'. It was suddenly comical. How preposterous some American names were.

He was talking to her over coffee before his lecture began, telling her how she seemed changed this morning at the same time as complaining about the price of everything in London.

She found a seat in the back and settled in. She liked the jokes and light banter he used to relax his students.

At one point he told them that the subconscious was much better at dealing with complexity than the conscious mind. And he wanted them relaxed for what he had to say.

This echoed what Lucas had once said to her about how a mathematician longs for those moments when the mind begins to wander. After a certain amount of time he can return to the problem and see the Beautiful Thing.

Gradually, a kind of hush weaved its way across the room. Janet closed her eyes. Just Bradley's voice, it seemed that she could hear Lucas' voice, like an echo. She could hear him chatter excitedly about his geometrical figures and how more geometrical figures could issue forth from his equations.

What had she been doing all of her life?

What had she done?

Had she perpetuated a state-of-being that had not allowed her to live within her own rhythms and parameters? Had centuries of fear, oppression, hatred, poverty and the brutality waged against her people somehow settled in her and made her complicit in that repression, even in the destruction of her own child?

Bradley Preston pointed to a diagram he had power-pointed of a slave ship, and next to it a price list. This, he said, was literally the bottom line. The enslaved, human beings, were considered nothing more than commodities; the guinea, for instance, had been created directly out of slavery, as was the phenomenon known as Great Britain and also the United States, France, all of the West while at the same time attempting to render an entire people null and void. The two went hand in hand.

Janet began to see how she had colluded in that thing that had begun hundreds of years ago. She was taking away her son's chance of freedom – his human right to be himself – taking it away in exchange for a life of safety, refusing to allow him to move beyond her scope of experience. Just as her mother had. And her father, in his way.

She had protected Lucas in order to save herself from the confusion and possible heartbreak of watching him live a life that she could not understand.

Sam was honest with her, Lucas, and himself with his insistence on Lucas's schooling 'in the community'. And all the time she could not face the question that always raged inside her: what community mattered outside of their son's own world?

The unrelated bits and pieces of her life began to assemble themselves the way the things in Lucas' bedroom made a pattern. She had taken the shadow lives of her mother and father – of her people – and lived them out. She had ignored the real life seething beneath the surface, that which was yet to have a name.

This life had had its own trajectory, its own pattern, just as her ancestors had woven the travail that had seemed useless and meaningless to their captors and oppressors and created a kind of genius which still had not been named.

As Nietzsche had stated, what had not killed her had made her strong, had kept her alive for the moment when she crossed the river and the new life had emerged.

Faster than she was aware, Janet began to mentally write a defence of their son to Sam, mapping out in as legal an argument as she could, the case for their boy's schooling in Wiltshire, away from what could happen to him on the streets around Morant Bay Road, offering in return – if he would accept her proposition – to become more engaged with his chambers' social life, give supper parties, organize charity events, be at his side as a loving, dutiful, quiet wife, his 'role-model wife'.

Anything to set Lucas free.

Tears began to roll down her cheeks.

They had come suddenly and she could not stop them. Her nose began to run, too, but she had no tissues. She was seated in the middle of the row and couldn't leave without causing a commotion.

She could not stop the tears.

They came from a deep place. Janet lowered her head and wiped her face on her sleeve. She was ruining her clothes. But it did not matter.

She laughed to herself. How could she think that she was different from Gloria-Loretta? She too, had attempted to control her children, shape them to her will, but Ayesha's natural stubbornness had saved her. Her daughter was a human being who would always hold on to herself.

Bradley Preston caught her eye just as it occurred to her that it might be better to slip out quietly before the lecture ended, and put a call in to Sam to ask how he and the children were. She needed to escape the hothouse of Professor Preston's talk, but his eyes would not let her, daring her to stay for the rest of what he had to say.

She, alive now to the game he was playing, remained.

With his strong voice, his flourishes, his jokes and asides, he was wooing her in front of 200 unsuspecting witnesses.

She knew that he was laughing at what he saw in her face.

He abruptly changed the subject.

He announced to the lecture hall that he would have liked to have lived from 1860 to the end of the 19th century. He would have liked to have danced with the Empress Eugenie, she dressed in her glorious white gowns by Worth, her pale Spanish skin and jet-black hair, glorious against the concoctions of the English couturier, this would have been, for him, a much more interesting life than living at Osborne with Victoria and her grandchildren.

He was one black man who had no dreams of nobility, of ancient kings and queens parading in stately lines through noble kingdoms. He would have preferred being a rogue, a vagabond, an incendiary, living through the siege of Paris in 1870. This would have been a life much more interesting than picking cotton in Alabama like his great-great grandmother had done.

If he had lived during the Siege, he continued, he would have played piano for the L'Orchestre d'Elmina whose music cleansed the souls of those who traded in the bodies of human beings. It would have been glorious to have witnessed their rituals and exculpations, to have heard especially the great incantation against Louis Napoleon himself that had led to the death, years later, of the Emperor's only child and son at the hands of the Impis during the Zulu Wars.

All of this was said with such breathtaking glee that some in the audience began to shift uneasily in their seats, unsure of where Bradley Preston was heading.

Even though he had a reputation for being iconoclastic – many of them were at the lecture because of this – yet Janet could feel a ripple of agitation grow from row to row like an underhanded Mexican wave.

And there was more.

Race, for him, was a 19th century construct as outdated as eugenics, counting bumps on the head, or howling at the moon.

After all, human beings had more in common than they did not.

In the end, the saga, the idea of race bored him.

Another thing: what point did DNA testing to trace their ancestry back to a particular place in Africa have for African Americans, besides some fairy tale sense of self and keeping up with the Joneses ?

Activity like that could only breed more fantasy, more speculation, more sentimentality. It would be much better for black people if they gave the world a gift for the 21st century: the erasure of race once and for all. And become human beings. Before it was too late.

And so, he said in conclusion, since the title of the conference was 'Othello: The Stranger', his thesis was that Othello was indeed a stranger – to himself.

Othello was his own victim, he said, just as anyone who takes skin colour as anything more than an interesting variation on a theme is their own victim.

This last statement was accompanied by the scraping sound of a chair being pulled away followed by the rapid exit of a tall, young, black man, followed by several white students, and a plump black girl who glowered at Preston as she ploughed her way through rows of people to the door, a manoeuvre that was as menacing as it was extraordinary, her large body moving in a surprisingly delicate and determined way past the rows of seats, careful not to bump into anyone, her eyes never leaving the face of the man who had uttered such things in the presence of white people, a man who clearly was a traitor and perhaps insane. But above all, Janet concluded, watching the girl storm out, she could tell by her expression that she considered Bradley just another misguided and faulty Yank whose books she would never read again, Janet convinced that if the woman had had an American flag to hand, she would have burnt it to a crisp.

As she slammed the door, Bradley Preston's face softened, almost as if he had regretted what he had said, as if he had spoken aloud a deeply private thought, something that he had not quite formulated in his own mind.

This was evidence of a reckless quality that Janet suddenly realized belonged to her, too.

Bradley Preston came towards her amidst the scattered but enthusiastic applause of the few people still in their seats.

He never took his eyes off her face.

And she held his eye.

And he held it the same way later that evening, reducing her again to giggles, the pure pleasure of laughing like a child, something she had not done for a long time.

She laughed at the irony of being in a soul food restaurant which had no black cooks and no black customers; the joy of this place, Bradley Preston explained as they entered Mamma Lou's Hot Soul Kitchen.

This was a place, he said, so implausibly huddled between the grand white villas of Holland Park that he had vowed he would make it his business to eat there every time he was in town. It had an unintentional surrealism, and he loved that. Its parody of African American cuisine for City types, the trendy and mega-rich foreigners fascinated him. The place was unthinkable and indescribable to his friends back in Philly. Its strangeness and audacity drew him to it and he wanted Janet to see it as well.

They would be the only black people in the place, living golliwogs or objets d'art, he said.

Deep in the back of the room – Siberia – they listened politely to the pretty Eastern European waitress apologise profusely about where they had been seated. She offered them two glasses of champagne on the house, and Bradley said that he was grateful that political correctness extended to free drinks.

He asked to see the bottle first before she poured, even when she explained that the drink was their house champagne.

His big face broke out into a mischievous grin after she had gone. Leaning in, he took Janet's hand, twisting it gently so that her wedding ring showed in the candlelight.

Running his index finger across the knuckle of her finger, he encircled it as the ring did. Then just as gently, he placed her hand on the snow-white tablecloth, not once looking at her face. He seemed to her to be deep in thought, not raising his head until the chilled glasses and the unopened bottle arrived. He immediately pointed out to the intimidated waitress that what she was offering was not champagne but a sparkling wine, since the wine came from Spain not France and therefore could not be champagne no matter what her manager had told her to tell her customers. Nevertheless they would have two glasses anyway to toast the end of the conference, and the end of Janet's agoraphobia.

Drinking deeply, grimacing slightly at the sharpness of the wine, and putting the glass down heavily, Bradley Preston began to ask her about her students. Happy to escape into the troubles of Latoya Richardson, Janet created a saga which was part Latoya, part fantasy, elated that she could lie to him. She wanted a tale which was as fantastic as possible.

278

She still did not have her bearings in the new world opening up to her, or with her new self. Instead of her usual hesitancy, Janet allowed the words to come tumbling out.

She held his attention, watching his eyes grow big in astonishment at the antics of an extraordinarily difficult student. She embellished it as much as she could.

She enjoyed herself.

As she spoke, Bradley Preston's recklessness suddenly became apparent to her again through the haze of the sparkling wine: his entire academic career was cover for a man who had known fairly early in life that it was best for him to keep certain elements of himself under control.

In the bad old days, in his country, he would have been lynched, left hanging on some tree in the forest. She had read about this, about how black men, returning from war or work up North, would be thought by certain powers-that-be, to be too above themselves to live. She had read how certain young men and boys would have to find their way to the North because their mouths and demeanours could bring their lives to a rapid end.

She was about to say this to him when they noticed a commotion at the front of the restaurant.

All activity ground to a quick halt as four young black men, one not much older than Lucas, walked up to each table and casually ordered its occupants to give up everything they had. She heard the whimpering of the man seated at the table next to them who had been bragging earlier about the multi-million pound deal he had just made. She heard a rush of water splashing on the floor from between his legs.

The thieves were fast and mocking and efficient. Two of them came to their table. Bradley caught their eye the way he had caught her eye in class. The boys stared at him for what felt like an eternity, then nodded and walked past them.

Bradley, his hand on her arm, led her through the restaurant and out the front door, flagging down the first taxi they saw. They settled back into the seat as the taxi sped off.

It had all taken no more the five minutes.

She asked if they should ring the police. Bradley quietly said not to bother. The police would be there already. London had more security cameras than any city in the world and the boys had already been filmed. They were doomed and would soon be captured. They would stand trial and be sent down. Certain newspapers would see to that. But, he said, for that one moment those boys had exerted a control that they would never be able to exert again in their lives. They were descended, he was convinced, from those who had gone from slave cabin to slave cabin, bullying, threatening, telling the enslaved to get up, and live one more day.

Like old soldiers, there had gradually been no need for people like that, but the flight or fight response remained among our people, he said.

Because of this, he had, he continued, decided in a split second that he would assist them, in his way. His decision, he said, had been followed by a sensation close to joy.

His hand closed over her knee as he spoke while her eyes looked straight ahead, fixed on the back of the driver's head. Janet stared at the man's neatly trimmed silver hair and at the photo of a white-blond child pinned to the back of the window, her face the face of Ayesha's doll.

She held that image in her mind while walking with Bradley through a darkened Soho street.

She held it, when a short while later, she allowed him to partially undress her in a passageway in the glare of a lone light from a barred window.

They were not far from the backdoor of a club.

People saw them, she knew that people saw them. Some glanced quickly, some looked longer.

Here they were. They were two black people, in practically full view. This would be the only one chance to see. She wanted them to see.

Soon she was unable to understand what Bradley was saying to her. It sounded as if he was talking in tongues the way the old folks did in

280

the Protestant church. This thought, blasphemous under the present circumstances, made her blush more than the man with the lonely eyes who stood transfixed as he watched them.

She wondered how many times he would recreate this moment in his mind, in his conversation, how he would embellish it, make it into legend.

Two black people, well-presented, having sex in front of him. Two teachers, one quite distinguished. They could be arrested at any moment. What would she say to Sam, the children, everyone?

Over Bradley's shoulder, Janet Bookman Baker saw an old woman in the window overlooking them, smoking, watching, her eyes barely open. She only opened them when the spectator had walked quickly away, after they had finished, his face flushed.

The old woman, obviously bored, flung her burning cigarette out of the window, barely missing Janet's head. As she bent over to dress herself, Janet brushed aside Bradley's tender efforts to assist her, leaving him to dress himself.

She allowed him to re-arrange her hair and then, as if they were beginning a first date, he took her hand and led her out into the glare of the bright, hard lights of the street.

She walked with him into the rush of people, and trembling slightly, she allowed him to put his arm around her shoulder.

It would be lovely, she thought, to think of this man crying.

The Arrow That The Bow Of Exile Shoots First

Professor Preston looks really jet lagged. He smiles weakly at me. I smile back. Hope he can do the show.

I have to do the usual stupid quizzes that start the show off. This one is about cars which I know nothing about so I leave that to the guy who is reading the sports bulletin.

I pose the question of the evening: "Reality TV, women's magazines, celebrity gossip. Are they manipulating our brains? Are we heading for totalitarianism?"

First up, the guy on the men's magazine:

"Take reality TV. You think it's big on screen? It's an enormous industry going on behind the scenes. Massive. You talk to some agent about getting an interview or a cover with their client. You're bidding and you have to wait to see if your bid gets picked up. And the ladies. If you have a women's mag, it's about the diet tips, the inside thing on the celeb's emotional life, future plans, beauty stuff; the tabloids divide the Reality TV person up amongst them, depending on whether a star columnist likes the person, or the editor does or whatever; we're all at war with each other, so if paper X likes the celeb, paper Y has to do the spoiler: like digging up the ex-con daddy or the weird sister. For the men's mags, it's all about tits: the one who's not afraid to get her tits out, show 'em in the Jacuzzi, or sunbathing or whatever. You get all that straight with the wannabe, then we can start the bidding. Totalitarianism? Brain manipulation? What brains? Totalitarianism? A price worth paying for fame."

The psychologist takes up the next point. He's just published a book called 'People On The Sofa Who Watch People On The Sofa –

The Great Big Dysfunctional Circle.' For Reality TV, his job is to ask questions about sexual fantasies, weed out the suicides. He tells potential contestants that he would never go on TV to expose himself, nor would any of the producers. The people he interviews want to think that they'll find the love of their lives, the attention they need. If only they can get on TV. Reality TV, he says, is better than writing sick notes for people who don't want to go to work.

The other guest is Lisa, born in 1984 she's an 80s fanatic. She's got the hair, big-shoulders…To her, totalitarianism is good. People need to be under control, she says. She says that the 80s look like hedonism on the outside, but it was really about control.

I think, too bad my mainly male listeners can't see her. She is wearing a black Azzedine Alaia dress plastered on. She's brought on a phone the size of a cosh adapted so that she can use it. She likes the feeling of it up against her ear.

She likes flashing money and she spends lavishly.

She's been writing letters to the Mayor of London asking for the old GLC concerts on the Thames to come back. That was when, she told us, the Thames had respect.

How does she know? She was an embryo!

Her least favourite headline in the whole world is the one for November 22, 1990 that announced the resignation of Margaret Thatcher.

She demands that the Tory party give her back to the nation. "Let the nation decide!" she screams on air.

Professor Preston breaks in and tells her that nostalgia is a country that never existed, that in the land of nostalgia, everything is always perfect.

But this is way above her head, where I think it should stay.

"Do you know what's great about that slim, grey book 1984?" he suddenly asks, "It's that totalitarianism is made out of everyday things: stripping down language that doesn't suit the government, for instance; and the triumphs will be the little transgressions made day to day: like reciting a fairy tale. Remembering what a word really means. But humankind always wants comfort, sureness, a straight line. Totalitarianism is ourselves."

After the show, Professor Preston walks me back to my apartment.

It is still dark and the air is cold.

I like the people on the street in the early mornings.

They are usually the mad ones, the ones who have nothing or who refuse to have connections with life as we know it.

There is a guy who waits for me outside the studio.

He always has a fresh blanket around his shoulders, usually in cheery colours.

When we're both in the mood, he tells me a little bit about his life and a little bit about the life of the city we both live in, which is the same thing for him.

For him London is a live entity, a living, breathing thing with its own mind and beating heart.

It does what it wants to and what it wants is anarchy.

He told me once that he could not ever see himself living in America, could not ever see himself functioning in a city with a grid laid on top of it.

He is out there when we leave, and immediately engages in conversation with us, as if he has known Bradley Preston all his life.

He tells his philosophy again and Professor Preston tells him that he must go to New York and live in Greenwich Village before the Brits take over. The streets there in some places are made out of cow paths and in some places it still has a feel of the colonial.

Our guy in the streets rails against his fellow countrymen, about how they like to turn everywhere into the place they left.

He asks me why we had left the US and Professor Preston says that in his case, the US had left him, but that he had run after it and is still running after it the way a baby set down on a street corner crawls after his mother. He says that he always uses that metaphor because one of his mentors at college had that abiding image of his own life;

at the age of two, he was set down in a street by his mother after the Nazis had ordered her to leave him behind.

Every inch she took, the mentor had said, he could still see in his mind in slow motion: the turning of her head to look at him every few steps, each look more and more gruesome, her face ageing before his eyes, her hair completely white by the time she had been thrown inside a truck which looked to him the size of the universe.

It was the story his mentor always told by way of introducing himself to his class. His subject was history and he warned them that first day of class that everything that had happened in the 20th century that had been catastrophic would be repeated again simply because as a race, human beings had learnt nothing.

The mentor had predicted the fall of Richard Nixon, something he had seen clearly during the time of Nixon's cloth coat speech in the 50s when 'Tricky Dicky' had defended himself against corruption.

He had seen it when Nixon had given his bitter farewell speech to politics after his defeat by JFK. And Bradley Preston says, lighting a cigarette in the dark and sharing it with my friend the dosser, his mentor had told them all that Nixon would do it again.

They were young. Too young to understand what they were being told. To them Nixon was just an old guy who meant nothing.

They laughed at another old guy trying to warn them.

His mentor wound up shooting himself on the day that Ronald Reagan became President, leaving behind a note that read: 'A Reagan campaigner rings a doorbell in L.A. and an old guy answers. The campaigner doesn't know that the guy used to work in Jack Warner's office on the Warner Brothers lot in the days Reagan was a starlet there. So the old guy opens the door and the campaigner says, bright as a button: 'Reagan For President!' And the old guy, used to sitting in on pitch meetings with Warner, immediately yells back: 'No, Jimmy Stewart for President. Reagan for best friend.'

And we all laugh loud and hard, me for the first time in a long time.

And Bradley Preston says, after we finish: "See, all I've got is my desire to honour my youth. I've got to honour the people who warned me, who told me. I must not forget them. I must not relegate them to history or to laughter and forgetting. That's my job."

We're walking and Professor Preston suddenly asks me: "Do you know Dante"?

"Not really."

He takes out a piece of paper on which he had scribbled down these words from the Comedy:

> ... *Tu lascerai ogne cosa diletta*
> *più caramente; e questo è quello strale*
> *che l'arco de lo essilio pria saetta.*
> *Tu proverai sì come sa di sale*
> *lo pane altrui, e come è duro calle*
> *lo scendere e 'l salir per l'altrui scale...*

Bradley Preston says "That's Cacciaguida, Dante's great-great-grandfather, warning him what to expect from exile... You shall leave everything you love most, this is the arrow that the bow of exile shoots first. You are to know the bitter taste of others' bread, how salty it is, and know how hard a path it is for one who goes ascending and descending others' stairs."

I wonder about this man, Professor Preston.

I wonder how much he knows that he and I are alike.

I wonder if his melancholy comes through to people.

His destructive nature, is that apparent to everyone?

He is capable of some very extreme things, of things that can bring certain situations and lives to a halt.

People like him are, in my limited experience, often very successful in the world.

They recreate the world in the shape of their sickness and they call it progress, peace, the way things should be.

People like us can sit in the back objecting, but it doesn't matter.

Some forms of madness have charisma.

He is telling me that he likes Paris because they have not polluted the skyline. You can still look up at the sky in the middle of Paris and you can still see it. Even if the sky is not as big as it is in America, you can still see it.

"I don't like skyscrapers anymore even though I'm a New Yorker. They're kind of what lured me to the city in the first place and what drove me away. I was a kid who loved old black and white movies. New York was skyscrapers and narrow streets that the skyscrapers made dark in the middle of an August afternoon.

I remember coming back one day from a month in Maine.

There weren't very many black people in Maine in those days, I guess, and I stopped traffic. When I got back to New York, my girlfriend, who took the trip with me, almost passed out from the pollution. She had a migraine headache for weeks. But I loved it. I loved the smell of the place. The pollution, the bad air. I was lucky enough to live in the Village and what you smelled was a combination of marijuana and amyl nitrate mixed with Italian cooking and hot dogs being sold on the street and it was all good.

But I had to be on the move after 9/11.

The day before, I was in the apartment of a friend, a rich guy who bought his apartment because he wanted to take girls to his place and point out the view. The World Trade Center was so close you could walk to it in fifteen minutes on a stroll, but far enough away to dream about it.

His place was in one of those New York buildings that look derelict from the outside with the graffiti scrawled all over it and overflowing garbage cans all around, but when you got into it, it was the Ritz: beautiful girls to greet you at the high-tech desk, call you up and after that, you ride up to a wide corridor with only two apartments on each floor. And in my friend's place, you walked in and there it was, right outside the windows: the Twin Towers.

I spend the night there. September 10, 2001.

I wake up the next day and I see the second plane go in. I won't say the cliché thing that it was like a movie because it was, but better than that. It took a few seconds to understand that what was happening in front of you was real. Oh, I forgot to say that my friend was Russian and he started talking in Russian, I had never heard him speak a word of Russian but he's babbling in Russian and suddenly the sky goes black. Black. No sound. Nothing.

I surmise, of course, that I've died, the only logical conclusion to come to. And what do I do now? Who do I talk to? Is there anyone to talk to?

The whole thing is images: the running crowd down below looking like one of those wildlife shots taken from a helicopter where you can see the wildebeest turn one way, then sharply turn another way and you don't know what's driving them because the turning is so perfect. I go down to the lobby and people run past, covered head to toe in dust. One lady comes inside the building – a black lady, I guess, and she walks up to me and calmly and quietly asks me the way to Brooklyn. She's walking home to Brooklyn! Right now. All I need to do is point her in the right direction.

People are being chased by a big, white cloud, so I go to a phone booth, light a cigarette and try to call. Who?

My mamma, who else?

I sit on the ground with my cigarette and can't figure out why the phone isn't working.

Then I think 'I'll just drive.' I can see myself driving upstate at top speed. Just driving. Where? To Toronto. Toronto. Another country. But there is no 'another country' now.

So I say that to say, even with all of that, I didn't leave. I couldn't leave. I can't leave."

And then he says to me in the cold London air, "Go home, Anna. I think of what the composer Elgar said in 1910 when he smelled and felt the onslaught of war: no matter how it looks on the surface: we walk like ghosts."

And with that, he drops me off at my place.

He asks me if I know a black British woman by the name of Janet. Janet Bookman Baker. She teaches at a college in South London.

I tell him that I don't really know any black British people. They don't let me. I ask why he asked. He says just curious. Being a hick, as if I would know every black person in London.

I watch him go away.

I wonder again if anyone will ever know this man who likes to reveal himself to strangers.

I don't go in, but on to Mr. Perfection.

I leave my shoes outside Mr. Perfection's door because you cannot wear shoes in his apartment.

He has this Filipino guy who does nothing but ride his scooter over from Harlesden, drop off a fresh pair of shoes, and pick up the ones Mr. Perfection needs cleaned and repaired, which he takes back to Harlesden.

Mr. Perfection likes Diana Vreeland, the chicest woman – as far he's concerned – who ever lived, next to Coco Chanel that is, who believed that the soles of your shoes should never be scuffed.

Mr. Perfection could be Diana Vreeland incarnated, something he wouldn't mind except it would make him seem gay, which he has an abhorrence of being mistaken for, not that he hates gays or anything, it's just that even the most discreet of them he believes are too obvious in their likes and dislikes and insistence on things.

Not like Mr. P at all.

No way.

It is in there, in his place, that I…pray.

I ask the Deity to take away Mr. P's sense of sight and smell momentarily as I take off my boots which I have not taken off for a few days due to circumstances not under my control like worrying about my feet being exposed to gamma rays.

The place is white on white in white.

Galactica.

I didn't know there were so many shades of white. The entrance room is vanilla, like "the colour of vanilla ice cream in the July sunlight of Little Italy in New York in the early 70s."

That's the name of the shade.

He invented it himself and has it patented.

He takes pains to explain to me that he doesn't actually know the colour he has described and which he owns because it doesn't actually exist but he's known about it since he was a toddler when his mother had bought an old pair of 70s baby coveralls called 'Oshgosh' which were in that colour.

His 'Summertime in Little Italy in the 70s' opened up into the main room.

No, he corrects me. "This is 'Swiss Hospital White'. I had a skiing accident and I didn't want to leave. It was wonderful."

Got it. Swiss Hospital White.

His main room has what looks like one of the refectory tables from Our Lady of Rocamadour, but very, very, very, very clean. Looks like a submission to the Turner Prize.

I stand there. I don't move. Am I actually having sex with this man? What happens afterwards? Are gloves involved, tissues, baby bed rubber mats under our...

His bedroom is what he calls 'Athens in August', minus the Mediterranean blue part: a blinding- headache/white noise/into-the-void-/Kurt- Cobain-when-the-shotgun-went-off white. It is so precise, so driven that it has a weird, awesome beauty.

All the mayhem going on in the world yet here's somebody who can comb through it to impose some kind of sense to it all.

Before I can compliment him, because I am truly awed, he gives me a lecture about his Egyptian cotton sheets, and the real problem in life – forget terrorism, war, global warming, AIDS – which is how and where to purchase the correct mite-repellents for his mattress.

His order and control is awesome!

Me just standing there gobsmacked drives him on.

He discovered while buying sheets that he has a terror of cords, of flex, he is a flexophobe; while in his favourite designer furniture shop dealing with the thread count in his sheets, a television without a cord catches his eye. It is as if every cell in his body relaxes, every part of his being gives a big sigh because that means ONE LESS CORD in his environment.

In spite of at that moment contemplating whether hedge-fund management can or should carry a health-warning, I succumb to his enthusiasm, his full flow, his total dedication to the cause of order and cleanliness.

His life goes like this:

Every Saturday morning he is up at 6 a.m. to begin the ritual of cleaning: on go the gloves, out come the various religious objects otherwise known as toilet cleaner and so forth to you and me, but for P, these things begin the Mass which does not end until midnight when he collapses in a quivering heap of accomplishment mixed with fear of a horrible reality: disorder will return. "Disorder", he is saying, "is bigger than order. Disorder lurks in the corners of every orderly situation, waiting to pounce. You put a stack of papers on the table and sooner or later they will be in a state of disorder. All the energy expended to create order, does that energy create anything else besides sweat? Does it create/release something besides…youck??? ?"

I say like the way an oyster, when irritated, creates the side-effect of a pearl ? And that side-effect is useful? Even beautiful?"

I think about this.

Soon, he predicts, there will be gadgets, little things that will sound a warning if even a microbe is detected. He cannot wait for that blessed day.

I follow him into his bathroom, decorated like that ice house in Dr. Zhivago minus the snow, and right beside the tub is…a fridge.

"For my vodka", P explains.

He leads me into another room – this one as empty as a gallery wall before a painting is hung – to show me his latest acquisition: it's a wall-size white canvas called Mountain Fastness by an artist who just died, and he's collecting her because the word is out that the price of her work will skyrocket, and his voice is suddenly developing this masculine version of a Valley Girl thing, what the Brits call upturn. In his mouth it doesn't sound great, a little too mid-Atlantic, like an actor from the RSC trying to do Neil Simon, but he loves saying Mountain Fastness the way he does because it's clean and being a synaesthete he says that the word is white, pure white.

That painting.

I know the artist.

Knew her.

She was the lover of The Girl With The Kaleidoscope Eyes.

Her name was Carol.

The last time I saw her was two years ago in August. In Krakow at the annual unveiling of the Black Madonna.

I am a Black Virgin anorak, ever since I was at Roc. There was one at the school, a statue with no hands and a featureless face in which you could lose yourself. My mother had a replica at home. Her prize for being one of Roc's Top Girls.

It's not there anymore.

It's gone.

I still look for her. That statue.

I go every year to a shrine of the Black Madonna. Europe has loads.

Krakow. There are trams and jazz bands in the Old Town. There is graffiti on the wall of a derelict building. It says 'Jews Out'. This is pilgrimage time, after all.

I go straight to the shrine after arriving at the airport. I walk like everyone else. There are girls dressed in black from head to toe. The chapel in the monastery is packed. I can't move. Everyone is looking at me. Do they think that the BM is here amongst them -or the Devil? What do these people see when they look at a living black woman? Do they see Her?

I want to ask this.

But I am swept along with the crowd.

I hear a monk speaking English with an American accent. He's from Chicago. I can hear it. I introduce myself. It's almost dawn and he's been praying all night. I'm tired and the flight, the charter, was hot and too full of prayers.

We talk about Chi-town. I ask him if I had come to his neighbourhood back home to see the BM, would I have been welcomed?

This is a belligerent question. It is out of order and hostile. But I want to know.

Of course he can't give me a straight answer because the straight answer would be 'ugh, well…'

I leave him and rejoin the throng.

There are old ladies who have made their way to the front of this scrum.

Two guys, blond and strapping, see me and without a word clear the crowd and get me to the front.

The old ladies are deep in prayer.

The cover is lifted off the icon.

A cheesy record plays with it.

The BM has the scarified face of an African warrior queen.

She is black and they are kneeling before her.

I kneel, too.

But I am not praying.

I am asking: what do these people see?

Is she a mirror through which they can see themselves?

I speak exaggerated American English which gets me a taxi to the Old Jewish Quarter.

There is a Jewish Centre at the entrance.

A big, strapping guy with a yarmulke on his head is hanging outside, talking to a little kid.

The streets still have the ancient names.

They are still there from the old days.

I had seen a Nazi propaganda film once about these very stalls.

In the film, the people are standing dead-eyed behind their wares as the camera pans them to a chirpy voice-over and happy music. I always wondered if they already knew that they were dead.

Now like all Old Towns all over the world, this one is trendy, too. Cool cafés, etc. The world moves on.

The lady known by everybody as 'The Girl With The Kaleidoscope Eyes' and Carol, the painter live in a warehouse space, part living quarters, mostly work space for Carol.

TGWTKE makes sushi. Carol greets me with her delicate painter's hands, her white hair tied back in a ponytail, her overalls splattered in paint. Just like a woman painter should be. She is quick and direct, old but younger than me. She is a selfish bitch. Her art, her expression is everything. Everything else plays a bit role. I know this type.

Carol is painting white on white, huge canvasses that she calls 'Give Me Amnesia Next Time'.

She is a woman who talks a great deal and is used to being allowed to talk. She knows the young rabbi, who works at the Jewish Centre. His only use to her is his body. She wants to paint him in the nude in a series she intends to call 'Don't Talk To Me About The Old Times'.

At first he thought she was joking. Now that he knows she's serious he avoids her. Actually she hates rabbis. Priests, ministers, gurus, imams, etc. all of them. But especially rabbis which she calls rebs. Her father was a reb, her brother a reb. They all backed the wrong horse, as far as she could see. If there is a god he's on permanent vacation with no forwarding address. Who could blame him?

I listen to Carol until she literally falls asleep in the chair. Out. Like a baby.

TGWTKE looks at her with that look of love. They must wake the dead when they're fucking.

We start drinking vodka as soon as we get up, Carol and me.

TGWTKE starts on lunch, something Italian and motherly.

Carol suggests we go to Auschwitz.

We're both pissed and this is no way to do that.

Which is why I say yes.

Carol had had two dozen relatives murdered there, including three kapos.

They were beaten to death.

On the way there, we see these old Poles tending to their gardens close by the camp.

How long had they been there?

They're so old.

It is a hot afternoon.

The gate has a cheery art deco sign curling across the top, and back in the day, an orchestra stood right on the inside to welcome you in.

Why is there so much dust?

Here, in this place, there is no colour at all.

It looks as if the colour has been rubbed out with a giant eraser.

And there are so many silent people, so many silent people, just walking, walking.

This place.

It is not the big edifice of evil.

It is not oozing menace.

It's got small buildings.

Barracks.

It's got industrial bread-baking ovens for Hans and Heidi to play with.

Quaint. Banal. Anonymous.

And it makes you want to vomit.

This is studied, calculated, systematized.

It was a place where everything was dedicated to distorting reality, ripping it to shreds and presenting something else to you. Ordinariness.

The place made evil useful, something you could write down in a ledger. A place of fog and night.

An old man who can't stop talking tells me that when he was liberated from here, he thought that he still had the body he had when he was ten years old and the Nazis put him inside. Except that when he got out, he was almost fifteen. He could never get rid of that ten year old's body. He can still see it, almost all of the time.

This place.

It is like a chess board on the stone floor of an evil troll high up in the mountains in a castle hidden by clouds.

The troll is up there manipulating it all.

For his own amusement.

You have to understand the troll thing if you want to know something about the Northern European.

I understand.

Because we're pissed.

Here.

Maybe that's the only way she can deal with it. She isn't sad or upset. It is a museum to her. She says.

The next day, TGWTKE tries to wake Carol, who is always up first to make coffee and have a fag.

She's dead.

Natural causes, they say later.

Sudden Adult Death Syndrome.

Adults can go like babies go. Don't you know that?

Now, I'm in, of all people's places, Mr. Perfection's sterile environment, standing in front of one of Carol's canvasses. P likes it. To him it is clean and blank.

How can I tell him what it's about?

What do you say to a guy when destruction means his Filipino flunkey has forgotten to show up ?

Funny how life and death dance together.

I can't recall anything about the sex except that it didn't include me and involved lots of tissues and a forest of 75 white iPods surrounding the bed, all playing in harmony, of course.

After I leave Mr. Perfection, I actually walk into a church.

A soft-frozen yogurt moment from my childhood.

Remember when soft-frozen yogurt was a big deal when you were a little kid?

This was one of those. Like when I used to escape to the mall where I was the one who would buy the yoghurt for everybody, I was the lost one, looking at the windows full of fake diamonds, all the time explaining to Deshann and Farista that, no way, I was not like my mother, that crazy lady who stood on the corner exhorting one and all to face the fact that there are more dimensions than this one, and that true beauty could only be found in the Fibonacci Sequence which gave off these gorgeous colours, mainly a spring green with a hint of rain and a really tender baby pink slowly turning to blush. This was the phase when I was actually Whitney Houston inside, hear me sing.

And Dad losing his mind upstairs.

What did I do in church? Sit. Just sit there.

There is the idea of Intelligent Design, in which The Creator is supposed to put DNA into things and let it get on with it, a deeply unscientific approach to What You Don't Know. This is what I've always thought but right now I'm thinking: wait a minute; there are things we don't know, and is it so stupid to surrender at the gate of our knowledge and let Somebody Else drive the bus?

I am saying to myself: 'Hey, I don't know everything, and we aren't meant to know everything because what would we be then? What? And this is where atheists mess up because what they do is create another religion with themselves as God which just goes to show that you can't help doing that. Making God. Or I mean believing in God.'

Sitting in church, looking at all the statues I ask myself: Am I a little thread in a carpet so immense that I can't even see the whole thing let alone where it ends? Should I just rejoice in my little corner of the carpet, my little part of the warp and the woof and leave it at that? Here I've been, trying to unravel something I can't even, or maybe even shouldn't, comprehend.

None of this is as morbid as it sounds. Thing is it's sort of exhilarating, freeing. High. So high that for just a minute I think my long-dead big sister is going to walk through the door and come and sit right down next to me and say – "Little sister, I've been looking for you."

I close my eyes, saying over and over again: Where are you? Where are you?

Waiting for an answer in this church, The Reply, all I can hear is the voice of Shelby Allen:

"Look, Anna. Everybody's doing a novel, ok? It's show business for ugly people."

"So is a rock band if you've done something else."

"No, Anna, that's real showbiz. You mean politics."

"Politics is show biz for ugly people."

297

"Anyway, what is writing now ? An art form? Please. So you had one tiny novel well-received. We go for the Sixteenth Minute. That's all that counts."

Shelby, the hot-shit assistant to my literary agent is talking, the one who wants me to go to London to write The Second Novel.

I am imagining what it would be like in London and how I can escape my destiny.

After I get back from church, where I just stared at the flowers on the altar, nothing more, she called me, talking in that breathless, mind-somewhere-else-voice that she's lately cultivated and tells me that she is giving up on getting them, her kids, to understand the Fibonacci Sequence and is going on, instead, to introduce them to the Zero and the Riemann Zeta Function, and get them to imagine the beautiful landscapes that this mathematical powerhouse can create. In your mind. That is after she gets them to understand how to make mental clock calculators, although she's afraid that with some of them having a criminal bent to their minds, they might figure out how to break open all the banks in Switzerland. However, that might be some kind of triumph. They're doing something instead of living, giving birth, raising kids, and sometimes dying right inside the house she and Dad live in, my house, where I grew up as a kid.

"But", she is saying, "I have to move on from the Fibonacci Sequence. You know, honey, I really tried. But they don't get the beauty."

Thinking now, with you, about how easy it can be, so easy to return home, no matter how chaotic that would be, just to go back to my own room, smell my own stuff, curl up in my bed, stare at my own ceiling, not re-live anything because I'm not talking about nostalgia here, but the acknowledgement of a fact, of a state of being: I LIKE MY PARENTS, I know that now. Yes, definitely, they freak me out, but what else can I do but go…wow….here it comes, home.

Home.

That's where I belong right now.

Going back to church, sitting there, suddenly, I believe in me, that little girl with the little pearl rosary and pearl-covered missal.

I believe in the candles, the booming organ welcoming me into a society that I had been told I would never quite understand, but that was ok because Holy Mother Church would envelope me in her bosom since faith was enough.

But then, when it all fell down, even then, God was there.

Yeah, that's true.

I'm saying this out loud to you: I have always held on to the possibility that I could find the un-findable.

I have forgotten how many times I have felt this, with how many people and in how many situations.

I'm outside now and there's the one they call 'Hey Man', the old hippy, the guy with the long hair, the droopy moustache, bad teeth and smoking roll-ups, the guy you see come rain, come shine, fair weather or foul, shambling down the street dressed like somebody who walked out of an Eagles' concert thirty-five years ago to take a piss and got lost in a time warp.

Because he's never changed he's now in style again, proof positive that we humans are a conservative species, herd-like actually, waiting for the pack leader to tell us what to do.

Hey Man probably figured this out years ago.

Even though he spends quite a lot of time in my subconscious, I have never spoken to Hey Man.

Montgomery Tourlaine had assured me once that this fugitive from The Twilight Zone was like himself, like me, an ex-pat, adrift, a fugitive. So the story probably is that HM is a fugitive from the Vietnam War, from Nixonian America.

The country he has left behind now exists only in his head.

Today, right now, I want to walk up to him.

Talk to him.

Sit him down on something stone here in Covent Garden Piazza and ask him what it was like to be young at a time when you could believe.

299

The crowds are making their way through the Piazza, eating, talking, buying, consuming and there's Hey Man, deep in his world.

I don't have the courage to walk up to the guy.

There are still people in this world who don't want to be noticed or clocked or talked about or thought about, who don't search for that sixteenth minute, people who are not drowning in the ordinariness of their lives, who, in fact, welcome not being known; able to remember life without IT, mobiles, Reality TV, cars that tell you how to drive, SMS; upgrading; fast-tracking.

Hey Man has this way of walking sideways in his platform heels, wide-leg trousers flapping around his ankles and just stopping at the top of the boot.

He brings into focus, into really clear sight something truly shocking:

I am guilty of doing the time-honoured, boring thing of hating what my elders love and naturally hating who they were in their own youth.

Me.

I head for the first open door. A bookstore.

Like librarians, my real heroes, bookshops contain my second bunch of heroes, not the people or conglomerates who own them, but the people who work in them, like the guy who is telling me where the fiction section is, classic fiction is what I need, the time-honoured stuff.

When I was small, one of the questions that I used to ask my father was why human beings repeated themselves, why, for example, if Tolstoy had taken us to one place, shown us something true, why is it that people didn't take up that ball and run with it, instead of repeating it or pretending that Tolstoy had not shown us what he had shown us.

Dad said: "Because it's hard".

At the time, I just thought it was one of his "don't bother me, kid, I'm working" responses, but now, standing in the bookshop, leafing through Anna Karenina, I can understand what he meant.

You've probably always known the answer to it.

You wouldn't be where you are unless you knew that.

And you know, all the time my Fem Lit prof railed about why Anna throws herself under the train, all that feminist stuff which I had believed, half doubted, I ask myself now, in front of you, why did she do it? My prof's conclusion was that it did not make sense, that it was wrong.

It is wrong if you go outside the world of the book. But in the world of the novel, in the world that Tolstoy creates, it is the only possible ending.

But then you know that.

My mom and dad had to cover up what I had witnessed that night because to have admitted it would have destroyed the symmetry of their lives, would have undone the noble lie they had woven for the benefit of their people. They couldn't be Role Models any more. And if other folks don't look up to you, point to you, then what's the point? So I, their daughter, had to be the virgin sacrifice to their lives devoted to an ideal, to a state of being that was more important than my shallow understanding.

I ask some the guy with a badge on his shirt that says "Go On Ask Me" if "AK" is included in the five books for the price of three deal.

I'm not sure that he knows what I'm talking about.

Then I see her.

She's tall.

Small head.

Like a ballerina.

Her eyes are big, open, slightly slanted at the corners.

She is staring at me.

The way you are now, but not out of exhaustion because I've been talking all night.

No, that's not the reason.

I know her. I don't know how I know her.

It's like we are in the same story, but we don't know it.

Somebody outside us does and that somebody is waiting for us to meet, waiting to see what we say, what we do.

I want to tell her this, but I turn my head away the way you're supposed to do in London. But I instantly regret this, so I turn around again, my motion knocking over a glass perched on one of the counters, breaking it. I don't know where it came from. I stoop down to try and clean it up.

When I'm finished, she's gone.

The guy with the badge is still talking to me.

We are all flotsam and jetsam, born of flotsam and jetsam, which is why we cannot recall the future, as Montgomery Tourlaine used to tell me over and over, why we cannot recall the state when the broken glass returns whole to the edge of the table simply because we are not of that state, it's too small for us to access, too small for us to enter. Chaos is the biggest state, the largest home.

The guy with the badge is still talking, things I have completely forgotten about, or do not choose to recall.

Maybe, I think as I listen to this guy rambling on, maybe it is beautiful, this state of disorder, the life we know.

The guy with the badge is still talking but I've walked away.

The woman who caught my eye is staring at me from outside and like a true Londoner, she turns her head when I look her way.

She moves on, swallowed up in the melee that goes by the name of Tottenham Court Road, taking with her forever my total conviction that she is indeed one with me in all of this that we exist in.

7.

Where were they going?

What was going to happen?

Tirian seemed to be immobilized and confused.

Her small face was once again impassive. She looked more and more like a child who had been thrown away.

Maybe she could be saved.

Maybe they all had a chance.

The flood had made the security devices in Paris unreliable, one of the reasons for its attraction.

Could she keep Tirian in the state she was in and escape with her and Saronia?

It was worth the attempt.

Suddenly that series of numbers – the Fibonacci Prime – came to her out of the blue. Saronia was communicating with her, bypassing Tirian and coming straight into her head. '5387'.

Jody recited the numbers.

The lights in the room went out. Then came back on.

The number was like a kind of 'open sesame'.

Jody saw that Tirian noticed right away what was going on, but was not quick enough to respond. She was still immobilized.

She was not quick enough to prevent the entire apartment being taken out of Ubiquity.

The numbers had neutralized all of the surveillance.

Tirian was stunned.

Jody thought: 'How long would she last now that her mission is on the verge of failure? This child, whatever she or it is, tried to kill me. Kill us…'

Jody remembered something one of her tutors in Elimination Systems had told her as they were having tea in his icebox – out of Ubiquity.

'Uncertainty, Jody. We humans don't like it as a rule. For instance, have you ever asked yourself what we really are – machines, computers? And that we, let's say, computers, have offspring that we don't acknowledge, but unfortunately are growing faster than we have a handle on?

Look, Alan Turing, who created 'Colossus', the first working computer and who helped break the German Enigma code and, well, won World War Two pretty much single-handed, thought we might be. We don't know. He also proved that we can never truly know what can be computed and what cannot be computed. Uncertainty, Jody. The great mathematician Gödel proved that there are things that are true but that can never ever be proven.'

'He proved that you can't prove something?' she had asked.

'Yes. A beautiful theorem. Except…we can't ever know if it's true. Not by logic. But Gödel also said that we have intuition, which goes beyond logic. And maybe I would add, the 'little flame'.'

'What's that?'

'Every one of us has to discover that for ourselves. If you're lucky, working for this outfit, you never will.'

'Where are you going with this?'

'Here. Now, if computers are, in the main, the sum of our human interactions, a record therefore of us, and they can generate knowledge based on this sum of human interactions, based on us, then…they are our offspring, our children. Just as much as our flesh and blood is.'

'Computers are our children?'

'Listen to me, Jody. Computers are not subtle. They have no imagination, no compassion. And because of that, they can have a ruthlessness, a precision that we will never have. We, unlike them, can walk forward. Into what? Into not knowing. And perhaps we survive. And perhaps we don't.'

Jody grabbed Saronia's hand.

"Mo…Mother, let's get out of here while the systems are down. Now !"

Saronia seemed not to be able to stand up.

"We're officially Undetectables right now! We've got to keep moving!"

"But I…"

Jody looked at Tirian. The child, or whatever it was, looked helpless. She looked like the feral child she herself had once been.

Jody grabbed her, and with her other hand, hurried Saronia through the apartment and out the door.

Their footsteps rang through the courtyard as they headed for the river.

The old-fashioned sandbags kept the Seine at bay, but further on, in the less wealthy areas where the flooding was strongest, the lawlessness was out of hand, and things would be different.

Without the automatic ability to scan anyone in the lawless areas, Jody knew that they would be fair game for anyone.

But she had to take that chance.

As she reached the water's edge, she noticed something. Someone was waving.

"Mom! !Look! Over there! Somebody's trying to signal us!"

In the twilight, Jody could make out the face of a handsome young boatman, waving at them and indicating that he was coming over.

Without her scanner, Jody could not tell who or what he was.

But she had no option.

She had to trust her feelings.

She insisted to the other boatman who was in line to pick up the next fare that she, her mother, and little sister had specifically asked for the young man rushing toward them in his boat. She lied and said that he had been especially hired for them.

The boatman was angry and mumbled something about the rules, but he moved on to take the next fare.

When the young man pulled up, Jody helped Saronia and Tirian into his boat.

She sank back into one of the worn seats.

'I'm in a new world. I'm out of Ubiquity, but don't even have time to see what it feels like!', she thought as she leaned forward and yelled at the boatman: "Can you get us out of here fast? I'll tell you when to stop."

The boat was not as tidy as some of the others.

The driver was playing very loud rock music.

"This is 'Les Idiotes.' Tu connais?" He yelled over the din.

Jody knew enough French to understand that he was using the familiar, a form of address reserved only for family, friends and people considered to be inferior to the speaker. "Tu" could also be a way that young people addressed one another.

He felt warm and comfortable.

She kept both Saronia and Tirian close to her. Tirian was still unsettled. She and Saronia were silent as the boat moved through the darkness.

She had no idea where they were going, but she trusted the young man.

"Je ne sais pas Les Idiotes", she replied.

"Ah, you are American then?" he asked.

"Yes."

"From where?"

"Chicago."

"The Windy City. I would like to go to America, but it's very difficult. You have to pass many checks."

"In France, too."

"Everywhere. I have the opinion that it is the young who will break down these barriers, who will say no. We will cross over and it will all be new."

For the first time since they entered the boat, Saronia looked up. Her face changed.

"Why did you pick us up?" Jody asked him.

"Why? It's simple. You are two beautiful women and a delightful little girl."

"Why!!!!!"

"Like I said, it will be the young who must break down the barriers, who must cross over. Don't you think sometimes that all of this protection we have made is merely an expression of the fear of death which comes to everyone no matter what. So you may as well be as free as possible and live a little on the edge, too. I say you must ensure that you are not living the life of someone else. My friends and I, we believe this. I have friends who allow me through the various zones. We live 'outside'. We all like to play dangerously, too."

"You're not going to answer my question, are you?"

"But I have. I said you might as well live as free…"

Jody closed her eyes. She relaxed as she listened to his voice. She thought: 'Either this guy is taking us to our doom, or taking us out of it. I'm going to believe the latter.' This was the first time she had ever relied on herself alone without drugs and devices.

Jody looked behind her.

In some parts of Paris, the lights were still on.

She looked over at the woman who she now knew was her mother. Saronia had withdrawn even deeper inside herself…Jody covered her and Tirian with an old blanket she found tucked behind the seat.

She would save Tirian, too.

If it was possible.

A glint of light bounced off the boy's neck revealing a medal around it. There was also a minute white rose tattooed on his sunburnt upper right arm.

Out of habit, Jody instinctively began to make contact with Control.

The boy could be a Virus.

But she stopped herself.

Control was now the enemy.

The boy was going too slow. They did not have much time left to be on an open waterway.

Soon, they would become prey for the Hunters.

They had to get into somewhere safe. But how. Where?

The boatman was leisurely recounting the time when his father, then a young man, had stumbled drunk into the Seine off the Ile.

He had not known he was in the water until he saw three pretty girls running along the shore screaming frantically.

He had thought that he was at home in his bed having a lovely dream about floating.

"Like all great rivers, the Seine is treacherous. She has a treacherous current which began to drag my father down. It was when he felt the water around his mouth he knew that he was not asleep. And he saved himself. With regret.

There were times he told me that it would be wonderful to be eaten by the river. Since we are mainly water, it is water that we become in the grave. Why would it be so horrible to make one's home in the water? After all, Paris would not exist if there were no Seine. To drown in her would be the same as going home. To drown in her would be to meet the one known as The Flute. Have you ever heard of The Flute?"

Jody kept her eyes on Saronia and Tirian.

"Something,…" Jody replied.

The boy interrupted her.

"During the time of Napoleon The Third, the nephew of the great Napoleon – but there were many who said that no, he was not his real nephew, but the son of someone else – but, in that time, on the rue le Regrattier, on the island we have just left, there was a great house, a maison close, with only black women in it. They had been the children of slaves and were the most beautiful women in Paris. Men would give anything to have a night with them. They were called collectively L'Orchestre d'Elmina and their most famous associate was a young, beautiful girl called The Flute."

"Yes, I have heard this."

"Good. As I said, she was the flute in this great orchestra of love. But their love held a secret and cost a great price. Even when she was an old woman, men still sought her out. When The Flute tried to extract her price from one man, she aroused his anger. He strangled her and threw her in the Seine. Not far from here. Over there. Close to the shore. It was 1910. The last time the river flooded this way.

And it is said that the women like her, who know and hold this Secret, and their children, especially the sons, can cause this river to flood. So, for me, The Flute has a descendant and he is bringing the river up to meet her people on the shore."

Jody looked at him. His back was broad and strong as he navigated the boat.

"Someone is causing this?"

"Mais oui. That is why I came for you. So that you would know. My father knew this story and I believe that he fell in love with The Flute as

308

a result. He would say that he would rather drown. Then he could join her. You see, his father and his father before him were what you would call 'contremaîtres' – overseers, and he could never forget this. He would not allow his children to forget it, either. That is all I have to say."

Jody stared at the boy. He had picked them up, carried them away from danger in order to tell her this?

She and Saronia and Tirian and he were suddenly part of an old story, heirs to an unknown tradition.

His people had been responsible for the enslavement of her ancestors.

Was this guy making reparation for the past by rowing them to safety now?

Jody looked at him.

Did reparations matter?

Was it possible for her to reconcile their pasts together, for her to forgive his ancestors and then move on?

Could she look at Tirian, who had been clearly her enemy, and forgive her?

Could she close the circle of hatred and pain, and in closing it, create something new?

The boat pulled up to one of the makeshift docks, in the dark.

Jody held her breath as she waited for the police to swoop down on the boat. She and Saronia were now officially Undetectables.

Her eyes locked on the boatman. He was for them or against them.

Saronia was quietly crying. Jody put her arms around her. To her utter amazement, Saronia looked up at her, a mischievous grin on her face.

Something was up.

The boatman ushered them off the boat.

He said nothing.

He was not going to give them away.

It was so dark that Saronia almost tripped and fell into the river. She had almost burst out laughing.

'The stress is making her hysterical', Jody thought.

Tirian had turned back into a mute, lifeless creature, numb and hollow eyed.

309

Saronia was giggling softly.

"Mom", Jody whispered, "Take it easy."

A small light emerged from the darkness.

The boatman handed them over to a young man who appeared and led them wordlessly over the wooden pathways into an apartment building, grey and tall and imposing.

Pumps were busily draining the water.

The draining work was being done by African immigrants, talking softly amongst themselves.

In the distance the Eiffel Tower twinkled red, white and blue.

The Mayor's efforts to keep the land around the great tower dry had been a success.

Jody took deep breaths. She must stay conscious.

The woman walking beside her, laughing at her own private joke, was her mother.

This was the woman who had given her away. The woman who had denied her her identity.

They were led into a large room.

It looked like a library lined with shelves full of books.

The strong dose of oxymorcin that Tirian had clearly swapped for what she had given her in the boat on the way to Saronia's, was working hard in her system to destroy her equilibrium.

'Keep awake.', she told herself. 'Protect yourself and your mother. And Tirian.'

Muffled voices seemed to be coming from another room.

Jody tried to imagine what could be going on, who was inside that other room.

No question that the voices were Anglophone. Some were American, some British.

The woman who emerged was tall and what could be called handsome.

Her grey hair was piled on top of her head and she wore a long, flowing black dress. The medal that the boatman had, hung around her neck, too.

Without saying a word, the woman offered them plush white armchairs and poured each of them a cup of tea.

"Exile or no, there's nothing better than a cup of tea." She laughed.

Her smile and warm Caribbean voice changed her sombre face and lit up the room. Confused, Jody absently tried to scan her. It was a reflex.

"No need for that here,' the woman said. "What I mean is", she continued, opening the curtains wider, allowing in the moonlight, is that we are all unprotected here. We are all Undetectables.

And I hope that you know now, Ultra, that whatever is thought to be fool-proof, there comes a fool who can prove it is not true. Ubiquity does not extend everywhere, no matter what it calls itself. There are people outside and who are free. There are people, like that boatman, who help us."

"Us?" Jody asked.

"I suppose that Saronia hasn't had time to explain. We've known each other for a long time. Ever since my brother lost an extradition case in London. Let me remember what the judge said: 'The Extradition Act of 2003 did not require mutuality or reciprocity. No evidence against a UK national was required upon a request from the US.'

Something like that.

And soon my brother was off. Swallowed up. I have no idea where he is, what's become of him. So it made sense to me to go where they could not reach me: France. Paris. And I met Saronia here soon after arriving. And we've been friends ever since."

Saronia walked into the woman's open arms.

"I had a feeling that we were coming to you. I just knew it. I just laughed with joy when I knew it." Saronia smiled.

Confused, Jody stood for a moment and listened to everything around her.

Whoever this woman was, whatever her business, the main thing was that Jody had to get her newly-discovered mother to safety.

And to figure out what to do about Tirian.

It was time to prepare herself, in every way, for a new world.

*What can be more absurd than the introduction,
in the first scene, of a child...?*

<small>CERVANTES,</small> DON QUIXOTE

Standing on the stairs of the Holland Park villa which Bradley Preston rented, Janet Bookman Baker took in the expanse of the street.

Its generous sweep was lined with imposing houses, many divided up, like Bradley's, into apartments for the wealthy.

She had picked up a message from the hotel saying that Sam had tried to reach her in the night.

She had listened to her voicemail, and heard Sam, quiet and contemplative, telling her that he missed her and loved her and that he was seriously reconsidering his decision about Lucas going to the local school.

The day that she had left for the Conference, he had been told by a small gang waiting for him outside the house that Lucas had disrespected them.

They didn't like the fact that he spent so much time in the library.

He did not 'kotch' at Burger King with them and that disturbed them.

Sam had paused after he had related that story, then said that they had been defeated, and it would be best to send Lucas away as soon as possible.

Janet had rung Sam back while Bradley was in the shower, talking to him as briefly as possible, telling him that she would see him soon and not to worry. They would find a way. The silence between them after she had spoken seemed to be one in which Sam was searching for her. And in that silence he told her that he loved her and needed her back in Morant Bay Road.

Then, after putting the phone down, she had looked in Bradley Preston's mirror at her nude body, staring at it, remembering something Lucas had said to her before she left: that he did not want to grow up to work in the City or be a lawyer like his dad, or get rich while becoming a movie star on the side, the desire of some of the guys he knew. He didn't want to go to the local school. He didn't want to watch the division of his friends. He wanted to go away to a new world.

When she had dressed, she checked her messages again.

Sam had left another message, this time on her mobile, asking where she was, if she was ok.

She had texted him back, telling him that she needed a little space and that he was not to worry.

She would return to the old narrative for Lucas's sake, for the sake of her daughter, for the sake of the family life that she and Sam had built.

Just as her father had returned to the old narrative of his life for her sake.

She would return. But like him, she would never be the same again.

And turning away from Bradley's place, she thought of what stretched before her.

Stumbling over a rocking pavement stone, she startled a very thin, chic young woman, clearly out to walk her baby to sleep. The woman kept her face straight ahead so that she did not see Janet at first, but after Janet tripped and bumped into her, she made an awkward jump which jolted the pram. The movement woke the baby up into a crying fit. Janet reached over instinctively to calm the child and the woman, laughing, thanked her and carried on with the baby, both of them disappearing into one of the private gardens that lined the winding road.

Strolling along, the late morning breeze ruffling her hair, Janet stopped to watch a game of tennis. She found herself studying the fine bodies of the two young men who were playing as if they had time on their hands.

One of them caught her eye and smiled at her.

She smiled back. Bradley and her time with him, her time with Tomas before that, already things of the past.

She directed her attention to a young man raking leaves beside a gnarled tree, taking in her stride the fact that she could look at him, openly, full of that feeling of watching him for her own pleasure, the same way she would feel on the first day at school, or those glorious days before her wedding when she had believed that she had resolved her life once and for all. The same sensation of pleasure and joy and open-endedness inched its way through her stomach as she watched the young man bend over to collect the leaves. She was aware for a moment, that she might go over and speak to him, that she might make a complete fool of herself because he would know, he would sense right away, that the foundation of her enquiries had nothing to do with leaf maintenance.

Janet gathered her coat closer around her, wheeling her suitcase past the boy. She turned and looked at him when it was safe to do so, when he did not know she was looking. Thinking to herself as she hurried along, that God only knew what people were these days. The boy with his slanted dark eyes, jet-black, straight hair and olive skin, so many cultures coming together, so much the future of humankind.

In the future, her colour would disappear and the colour of the little blonde baby in the pram would disappear and all that would be left was what the boy who was raking the leaves looked like. And if everyone looked roughly the same, would it end the wars, the brutality, the hatred?

The beautiful boy picked up the leaves with the same sweeping gesture that Bradley had had the night before when he swept all the glasses off the dining room table in his rented flat.

He had laughed like a child as he walked around in someone else's home, destroying someone else's glass and crystal. He had invited her to join in, had insisted that she join in.

He had handed her one of the expensive-looking crystal glasses, ordering her to smash it in the fireplace. He had told her that the neighbours were much too English to complain.

Bradley had directed her into the study where two glass unicorns sat half-hidden behind a large copy of Paradise Lost.

She watched him as he swept them to the floor.

There had been moments of fleeting guilt as she followed him around, breaking what he had not broken, enjoying the sound of the smashed glass.

She had revelled in the look of it on the wooden floor. Being with him, she had thought of what they would do in the house of broken glass. She had been awestruck at his coolness at the destruction, mixed with a maniacal brusqueness that transformed itself into ardour for the state that he was creating, the damage he was inflicting.

He had moved around as silent as a ballet dancer, picking his way across the landscape he had created. It was all silence except for the sound of their sojourn through the universe he had created and the tiny beeper in his watch that kept ringing at strange five-minute -intervals. It soon became a part of the general mayhem.

Janet had taken off her glasses to be destroyed in their orgy of smashing and breaking. Gloria-Loretta had always said that her inability to see had been in her mind. She had always said that Janet had simply not wanted to see and Janet had known, on that night of broken glass, that her mother had been correct.

Janet had deferred to requests for pauses in their lovemaking – hardly the word for what she and Bradley had got up to – so that he could distribute shards of glass on the windowsills, and the mantelpiece, the staircase, and the passageway to the bed.

She had gingerly made her way on bare feet to where he slept, the shards around her feet not her broken marriage vows, nor the rules by which she had been raised, or the caveats she had passed on to her students and others, but bright, glittering lights which pointed the way to tomorrow.

As she walked along, Janet thought of Lucas.

Last year she had taken him to a lecture he had insisted on attending about the work of the mathematician and cosmologist, Carl Friedrich Gauss.

He had said to her on the bus home, talking so quickly that he had been gasping for air, that Gauss had questioned the idea of the world as it had been formulated by the Greeks. He had said that it was possible that there were parallel worlds, which could intrude on our own and that we would interpret that as hauntings, visitations, ghosts. Gauss had ripped the veil.

She had tried to calm him down, making the grave error of telling him that most people would never understand him, that he must try,

315

somehow, to be a boy like all the others. She had told him that what he had said about Gauss could not be true.

All the way home, Lucas had grown very quiet. And just before she had tucked him into bed and kissed him goodnight, he told her quietly that there were some things that were true but that could never be proven.

Suddenly a little girl who resembled Ayesha crossed the road in front of her.

The child had Ayesha's round face and thick, nappy hair, hair just as unruly, just as defiant as Ayesha's. The girl was practically her twin. She had the same air of self-containment as her daughter. But this child walked with a slight limp, her left foot dragging slightly behind her.

Watching the child, Janet recalled the paediatrician who had told them, when Ayesha was three months old, that she would have to have a slight correction to her left foot. If she did not, she would have a limp.

She and Sam had discussed their options. Sam had cried pitiably at the thought of his little girl having to have a general anaesthetic.

It was the first time Janet had ever seen him cry.

It had been astounding to see his face, usually so calm and composed, crumpled and distorted. His was a face unused to tears. Janet had felt so full of pity for him that she had, at one point, suggested that they not go through with the procedure if it would cause him such distress.

She could not help thinking then, in the back of her mind, that he was weeping for more than Ayesha, but not daring to say so.

From time to time after the correction had been made, Sam would make some comment about how fast Ayesha walked or how good she was at games.

He had relegated the entire episode in the hospital, along with his deep distress and the exposure of his vulnerability, to the past. He had never faced up to his inability to go to the hospital to see his little daughter right after the operation, nor his fear of touching her until she was well again.

From time to time, Janet could still see, at particular times, his eyes, old and clouded and heavy and frightened whenever he had looked at his broken child in her crib, her little ankle and foot swathed in bandages.

Now, in the person of the child in the road, a stranger, there was before her the embodiment of that parallel world that Lucas had talked about, opening up unbidden before her.

Adjusting her eyes as best she could, taking in the blur of white buildings and the wide, tranquil streets, Janet followed the limping child, who was singing to herself. Her own ears had become strangely better with the loss of her glasses and the diminution of her sight. She recognized the melody as part of a tune that Ayesha used to sing over and over, a tune from a children's show, innocuous, vapid, yet unforgettable.

The child sang over and over, louder and louder, dragging her foot, her voice like Ayesha's, too, only a little deeper. Mixing with her voice, was that old memory of Sam weeping at his inability to change things for his child, to make things better, standing over their baby daughter's crib, weeping, with the smell of the jail cell on him, with that whiff of poverty that often came into his Chambers with his clients. Sam, a man who had once taken a loaded gun off of a client, could only look at his little girl then and weep.

His tears were a coda that rang through her head as she followed the child down a short passageway and into the courtyard of an estate, discreetly tucked away behind the posh apartments and houses of Bradley Preston's part of Notting Hill.

Low-rise, the estate had a midmorning hush. There was only the distant sound of a radio playing, then applause, followed by a melancholy Irish voice talking to the audience.

The child stopped to listen to it, then turned abruptly to face Janet, in that gesture instantly making it clear that she was streetwise, stranger-danger alert, ready to confront the woman who had been so clearly following her.

Forcing an easygoing air, Janet smiled at the accusatory face of the child, a face too old, too wise.

To appease her, Janet asked her name, in a bright, casual voice.

The child replied monosyllabically, her eyes frozen over, her mouth hardening, the fat clouds casting fast shadows as she hurried up the stairs and away.

Janet continued on her way, adjusting her eyes to what was ahead.

She stopped at a bookshop in Oxford Street. She didn't know why. She couldn't read very well without her glasses. She strolled through the shelves, trying to hold on to the last few days that she had spent on the North side of the Thames, the feeling.

Suddenly, she found herself looking into the face of a young black woman, tall and what Gloria-Loretta would have called burly.

She was dressed in a greatcoat, too heavy for the time of year.

The young woman had a lion's mane of dreadlocks and large eyes like her own.

Janet was convinced that she knew her, convinced that they must speak.

She started to approach the girl, but instead turned her head away quickly and moved on. She moved so quickly that she almost took the book she had been leafing through out of the store.

Outside the shop, composing herself, she glanced once again at the place where she had been. But the young woman had moved away, suddenly to reappear in another part of the shop. And looking up and out of the window, their eyes met again.

Both frightened and exhilarated and unable to understand why, Janet walked quickly away in the direction of Waterloo Bridge.

Towards home.

The day began to close in, the sun hidden behind the clouds, the crowds rushing along.

No one looked at one another.

No one glanced at her, and she longed to see them all. One by one.

Janet was returning now to the way she had been, back to the place she could not leave. She would pick up what she had left behind.

She had entered the world.

But who would she be when she returned?

3

...till one day their earlier self walked like a ghost in its old home and made the new furniture ghastly.

ELIOT, MIDDLEMARCH

Returning to the old narrative, its flow and shape, its state of being, Janet Bookman Baker settled into it once more as she watched the September dusk gather over the river; its grey-blue light a soft curtain which released a small mist that hovered on the surface of the river; and a barge, black against the dying light, moved slowly towards Westminster, she taking it all in as she stood on Waterloo Bridge, about to cross over to 'her' side, watching the boat; the boat lonely, and proud with it, making its way west; waves the colour of slate suddenly emerging, the river's treacherous undertow asserting itself and its supremacy; London existed because of its masculinity; the river still ran beneath the city, was the city, and it could emerge and take the city with it – most of the world being water – and so many destinies had depended upon water; and as if emerging from a dream, Janet recalled again that last letter from Abena Assantewa which had begun with a quote from a journal of Ralph Waldo Emerson written in 1857 : 'a good field hand was valued at £500, but...a Mulatto girl...if beautiful and sprightly witted at £2,500 and upwards', 'the erotic', Professor Assantewa had written, 'always a factor of enslavement for good, Christian God-fearing men; men who had built great London alongside the Thames.', then : 'I'm tired, Janet. I feel as if I'm writing in the void, living in the void. All my decades of work, the years of my youth, nothing, nothing.

If my sister could have just said that she forgave me.

If only I could have seen who she really was....Earlene'.

Earlene. Had she, Janet asked herself, isolated parts of her life to such an extent that she had not been able to see what her life had been weaving; that the Earlene of her father's letter – the name she

321

had blocked herself from remembering – and Abena Assantewa's sister were one and the same person; Abena's Earlene, a woman who had washed and cleaned for nuns, a mentor for schoolgirls, who had lived only to help others; Earlene, in whose name Professor Assantewa was rendering one last service to the child her late sister had loved above all else; Earlene, the sister Abena had belittled all of her life until the end, until she had learned that there was more in life than she could order and articulate, and that through this love she had come to know her; this great feminist activist Abena Assantewa, who had written books, had made hundreds of speeches, a woman who had been a confidante of Presidents and Prime Ministers, who had lived her life in the spotlight, had discovered, almost when it was too late, that hers had been a life which had been nothing compared to her sister's life of sacrifice, of goodness, of anonymity, and shadow; and she had ended her last letter with a lament: that it broke her heart to think that Earlene had never known what it was to love the way a man and a woman could, or to receive love the way she had; she herself now slipping into a twilight world in which she might be shown a way to understand her life, and how she had come to live the way she had.

The way she had walked from the bridge, rolling her suitcase behind her on the long trek home to Morant Bay Road, playing Professor Assantewa's last letter over and over in her head, made Janet exhilarated; she had finally seen that invisible world which held the connection that had always bound her to Professor Assantewa; she had crossed the water and all was becoming clear and with this revelation had come another gift: liberation from having to be strong, to be cheerful, to be good; from having to pay constant attention to the rules; free, no longer afraid of the darkness that had by now fallen, causing the streetlights to come on, beautiful and warm; she, no longer afraid of the people who passed by on their way home, moving in and out of the light; she, no longer afraid of the general atmosphere of the streets and the houses that surrounded them; definitions shifted continuously; that neither art, music, not great books, nor even God could prevent; Janet no longer able or wishing to stave off the inevitable.

Inevitable, she thought, as she walked through the door of her home, that the house should look different; without her glasses it had become a soft, ethereal place; as she walked slowly down the hallway, utilizing her memory, her brain, attempting to get back the old familiar things; slowly hanging up her coat on the hook by the door, momentarily relieved by its suburban familiarity; Ayesha leading the charge to her, her warm little body wriggling with excitement, demanding to know where her mother's glasses had gone, why wasn't she wearing them; demanding that Janet ring the police, yet telling Janet how pretty, how new, how different she looked without them; Janet knowing that her clever little daughter had sensed the change in her; Lucas plying her with a thousand observations on how the world worked; his latest discovery; that there were more dimensions than three, a fact mathematically proven; that it was probable that events were occurring that the average human could not perceive and when those other dimensions collided with our own from time to time; they could even seem mystical, disconnected; but they were, in fact, perfectly connected, even beautifully so; and since reality was a collective agreement hard-wired to the brain, humans could just simply decide to change the agreement, and if it wasn't for fear of change and custom, they would; if he could "see" these other worlds through his calculations, others must have, too, since no human evolutionary event was isolated; the ability to do so might even be inherited, like red hair, 'selected' because this ability would have been necessary for the survival of the species; but, he asked himself aloud as he walked her into the dining room, what sort of environmental conditions could force a segment of human beings to see and work with these other dimensions; what if he had inherited this ability to go beyond what could be seen, and tasted, and heard and felt, and thought about in the typical, lazy way; the countryside would give him the peace and quiet he needed to explore, to work, couldn't she, he begged her, talk to Dad again, couldn't she convince him; the childminder greeted her at the entrance to the dining room, a local girl whose family had fled a militia in East Africa, and who was trying to explain to her over the din that Sam had to stay late at Chambers and had asked her to come over to sit with the children; Janet assuring her that she was grateful for that; fumbling in her handbag for the money to pay her because she could not see clearly – one hand searching for her wallet, the other wrapped around her children; astonished by her own calm, her lack of remorse for all that had happened, for all that will happen in the future; watching the childminder gather her things, a tall, timid girl, much the way she had been, who talked about her university course as if to assure Janet of her worth, that she was more than a servant; Janet wanting to undo the girl's tight, straightened ponytail, the carefully applied make-up, the propriety; wanting to sit her down and tell her that to look the way she did had its rewards in the outside world, but not inside; the childminder, a good church girl whom she had seen walking past the house every Sunday with her Bible, spoke now, quite out of the blue, about something that Jesus had said, something Janet would have listened carefully to just days ago; but now, instead, wanting to stop her, not out of disrespect to Christ; but wanting to send her out of the house with a quotation from St. Augustine that her father had said to her: 'Heretics are given us so that we might not remain in infancy'; instead, showing the girl out, wishing her well, watching it begin to rain just as the girl stepped out into the street, rushing out to give her one of the spare umbrellas, then spontaneously kissing her on the cheek, thanking her again and sending her on her way into the deep, dark night.

The deep, dark night seemed to envelope everything as she re-read Abena Assantewa's last letter, astonished that she had not understood before that she herself held the key to Professor Assantewa's dying in peace; she would go to her, go to Paris and hand that key to her.

To her, Sam's silent slipping into bed later; the perfunctory kiss and over-chattiness the following morning at breakfast, his deep, at times intense listening to Lucas' one-way discussion on the quintic and its beautiful mathematical conundrum; a sign to her that her husband was not yet ready to talk, not even to acknowledge the overcoming of her phobia and what may have been released in her as a result; only after a pause in Lucas' lecture did he talk about his latest client: a young man who was HIV positive and who had set out to infect all of his white lovers, male and female; a case which he believed would be his toughest yet; Janet surprised at his frankness and rough candour in front of the children, the content of what he had said mercifully lost on them but a riposte to her, a demonstration that he, too, could be reckless, this a surprisingly feminine gesture that she liked; hurrying Ayesha out to the school bus; helping her daughter on, she turned in time to see Sam, who, without a word, drove off, following the school bus; and she, standing, watching him turn the corner and disappear, knowing that their life together, as it had been, was closing.

Closing her filing cabinet, locking it, gathering the things she would pack before she left JLU for good, Janet looked into the mirror she kept on top of it, and that had once belonged to her mother's mother; Ayesha had once asked her if it was a magic mirror capable of showing things far away, or which were about to come; now gazing into the glass, its surface seemed to open like a fan and a great rush of blue-green spread over the expanse of it; the Caribbean Sea; noon sunlight dancing on its surface, this sea that had greeted those of her ancestors who had survived the Crossing and the Cross, this sea that nourished the island her mother had fled to in grief and pain and defeat; Janet, staring at the new reflection, whispered to Sam to take care of their children, imbue them with the calm steadiness that he had, guide them through life when she was away from them making her sojourn, and when they asked, to tell them that their mother was not a bad woman, but a woman who had taken to the road.

The road, she thought to herself was her destiny, a realisation that made Janet momentarily stop packing, and suddenly Latoya was standing there, her eyes shining, Janet seeing for the first time an air of Puritanism; seeing that the woman was a true bluestocking who would, in a few years time, burst forth into a full-blown bore; Latoya beginning to announce in a doom-laden voice that she intended to become a teacher, not a professor, and also, she was giving up fiction, since fiction was a lie and the world needed the truth; her sudden sweep of the hand breaking a glass perched on a bookcase; and, bending down to pick it up, she cut her finger.

Her finger, the tip of the index, blossomed red, and out of reflex, Janet found her First Aid kit, picked out a plaster and carefully bandaged it; Latoya allowing her to do it, watching her closely, thanking her rather primly and before she left as abruptly as she had come, announced that she had been reading the life of Mary Seacole and had learned through the great woman's story that it is always best to pitch your own tent.

'Pitch your own tent', Janet said over and over to herself as she walked home with what she could carry from the office, recalling the story of the black woman who had been prevented from nursing the soldiers of the Crimea by Florence Nightingale and, undeterred, had set up her own hospital on the edge of the battlefield, a woman who would not allow anyone to erase her from history.

History was a kind of trajectory, not myth; her own life was taking on the property of myth: Latoya, her children and husband, her mother, Tomas, Bradley Preston, she herself, all of them had emerged from an unbroken link, connected; and in that moment of realization, she could see Lucas' face old, see him the way he would be long after she was gone; and at the same time, she could feel herself holding Ayesha, her face against her daughter's thick, coarse hair, inhaling the smell of the coconut pomade that Gloria -Loretta sent back every month, her daughter's fat little arms around her neck and basking in the joy on Ayesha's beautiful face.

Face the fact – she almost said out loud to herself as she entered the Common on the way to Morant Bay Road – that it had been arrogant of her and Sam to believe that they could live in her old neighbourhood as if they had not changed, as if it had not changed; she and Sam as authentic as Marie Antoinette at the Petit Trianon – living in their grand house with its professionally designed garden; how absurd it was to believe that they could have set an example for people who had to live lives that she and Sam had worked hard to avoid.

To avoid the people, they had used them as a façade and now that façade was crumbling; and the one person who had consistently seen past her charade had been Latoya.

Latoya Richardson was suddenly standing at the corner of the street, as if waiting for her, leaning against a building, her head cocked, her eyes looking straight into Janet's, all this clear to her even without her glasses.

Without her glasses, Janet could not see the subtle changes of expression on Latoya's face, as she walked up to her making light conversation about, of all things, the weather; Latoya walking along with her and entering the Common; Janet becoming more and more apprehensive; Latoya now practically shouting something about how she could understand the innate conservatism of human beings; always best to be conservative; she herself planned to get to know the Conservatives in her area, not because they were interesting but because they were real; anyone who thought that human beings were anything else other than conservative did not understand; she might even work for them at the next election, the Conservatives; Latoya, clearly in some sort of mania, a strange smell emanating from her, like something feral; she reached out to Janet's face; in reflex, Janet stopping her; Latoya rocking back on her heels, and then both of them falling to the ground, Latoya on top; in the back of her mind Janet observing the absurdly see-saw motion of their girl-punches, young boys gathering, some taking photos with their mobiles, a few calling out to them, the sound of a dry twig snapping, the weight of Latoya's thrashing body taking the wind out of her; the rapidly growing crowd, baying, taking sides, giving Janet an extra bout of strength which enabled her to push Latoya off her, and both of them standing up simultaneously; she shaking her former student like a rag-doll, part of her exhilarated at what could only be considered an appalling and ridiculous spectacle; and leaving her former student to wipe away the blood from a cut over her right eye, Janet Bookman Baker walked in the direction of home, the sunset shining in her face.

The sunset shining in her face, Janet felt a new kind of energy; the High Street had a vibrancy she had not seen before; beautiful, one road filled with flower stalls; the record shops, the takeaways, the last shoe repair for miles around, all in what seemed to be suspended time, and she in a gentle delirium that gave her energy and direction and made her a part of the last surge of summer before September passed and autumn set in; an oddly foreign humidity enveloped her underarms and forehead, blurred her vision, made her bold so that she looked directly into the eyes of passers-by who interested her, saying hello, smiling, not considering what they might think of her, what she looked like; old Mrs. Perry, waddling down the street, her ubiquitous brown felt hat set at its usual rakish angle, the one called 'naughty' by everyone; there were times in her early girlhood when old Mrs. Perry, a twinkle in her eye, would summon her over to the front door of her small house, still bomb-damaged and full of Vera Lynn, smelling of cabbage, lye soap and hard work; good old Violet Mary Perry, who had lost two sons in the war and a husband who had gone quietly mad one day alone at his allotment; a woman who called her new neighbours 'the dark people' and who had voted Churchill out in '45, bragging about it even though she had cried for three days at the news of his death and would never hear a word against him; a woman who answered a question when asked and had never told a lie to anyone in her life; born within the sound of the Bow Bells and proud of the fact that hers and her ancestors' faces were only fit for cathedral gargoyles, those monsters the real protectors of England; a thin, tall woman with dyed black hair and brows who would puff away on her cigarette as she shared confidences with Janet back then as if she was a grown woman, convinced that as a dark person she was learning about life early anyway because that was what was done amongst the coloured; Janet seeing again those times on the doorstep where she heard stories of the War and its aftermath, not heartwarming tales of men and women of cheerful stoicism, but tales of thieves; shirkers and spivs; and during the waning days of the war, there had been an epidemic of girls and men in full congress in broad daylight on the Common; that old cliché of living for today made graphic and real, after all, no one could be sure whether they would be alive the next day; the greeting before parting after a day's work was 'good luck'; and feeling one with the old lady for the first time in her life, she wanted to stop and speak but if she had, she would have told the old lady – who would have understood – that locked inside her had been a scream that masked a howl, released now, bringing down her old and useless image.

Her old and useless image, gone, she thought to herself, and there was Sam standing at the entrance of their home as if he had expected her at that very moment, the door behind him opening into a cavernous darkness she had never seen before, the house that they had both once considered the symbol of their victory, revealing itself to her as nothing more than an exercise in sound middle-class principles and good judgement; exemplified by the fresh tulips he had brought home, already curving downward in gentle arcs in the vase at the entrance to the stairs, Sam – his face younger and more vulnerable than she had seen it in years- smiling and kissing her on the cheek as he eased her jacket off, his hand trembling, the slight smell of drink on his breath, his glasses pushed to the top of his head, avoiding – she could sense it – asking her where hers were; still in his suit, his tie loosened, full of that air of sadness and confusion that he would on occasion bring home from Chambers; leading her into the dining room, pouring her a whiskey with inhuman precision, the drink so clearly a refuge, asking herself why she had not noticed this before, taking in the atmosphere of the dining room, the state of things in general, this room, notwithstanding their robust and concerted family life, maintained a Stygian gloom that she had always tried to dispel with lighting and for a time candles, but it never went away, along with an uncharacteristic dampness that some of the old people would say indicated that the room was haunted; thinking of this as she caught Sam looking at the specks of dirt and minor scratches on her right arm; slightly tipsy, he inspected her arm muttering 'picaro' which he corrected to 'picara'; a new word, he explained, that he would use to describe her to anyone who asked him who she was, what her essence was; pouring himself another drink, he continued with the etymology of a word which implied 'wanderer': 'picaro' being the root of picaresque, picaresque being the true nature of the novel, the novel being the chronicle and accumulations, the discovery and the discards of the wanderer; at least, Sam continued, that was what his new pupil in Chambers had said to him just the other day, in a move, no doubt, to demonstrate that he had a 'hinterland' – a life beyond work – so he had pulled out of the blue an utterly pointless and useless fact to impress him.

To impress him with her own knowledge of the obscure and useless, Janet told him about the French use of the word nègre in relation to writing which led her to reveal that she had learned this from Abena Assantewa, the celebrated African American writer and public figure with whom she had been corresponding for months; now tipsy herself from drink, she told how the letters had arrived, out of the blue, as if Abena had been guided to send them to her; she had found comfort through their exchange of letters, and a solace that allowed her to reveal a self that she could never share with anyone else, not even with him; she had become dependent on the letters, they had begun to form and shape her without her being aware of it, and through them she had been re-born; if only she could give Professor Assantewa something comparable, but that was not possible; she was convinced that Professor Assantewa was in Paris nearing the end of her life, and no one, most of all him, could understand what she felt about this dying; Janet saying all of this in a rush and tumble of words, a part of her watching herself break the pledge that she and Sam had made early on in their marriage that whatever major changes occurred, the other partner would know; she marvelling at how he listened without comment aware that she was making Sam sit and listen to the history of her secret self; exposing herself not only to him but to herself, stripping away her own scaffold, readying herself for all that would come later.

Later, she and Sam made love, her aggression a surprise to them both, surprising, too, was the discovery of a red birth mark behind his ankle, something that she had not seen before; in the calm almost

330

monotone voice of a man who had recounted his story a hundred times, Sam told her how, as a boy, his mother had thought the birthmark some sort of curse and had sent him to be exorcised; the big, brooding pastor with the few words turned out to have been his natural father, a man who had run away at his birth and whom his mother had excised from the family saga; sending him to the man had been a perverse act on her part; he a spitting image of the man who never once acknowledged their connection; his father's talking to God like an equal, explaining to the Deity that he wanted the cursed mark removed from the young man who had been sent to him and some time later on, considering the Devil to have finally departed, leaving God to render him whole even if he had not been left blemish-free.

Free, at eighteen, from the control of his mother and stepfather, Sam had set out to develop a relationship with his natural father, a man who wrestled with the Devil at night, arguing with him not over sin, but freedom, the freedom to choose to go down to the infernal regions if it meant burning there as a free man; not the frightened supplicant of an all-powerful Deity; to want to risk damnation, he would say to Sam, seemed to him to be the highest form of love of God; by fighting God's power he would demonstrate a love so strong that it would free God from having to be The Eternal Being and leave Him simply to be loved for Himself, whether there was a heaven or a hell; in the end, his father had accepted both God and Sam, who by then was travelling back and forth to Dudley to see him, sitting in the congregation listening to the four-hour sermons that he would spend hours unpicking at night; later, when he was older, attending his father's church, offering, needing, to serve the man who never once called him 'son'; needing to stand with him on street corners when he exhorted passers-by to come to Jesus; his father telling him once, after his nightly wrestling match with the Dark and the Light, that he was glad that he had found Jesus Christ well before he had discovered Christians and Christianity; disgusted by their pomp and circumstance in the name of a man who had been born in a stable and who had died like a common criminal, rose from the dead and first showed himself to a former prostitute; if Christianity was about anything it was about being on the road, the dust on your feet, eating what was given to you, sleeping rough; his father's insistence on the primacy of his own point of view and his way of seeing things, had, at the time been quite astonishing because it had mirrored his own disposition, even now, and made him wonder from time to time how it had come to be that he was so much like a man who had never been a part of his life from his birth until the day of the exorcism; and now, fifteen years after his death, he still continued to wonder about connections and links that could not be seen, connections that shaped and defined and ruled things: both he and his father would rub their chins when deep in thought; they both had had that nervous itch on the back of the right hand when things were not going well; Sam, haunted for years by the fear that he might turn out like his father, that he might leave his family, too; this fear the source of his over-parenting, over-husbanding, over-involvement with his clients, the latter rendering him, in his opinion, ultimately an ineffective lawyer; even as he was overdoing everything, there lurked in the back of his mind a nagging voice, his own voice, telling him to drop it all, run away; the truth being that not a day went by when he was not tempted to vanish, disappear; the struggle to resist was the source of the little colds he acquired in mid-winter, positive that Lucas copied his cough through empathy; and all the while Janet listening to a voice that she did not recognize, Sam's voice, a new voice flat and low, nothing in his eyes.

In his eyes, Janet saw reflected a man she had never seen before; a man who had come to understand that he had been taking on more and more extreme clients, hopeless cases, spending more time than he should meticulously preparing arguments for hopeless cases, earning more and more in Legal Aid; doing it not for the money but for the sordidness of it all, choosing to work with ever-more low life solicitors, many of them looked like criminals themselves, the way some dogs resembled their masters, the solicitors tending to imitate the facial expressions, the ticks and particular mannerisms of those they represented; fascinating how their features changed from proximity to crime; which led him to question what effect environment had on human beings, he himself had taken on that air of menace and violence that surrounded his clients, could violence be the real reason why he wanted Lucas to attend school in the community – not the community's violence – but his own?; did he want to see his son struggle so that he could go through the struggle with him, and in that way prove himself over and over every day so that he could begin to feel again?

To feel again was what he wanted, he said, what he needed, so much had been hidden within him. Listening to him, Janet had a great craving for a cigarette which led her to open their bedroom window, and there, under the small lights he had set up, Tomas' garden glistened in the night and closing the window and drawing the blinds, Janet Bookman Baker returned to the bed she shared with her husband, as she sat beside him, cradling his head in her lap, Janet said 'yes'; 'yes' to her sleeping children; 'yes' to the house and the neighbourhood; 'yes' to her fragile and lovely husband, his face beneath her beautiful, solemn and still.

Beautiful and solemn and still in the morning, the river was easy to get down to at low tide.

At low tide, Janet joined the elderly and those not so elderly, their faces fixed to the mud and searching, delighting at the merest hint of metal shining against the mackerel sky; shoeless along with the scavengers searching for their fortune in the debris and the wet; making her way to the water's edge, the river no longer her enemy, now her friend and helpmeet; wondering, as she stood there gazing, just what it would be like to wade in, to let it wash over her head, to feel its heaviness and its darkness enveloping her, pulling her down, washing over her, taking her down to the booty and the corpses, then releasing her and she, without water wings, would have the knowledge of riding the water, high on top of the waves, her black skin wet and dripping, silver against the grey light, she would ride the Thames as it poured into the sea and the sea into the ocean, the ocean carrying her back to the Ancient Land, where she would emerge on land as The Returned, draped in cowry and sea shells, a million tiny bells trembling from her hair and her fingertips, the trees bowing in her path and waves parting in the near distance; and there she would see her father once again, recalling what the obeah woman had said : that when she stood in the mud of the river, she would know a secret and that secret would open a door that would never close.

Close by the river, she thought about her mother, a woman whose husband, if not in body but in spirit, had left her, taken himself to another place inside himself, left her alone with the house and the pots and pans, left her to glory in her fixtures, her lovely garden, her obsession with the correctness and order of life, left her nothing but herself, her daughter, and her own efforts to re-build her sense of herself brick by brick, defend her identity, her self-definition, her honour, when she had been raised to do nothing at all but be a helpmeet, an appendage; but in the privacy of herself she had survived, carefully, secretly, putting away bits of herself, inwardly laying low until the time came when she could step out into the light and be free.

Free, Janet thought to herself as Morant Bay Road came into view, giddy from the realization that she had got her mother all wrong, completely wrong; not some harridan, or monstrous, a figure that she had constructed from nightmares, but a woman whose life was dedicated to tending her own flame now.

Now she climbs the stairs to Ayesha's room, her daughter away at a friend's house, her scent still lingering, Léopoldine, her black doll prominently rested on the pillows at the head of the bed; the doll's sharp dark eyes staring directly at her as Janet walked out of the room, and on to Lucas's room filled with his usual collection of maths books and equations, piles of clothing and an orderly patch where he sat and wrote and thought; tidying it out of reflex, Janet stopped and looked around, her eyes trying to see with his eyes, following what she could see as a system within the jumble, a trail leading to the corner of his desk.

The corner of his desk was cluttered and dusty, but beneath a pile of papers there was her father's missing copy of Paradise Lost, its bookmark was a photo of Milton Bookman holding his grandson, Lucas.

Lucas had had the book and the photo all along and had never told her, making him clearly the heir, and not Ayesha, to the Bookman family's genius at keeping secrets, she stunned that her son had had a secret life, that even her child had developed a façade to cover his real self, tucked in a neat and hidden corner of his room. This, she suddenly realized, this was the reason he had to go away to study, to be free to discover his answer.

An answer to the riddle of her father's disappearance that weekend decades ago was what she was after, Janet had told Janey Francis when she rang her up the following morning; Janey promptly suggesting that they meet at her new cake and tea-shop behind Taken As Red, The Crimson Dalliance.

The Crimson Dalliance was decorated in Janey's trademark red, its vibrancy practically eye-watering; Janet sitting at a corner table, watched Janey behind the counter glowing, while one of her flamboyant ladies served at table, leaving some sort of glitter in her wake as she moved around; Janey, as usual, easy in her skin; the entire place filled with women easy in their skin, black women of all shades and hues, glorious, ethereal, as if they had come from another place, from another world where they were considered beautiful; come from another world simply to eat at Janey's place; there was a whistling woman reading the serious press at a table next to Janet's, making a sweeping gesture as she turned the pages, scrutinizing every word carefully, whistling audibly and arrogantly, causing Janet to recall the old Medieval admonition about a whistling woman: 'a whistling woman like a crowing hen, never comes to a good end'; this entire room, she thought, was full of women who would have been considered, hundreds of years ago, to have been the cause of bad harvests, blights on the land, and malediction, in other words, all in their own way, each woman was a disturber of the peace, just as Janey Francis was…just as she was.

Just as Janet was about to leave – convinced that Janey had changed her mind about talking to her – she appeared asking Janet if she would like to go to her Scarlet Palace, the outdoor extension in what had been the garden, a refuge that allowed her to enjoy her Cuban cigar – lawfully – she added, and before Janet could respond, she found herself following Janey as she made her way like a serpent through the tables and out of the Dalliance proper into another atmosphere just as red, but full of smoke and low-key reggae; and sitting down at a side table, Janey lit a Churchill while at the same time telling her that she liked to smoke it like a Cuban woman on the point of pouring libation to a river goddess, except, Janey Francis laughed, she personally had no god nor goddess; nothing but her own rules.

Her own rules had led her to this moment, she said, and now they impelled her to tell what she knew about that weekend long ago and to reveal her part in it; Janey Francis, speaking slowly and matter-of-factly, her voice conspiratorial yet as light as a feather, forming Os with the smoke of her cigar, from time to time watching them curl and vanish, a woman, Janet observed with a pleasure and approval that surprised her, who loved tobacco smoke and the culture that went with it.

Tobacco smoke and the culture that went with it, Janey Francis began as she served Janet a strong yet delicate Caribbean coffee tickled with a soupçon of rum, was alien to Milton Bookman, a Puritan by nature, who had found himself in a situation that his natural Puritan nature had fought; that nature evident in how he had argued with members of the book club, for example, a man addicted to detail and accuracy; this was true of her father, Janet admitted, both of them laughing together at the memory of her father, Janey offering her a puff on the cigar, instructing her on how to take it in, the smoke and aroma heady, intoxicating, making Janet slightly dizzy, speedy, beautiful.

Beautiful, the man was beautiful in his insistence on control and the proper way of doing things, of being, Janey Francis continued, her eyes constantly fixed on Janet, almost singing her father's name as she listened to Janey Francis tell her that Milton Bookman had been a man who had expected everyone else to be the way he was; he must have run his wife,

Gloria-Loretta crazy, and Janet laughed again, remembering the times she would see them locked in verbal combat over the proper way to dry a dish; and that book club he conducted on his bus once a month, a wonderful thing, but also a vehicle for the exercise of his ego; to see him and the other gentlemen who attended the club clash was a hilarious thing to behold; old elk banging their antlers against one another, argument being the only thing that he and a certain elderly male member of the book club could ever agree on.

On the day the gentleman had joined the book club, Janey Francis said – offering Janet another smoke of the Churchill which she gratefully took – the old man had announced to everyone on board that his grandfather had been a famous Victorian explorer, someone right out of Rider Haggard who had, in childhood, been shown a map of the world with blank, empty spaces and had taken it upon himself to go out and fill in one of those spaces, which was why he had gone to Tibet, since Tibet was one of those blank spaces on his grandfather's Victorian map; and how glorious it must have been, the old gentleman had told the entire book club in a booming voice, for a man to confront a map full of blank spaces, how glorious and good those days long ago must have been when the world made sense and everyone and everything had a place; his grandfather, determined to make his mark, had walked through the capital city of Tibet and had found himself surrounded by applause everywhere he went, wave upon wave of applause, the sweetest sound he had ever heard in his life and he had never forgotten it; that greeting in a far away place being the first thing that any of his grandchildren learned about him; well, Janey laughed, almost choking on her cigar smoke, Milton Bookman had listened patiently with the look of a coiled viper about to spring, and waiting until the story had finished, filled in the blank space in the old man's narrative that he had not known was there: that the clapping his grandfather had received was not a sign of welcome and praise but a gesture of repulsion: the applause was an appeal to heaven to expel the 'white devil'.

The white devil, Janey added, now slowly smoking her cigar and savouring it with a kind of masculine relish which was all female, stared past Janet into the distance, the white devil, she said, was the expression the Tibetans of the time used, not Milton's own reflection on the story-teller or his grandfather, a detail that her father had neglected to mention to Janet when he had explained the source of the Tibetan's reaction, the old gentleman, after being told the source of the clapping instantly took offence, which was what Milton wanted because the man's anger had disempowered him; Milton, of course, being an extremely proud man did not calm the man or bother to explain any further meaning, Janey Francis said; Janet smiling at the memory of her father's telling of it, the way he had embellished it for her, the way he had made himself look like a hero against some smug racist instead of an arrogant bore; but Janet had not come to hear what she had known already.

She had known already that Janey would have another tale to tell, a tale that would be different from the one she had carried inside for most of her life, the story she had told herself over and over again in order to justify and explain so much that had not been good in her own life, a tale that she had wilfully re-constructed and now she had come to hear it in its entirety, in its truth; Janet waiting, now as the day began to fade and she could see that Janey had designed the place to catch the western light, the dying light, the light of the afterworld, 'the country of the young' as the Irish called it; Janet mesmerized by the way it glistened and shimmered and rippled and flowed as Janey, finishing the last of the Churchill, began, as if talking to herself, to recite a portion of what Janet recognized as Wordsworth's The Ruined Cottage: "Oh sir, the good die first…And they whose hearts are dry as summer dust…Burn to the socket. "; and Janey Francis' eyes grew soft and she almost whispered what she had to say next: that Milton Bookman had seen himself, in the end, as nothing but dust, a broken, useless man who had loved his wife, loved his daughter, but who had lacked the courage to keep the one woman who had been the love of his life, a black American girl by the name of Earlene who had been a passenger on his bus one rainy afternoon decades ago, just one afternoon; a skinny, haunted-faced girl with a cheap, battered suitcase and carrying a small black statue, her good luck, she had said; lost and frightened, she had caught Milton's bus, not knowing where she was going, and as Milton Bookman collected her fare, their eyes met and they experienced what the French call a 'coup de foudre', and he had brought her to Taken As Red because they had not wanted to part, and they had stayed in the spare room in the back of her shop that weekend; but something happened that she did not understand: he left Earlene and went back to his life; she did not know what happened to Earlene, she had probably gone back to America, married a man there and was a grandmother now, round and happy; but Milton had never recovered, so that gradually, right before her eyes, he had withered and died, reminding her in the end of Wordsworth's poem, having read it in one of the books someone had brought along to the book club; the poem described her, how she was like dust, having lived long past Milton Bookman, the man she had loved but could not have, long past him into a future she could not see, just a performer on a stage that she had created, and one day, the curtain would come down, and yes, she would have hundreds of mourners, but -"live your life, Janet"- drowning the rest of what she had to say in the hard, bitter taste of the coffee.

The hard, bitter taste of the coffee had brought back to Janet's mind the little statue on her father's desk, black, its hard, crude carving chipped in certain places, dark yet managing to release a brutal whiteness that had made the statue seem like a black hole into which prayers could be emptied and she had done so; recalling how she had, as a child, been drawn to it, drawn to its ugliness; remembering, too, her father's obsessive protection of it, the way in which he had kept it slightly out of reach; she knew, even at a young age, that the statue was more than just something left behind on his bus as he had always told her; the statue had something to do with that lost weekend and with Janey Francis and the mysterious Earlene whose letter he had carried until the moment of his death; and whose story of loss she had imitated in her own way.

In her own way, Janey Francis had continued, she had made a refuge for Milton Bookman, giving him a place where he could escape his life and recreate his true nature; that nature coming to full flower one hot, rainy night in August, a Friday evening many years ago, when he had come to her shop with Earlene, her big, halo-shaped afro, her eyes like the eyes of a doe, her fragility and beauty overwhelming; he and Earlene had made plans, right at her kitchen table, to run away together to Paris, live there, and in the fullness of time, take the children they had made together back to Africa, but never deserting his Janet, he would come for his Janet; as he spoke of his plans, Milton Bookman's face was as clear and as happy as she had ever seen it; Janey could remember watching Milton and Earlene together; thinking now how easy it had been for her to want to protect their happiness, protect his happiness, his peace, his clarity.

His clarity, that fateful weekend had caused her to review her own life, and that was when she had decided to expand her business, branch out, live to the hilt, be free, happy, and she had told Earlene that she intended to change her life, and the American girl's big beautiful eyes had filled with a sadness that Janey would never forget, as she said – out of the presence of Milton – that she was changing her life, too; she was returning to America where she belonged and that Milton must return to where he belonged, to his wife and child; and while Milton slept, Earlene had told her that she and Milton had walked to the river a few hours before where she had told him her decision.

Her decision, she had said to Janey, had also been a part of forgiving her sister Abena, a professor who had no contact with her because she was ashamed of her; it was the weekend in London, with Milton that had made her see that she had to return to America to make it right with her sister; going away, far away, was the best way that she could hold on to Milton forever, to what they had, to what they could have had; away from him she could be with him until the hour of her death and beyond, and if it was God's will, she would be free to find her sister and tell her that she loved her; it had been so hard, Earlene had said, to tell him, impossible to find and form the words; when she had told him her decision, he had said that he hated everything connected with that moment: Waterloo Bridge where they had stood when she told him; the sky above and most of all, the river; he hated the river because he did not have the courage to plunge into it, he hated it as his wife feared it – that

340

hatred and fear of the great water was what he and his wife could have together; that moment, listening to Earlene, had begun Day One of the rest of her life.

Her life, Earlene had said that day decades ago, leaning against the sink, the dying light of the hot August sun illuminating her hair, would be a life dedicated to working for others because she had caused enough pain; and before Earlene had gone forever, she had asked her to give Milton Bookman a little statue, a Black Virgin, a gift she would have to make reparations for because she had taken it without permission; she had needed it to insure her safety, someday, it would return to where it belonged, Black Madonnas always did; and she had also left behind an antique too, an antique of a black woman to give to Milton which he had refused to take, she, Janey having had to eventually give it to the rag and bone man in exchange for some beautiful red-handled enamel kitchen-wear made in the States during the war; she had seen no use for the photo, it hadn't fit her purpose or her decor; but what she had not exchanged had been Milton Bookman's secret.

Milton Bookman's secret, Janey Francis finishing her cigar said, had in a sense defined her own life; she was happy to be the "other woman", she had wanted to be; and laughing a hearty laugh, she asked Janet if she would like a little rum to help her on her way.

On her way into the house, Janet watched Edna Saddler digging in her garden, Janet standing half in deep shadow, half in mottled light, could see the old woman, her face the colour of mahogany, her ancient hands with their spidery veins, big, mannish, yet full of grace, digging and pulling and plucking, oblivious to the gentle rain that had begun to fall, washing the dying leaves and the dying grass and the green conifer trees, robustly spring-like and eternal in the dying summer.

In the dying summer, Tomas had told her, in that conjunction between autumn and the end of the heat and humidity, his stepfather had planted two evergreens as a reminder of his Bavarian homeland; the evergreens had caused Tomas to imagine himself there, in a land of mountains and conifers, subject to a mad king whose Versailles he would lose himself in; gradually, his dream of the Bavarian garden had turned to revulsion, to fear anytime he had come near the evergreens, that fear had been a driver in his childhood, had sent him into the Army and war, and which had eventually faded, turning his stepfather's trees back into the benign refuge he had intended.

He had intended to let her know that he was going away, Janet told herself as she walked into the house; he had thought it best to simply go, leave her to return him to where he belonged in her life: in the worlds of her imagination and of her heart; in their own land where they could reside in the wind.

The wind picked up and Mrs. Saddler returned to her house, looking from side to side in case someone was lurking in the shadows, her face beautiful and hard; and Janet thought of Tomas, and in thinking of him, she recalled another of her father's favourite poems: '…and so it was I entered the broken world to trace the visionary company of love…'

Love, Janet knows, is what Sam is talking about; after she tells him that she must go to Paris, to Abena, and she was not sure when she would return, but she would, she would come to the children, to him, to their life; she is glad that she has no illusions, while Sam, as if in another place, talks of a client he had long ago who thought herself a descendant of the Queen Of Sheba, exiled in a world of barbarians, and this lineage had given her the gift, no, the curse, of hearing the truth behind what people said; a woman who had fled to Paris, where she had thrown herself into the Seine, and there were times when he thought of her, floating like Ophelia; and he was with her, too, floating on the water.

I See America Through Their Eyes.

Showboat.

At last.

Showboat's boat is a small yacht, lights strung across the prow.

Lights up the night.

Drunk people hanging around trying to get inside.

Security guards at the gangplank.

Nightime in London.

Another largish crowd of people wait patiently in a light rain. They are laughing and talking among themselves. They've got invites.

Would rather have the pissed crowd, but it's live with a ten-second delay, so maybe not.

I wear my coat, of course, plus a pair of jeans and a t-shirt with a George Bernard Shaw quote: *Fashion Is Nothing But An Induced Epidemic*.

It's the only thing I have clean.

A girl with a clipboard leads me through the crowd.

She's not sure, but I have the email.

There's a long counter and stools with high backs that surround it.

The camera track circles the counter and there are stands for the audience.

I can see the presenter reading a sheaf of papers at the counter.

He's wearing glasses and looks like an accountant for a rock star.

I've never seen him before but obviously the guy's a big deal because lots of people are fluttering around him.

Wish I knew who he was.

For a second.

They take me into a room full of lights with a make-up lady with an apron full of brushes and a cheery expression.

She tells me right away that she doesn't have a foundation for my skin, that this is always a problem with black girls.

She's been a make-up artist for twenty-five years and in the old days, she just made everyone lighter-skinned-the-handful-who-were-on-air-but-now-things-have-to-be-more-subtle.

She tells me that I have great skin, 'all black girls do, I want to come back black'.

I tell her that first, she'll have to suffer.

She seems to accept this mission.

Another make-up artist comes in who looks exactly like my make-up lady and they start gossiping about who has had a face lift, who has had botox, fillers, a nose job, hair transplants, boob jobs, chin re-alignments, tooth implants.

I'm thinking that this information could be of use to someone somewhere for the purposes of me making a little money, but I have never heard of anyone under discussion, so…

The lights around the mirror are very strong and I can see my mother's face looking back at me and sometimes my father's.

The faces go back and forth.

Yikes.

The make-up ladies then abruptly switch to tales of their individual visits to the US, and how much they enjoy Americans.

I see America through their eyes and it is a place of wonder, big food, big fun and great manners.

America sounds, through them, a beautifully naïve pleasure dome, a nirvana away from the travails of this sceptred isle.

It is the place I was born in and am returning to.

I feel excited and scared in a good way.

What will I sound like now to people in my homeland? Will I suddenly, in the midst of shopping in some monstrous mall, wish I was back in the high street? Will my 'a' slip, will my consonants sound too precise and sharp so that people will think I'm stuck-up? Should

I start slurring them now, making them soft now? I wish those ladies could go back with me, escort me off the plane, show me what they see, let me feel what they feel.

I will be a foreigner there, and I need guidance.

My made-up face is lighter than it usually is.

Fab. It's a mask that I can hide behind.

Suddenly there's a timid knock on the door like the ones we used at Roc when we wanted to talk to Mother Superior. It intrigued me, made me sit up straight.

It's the guy I saw earlier in the studio. He introduces himself as Carson Quinlan.

And he's American.

That really makes me relax and I can tell that he relaxes, too.

We do the usual American thing about where are you from.

He's from L.A.

I ask him why he's here in London and his face goes really dead so I leave it.

He straddles the chair and looks me straight in the eye:

"Ever done 'live'?"

"Never been on television."

"Good. I like folks like you. Just say what you want, no bad language and it'll be over in the fastest thirty minutes you've ever had in your life. I go back and forth. Just look at me, not the camera. And that's it. Do you know the show?"

"Nope."

"Even better. The audience is vocal and rowdy so don't let them scare you. They're some of the coolest people in London, so if they react, you're made."

Yes, I can sense a weariness in the guy.

He tells me that he's married to an English woman who saved his life, and they have three children, "four people I love more than anything in the world, so I'm here and it's been good. I just miss proper hotdogs and any kind of beach."

He leans in further, conspiratorially.

345

"The people behind this show don't get it yet. The 'back-in-the-day-brigade'think I'm dumbing the channel down, let alone this show. I had a column back in New York and my job was simple: to fellate celebrities in print. Period. In my column, they never did anything wrong. They were never ugly. Never fat. If they were ax murderers, my column blamed the ax. But there's resistance here about that and it tires me out. Look, if this show continued the way it was going with the last host – the Oxbridge guy with the long, thinning blond hair, really smart but when you listened to him you felt stupid – it wouldn't be here. Nobody wants to feel like a dork anymore when they watch TV. He made the show into a debating society, you couldn't understand what they were talking about half the time – Heigel Shmeigel, and worse – the people on it were ugly."

"Ugly?"

"AWA," he said, "Ageing Without Assistance."

I was really stunned.

"Plus – and this is real bad – they were critical of everything. I mean, this is a critics' show, not a criticizer show. It's infotainment."

I asked him if the people he talked about paid him.

"Of course not! But nobody is going to risk a $50 million movie with a bunch of critical people. That doesn't work. You can't have hate when you're dealing with celebs! What's wrong with beautiful? This show is all about the People. The People see themselves, ok at a higher level, but we're American. We understand aspirational."

Actually, I don't, but I listen with as wise a face as I can.

My two fellow panelists arrive.

They just get something slapped on and they're out.

They're men.

They've done this before so they know not to trip on the cables.

They've both written books which I've skimmed before I came on.

One of the guys is called Spikey, a 'brother from the community', an ex-mugger who's written a bestseller called 'Going Out To Eat'.

"If you like what Carson likes, the camera'll stay on you and Carson will only talk to you." Spikey says.

"I don't understand."

"Hey, all these people are hooked up. It's a game."

"This isn't real?"

"Real? Telly's not real."

He switches gears by telling me about the adventures of him and his former mates on various mugging excursions on the Underground. He gives me tips on which stations were the best pickings.

The other one is Teach, a musician-guru who's plugging a book called 'The One', about...'how James Brown turned popular music around. Before him, pop music began on the upbeat. Brown began it on the downbeat – the funk. The Funk – one, two, three, four – bam, bam, bam, bam, 'Get up, get on up. Get up, Get on up...' Rap, soul and their offspring are downbeat. Reggae is supreme downbeat."

Ok.

I'll have to re-read this one.

The show starts.

Good old Carson turns into a TV monster, the heat and light coming off the guy when the floor manager cues him is blinding. His eyes are bigger, his mouth is bigger, he grows taller. The lights are hot and I start to sweat.

But I'm keeping the coat on.

The first guest is on a live link, Marcel something or other.

He's talking about a book he's written about French TV and he's talking in French. Very fast. I'm gradually understanding a little bit. He uses 'con' a lot which makes Carson twitch. I want to tell him that it doesn't exactly translate as "cunt", but this is the one forbidden word on TV so I can't say anything. The French guy thinks that if Flaubert were alive today he would be on TV. Voltaire certainly would.

Scary fucking thought.

Next comes the novel set in Renaissance Padua which we all hate.

We hate all of the meticulous research that went into it; we hate the industry that's grown up around it, we hate the novel for the money it's made, its massive readership. We, without consulting one another, have decided that we are the ones who will crash this runaway train down to earth. We are on telly and we have the power.

I say something that Carson likes.

The cameras stay on me.

Everybody else is wiped out, non-existent, just like Spikey said.

There is something exhilarating about this.

This is a blood sport and the audience is baying.

We're all goading one another, and the high is amazing.

I can see how people can get addicted to this, how they can want to do this more than anything in the world, the camera whirling around, the lights.

Suddenly, a small quiet-looking woman, like your favourite high school teacher, comes out of the audience.

It's……the author of the Renaissance Padua crap!

She has this compassionate look on her face.

She feels sorry for us.

She feels sorry for us three losers who are putting her book down, and afterwards we will return to our hovels while she's chauffeured back to her five-star.

She's smiling and Carson asks her about the book and she spends a minute on the usual stuff and then she changes the whole thing, at least for me.

"In researching medieval Padua, Florence, Venice, I faced something through my research that I didn't want to look at. Maybe our species is hard-wired to be sexually attracted to children. As we have become more conscious, I've noticed that the age of consent has risen. It's not acceptable anymore to marry a 10 year old child. But it used to be. In some societies it still is, but not practised. A Venetian bride would have been considered old at sixteen. Over the centuries, we've developed a taboo, a revulsion against sexual contact with children, but how deep does that go? Another thing: there's pedophilia and also pedophobia, very real in the 70s with all those movies about children possessed and children as devils. Maybe hatred/attraction to children is like war and eating fat, it's hard-wired. Above all, through the book I was able to face the abuse that I suffered at the hands of my father. He gave himself a heart attack when I was ten to stop himself. He was a scholar, a bright man. I've forgiven him. Kids are always at the mercy of adults. And maybe civilization itself emerged and emerges as we become more aware of our duty of care to them."

She stops and you can hear a pin drop in the studio for a few seconds which in broadcasting terms is called 'dead air', the ultimate vacuum that must be filled and being a broadcaster, I plough in faster than I can think.

I talk about Earlene and how she cared for me, and how she kept the atmosphere clear for me and my life and how she made blueberry pie for me and how I long to make that pie again and this is shocking as I watch myself talk about Carl Cookson and my father's accusations about him which were not true and how Carl came over and fought with my dad and how my mother and Earlene tried to stop them and the next day Carl was dead. He had killed himself for Earlene – and me, too; he loved me, too – then Earlene, my Earlene, was gone, all because of me, all because I wanted to cross the picket fence that divided me from the rest of the world and spend time with the nice man next door, with the two of them, the two who showed me everything.

Carson 's mind is blown, so he moves quickly along to the next item.

This is a webcast called 'Faustina TV' about a girl and her everyday life……in my home back in Chicago!

Faustina is one of the Langdale X People's molls and she is taking us on a tour of where I grew up.

There's my mom in the front room with a blackboard teaching mathematics to a roomful of gangbangers.

My mother.

She looks ethereal.

Transparent, as if she has left this world.

Next Faustina is showing us her street, the street I grew up on, a street once full of lawns and bikes against fences, and nice cars, and there is nothing now but rubble and slums…and our house alone.

Our house is standing alone.

Faustina shows my dad whom she calls 'The Phantom'.

That's what he is, standing at the top of the stairs leading to the master bedroom, dressed in a tracksuit, his face and eyes haunted.

I don't say anything.

I have no comment, even though Carson is trying to get me to say something.

He doesn't know that this belongs to me.

I say nothing.

I've said enough.

My dad.

I remember once when his face was like that when I was a child.

I saw him go into his own world.

I knew in my heart and soul that something was wrong then, that something was going to be wrong in the future.

That day he broke every glass in the house. Every one.

Mom left and was gone for three days.

While she was gone, Earlene took me and barricaded us in my room.

To calm me down, she began to tell me the story of a little girl in the future. The little girl was trying to find her mother and father.

The future world was not beautiful. It was not good.

She never told me the ending.

Then, she told me about her sister, a famous professor who was ashamed of her and who she prayed for every night.

She said that she wanted, almost as much as she wanted me to be safe and happy, for that sister to find the peace she was searching for.

She prayed one day, before it was too late, that they would meet again.

And you're smiling. Because you know.

I don't take the car they've laid on.

I walk home.

I see a car coming.

For a split second, I have to make a decision.

I see the driver's face.

He is innocent.

I stand back from the curb.

I am tired.

I start counting the money I have.

I have to see if I have enough.

Because I am going to Paris.

I have the address, the door code.

She wrote it at the end of the last instalment.

I am going to the apartment of Abena Assantewa.

I'm going to thank her for the story.

I am going to tell her that we can both put Earlene to rest.

I know that she brought us together.

But you knew before me.

Your sister, Miss Africa, made sure that I got the story every morning.

And that I didn't miss it.

And that I came here in the end.

Thank you for taking care of her, for keeping her for me.

For me.

I am standing alone in the full-length mirror.

I am naked.

After all these years of dressing and undressing in the dark, I am now in the light.

These days, yes, I would be and am considered fat. Not cat-call-in-the-street-fat, but well, if I shopped I couldn't just walk in and do it.

I pinch a roll of fat on my waist and on my kneecaps. Rubens' paintings flash before my eyes and I'm not flattering myself here by mentioning my body and Rubens in the same breath, just saying that the images flashed by. Also, I think of Hemingway's description of Brett Ashley, but he's describing the body of a drunk who doesn't eat. Brett is about streamlining, which is the form – with the exception of the 50s – of the 20th century.

They say that fat is down to pollution, which must be true because the US is the only country in the world where the poor people are fat.

I have to keep that in mind.

I put on a short, tight, black, sleeveless, low cut dress that I bought at Oxfam once while pissed. It stops just above my knees.

My…cleavage…shows.

Why am I doing this for an old man?

I run my fingers through my hair to make it more Medusa-like.

I find an old tube of lipstick that I've had for too long, prick a fresh opening around the crusty top until something fluid comes out that I can use, and putting on a pair of high-heels I was given at work as a joke birthday present, I stand and look in the mirror once more.

The person looking back at me in the mirror looks like a clown, an alien, but this is a special occasion.

What does Professor Assantewa say in her book, 'Dead White Females'?: 'Most women – no matter what their ethnicity – see their bodies as ornaments. The body is static, only existing to be seen and presented to be seen by others. We do not see our bodies as dynamic, moving, changing.'

I don't see mine at all, except in anger and terror.

Until now.

And your sister. I made that mistake with your sister.

She'd come to work and I'd judge her as just one of those high-end Afro-Brit girls, just a bunch of blonde-streaked extensions, lipstick and weird name. But she guarded me. She made sure that I had Professor Assantewa's story whenever it came through.

Yours is easy. Yaa.

Yaa who takes care of Abena Assantewa.

Yaa who's been sitting with me and listening to me.

You're like the invisible sister who grew up unknown to me.

But who was always there.

I wasn't ever on my own, was I?

Before I leave for Montgomery Tourlaine's place in my new clothes, Dan sends an email saying 'Tell Me A Story' has been won by a fashion editor who set her tale of a woman trying to write a literary novel in modern day London. North London.

It's a comedy.

I waddle across the corridor in my strange clothes and knock on Montgomery Tourlaine's door.

He opens it.

He is in an old suit and wearing a bow tie.

I can see candlelight in the background.

I love the flames.

He leads me down a dark corridor lined with books into his small front room which is brown and oakey and is full of dust.

I sit on his couch. It sinks down almost to the floor as he hands me a small glass of sherry and some Ritz crackers.

On the wall over the bookcase are some framed quotes:

I am myself astray in life as on an endless beach where I was alone. *In Search Of Lost Time*, Proust.

When we are born, we cry
That we come to this great stage of fools.
King Lear.

I assume that these quotes mean something to him.

I don't ask.

While I drink the sherry he reads the latest musings from a crony living in Greenwich Village:

'Femi-nazis…They finally chased me out of the university with their fiery broomsticks! Why? Because I didn't teach women writers. I teach writers, not women writers! Women! Women turn great writers into monsters. They tried to ruin Ted Hughes. What have women done of importance in this world! They didn't create civilization! They squatted, holding up the herds and the armies and that's it. That's it! We need women for our primal urges, and dynasties. I envy homosexual men. No wonder they're called 'gay'. No women!'

How do you tell somebody who's your friend that his friend is an asshole? But he beats me to it.

"He's an asshole", Montgomery Tourlaine says.

He reads on: 'I've got students who plagiarize left, right and centre. Some student in my French class copied Jacques le Fataliste as their pastiche of pre-revolutionary writing, as if I wouldn't know! Everyone talks about 'community', but what about the community of the dead? Is Diderot fair game because he can't sue? And my son, my own son. He doesn't have complete thoughts anymore. 'Ignore' and 'cancel' rank just below Holocaust Denial as the two nastiest words in his vocabulary. He can answer right away but he can't THINK. High speed is what counts with this guy.'

I can't remember the rest because the sherry was kicking in. It made me stop trying to tug down the bottom of my dress. I didn't want to be ribald. Not in here.

Montgomery Tourlaine's eyes grow soft. In his mind, he is looking at New York City.

"When I went there at the end of the 70s, there was Times Square. I went to a peep show my first day. Took a blonde girl standing on the street corner, the 'Minnesota Strip', they called it, in with me. We watched a window with a dumb waiter that opened and there would be a girl flashing in there. Fleeting beauty. A face like I imagined the face of Tess of the D'Urbervilles to be. Innocence complete. With her leg over head. Now New York's got all these weird names for neighbourhoods. I don't know how I'm going to get around if somebody says 'Noho', 'Nolita', what the hell is that, I just know the Bowery, mate. I mean, man. I mean."

He looks around his little room with the strongest, longest gaze I've ever seen him have.

He's holding on and he and I know that.

He's collecting and assembling all the days and nights spent in his little flat.

Once he leaves London he's not likely to ever return.

He's got to get a job so that he can have health insurance.

So that he doesn't die old and sick and alone, and away from his native land.

We eat in silence.

A really nice chicken meal and I drink more red wine than I should. But that's because I'm trying not to cry.

He plays Charlie Parker and Ornette Coleman as we sit on his couch in the dark.

"Anna. What's your future here in London exactly?"

The thing to say to an older person who asks you a perfectly respectable question is that you hadn't really thought about that, that you were taking it day to day instead of saying "what future?"

Which is what I said.

"Let an old man say something. I know it's cool to see the world. I did it. But the world isn't a nice place now. I was editor of the college yearbook. I wrote the clever captions under people's pictures. I was the one who announced that I had no intention of being wealthy or famous or the name on everyone's lips, all I wanted to do was keep moving. I know two famous people now, two people from my year, one on TV and the other married to a celebrity, and if I were to call her up right now she'd pick up the phone and if I said that I needed a place to stay she'd put me up in Martha's Vineyard or wherever she lives with her rich husband, so it's possible to go back and to go back in style."

Munching on Montgomery's pretzels, I imagine him wandering through the Manhattan of strange names, of an eaten up Little Italy, of all of his haunts and spaces of remembrance that are now condos and places for those who have money.

I'm scared to tell HIM that this is the way it is.

I don't have the right to tell him the New York City he left thirty years ago isn't there anymore.

Nowhere is 'there' anymore.

You don't have to be old to know this.

I don't know if returning will be a shock for him.

I don't know if Montgomery won't fit right in, wear a flag lapel pin, I just don't know.

What he's telling me is that this isn't the Twenties.

"The Lost Generation" has been lost a long time and there's no virtue any more in staying on the outside when the outside is the outside because NOTHING IS GOING ON. My choices don't make any difference to anyone.

They don't even mean anything to me.

I say this to Montgomery while he sorts through his books.

I believe that he is listening to me, really concentrating.

He can carry a piece of me back with him.

Maybe I can help him by providing a tragic heroine for his inevitable memoir, the section on the smelly young black American girl next door trying to fight against acquiring a mid-Atlantic twang.

I picture him working away on his old egg beater occasionally looking out of the window at some playground close by the Hudson River and the little children alive and well there.

I imagine him slowly realizing that he has to fictionalize his memoir because who would believe that I ever existed?

If it does well, I could become the lead character in a television series.

We would have our partnership, me with a nice apartment in the West Village or Soho or wherever, he owning that building near the Hudson that once looked like a flophouse which, I bet, if it even still exists is something he would not even recognize. Or rather, Montgomery would recognize it. We stand together in his mirror.

Even though he is thirty five years older than I am, I look old next to him.

I look like something aged and tired.

I don't like standing next to him, I don't like the comparison that I'm already making, me, the product of a nervous, worried youth and he, the product of a youth that didn't give a damn, or at least gave the appearance of it.

Or maybe they cared too much and their caring unleashed the other thing, that thing that locks you down in perpetual pursuit of the life…of life that hasn't been lived yet.

Next to him, I look bizarre, lines already around my mouth, the neck is sagging a bit, too many toxins.

Anyway, we're both pissed.

He says that I should call home.

It's the alcohol that calls Chicago.

My dad answers.

I don't recognize his voice but I know it's him.

He says: "Earlene?"

The alcohol says: "Yes."

"Va plonger en beauté", Montgomery Tourlaine says.

Yes, I will go down swinging…

I don't put the phone down, horrified at what I've done to a man in dementia.

I wait for him to speak.

I remember every word.

He said : "Earlene, I just couldn't accept it. I tried. I prayed on it. But I just…Carl was taking both you and Anna anyway from me. Anna spent every afternoon over there with you. I could see you, both of you, sitting on the porch reading together. I couldn't take it. Then you tell me that you're going to marry him. Why would you marry a man like that! He was a bum, Earlene! I tried to get it all out of mind. But I couldn't. I prayed on it. I was willing to leave my wife, my child…for you. And you tell me you love a man who doesn't have a job, who claims to be getting a soldier's pay, but he's nothing! I told you that. That day, when I saw Anna, my baby, kiss him…He kissed my child! I went over there and I fought him. He beat me. After that, I went home and took Anna's crayons and paper and wrote signs that I put on every tree, up and down the street. I said that he molested children. I said that he was a monster, the plague. Earlene, I swear, I thought that he would hit the road. I didn't think he would kill himself. I didn't know he had a gun. I didn't think that Anna would find him. You left. You left me. I didn't think you would go. Where did you go? Where did you go? I'm still here. I'm still here, Earlene. There are people in my house. I don't know these people. Help me, Earlene. Come home, come home, Earlene."

I hang up.

I stand still for a long time.

I don't know for how long.

Seconds.

Days.

Montgomery Tourlaine tells me that he's come to the conclusion that

357

he does believe in God and so should I. Since there are no other beings out there, the story of God coming to earth to redeem us makes sense. We're all God has.

He says that he is flying into JFK with a quote in his heart:

"I think, from Jefferson: 'A little patience, and we shall see the reign of witches pass over, their spells dissolve, and the people, recovering their true sight, restore their government to its principles.'

"Anna, you know what I've learned all my years overseas? Utopia is an infantile state of being."

I sleep for forty-eight hours.

When I get up, there's a note under the door from Montgomery Tourlaine:

"Back in my day, your parents weren't your friends. They were your parents, the old people, to be escaped from at the earliest opportunity. And when you got out you were out. But you, you go back. Thanks for not being a non-smoking, goatee- wearing, green-fascist. Here's looking at you, kid."

He was gone.

An email in from the Renaissance woman from Showboat. I don't know how she got my email. She's going to stalk me.

"Already I've done 810 pages set in the modern buildings and sites where Jack The Ripper committed his murders. I'm working from the official victim list known as the 'Canonical Five'. It goes: Murder One: Mary Ann Nichols, Buck's Row which is now called Durward Street, the large school there in 1888 is now a hostel; the second murder site, Hanbury Street where Anna Chapman was murdered is gone, replaced by the Truman Brewery. Truman Brewery is now an arts and recreation site; the third, Henriques Street, where Elizabeth Stride was mutilated, has been demolished and a school built; the fourth site, the only one in the City Of London – Mitre Square – still exists, but not the way it did in 1888. The place where the body of Catherine Eddowes was found is called 'Ripper Corner' and has a bench and a flowerbed; and the last, Millers Court off Dorset Street was demolished to make way for the extension of Spitalfields Market. Nuns used to live there, but they left in the 1990s."

Saul Bellow had a term for somebody like her: 'Facts and figures'.

I go out to Comfort to have a fry-up and think what my next moves will be.

In the booth behind me three woman are arguing. Sounds like mother/daughter/aunt and let's say that this is what it is.

The mother looks like she's in her late forties, been out clubbing – and she doesn't look great – moaning for a fag at the same time yelling at her daughter, who looks close to my age, that she can't handle the 'Saffy' thing from her any more and she ought to chill out and stop collecting replicas of her childhood toys. Auntie – I think auntie, anyway – auntie is talking about how she's gone back home, left the high-powered job and become completely immersed in raising the kids she helped make; cleaning, vacuuming, scrubbing toilets, preparing dinner, not letting her husband do anything around the house because that is her job. It was all about being swept off her feet by a rich City lawyer, which happened, so why should she stay slaving and being like her best friend, still at the office, living in a miniscule studio in Docklands, having casual flings, talking like a yob, and listening to CDs when she's not with her girlfriends. The mother yells at her daughter: "What do you want?"

I want to say: What she wants is boundaries.

Back home. A letter from Mom on her stationary with Sojourner Truth's photo at the head of it.

She's meeting me at the airport when I get home.

Oh, and she heard Dad on the phone to me.

I'll be in Chicago, and I won't be able any more to travel around Europe looking for my Black Madonnas. I won't ever see 'La Moreneta – the little dark one' of Montserrat; or Our Lady Of Rocamadour or Einsiedeln : 'Negra sum sed formosa'.

I won't be back over here.

My mother taught me Ghanaian names when I was very little. She dreamt of Ghana. And Earlene would bake blueberry pie.

I want to cook one.

I will cook one.

Is that what this journey's been about, baking a pie?

8.

The room was dark and there was a roaring fire in the fireplace.

Jody closed her eyes.

"I could stay here forever. I want to stay here forever."

She could see Tirian sitting and watching her in the shadows. Her arms were wrapped around her knees. Her big, baby eyes looked old and sinister.

Saronia sat staring into the fire.

Her friend was talking:

"I think about everything we were. Us Nonas. We had so many dreams. Back in the 60s and 70s, we thought that we could do it all, be it all. So many people drugged out or got killed or just gave up. We grew up and then what was the next battle? To keep living. No matter what. And what did we leave our kids, our grandkids? I don't know. A world full of fear. Full of greed. We marched for an equal society but what's the world like now? It's full of fear. Kids roaming a big city like New York with no mothers, no fathers. Little kids living in a big garbage can, hemmed in on all sides. When people live like that they bust out. Those kids are killing each other because you can't cage human beings up, give them no hope and expect them to act civilized. This is the world we Nonas made."

Saronia turned and looked at her. "I'm a Nona and I'm sorry, Jody. I'm sorry."

"I found you. That's all that matters", Jody said. "Will you...will you hug me?"

Saronia opened her arms and Jody crawled into them. She closed her eyes. She saw again the image of the two people over her crib.

"...I wish that David Frederick was here. Then everything would be ok.", she said.

They remained that way for an hour while Tirian sat huddled in a corner like an immobilised machine.

Saronia's friend re-appeared with food.

"Where are you all from?"

"Everywhere. We move people on a network, like the old Underground Railway network during slavery times in the United States. We call the network 'Sojourner Truth.'"

I know that name. Mom…Audrey, my foster mother told me that name. Sojourner Truth, a former slave and abolitionist. And fighter.

"We like that name." the woman said. "It's beautiful. It's on the moon, you know. They named a space probe after her. I like the name because I can see it."

"You can see names?" Jody thought.

"Oh yes. 'Sojourner Truth' is a silvery pink. Very beautiful. Very beautiful."

"You heard me? I thought that this was an icebox", Jody said.

"We have friends. We're not completely off the Grid. Jody, science has found a means by which…people can change themselves into whoever they want. Whoever. It's only for the elite. It's way past 'Avatar'. Listen, if we were created in a Big Bang, like everyone believed we were, why is it that our universe began in such a low entropic state? It should be much higher."

"I don't understand this."

"Entropy. Disorder: what cannot be used. Debris, there should be a lot of that, if we were born in a huge bang. But there's not a lot. We've discovered that: our little universe is not the direct result of that Big Bang. We're an off-shoot of it, which is why our entropic state is so low. We don't know the dimensions of the sea that we're on. But we know that we are on a sea. It's not sci-fi, Jody. There is a parallel world to match ours. The people in charge, who know this, they have no values except the furtherance of their own power, their own ascendancy and they're Nonas like me. They intend to live and play forever. No matter what the cost. They take people's lives and manipulate them. They create false hopes, desires, goals. We've lived too long. And in living, we've betrayed our own

youth. We've lost our ideals, our promise. We've become the fascists we railed against, when we were young. I'm trying to make amends before I die".

"That's what my husband says all the time", Saronia said. "and Bogle always says this;

"My child that was lost to me has returned."

Jody looked at Tirian.

The child seemed lifeless.

Jody did not allow herself to think, only be in this small band of family.

The night passed, and the next day had turned into night before she began to wonder:

'Had what Saronia's friend said been true? Was there another level of science, of reality, that she knew nothing about?'

Two figures came towards her from out of the shadows of the room.

One was Saronia.

Behind her was a tall, distinguished black man with long, flowing grey locks. Very fine gold threads glistened in his hair.

Jody knew his face, but she did not know how.

It was as if his face had come out of a dream she had been dreaming since she was a baby, the dream that was always there, just on the edge of her consciousness.

"Jody," Saronia said, "This is my husband, your stepfather, Bogle."

She swallowed hard. Would she ever get used to her new reality? She felt awkward, clumsy.

"'Bogle.' That's an unusual name."

"I call myself after Paul Bogle, the Jamaican freedom fighter. The hero of the Morant Bay Rebellion in the 1860s."

"I've never heard of him."

"He was a great man. Driven to free his people."

"Did he succeed?"

"Ultimately. Ultimately we always do. Saronia here tells me that you want to help us get back to the States. It's home."

"I don't know if I can."

He smiled. His face was beautiful. She loved his face.

362

"One step at a time. We can wait for the next boat. Some of our people should be on it. Running. Always running. I don't want that for you."

Jody's eyes filled with tears. Bogle took her hand and recited to the melody that she always heard in her head:

"Big whorls have little whorls:

Which feed on their velocity

And little whorls have lesser whorls

And so on to viscosity."

"What does it mean?" Jody asked.

"It goes on and on until it thickens and no longer moves."

He led her to the couch. They all sat down together.

"Jody, let me tell you something. It's important. I want to explain. My friends and I started as students in the 60s and 70s. Questioning. When we didn't get answers, we started looking. We discovered things like the biggest cause of death for pregnant women, married and unmarried, poor and middle class, is murder. By their partners. It was being tolerated for a while by the government in ethnic minority areas. We looked into the data mining that began in the early part of the century. We found organizations that had web links to organizations that had web links to other organizations that may have had, at one time, a link to a suspect organization, suspect according to the government. If that was true the entire chain was shut down. They never knew why. Nobody knew that government had access to all their data. So it gradually became the situation that we have today, that we take for granted today: you never know who's accused you. That's when Orwell's world began, after the First Outrage in 2001.

In time, people were born and grew up who never knew life any other way than one of constant surveillance, informing on one another.

They didn't know what being out of the spotlight was. Gradually, they didn't want to know. So, the small group of people who took charge of every aspect of our lives, who determined whether we lived or died, used front groups to make reality television programmes in the early part of the century creating a population willing to invade its own privacy.

One thing led to another. My friends started investigating various things after the end of the first phase of the Long War in 2012: the Great

363

Pandemic; 2022 – the Eruption of Vesuvius; 2030-End of first phase of the re-colonialisation of Africa and now 2044 Paris is flooded. We know that this is all connected. We're finding links every day. We want to make connections. That's what makes us threatening. Full Spectrum Dominance wants people to think that what happens is random. Anybody who tries to demonstrate connectivity is the enemy."

"Is that what you try to do?"

"Yes, Jody. That's what I try to do."

Tirian woke up.

Jody went to her.

For the first time Tirian allowed her to touch her.

Bogle joined them.

He stroked Tirian's hair.

"About 50 years ago", he began, "scientists started to look at what they called "foetal programming," how the egg, through signals from the womb or the genetic code, shapes itself to survive in the environment it has to exist in. For example, human beings are programmed to eat fat because for most of our history we've starved. If your grandfather was starving then you're programmed to stuff yourself, simple as that.

What they discovered in "foetal programming" is that the womb gives the developing egg the signal that the environment in which the new human being is entering is one in which it has to defend itself. If that's true, a person could be born fighting. And not knowing why they're so aggressive, or frightened, or why they eat so much.

This science is called epigenetics, the science of studying the genetic instruction manual. FSD has perfected epigenetics.

They use it to eliminate 'viruses'- anyone they consider an enemy.

FSD has assessed that environmental factors, like violence, deprivation, fear; can travel through generations. This can create a certain type of human being. An 'undesirable' human being.

Instead of changing the environment so that no more human beings are born into situations in which they are enslaved, threatened, or frightened, FSD simply…eliminates the people."

He stopped and walked over to the window.

"How did you…" Jody could not continue.

"How did I discover this? Have you forgotten what they taught you in your training? I had the same. 'No system can be both consistent and complete.' Remember, Jody, we can never know, even if we've discovered 'The Answer', that the tools we used to find that answer weren't flawed in some way and therefore the solution is flawed. In other words, make a lock and there's always somebody out there who can pick it. That's because the lock creates simultaneously the formula to pick it. You just have to find it. And when you find it, someone's making the lock to defeat that formula. 'And on to viscosity.' It never ends."

The light changed and she could hear the pumps in the courtyard removing the water. All of her senses felt heightened.

Bogle lowered his voice.

"We stumbled on epigenetics……your…mother and I.

"We?"

Bogle took her hand.

"Saronia isn't your mother. Saronia gave her own child away. They've used her guilt to make her think that child is you. But…you're my child."

"I'm your child?"

"Yes. Your mother was a brilliant woman, a great mind. You look just like her. She found out many things. She could always keep one step ahead of them so, FSD 'disappeared' her. And me. They thought they did.

You were a baby. You were given to a family, high officials in FSD. Those people took pity on us. Your mother asked that you be given some numbers and a melody, as a gift from her. This was a code Jody, numbers to help you get out of Ubiquity. Be free. She taught me another technique. How to transmit an image.

I could communicate with you, let you see us, as best I could.

I had to let you know that one of us was still alive, still taking care of you.

I have friends inside FSD. They kept me informed on your coordinates, your scanner details, your Regular. So that you would never forget us."

"But I don't look like you."

"A rogue European gene floated up to the surface and made you. It happens from time to time…But you're mine…daughter."

And now she could see it. She could see the resemblance in the eyes, the mouth, the curve of the cheek.

She could see The Image now too, of her parents standing over her, watching her, protecting her.

"Where is my mother?"

"She's dead, Jody. She's been dead a long time. Saronia here has kept me going. And keeping track of you, that's kept me alive."

"I want you to meet David Frederick, we're going to…"

Bogle stroked her face.

"David Frederick is dead. They've killed him. Do you remember that you were told that certain high-ranking Ultras have the ability to morph into other human beings? One of them killed David, took on his identity. He never returned to you. And there's something else that FSD is doing, something more horrible than they've ever done. But we don't know what it is. Yet."

Jody stared at the man who was her father for a long time. The truth was about to begin, a truth whose consequences she could not determine.

She and Bogle held one another.

Jody felt a peace she had never known before.

Soon there would be other sounds that she could not imagine.

As Undetectables, they would discover the true reality in which they lived. The veil known as Ubiquity would be lifted, revealing whatever was behind it.

And who was behind it.

They would also be open to the Hunters.

But she had found half of her family alive.

She had discovered who she was.

She thought for a moment about her Regular.

Maybe Maisie Blue would come bursting through the door with an army of renegades. Maisie Blue would save her.

But she would have to find her first.

They would have lost contact, lost their connection.

"You have been lost and now you are found. You've come back to me."

She allowed her father to hold her.

Bogle took her over to Saronia, who had given them space to be together.

He put his arms around her.

"Saronia, I'm sorry that Jody isn't the child you gave away. I'm sorry that all that was dug up again for you. But you're my wife. You kept me alive. And Jody belongs to you as much as she belongs to me. Don't you forget that."

Tears filled his eyes and he suddenly looked old and weary.

"When I got confirmation that they had killed your mother I wanted to come out of hiding to claim you. But I thought about all of the people I might betray if I was caught. Please forgive me."

"I do, Dad. I do." Jody said.

"You're just like your mother. My mother – your grandmother – was descended from a woman who belonged to an organization called L'Orchestre d'Elmina. It had great power, but some of them handled this power very badly. They were full of hatred. I've tried not to be like that. Because if we – you and I – who are descended from these women, if we can – connect, reconcile, then we can reconfigure the world."

"And that's our problem."

Control was standing before them.

Jody did not need to ask how he got there.

He had the power.

"We can't let you reconfigure history. What in the world would happen to us? Nonas like you, Bogle, never got it."

"That's why they call you Control, right?"

"Your first correct observation. Oh, and that 'other thing' that you suspect that we're up to? We're working with the cytokine storm. It may have caused the 1918 flu pandemic – and did cause the 2012 pandemic. We've analysed it. The cytokine storm is the systemic response of a healthy immune system to what the body perceives as an invasion. Things just go right over the top. About 150 of what they call inflammatory mediators. Tears your body down pretty fast. The old and the very young are pretty resistant, but people your age, Jody, in the bloom of life-bang!-you're gone."

"So you're developing that to use as another means of…"

"Keeping order, Bogle. Keeping order."

"Where's Tirian?"

Control smiled.

"Jody, look. You know how we Nonas are. Bogle knows. Play, play, play. We were very spoiled, we Baby Boomers. We never stop playing. Got to keep drinking from that Fountain Of Youth and nothing's better than a kiddie game. So I just had to try out the new morphing facility we have. Hey, come on. I'm entitled. I gave FSD everything. Everything. I'm entitled. They let me play with our developing morph technique. I was a guinea pig. It was a risk, but it was great. But…well, I had a little sister, and boy, did she live good. She was the only girl. I'm greedy. I wanted what she had. I guess I always wanted to know what it was like to be a little girl, they always looked like they had the most fun."

"You were Tirian?"

"Well I still am. Come close. Look at the eyes. See? Just a kid at heart."

Jody moved closer to Bogle and Saronia. She held their hands.

"Why?" she asked.

"Oh well. I'm always stuck behind a desk, metaphorically speaking. I never get to go on the hunts anymore. I just thought it might be fun to go on this one."

"A hunt"? Jody asked. "A hunt for what?"

"Simple. You're his kid. We couldn't find him. Those Stockies are really smart geeks, they're always blocking us. But, well, I thought since we know that he'd been looking for you and you worked for us, hey, you could smoke him out. And you did. Including his whole network. Anyway, I'm always happy to be in Paris. Who isn't?"

Jody let her mind run through the room, searching for any possibility of escape.

If they could get outside, they could find a river taxi.

But she knew that her father was not going to leave Saronia.

And she was not going to leave her father.

"This is not just about finding me." Bogle said.

"Bogle, you were always a smart guy. You're right. It's not simply about finding you."

Control looked at Jody.

"It's about you, too."

"Elimination Systems…"

"That whole thing was my idea. Great name, huh? Created the whole thing, just to contain you. Through your father, here Jody, you're a virus. He's descended from the Orchestra…and so are you. We can't have that. We can't have natural-born rebels running around. We think you people might have some genetic pre-disposition toward that. We'll take a look.

But my job is to eliminate viruses in the system.

FSD is writing a new narrative for the world. In time, any story outside our narrative, won't be a narrative at all. We are the connection. There is no other."

"And my wife?" Bogle asked as he drew Saronia close to him.

"I'm afraid she's collateral. Stuff like that happens in war time."

Jody, Bogle and Saronia stood together.

For a moment, Jody thought that she saw something in Control's eyes. She thought that she saw something that looked like envy.

"You were my mentor. You were like my father. I don't understand how you could…"

Control smiled.

"Do you remember when I told you that I loved the play The White Devil?

"Yes."

"And I couldn't remember my favourite line in it?"

"Yes, but what has that got to do…"

"That's my answer to your question. That line I forgot. It's delivered by a character called Count Ludovico. Some say he's the bad guy, but for me…"

"What's the line, Control?" Jody asked as she drew her father and Saronia close to her.

"'I limn'd this night-piece, and it was my best'. Negation. Pure and simple. My mark on the world. My way of saying 'Look at me.' I'm a Nona, after all."

They sat together for a long time, the three of them.

There were no lights, no moon, only the glow of the candles that Bogle had found.

Bogle, Saronia and Jody were alone.

"What do we do now, Dad?" Jody asked Bogle.

She crawled into his arms.

"The world is crazy", Bogle replied.

"What we do", Saronia said, "Is what Bonhoeffer the cat would do."

"What Bonhoeffer would do? He'd sit by this candle, if it was dark in the woods," Jody said. "I remember the story you wrote, about when he got lost. We have to keep a little flame burning. Keep a little flame burning."

About Saints

Parents tell you lots of things, ever think about that?

I was told by my parents that rivers and lakes were bad things.

Rivers in particular were graveyards, the resting place of the dead.

Their own childhoods were filled with stories of dead bodies of black women found floating in the water.

The river was where you went to meet your fate.

For that reason I never learned to swim, although in my mind I am swimming all the time.

I am swimming in great currents of water in which I let myself go and allow myself to be carried by the waves and the momentum of flowing water.

To say that it is beautiful, to say that I am one with it all, is to understate the experience.

I'm not afraid to close my eyes in it, to give myself up to it.

And I see my parents standing on the far shore, hand-in hand waving at me, encouraging me to go further on the river, to see further.

They love me and I love them.

I can tell you this and I don't have to explain: I want to go back home, get my hands dirty.

I figure if I can feel empty, I can survive, the paradox being that the truly American thing to do is travel.

So that you can go home again.

Don't take sides, here. Listen to me.

Remain neutral just a little longer.

They say that certain endorphins are released at the moment of death, that is if you have a serene death and you're not killed in some terrible way, that at the moment of death the brain makes you high, and this, I believe, is what makes the out-of-body experience with the long, white tunnel and the light and the bliss.

The bliss.

I hope that Earlene had this.

If she's dead.

I feel that she is.

I hope she went in bliss.

But who could tell me that?

It's too late.

Once I had a war with a guy about saints.

It was stupid.

We met in the only time I've been in a chat room.

Afterwards he started sending me abusive stuff quoting from the Summa Theologica, then I hit him back with Averroes and it got very abusive and sick, Latin and Arabic all over the place, but my point is this: I had stopped eating sugary crap. Just like that. I was OCCUPIED. With other things. And I was told this would happen by Earlene when I was a little kid. She said: "Anna, you just need to be occupied."

"You just need to be occupied".

I can be.

I can work with my mother.

Take care of my dad.

I can be in my country.

I can do that.

Gosh, clarity can come at any time and re-emerge out of the strangest circumstances.

Picture this: the street that I grew up on was once lined with trees.

We lived in what you could call middle-class respectability. Like the British middle-class.

There were lawns and fences.

Kids had bikes parked right inside the gates.

People leaned over porches and talked with one another.

Dogs chased balls in the street.

Dads came home from work, swinging their lunch pails whistling like people from some old Disney cartoon.

No, this is true.

This is where I grew up. Our house is the only one left standing now. The rest are burnt-out shells or crack-dens or squats. The chaos is encroaching. It is creeping up the street to our house. It will engulf us sooner or later.

I want to be there when it does.

On my way here I passed through the Piazza.

Hey Man was sitting on the ground.

He had a sheet spread in his lap, an upside down hat and a sign: 'Host Corporate Function In Exchange For Food.'

I squatted beside of him.

I said:

"Yeah, I'm going back to my parents' house.

I'm going to cook, and help keep my dad clean, and maybe bring babies into the world, and plant some flowers like Carl taught me, and just keep my head down. Vanish. Be nothing. Leave no footprint."

He looked at me for a while. Then he said in a voice as clear as a bell:

"It was Flaubert I think who said: 'Be regular and orderly in your life like a bourgeois so that you may be violent and original in your work.'"

And so I understood.

I can be there, be with Carl and Earlene, be in Carl's garden, listen to him play the blues. Know that he loves the two of us. I can only be there, be with them if I live an orderly life. If I have ritual and rhythm.

You know, I don't want anything.

I don't want to be rich.

I don't want to be famous.

373

I don't want to be fulfilled or find the love of my life.
I'm just here on this earth.
And then I'll go.
And nobody will know that I've been here at all.
I don't want to disturb much.
That's the least I can do for this earth.

The steward in First Class poured her a glass of champagne, Janet
grateful for the re-fill; it emptied her head momentarily of thought
and the chattering of the Irishman seated across her table talking
about Joyce and all of the pubs he knew in Paris; quoting Joyce and
Yeats and Heaney as he opened up cans of drink and sipped them
one by one, delicately and beautifully like a dowager; his monologue
leaving poetry and turning to a phenomenon he had recently seen on
French TV : the Minka Sisters, extraordinarily gifted twins, teenaged
maths prodigies who lived on an estate on the outskirts of Paris with
their mother; African French girls, geniuses at equations, clearly
carefully nurtured; they wore their hair short and natural, why didn't
more black women do that, he asked; she, too relaxed by the
champagne to tell him that his question was impertinent, merely
smiled, moved by his big, eager face, a face eager for conversation,
and what, Janet imagined, was a bit of solace.

Solace was what she could not offer him, only her reluctant
attention, trapped as they were together on the crowded train, their
two-seater much too small, her attempt at avoiding touching the top
of his knees futile, and all the while the anonymous Irishman regaled
her with anecdotes, like – she could not help thinking – a cliché, a
pleasant cliché but a cliché nevertheless; story after story tumbling
from his lips, stories that encompassed the lives of his family and
friends, going back further still to an Ireland he could not know, but
did know in his bones and in his blood.

Blood had been his destiny, he was saying, blood was the wages of
his father's life and his father before him; his grandfather ages ago had

suffered the fury of his neighbours, their rotten fruit and vegetables hurled at him when it had been discovered that he had been a part of the Easter Rising; his neighbours cursing him because they had had sons who had died on the Somme, and a war was no time for a revolt; he smiled as he recalled his grandfather's ironic chuckle as the old man recounted how the British had made martyrs of the leaders by shooting them: one was so ill that he had had to be executed seated in a chair; his own father lamenting the fact that he had not gone inside the Maze with Bobby Sands, that he did not have the courage to starve himself to death in the name of freedom; the tragedy being that his own life had been blighted by living with a man who had had regrets.

A man who had had regrets, Janet thought, a simple definition of her own father's life.

Life, the Irishman said, had therefore been for him a journey towards his father and also away from him; no one could understand what he meant by that; he was hoping that she might because that lack of understanding had created a great loneliness in him that he believed would never be assuaged; but, lately, he had been reading the letters of his great-grandmother who had gone to America on what his people called 'coffin ships', wretched boats that had taken people out of Ireland during the famine and it had given him hope and courage to read how she had managed to survive that practically fatal voyage across the ocean, and it had given him a connection, a link, to the living and the dead of his people, to all of humanity, which could, from time to time, take the loneliness away; but then, stopping abruptly, his eyes became heavy and he sank down into himself, and slowly the space between them became a place of benediction, completing her healing, and she hoped, healing him, too; there was, for that moment, only the two of them in peace; his knees partly opened as he fell into sleep, his face still, full of sorrow, almost beatific in repose.

Almost beatific in repose, the young woman in Professor Assantewa's apartment introduced to her as Anna, did not move at first, then stood up and smiling, extended her hand; the young girl in African garb who had introduced them vanished, leaving them alone to make conversation as they both waited to be taken in to Abena Assantewa; Janet, nervous, surveying the room, very Parisian; orderly, coordinated, with touches of eccentricity, a discreet African air, and a library stuffed with books which made the room almost Proustian.

Proustian was an idiotic way to describe Professor Assantewa's library; angry now that she was intrigued by the young North American's voice; intrigued by the affinity she felt with her, one, that as far as she could see, had no foundation, and yet, she knew, that before the day was over, she would know the root of that affinity, and that knowledge would bring her peace and the end of this sudden and shocking onslaught of nervousness.

Nervousness led her, as an attempt to make conversation, to recount her discovery of a discarded music magazine beneath her seat on the train to Paris, the magazine turned open, she said to both young women, to a curious article about a new band made up of young, black, female maths undergraduates who had named themselves after a book by her son's favourite quantum mechanic, Professor Seth Lloyd of MIT's "Random Atomic Acts".

"Random Atomic Acts", she chattered on, stated that their intention was to make music that expressed themselves unmediated by categories or definitions; their inspiration being a section on the subject of diasporas from Professor Lloyd's book: '...as living creatures, we operate almost entirely on entropy increase: the chemical reactions that our cells use to survive operate by increasing entropy; increase in entropy is the force that drives us forward; entropy is the force behind Diaspora,...' those words, Janet said, the musicians said had spurred them on; she understanding this completely since it was not unusual that mathematicians were often musicians, there being a great tradition of this; take Einstein for example; her son was going to be a mathematician but did not play an instrument.

An instrument, the taking up of it and the mastering of it, was second nature to them, the girls had stated in the article; going on to make the point that mathematicians use the word 'beautiful' more than artists do, they have less fear of it; they- 'RAA' -had made the decision to be beautiful and musical, to become examples of the force Seth Lloyd described, agents of entropy in order to advance their people and the whole world; that quote from their interview, Janet said, had been lifted out of the text and placed beneath their photo.

Their photo – three black girls in their early twenties, confident, beautiful, free and brave, made her think, Janet said, of the future.

"The critic had some doubts concerning the viability of the band's existence outside its 'normal' parameters. Doubts concerning the future, RAA's future…" she continued, warming to the subject, hiding herself in it, lecturing the two young women, unable to stop being the professor; until the young girl called Anna spoke up, and when she did, Janet knew who she was.

She said she was not surprised at all by the critic's doubts – black girls weren't considered capable of making anything other than soul or jazz and RAA played 'Nu-Slack'; she knew RAA's music…

…make me a garland; to please me at the glass I here adorn myself…

DANTE, THE DIVINE COMEDY

Music flooded the garden as Sam placed the food that he had cooked on the table; Lucas settling down, arranging a seat next to him for his mother; asking Sam when she would be coming home, and Sam telling him soon, she would be calling before they went to sleep; calling Ayesha to hurry and come to eat, there was school tomorrow.

Tomorrow, Ayesha announces, marching into the garden with her determined walk, she's planning to take the photo Janet had given her to class for history day; she had never seen a photo of a black woman taken so long ago; Sam taking it, studying it as Ayesha lights the candles, Lucas chattering away about matter/anti-matter annihilation; and then, with the photo still in his hand, Sam calls his children to study it with him by the light of the candles; there is something in the eyes of the woman that he wants them to see; he places Janet in the midst of their gathering, the children close to him; his left hand on her chair, and his right tracing the face beneath the glass covering the photo; the children asking questions; and the sky filled with shooting stars.

Thanks to to the poets Derek Walcott and Robert Rehder who through their words make the invisible visible; to all at Picnic Publishing; to John Schwartz at SoapBox; to Spencer Hanson and David Duff of the Gate Cinema Notting Hill for the constant supply of popcorn to sustain me during the long writing hours; to the two guys who kept me connected, the best newsagents in the world: Yogesh Rajkotia and Raj Rajkotia of Holland Park News; to Seth Lloyd, Professor of quantum mechanics at Massachusetts Institute of Technology and author of "Programming The Universe", who told me that my idea about entropy and the African Diaspora sounded about right to him; to Professor Marcus du Sautoy, Sir Andrew Wiley, Stephen Hawking, and Simon Singh, mathematicians who brought me back to my childhood love and passion for mathematics through their determination to make their own genius accessible to the likes of me; to the Women of Africa, north and south, east, west and the centre, both on the continent and in the Diaspora who give me courage and make me happy and proud to be one of them; thanks to my dear brothers and sisters, and to Fred Momar Fortas, the brother my mother did not birth"; to all those-and they know who they are – who said "no" and "stop" – they ushered me to where I am meant to be; and to my agent and friend, Judith Antell who arrived out of the blue like an angel and through her own brilliance and belief made this book possible.